The First Time at Firelight Falls

She was a devil woman.

"I'll kiss anything you want me to." He made it sound like a blood vow.

She gasped when he slid his hand up through her hair and held her fast. This time he went in for a take-no-prisoners kiss, designed to melt bones, stop time, erase the memories of all kisses that had come before, what-the-fuck-did-they-have-to-lose kind of kiss. Molten, savage, skillful. They were on the clock.

He was a guy who knew how to make a point, and he never half-assed anything. Clearly, neither did she. Silk, heat, tongue, lips—the taste of her roared through his bloodstream, tightened all his muscles. He curled one hand into the edge of his desk, a reflex against floating up to the ceiling, because suddenly whatever boundaries he'd once had melted away. And damn, she gave as good as she got. It was a hot, deep, dangerous tangle of tongues, the slide of lips. When she moaned softly, low in the back of her throat, guttural, helpless pleasure, he slipped his hand from her hair and sank backward into his chair.

One second before the bell rang.

By Julie Anne Long

JULIE ANNE LONG

THE FIRST TIME AT FIRELIGHT FALLS

A HELLCAT CANYON NOVEL

THE FIRST TIME AT FIRELIGHT FALLS. Copyright © 2018 by Julie Anne Long. All rights reserved. Printed in the United States of America. No part of this book may be used or reproduced in any manner whatsoever without written permission except in the case of brief quotations embodied in critical articles and reviews. For information, address HarperCollins Publishers, 195 Broadway, New York, NY 10007.

First Avon Books mass market printing: June 2018

Print Edition ISBN: 978-0-06-267290-2
Digital Edition ISBN: 978-0-06-267291-9

Cover design by Nadine Badalaty
Cover photographs © All Canada Photos / Alamy Stock Photo (background); © Peopleimages/Getty Images (couple); © TRphotos/ Shutterstock (waterfall)

Avon, Avon & logo, and Avon Books & logo are registered trademarks of HarperCollins Publishers in the United States of America and other countries.

HarperCollins is a registered trademark of HarperCollins Publishers in the United States of America and other countries.

FIRST EDITION

18 19 20 21 22   QGM   10 9 8 7 6 5 4 3 2 1

ACKNOWLEDGMENTS

My gratitude to my editor, May Chen, because her delight in the story, her humor, and her sharp wits make working with her such a pleasure; to the brilliant staff at Avon who work so hard to make sure the books you love find their way into your hands, and have beautiful covers and well-proofed insides, to boot; to my agent, Steve Axelrod; and to every lovely reader who reads this book.

THE
FIRST TIME
AT FIRELIGHT
FALLS

CHAPTER 1

"It's about a *prostitute,* Gabe."

Jan Pennington flung her handbag on the floor of his office, whipped off her bright yellow sweater and draped it over the chair with the flourish of a magician with a cape, then sank with such a chummy flop into one of the chairs opposite him that it scooted back on its wheels.

Gabe Caldera wasn't the least surprised that Jan was the first person ever to say "prostitute" in the principal's office of Hellcat Canyon Elementary. He'd come to know her as many things, among them a truffle pig (when it came to rooting out controversy), a whetstone (for his patience), and, as president of the PTA, an undeniable asset to the school. Patton had never enjoyed his power more than Jan did.

The sweater fling, the chummy chair flop, the "Gabe" rather than "Mr. Caldera"—most days all the little strategies parents employed to assert dominance and declare territory amused him, even aroused his sympathy. He understood all of it was an attempt to corral life's uncertainty into some sort of manageable form. But every now and then he wanted to seize them by the shoulders and shake them and tell them all to lighten up, for fuck's sake, and just enjoy each moment. Every human was dealt a finite amount of them.

He knew the woman already occupying the other chair across from him only in terms of moments, all of them indelible for no rational reason: the time after a soccer game when he'd seen her walking with her ten-year-old daughter, Annelise, back to the parking lot, and they'd suddenly erupted into a goofy dance, complete with hip bumps and disco twirls; the time he'd seen her slip into his secretary, Mrs. Maker's, office and slip right out again, stealthy as a doe, her face alight with secret pleasure. He'd gone in and discovered she'd left a vase of fluffy geraniums and a birthday card.

And then there was that time she'd brought her daughter's forgotten lunch to school and she'd paused by the benches outside the cafeteria, watching a blue jay and a squirrel squabble over a stray french fry. He stood beside her in silence until the squirrel finally absconded with the fry, the thwarted, enraged jay squawking and strafing it all the way across the blacktop.

"I was rooting for the blue jay," she'd said to him, turning on him a smile of such dazzling, wry warmth he could swear it permanently changed his body chemistry. And then she'd pivoted and sailed off again, all slim quickness, red hair tossed and fluffed in the breeze, the ubiquitous giant handbag characteristic of moms everywhere thumping merrily off her hip.

She made him restless in a very primal way. As if his

skin felt a little too tight. Which was how he suspected a werewolf felt during a full moon in the minutes between the time he'd transformed from a naked human into a savage, lustful beast.

In short, he welcomed nearly any controversy that resulted in Eden Harwood sitting across from him now.

"It's about a prostitute, but it's a song from the musical *Man of La Mancha*, Principal Caldera." Ms. Harwood's words had the soothing cadence of a hostage negotiator. But the knuckles curled into the handle of her handbag perched on her knees were bloodless from a death grip. "It's quite a famous musical. The one featuring that song everybody knows? 'The Impossible Dream'? Annelise heard the soundtrack at my mother's house and fell in love with it."

Speaking of impossible dreams, Gabe's was for Eden to really *see* him, not just part of her busy life's scenery, like the parking lot or a tree, but as everyone else did, which was—how had his friend Mac Coltrane put it?—a "conspicuous bastard" who was usually "knee-deep in fawning PTA moms."

He was pretty sure Eden's spine wasn't quite touching the back of the chair. Her posture in fact suggested a runner prepared to bolt at the sound of a starting gun. Her pale pink sweater was exactly the color of her lips. They both looked distractingly soft.

"It's still a song about a *prostitute*, Gabe." Jan's big dark eyes glowed with injured self-righteousness. Her foot began a sort of spasmodic pendulum swing, and light bounced from the polished toes of her pumps. Ironically, given today's complaint, her perfume was making his office smell like a bordello.

"As it so happens, I'm familiar with the song. It's called 'It's All the Same,'" he said idly. Finally. The first words he'd said to either of them.

Eden's eyebrows shot upward.

This seemed to give even Jan pause.

"A navy SEAL *and* a musical theater aficionado," she purred finally. "You are a true Renaissance man."

"*Ex*–navy SEAL," he amended modestly. "And I'm hardly an aficionado. You . . . pick up a thing or two by osmosis." He waved a hand, as if the air was simply full of songs one could intercept if only one had the right antenna.

Gabe had in fact reluctantly absorbed every word to every song in *Oklahoma* and *Rent* as well as a few others thanks to a long-ago musical theater–major roommate. The one about the surrey with the fringe on top was his secret go-to shower jam. That, and Soundgarden's "Black Hole Sun."

"*Anyway*," Jan pressed on, "imagine my shock, Gabe, when I was in class on my parent volunteer day and heard *my* daughter Caitlynn singing that song about a prostitute with her friends! In front of the class! I'm sure you'll agree they're all much too young to sing a song so . . . so . . . so . . ."

She fanned her fingers in mute outrage.

". . . sexually cavalier?" Eden supplied evenly.

That was definitely the first time anyone had said *those* words in the office.

The occasion was marked by stunned silence, total except for the faint clunk of the second hand moving three places around the old wall clock.

"Rawly despairing, with just enough hope to be heart-breaking, depending upon who's singing it?" Eden continued conversationally. "Impactful, without being the least explicit? Unforgettably catchy?"

The kinds of things Eden Harwood said out loud made Gabe yearn to know all the things she didn't say out loud.

"*Inappropriate* was the word I was looking for." Jan, who'd been watching Eden in unblinking astonishment for a wordless moment, sounded a little parched.

"Okay, so if I understand the issue correctly, Jan, Ms. Harwood," Gabe interjected pleasantly, "Ms. Harwood, your daughter Annelise learned a song from the famous musical *Man of La Mancha*, a song that on the surface seems rather racy, but isn't explicit. A sad and compelling song sung from the point of view of a prostitute, but one that could indeed seem startling when delivered by a ten-year-old. And during recess one day, she taught the song to all of her friends, including Caitlynn, whereupon they decided to sing it in an impromptu talent show rehearsal in front of the whole class, with the goal of singing it in front of the entire school for the talent show. And you are alarmed by this turn of events."

He found every bit of this—*every* bit of this—really, hysterically funny.

But he could teach a master class in even-toned neutrality.

Jan lowered her voice and stage-whispered, "A song that contains the words, 'I'll do you and your brother.' *And* it includes . . ." She paused at such length that even he began to feel a little caught up in the suspense. ". . . the word 'breast.'"

Oh, for crying out loud.

Days like these made being a navy SEAL seem definitely easier than being an elementary school principal.

He didn't so much as twitch an eyelash. Commenting on the appropriate context for use of the word *breast* was land mine territory.

He benignly regarded Jan while silently consigning her to hell.

Eden cleared her throat. "With all due respect, Jan, Principal Caldera, that isn't precisely the lyric. The singer of the song—the character Aldonza—says she'll 'go with' you and your brother. Not . . . *do* you and your brother. She never says what she intends to do *with* them. It's all rather euphemistic and dependent upon context. And the word *breast* is used figuratively—as in she feels hatred in her breast for the men she goes with. She never says that men are *feeling* her breasts. Or anything of the sort."

Gabe's scalp tightened. He reached for his signed Joe DiMaggio baseball that he kept on a little stand on his desk and hefted its comforting weight once, twice. He tried hard not to think about the last time he'd felt a breast that wasn't his own.

Eden, he was pretty sure, was masterfully fucking with Jan.

And maybe even with him.

For the sheer entertainment of it.

His yearning, spiky *liking* for her dialed up another notch.

"As if a *figurative* breast is better!" Jan always stuck to her guns.

This was the kind of tenacity that made her a brilliant asset on the PTA. And a stone-cold pain in the ass in every other way.

"When Annelise asked my mother where the singer intended to 'go' with the man and his brother, my mother told her it was to go ride the bumper cars," Eden offered mildly. "Annelise seemed satisfied with this answer. She loves the bumper cars."

Gabe bit down hard on his back molars so he wouldn't laugh.

Eden's expression seemed innocent. But that glint in her eyes had gotten a little dangerous.

Jan did not look amused.

"Gabe . . ." Jan leaned forward and slid a hand across the polished wood surface of his desk toward him, almost beseechingly. The sun struck a glint from the big rock in her wedding band. ". . . you can understand why it makes me wonder what *else* Annelise Harwood is exposed to and might therefore expose *my* daughter to."

His expression, he knew, didn't reveal a thing.

But just for an instant a rogue surge of fury stopped his breath.

This was infinitely petty and utterly groundless. While it was true that it was said that no one knew who Annelise's father was, except, presumably, Eden, Jan's implication was that even Eden might not know. That Eden Harwood might have "gotten around," so to speak, and heaven forfend a woman should get around, because that kind of thing could lead to ten-year-olds singing show tunes and other kinds of crimes against morality. Gabe didn't give a crap about any of that. He sincerely hoped Eden Harwood had thoroughly enjoyed every minute of her life.

Eden was frozen, too.

And then her finger twitched on her handbag.

It occurred to him that she might have kept a tight grip in order to clock Jan Pennington with it should an opportunity arise.

It was time to end this.

He put his baseball back on its stand.

And then he slowly leaned way back in his chair and stretched his arms up casually, leisurely, and crossed his arms behind his head, which made the wall of his chest expand beneath his practical yet manly polo shirt. He smiled warmly, inclusively, with great, chummy affection. "Aw, *c'mon*, Jan."

Just like that, Jan visibly melted around the edges like ice cream left in the sun.

"I know you love and worry about your daughter, Jan. As do you, Ms. Harwood. And worry can be this . . . ever-present free-floating thing—sometimes it just needs something to land on." He gestured with one hand, as if worry was indeed in the very air around it. Both women tracked it with their eyes. "But in the end, it's just a song, isn't it?" he said almost tenderly. "Far, far more controversial songs exist, and Caitlynn's bound to encounter them one of these days on a car radio or a loudspeaker at the roller rink or who knows where, because no mom, as much as she wants to, can be everywhere. Right? You all work so hard, and you're so busy as it is and no one can possibly expect you to be omniscient and omnipotent."

Jan nodded breathlessly, enjoying this interpretation of herself.

Eden seemed rapt, too. She wasn't blinking, anyway. But the corners of her blue eyes—blue like a spring sky after rain, blue like a favorite pair of jeans; he'd entertained himself with metaphors for them practically from the moment he'd seen her—scrunched a little in what looked like . . . wry amusement? Skepticism?

And as much as he'd like to linger in the beam of her gaze, his job, which he took very seriously, was to distribute wisdom and sympathy equally among the two of them.

He shifted his eyes back to Jan. "You both love your kids, of course. Who wouldn't? They're terrific kids! They're both incredibly bright and hungry to learn. This school is lucky to have them attending. And you know, happy kids are going to sing and dance, especially if a song is dramatic. If Caitlynn is curious about what the song means, maybe you can use this as a teaching moment—an opportunity to make sure she knows that not only should a woman value herself, she deserves to be respected and cherished, which the poor woman singing the song in the *Man of La Mancha* patently was not."

It was quiet again.

Then before his eyes, rosy spots slowly bloomed on Eden Harwood's cheeks.

His heart gave a sharp kick—bam!—like a net taking a soccer ball. He stared at her, fascinated. What had caused *that*?

Jan was nodding along, sagely.

"Or you could just tell Caitlynn it's a song about a lady who's going to the go-kart tracks," he added idly. "Save the rest of the explanation for when she's a little older."

Eden made a little sound and looked down at her lap swiftly.

Jan heaved a great sigh, which evolved into a little laugh. "You're very wise, Gabe."

He shrugged modestly, with one shoulder. "That's why they pay me the big bucks."

Eden pivoted abruptly in her chair toward Jan Pennington.

"I'll have a word with Annelise to let her know it's not necessarily an appropriate song to sing at school, Jan. In front of a mirror with a hairbrush microphone, maybe. But not at school."

"Thank you," Jan said beneficently, a wounded party making a noble concession. "That would be most appreciated."

And then Eden laid a hand gently on Jan's arm. "And please feel free to speak to me directly about anything that concerns Annelise. We both know how busy Principal Caldera is, and wouldn't it be lovely if we could make his job a little easier by not taking up more of his valuable time?"

She gave Jan a small but radiant smile.

Damn. Well *played*, Ms. Harwood.

Gabe could have interjected self-deprecatingly—*My time is your time! It's no trouble at all!* that sort of thing—but frankly, he wanted to see how Jan parried this. Because Eden had just turned leaving the principal *alone* into a virtue, when bothering the principal was Jan's hobby.

And God only knew Jan wanted to be associated with the virtuous.

He could almost hear the fan blades powering Jan's brain whirring.

"Of course," Jan said finally. Rather creakily. "Thank you. I'll do that."

Eden's little smile evolved into a full-on beam. She turned abruptly back to Gabe. "Thank you for your time, Principal Caldera, and I apologize for the inconvenience of holding you after school for a meeting. Good to see you, Jan. I'm so sorry to rush out, but I need to get going or I'll be late to relieve my babysitter."

Whoosh. She was out of there.

E den's purse had been vibrating for the last few minutes of the meeting.

Naturally it stopped the minute she got out into the hall.

She took a few more steps.

It started up again.

She screeched to a halt, the soles of her sneakers squeaking on the hall linoleum, and rooted for her phone, which in a fit of haste she had uncharacteristically chucked into the depths of her bag instead of utilizing the cunning little side pocket. Her hand swished through strata of Kleenex, scrunchies, hand sanitizer, a half-eaten Snickers bar—"Yes!" she exulted when she found that, then stuffed it into the pocket of her jeans—a pair of Annelise's socks . . . aaand the phone stopped buzzing.

"Byeeee!" Jan Pennington singsonged cheerily as she breezed past her in a cloud of Chanel. Jan always smelled great; she'd hand that much to her. "See you at the carnival decorating committee meeting, Eden!"

Jan's kitten-heeled pumps click-click-clicked like dainty hooves as she vanished down the now-empty hall of the school, and then the huge door at the end of the hall thunked open and she was gone.

Oh, crap. She *had* signed up for the carnival decorating committee, hadn't she?

Well, she ought to be good at that, given that her life was essentially a hybrid of Whack-a-Mole and Schedule Tetris. Guitar lessons and soccer practice and Hummingbird scout meetings and homework and the dentist and the doctor for her and Annelise, not to mention other people's weddings, deaths, birthdays, and marital spats, all the things that kept Eden's Garden, her florist business, profitable.

And as for Jan, well, she'd sussed her out from the moment they'd met at one of Annelise's Hummingbird meetings. Helicopter mom, a bundle of nerves and restless, vague unhappiness wrapped in a cheerful candy coating and all tied together with a control-freak bow. She always tried to ease the discomfort of feeling inadequate by attempting to make other people look just a little worse, and Eden was an easy target—too busy to form any mom alliances.

Jan needed to be the first to know anything about anyone, and had a knack for ingratiating herself with people she thought might have some kind of influence or status.

She sighed. If only Annelise and Caitlynn hadn't decided to be *archrivals*.

But what softened Eden's attitude toward Jan— toward everyone, really—was that she felt just a teeny bit of tender pity toward everyone who didn't get to live with and know Annelise. She was pretty sure she had the best kid in the world, and she could think of nothing at all she'd done to earn that particular blessing.

So Jan didn't scare her a bit.

Principal Gabe Caldera, on the other hand, scared the crap out of her.

All six foot infinity of him.

Big-shouldered, smoldery-eyed, bass-voiced, easy-charm Principal Caldera, around whom women collected the way fruit flies had swarmed the peach Annelise had left in her backpack for a couple of weeks. At soccer games (he pinch-hit as coach), at school open houses, at PTA meetings—sometimes it seemed the only reason he seemed visible at all was because he was tall. His behavior, however, always seemed beyond reproach. Not one whiff of scandal.

She actually did know *fear* wasn't precisely the right word. It was some other emotion that shortened her breath and kicked her heart into an approximation of a gallop. (She could hear her brother Jude now: "Hearts don't *gallop,* Eden. They *beat*." Which was the kind of thing that made her and Avalon and their other brother

Jesse want to *beat* Jude. But that would deprive the community of a fine cardiac surgeon.)

Eden didn't have room in her schedule for emotions she couldn't identify. She couldn't delegate emotions to her mom or her sister, or reschedule them or negotiate a favor-trade, the way she could everything else in every square on her magnificent kitchen whiteboard, liberally and whimsically illustrated by her and Annelise.

However . . .

Last Christmas she'd been Room Mother for Annelise's classroom lunchtime Christmas party, and as she was leaving at the sound of the recess bell, she'd seen Principal Caldera standing in the hallway, deep in conversation with a teacher, students swarming and eddying around them as lockers were flung open and slammed shut.

And suddenly from the opposite end of the thronged hall some little bastard appeared, gleefully running, slaloming through the crowds. Which was strictly against the rules, for so many obvious reasons.

Seconds later, time suspended in the way it did when you're about to witness a disaster you could do nothing about: another kid was just about to open his locker right into the damn kid's face.

Suddenly Principal Caldera pivoted, stepped to the left, shot out an arm, snatched the running kid by the coat collar, and hoisted him straight up into the air. Literally plucking him from the milling stream of kids. Thereby saving him a certain concussion or expensive orthodontic surgery.

As far as Eden could tell, Mr. Caldera hadn't even

turned his head. Or blinked. She had a hunch his heart rate hadn't even elevated. There had been no evidence he'd even seen that kid coming.

She knew then that all the while he must have been eyeing the entire hall the way Joe Montana eyed a football field.

From time to time, say, at a stoplight, or while she was washing dishes, she replayed that moment in her head: that sidestep, that arm shooting out to pluck the kid from danger. It was unnerving and soothing and thrilling all at once, in a way she couldn't quite put a finger on. Except that some part of her she'd scarcely been aware of, a tiny part she'd unconsciously apportioned to remaining tensely hypervigilant the entire time Annelise was out of her sight at school, relaxed. She felt ever so slightly . . . lighter.

Her phone vibrated again right where her hands were rooting in her purse.

"Gotcha!" She captured the phone and fished it out. It was her sister, who was staying with Annelise at the shop on Main Street while Eden attended the meeting. "Hey, Ava. Sorry. The meeting ran a little longer than I anticipated. On my way. I might even go at least five miles over the speed limit."

"No worries. I just talked to Mac. He'll meet the contractor up at the house. He's expecting a friend to come over and help with hacking some old stumps out of the field, but they can spare a few minutes away from his company." Avalon and Mac were building a new barn on their property for their goats and a few other animals they hoped to welcome into their fold, hence the necessary field-clearing and stump-hacking. "Leesy and I are having Popsicles. Hope that's okay. So what happened?"

Eden sighed. Leesy had clearly just talked her auntie into Popsicles before dinner, usually a pretty significant no-no, but Eden would let this one slide. Avalon was helpless against the charms of her niece.

She hesitated. "Let's just say the principal defused the situation."

"That big hot guy we saw at Annelise's soccer game?" Avalon said with relish. "I'll just bet he did."

Avalon had recently reunited with and was freshly installed in a gigantic Victorian love nest at Devil's Leap in Hellcat Canyon with her first and only true love, Mac Coltrane, a turn of events that had astonished—Avalon often astonished people—and ultimately pleased her family. She was back in Hellcat Canyon to stay, which was fabulous for many reasons, not the least of which was she was now an option in Eden's game of Schedule Tetris and even voluntarily went to the occasional soccer game.

"I somehow don't think that's the last I'll have to deal with Jan Pennington, though."

"I met Jan Pennington," Avalon said thoughtfully. "If Jan Pennington was a dog, she'd be the anxious kind who pees a little every time the doorbell rings."

Eden laughed. "Everyone needs a nemesis, right? She'll keep me on my game."

"You could totally take her, you know."

This was an old and stupid and much-loved joke between Eden and Avalon. It started when they were kids when Avalon, already in a cranky mood, had crashed her hip into her desk in her bedroom and bellowed "STUPID DESK IN MY WAY!" and Eden, her voice oozing faux sympathy, had said, "I bet you could *totally* take that desk."

For pretty much no reason, it still cracked them up.

"Oh, I know I can. See you in a bit, Ava."

Eden pressed the call to an end and deliberately installed her phone in the correct little handbag pocket. She stared for a moment down the hallway she'd once thought she'd left behind forever, more than a decade ago. It was rather dreamily lit courtesy of the tall window at the end of the hallway, and for a moment of vertigo she was back in school again, the entire world—and a few really great guys—at her feet. The same gunmetal-gray lockers, the slightly less gray floor. Redolent of literal student bodies—sweat and gum and fruit-flavored drugstore lip gloss—with a top note of disinfectant courtesy of Carl the janitor's mop.

Frankly, it wasn't the song from the *Man of La Mancha* that worried her.

It was the song Annelise had written last night: "Invisible Dad."

And boy, if Jan Pennington knew about *that* song. Talk about gossip fodder. And Jan used gossip like currency.

"I *could* totally take Jan Pennington," Eden muttered to the bank of lockers in front of her.

"With one arm tied behind your back, even."

She whirled around.

Oh shit.

Gabe Caldera was standing behind her, incongruously backlit by the beam of light from the hall window, which was exactly the way she'd always thought an angel visitation would be staged.

They stared at each other for a full, silent three seconds or so. It occurred to her that she'd happily go on doing that indefinitely. She'd better speak.

CHAPTER 2

"**W**ere you a navy SEAL or a ninja?" she said finally. It emerged a little more irritably than she'd intended.

"One doesn't necessarily preclude the other. But I'm not at liberty to divulge."

His eyes literally seemed to fill with lights when he was teasing.

And they were green.

"Wow Green," she would call it. Because she was too tired for metaphors, and because she couldn't imagine a better description.

She was staring again. She needed to say more words. "Um, thank you for your time today. And sorry for the inconvenience."

"Any time, Ms. Harwood."

"Hopefully there won't *be* another time." This emerged a little more adamantly than she'd intended.

To her astonishment, he looked faintly stricken for a split second.

"I mean . . ." She touched his arm gently, an instinct to

take that expression from his face. "...I hope Annelise's behavior or song choices won't inspire more meetings."

He glanced swiftly down at her hand, and she pulled it back swiftly.

It had felt a bit like touching a brick.

A brick covered in warm, smooth skin.

A fraught, interesting little silence ensued, and a breath-stealing sensation skittered up her spine.

"Well, she's a live wire, Annelise," he allowed diplomatically. "A real crackling little person. Very inventive. The recess game where they all pretended to be tomato worms, for instance, was her idea. Though she wasn't one of the brawlers."

Annelise's Hummingbird troop had learned all about tomato hornworms during an agricultural excursion on Mac Coltrane's property up at Devil's Leap—and had decided to play Battle of the Tomato Worms at recess. Apparently the mock battle had become a real battle, and a few Hummingbirds had wound up in the principal's office for kicking and pulling hair. Annelise may have thought *up* the game, but she hadn't turned it into a riot. Like her beloved cat, Peace and Love, Annelise was kind of a pacifist. Probably because she didn't have any siblings to brawl with. Though she wrestled like puppies with her Uncle Jesse when he was back in town, which wasn't enough to suit any of the people who loved him. He was forever traveling on behalf of Redmond Worldwide.

"So what you're saying is I can count on a few more visits to the principal's office over the years," she concluded.

The principal grinned. "Ah, we'll just take it as it comes. She's an awesome kid. A total delight. Her teachers love her. And it's a privilege to watch her thrive and challenge herself academically and in the world."

Eden was tempted to lean into these words like a flower leaned into the sun—what mother wouldn't?— and yet she was perversely reluctant to be charmed. It was like the first time she'd put big-girl shoes on Annelise. Leesy had been *astounded*, as outraged as though she'd strapped anvils on her instead of little sneakers. And she'd refused to take even a single step forward without being tugged like a water-skier, howling.

Of course, now the girl was *nuts* for shoes.

But yeah. Principal Gabe probably said these kinds of things to all the moms. God only knew complimenting a kid was a foolproof ingratiating and disarming technique. She wondered if they taught that tactic in the SEALs.

For some reason, the word *we'll* was echoing in her mind. Like something she wanted to hoard and take out to mentally caress later.

"You can call me Mr. Caldera, by the way," he added. "'Principal' isn't often used as an honorific."

He was actually giving her shit! The nerve!

She liked it a *lot*. She all but loathed reverence.

"Wait—so what you're telling me is it's *not* like Your Excellency?" She furrowed her brow in mock confusion.

"I'll happily answer to Your Excellency, if that's what you prefer. It's not like the shoe doesn't fit. My friends—and maybe one or two, let's say, overconfident others—call me Gabe. So feel free to call me any of those things."

*In*teresting. She was pretty sure this was a subtle dig at Jan Pennington. But he'd said it with such humor and subtlety that she could take it any way she chose. A canny man, this Gabe Caldera.

She liked this, too, which was probably unworthy of her. And maybe this was also unworthy of him. But he was making it clear where his allegiances lay.

"Well, I'll take my options under advisement," she said.

"Great," he said, smiling.

"Great," she parroted brightly. For no reason. Unless it was because she hadn't had a frivolous exchange with a hot man in ages and in the interim she'd become a dork.

Heat crept up the back of her neck.

"Great!" he echoed. Then looked startled and a little abashed, as if he couldn't figure out why he'd said that.

Well, look at that. She'd infected the poor guy with her own dorkiness in mere seconds. And it was pretty difficult to imagine a circumstance in which he wouldn't feel utterly in command.

She was tempted to touch him again, a gesture to take away his discomfiture. She thought better of it, given that her cells were still on vibrate from the last time she'd touched him.

But the image of him plucking that kid from danger flashed into her head again and . . . some gut instinct made her want to rescue him.

He rescued both of them. "I thought for a moment you were tempted to deck Jan with your handbag."

Add mind reader to his résumé, she thought.

She gave a short laugh. "You know, I do understand her concerns. I mean, I probably wouldn't love it much either if I heard my daughter belting that song out of the blue. I probably would have gone about addressing the issue differently, however."

"What would you have done?" He sounded genuinely curious.

"I wouldn't have gone straight to Your Excellency, let's put it that way. I'm good at handling things on my own."

"Of course," he said easily, after a little pause. "No question. I can see that."

"But that doesn't mean I can't wield this like nun-chucks in a pinch." She gestured with her plumply full handbag.

"Good to know, in case we ever find ourselves on the same side in a street fight."

"Or in the produce section at the Hellcat Canyon grocery store on coupon day. Same difference," she added.

"The two of us in our rubber-soled shoes would be nimble as hell. We could totally take those gals from Heavenly Shores Mobile Estates."

She laughed, delighted. Damn it all, anyway. Like sunlight, true charm always found its way in through any little fissures and chinks and structural weaknesses.

And on the heels of the laughter, she didn't like the reminder that she had any weaknesses. She needed to be a fortress of competence for Annelise's sake.

"You know, I thought you subdued Jan pretty well with your own weapons," she said thoughtfully.

After a little silence during which they stared at each other.

"*My* weapons?"

"Yeah, you know . . . this bit."

She flung her arms high in an imitation of his long, leisurely, chest-expanding, woman-mesmerizing stretch.

And then crossed them behind her head.

She held his amazed gaze the entire time.

She hiked a brow. A silent way of saying, *I'm onto you, Gabe Caldera.*

Then she pivoted, turning her back on his expression of wonderment and dazzled appreciation, and took off at a brisk walk down the hall, with one final wicked flash of blue eyes over her shoulder and a casual flick of her hair.

"Hey, Avalon . . ."

"Mmm?" Avalon was perched on one of the lushly upholstered little wheeled chairs pushed up against the round antique oak table where Eden held little conferences with demanding brides-to-be. She'd decided she could hang out for a few more minutes. But then Eden's flower shop was such a pleasant little cocoon that guests always seemed to want to linger: the high walls were painted a soft shade of dusty rose; the window sheers floated like pretty ecru ghosts when a breeze wafted in; it always smelled wonderful. Annelise was upstairs in their apartment, supposedly getting her homework underway.

Eden was leaning over the counter of her shop scrolling through phone orders. Behind her and along the wall, tall thriving plants—as well as vivid, enticing blooms in buckets and vases inside the windowed fridge—waited for new homes, eager to soothe or lighten someone's heart. She was having a pretty great week, sales wise. She could give her assistant, Danny, more hours, if he wanted, and Danny, who was nineteen and hands down the most enthusiastic person she'd ever met, basically Tigger in Chuck Taylors, would totally want them.

"Okay, I don't want you to make a big deal of this . . ." she began.

Avalon levered her head up alertly. "Did that mole on your butt finally go funny?"

Siblings knew way too much about each other.

"No. I think . . . I think Principal Caldera might, um . . . like me."

Wow.

She felt exactly the way she had when she'd been caught passing a note to Timmy Cohen in her first-grade class that included two check boxes. *Do you like me? Yes or No.*

Avalon went still. "*Like* you, like you?"

"Yeah."

Avalon's face slowly illuminated with a sort of mischievous glee.

So help her, if Avalon teased her right now, Eden would roll her right out the door on that chair and out into Main Street traffic.

"Okay, let's hear the supporting evidence," Avalon said carefully. Wisely.

A strummed A minor came through the vents. Leesy was upstairs playing her guitar and probably admir-

ing herself in the mirror while she did it. She'd do just
about anything to postpone the math homework.

Eden would be up in a second to put a stop to that.

"Today after the meeting when I talked to him alone
he got a little . . . not stammery, per se, but kind of . . .
when we were talking. I think . . . I think he was flirting."

She lowered her voice on the word *flirting*. She felt
raw and patently ridiculous. She'd always been the loft-
ily wise older sister, the one who made sound decisions
and thoroughly studied for every test and *never* overdid
anything, rather unlike Avalon, who was legendary for
overshooting marks.

Then of course, Eden, the wild card, had gotten mys-
teriously knocked up ten years ago. Which trumped
even that time Avalon had tried to jump her bike over
Whiskey Creek.

"Are you sure he didn't get stammery because your
second shirt button came undone again, like that one
time you accidentally flashed Jeffrey the UPS guy when
he came into your shop? I mean, your boobs aren't very
big, but a boob is a boob as far as men are concerned."

Eden sighed. "Why do I even talk to you?"

"Because I'm your best option for adult conversation
at the moment."

"I guess it all depends on how you define 'adult,'" Eden
returned placidly. "But I was wearing this." She gestured
at her pale pink cardigan. "Polo, cardigan, jeans."

"Hardly a Nicki Minaj–caliber outfit, but who knows
what floats his boat. But that's a great color on you.
Makes you look kind of ethereal and Nicole Kidman-y."

"Wow. Thanks. Gosh." Eden was genuinely touched.

"Which is a *lot* to ask of a color. So."

Eden snorted.

But Avalon was staring at her as if she was piecing a puzzle together. "But I think you know it's a great color on you . . ." Avalon said slowly. "Which is *why* you wore it. I bet you subconsciously *wanted* to make Principal Gabe stammery," she pronounced with the triumph of Columbo announcing the killer. "Or you hoped you would."

That right there was why she talked to Avalon, who knew her better than she knew herself.

Damned if she was going to admit it, though. Not even to herself.

It *might* not even be true.

She was too tired to stop to think about the nuances of those kinds of things, anyway.

"Pshaw," was what she said.

"Did you just say *pshaw*, Grandma?"

"I thought it was due for a revival."

Like her libido.

"I'm saying you *like* him, like him, too."

Eden shrugged. "I don't know him well enough to *like* him, like him. I never thought of him at all beyond the fact that he's the principal of Annelise's school. I don't have *time* to have subconscious thoughts about anyone."

Even as she said that, though, something about it felt like a lie. Which forced her to acknowledge that, thanks to that hallway rescue she kept revisiting like a favorite song, awareness of Gabe Caldera had been a constant low hum in her life for a while now.

"He's just . . . easy on the eyes, that's all," she concluded with insincere offhandedness.

"Were *you* flirting?"

"I'm not sure. It kind of felt like that scene in *The Wizard of Oz* where the Tin Man has lockjaw and Dorothy has to oil him. You could practically hear the creaking sounds as I attempted it."

"Did you flick your hair?"

"Why?"

"You always flick your hair when you're flirting."

Huh. She hadn't known this.

"You know," Eden said slowly, "I'm sure it's possible he flirts with everyone. If ever a guy knew how to use his physical charm to manage a situation . . ."

Gabe Caldera was built like a wall, maybe. And he'd *felt* like a wall when she'd touched his arm. She could probably hook her hands over his uplifted forearm and do pull-ups.

But that fleeting stricken expression when she'd said she hoped never to be in his office again . . . she knew instinctively that he was *not*, precisely, a wall.

Which reminded her: nascent lust was one thing. It was all well and good to bask in attention.

Being responsible for yet another human's feelings was another thing altogether.

While Avalon had always been a heart-on-her-sleeve kind of girl, Eden was a cards-close-to-her-chest sort. Good with a feisty, sexy comeback and the occasional come hither stare, but a little cool, a little hard to get, a little hard to know. She sometimes thought it was *because* Avalon had a fools-rush-in tendency—in the family's emotional balance sheet, someone had to offset the excess. Eden had always understood her own appeal, and she'd closely guarded her heart and nether regions even eons ago when she was dating up a storm; the few hearts she'd broken had never haunted her conscience long.

But now, secretly, she was appalled to have broken any. Since Annelise was born, her emotions seemed permanently more tenderized, more porous and pliant. Another human's feelings were a sacred trust. She did not gamble with them anymore, not hers, not anyone else's.

Besides, who had *time* to gamble?

"Is he that kind of guy?" Avalon asked. "The flirts-with-everyone type?"

Eden mulled. "I dunno. He seems like a pretty straight shooter. Flirting with everyone would be a risky game for a principal."

"That's funny. Dad called him a straight shooter, too. Chatted with him at Annelise's soccer game. Said he was a guy's guy."

"Well, I guess it was only a matter of time before I started using Dad-isms."

"You did inherit Dad's ass."

"Ha."

Eden was tall and lean, like her dad of yore. Dad of present day now sported a significantly more pillowy torso, which made his bear hugs even more engulfing and excellent. Avalon was built more like her mom: short and curvy.

"Well, since you've been so busy, Eden, the first

thing you should know is that sex has changed a lot in ten years. You may need to brush up."

Eden glared at her. "I hope it has levels now, like Candy Crush. I'd totally ace it."

"You can always fire up your Kindle and have it read instructions to you while he's going at it."

"Ha ha."

But wait—could she?

Suddenly the very notion of her having sex after all this time seemed akin to those people leaping from wheelchairs at Lourdes. Glorious, sure, miraculous, sure, but the probability seemed awfully low.

The shop door jingled merrily, and they both lit up when Casey Carson walked in. She was the sunny, blond, Valkyrie-statured owner of the Truth and Beauty Salon across the street, the town expert on what women were paying to have done to their hair everywhere on their body, whether it was sleekly flattening it, streaking it in pastel shades, yanking it out by the roots, or pruning it into discreet shapes.

"Hey, Casey," Avalon said slyly, "is vajazzling still a thing? Asking for a friend who's thinking of getting back into the dating scene."

Eden shot Avalon the kind of wrathful look that used to send Avalon running, squeaking in fear, when she was a kid.

Avalon appeared made of sterner stuff these days, more's the pity.

"Only for the mistresses of kinky oligarchs." Casey considered dedicated consumption of fashion magazines and gossip websites part of her job responsibilities. "I've only had one vajazzling client in the last six months. In uncertain political climates people tend to stick with the classics. A nice wedge." She made it sound like brie. "Who wants to know?"

Eden gave Avalon the hairy eyeball, *daring* her to say anything.

"It just came up in casual conversation," Avalon wisely chose to say.

And yet Eden was absurdly relieved to know her nether regions were still au courant.

"Glad I could help!" Casey said cheerily. "See you at the Chamber of Commerce mixer this week, Eden?"

"Natch."

"And oh—don't forget that Jan Pennington needs to know what your raffle entry is by the end of the week. She just called to remind me."

Eden sighed. "I think of nothing else."

Casey laughed, and a few seconds later jingled on out, the delighted bearer of a tall arrangement featuring blue thistles and calla lilies and a big waterfall spray of greenery, like something a Martian would set the table with on Martian Thanksgiving.

Eden turned to her sister. "What did I ever do to you?"

"Well, for one, you told me to name my Barbie 'Toilette' when I was eight because, and I quote, 'it was a pretty French word.'"

Eden slowly smiled. "That *was* one of my better ones."

Toilette had been passed on to Annelise (who rechristened her "Winter") along with all the other off-brand Barbie-esque dolls she and Avalon had played with when they were kids (their parents had four kids and they weren't rich), including the one she and Avalon called Scrotal Ken. Their brother Jude, a stickler for accuracy even at the age of ten, had taken umbrage at the smooth area between Ken's legs and had drawn, in ink, an anatomically detailed penis and scrotum. He'd drawn a heart on him, too, complete with valves, and had just begun drawing a pancreas when her mom bolted into the room in response to Eden's outraged shrieking and put a stop to it.

Eden had forgotten about Scrotal Ken until her mom excavated him from the attic and passed him on to Annelise. He was wearing pants when that happened. When Annelise inevitably decided to put different clothes on him, Eden used his confusing body art as a teaching moment: boys had different privates than girls, and that a penis on the Ken doll wasn't dirty or bad or anything to get worked up about . . . but that her Ken doll probably ought to keep his pants on in mixed company (a good rule of thumb in life, in general), and private parts were private. And so forth.

"So what are you going to do about him?" Avalon said.

"Who?"

"You know exactly who I mean."

Eden felt a twinge, breathless, delicious and scary, when she thought about "him." An ancient sensation. She'd have to go back to her teenage years for the last time she'd felt *that* sort of thing.

"Oh, nothing. I'm too busy for anything like that. I hardly ever see him anyway, and then only in passing.

Forget everything I just said. I was just . . . I guess I was just making conversation just now."

Eden let the word *anyway* slip out on a yawn, just for that extra frisson of faux nonchalance.

She resumed sorting and filing the day's flower orders and idly reviewed the little messages that went with them—"Happy Birthday," "I'm sorry," "Congratulations on the promotion!" with great satisfaction. She loved being part of everyone's happy occasions as much as she loved prospering. She paused when she came to one that said simply, "You. Me. Forever."

Normally those words would have slipped right past her awareness like so much scenery on the highway, nothing more than part of the bookkeeping that kept the shop running. This time they snagged in a teeny little pothole.

A pothole lasered there, if she had to hazard a guess, by the charm of Gabe Caldera.

Forever. She didn't use that word much. Days, even weeks seemed to go by in a seeming eyeblink, and if the notion of a husband so much as flitted into her mind, it met the same fate as any flies that managed to find their way into the Misty Cat Tavern, slaughtered by the fan blades of her schedule. Her life had a sort of ceaseless momentum. They were good, she and Leesy.

And sleeping with a guy like Annelise's father was meant to be like skydiving or walking around topless at Burning Man—something one did once, for the experience, a memory to sock away and whip out when she wanted to shock her grandchildren. He'd been gentle but intense, intelligent enough to startle even her brainiac self a couple of times, and full of the misty philosophical bullshit that had passed for wisdom back in college and had once been her catnip, and which she now viewed with great suspicion. They'd spent about three hours in soulful conversation and one hour boinking.

He was long gone by the time that pink plus sign showed up on the stick. And she did, out of a sense of moral obligation, try to get word to him. But she'd never heard back.

Which was actually more than fine with her. Because instead of turning her life into a shambles, that pink plus sign was shockingly sobering. And she realized instantly that while he might not be the last person on earth she'd choose to father any of her children, he certainly wasn't anywhere near the first, either. And as time went on and the more real Annelise became to her, the less real he became.

Until it was often easy to forget he'd ever existed at all.

Turning up suddenly pregnant was uproar enough in her family and the town at large, without telling anyone who the father was. She'd never regretted her decision to keep it a secret. Her priority was Leesy's happiness, and part of that was making sure she grew up in peace and safety.

She'd explained the dad thing this way to Annelise when she was six: "Leesy, you know how there are lots of different kinds of flowers in the shop? And some flowers have a lot of petals, and other flowers have just a few, and some are just kind of floppy, like poppies, but they're all pretty and they're all exactly perfect in their own way? That's how families are. Some have dads, some don't. Some families have one dad, some have two dads—you know, like Matt and Darius at Canyon Collectibles? Some don't have a dad, but they have cousins and uncles and things. Families are made up of different parts, but no kind of family is better than another kind."

"So a family is like a bouquet?"

"Yes. That's exactly right."

"And sometimes you can all of a sudden add a new flower to your bouquet, like Rosemary at the Angel's Nest, when the foster girl lived with her."

When Annelise said things like this—blindsiding in their depth and sweetness and innocent soulfulness—Eden's reflex was to turn to someone and say, *Do you see how freaking cool she is?* Fresh deliveries of love and awe arrived pretty much daily in nearly unsustainable quantities. It seemed as though someone else ought to bear witness to the wondrous evolution of Annelise Harwood, to be a mutual memory archivist.

"Boys must be the stinkiest flowers," Annelise had added thoughtfully. "They're . . . collieflowers!"

She was really funny, too.

When had the need to share become an ache?

You. Me. Forever.

She smacked that order slip on the counter a little too abruptly. She suddenly realized that it had been quiet for a long time.

She looked up.

Avalon was frowning at her.

"Have you been frowning at me this entire time?"

"Yes."

"What?"

"Nothing," Avalon said. After a moment. Apparently after reviewing the options for things she could have said, Avalon had opted to be sensitive.

And this was almost worse, because when Avalon decided to be delicate, it meant she considered Eden's feelings raw and unwieldy and unpredictable indeed. Which only made Eden realize that from the perspective of men, her game, such as it was, did feel sort of wobbly from disuse. Practically atrophied.

"Well, I better get going," Avalon finally said. "Come on up to Devil's Leap when you get a chance. I think our donkey is arriving today!"

And with those enticing words and a wave of her hand, Avalon jingled out the door.

CHAPTER 3

As it so happened, a half hour later Eden and Annelise were roaring up Main Street to Devil's Leap as if her flower van was a wartime ambulance.

"Why didn't you *tell* me you needed trifold poster board to finish your report tonight?" she fretted.

Actual Aztec mothers had probably asked rhetorical questions much like this. Because there was only one possible answer. Which was: "Sorry. I forgot."

Annelise was bummed. She genuinely suffered wounded pride when she screwed up. But she did forget things, now and again. To bring her lunch to school, at least once a month, for instance.

Eden sighed. "Never mind."

She took a deep breath and rummaged around in her psyche, trying to whip up a little cheer. "We're lucky that Auntie Avalon has some leftover trifold poster board. You're usually so good about remembering I'm just surprised, is all. I know you'll remember next time. It just takes practice."

This wasn't the least bit certain, but Annelise shifted in her seat, thumped her heels a few times, more cheerfully. She was definitely more resilient than Eden had ever been. Eden had always known how to indulge in a strategic, self-flagellating brood.

"Becky Gordimer today said her dad hightailed it out of town four years ago and her mom hasn't seen him since," Annelise said suddenly.

Eden tensed. "Huh," she said brightly. "How about that."

She took the next corner at Jamboree Street a little sharply.

Annelise sometimes came at questions about her dad sideways, out of the blue, with a delicacy that was both funny and poignant. She was already so aware of the nuances of people's feelings.

"Mom, what does that mean, *hightailed*?"

"Hmm . . . well, maybe it means running with your tail in the air to catch the wind, like a sailboat. You know, like when Peace and Love takes a fright and his tail gets all big and poofy? Like that."

Annelise burst out laughing. "That is *hilARious*. 'Cause he was scared? Like a cartoon!"

"Pretty much." Eden was always a little extra kind to the Gordimer kids to offset the terrible father, known more for keeping a stool warm at the Plugged Nickel than their house warm in the winter, and because there always seemed to be something dripping from their noses and fingers, and she felt a little guilty for thinking them charmless. Eden was a loving mother. She wasn't Mother Teresa.

"We can Google *hightailed* to find out for sure when we get home, Leesy."

"Excellent!" Annelise *loved* to know things, and once she knew it, boy, was it in the memory banks. "Guess Mr. Gordimer wasn't her destiny."

"Destiny" was a new and beloved concept, too. Where she'd picked it up, Eden wasn't entirely certain, but Annelise was captivated by the drama and romance of it.

"Guess not, sweet cheeks."

Eden flipped the left turn on the road that led up to Devil's Leap.

The Lumineers were singing "Ophelia" on the radio. Usually Annelise liked to sing along to that one. The fact that she wasn't meant she was still mulling something.

"Is that what happened to *my* dad? Did he hightail it?"

Eden's heart twinged. Oh, crap.

Annelise was trying to sound casual, but a little worry had crept through.

"Um . . . well, not precisely. He didn't leave because he was scared. Not at all. He just left town quickly because he had a . . . previous appointment."

"Oh."

"Appointments" were boring things or things to be dreaded, in Annelise's book, involving dentists and doctors, and it was pretty much guaranteed to be a topic ender.

But Annelise wasn't six anymore. Eden couldn't keep diverting her with hairpin topic changes or holding out shiny objects.

Eden sighed—surreptitiously, a slow release of breath—because Annelise was keyed into sighs, too.

But for now, Eden suddenly knew exactly how to end the topic.

"Auntie Avalon said their donkey might arrive today," she said. "We can go and see it."

"A *donkey*? No. *Way*."

"*Way*."

When Eden and Annelise pulled up to the gigantic rose-colored Victorian house at Devil's Leap where Avalon now lived with Mac, she'd had a text from Avalon.

> We're out near the goat paddock! I told Mac we should name the donkey after him. You should have seen his expression.

This was followed by an emoji of a little yellow face laughing tears.

Eden snickered.

Avalon and Mac definitely gave each other a run for the money.

> P.S. You guys might as well stay for dinner. It's just spaghetti. But you have to eat.

This was true.

And now that they were here, Eden realized how pleasant it would be to just linger a tiny bit outside the confines of her usual schedule.

When Avalon bought the house at Devil's Leap, she'd discovered Mac was the caretaker, and he lived nearby in a cottage with a small herd of goats, some chickens, and a homely but dignified long-legged cat. Avalon had adopted a tiny, ancient fluffy dog, and they were adopting more animals and making plans to set up programs for at-risk kids and veterans—and presentations to local investors and vendors were the reason Avalon had trifold poster board. After the biggest upheaval in her entire life, Avalon was living her dream.

And Devil's Leap was heaven for a kid. Vast, rugged, wooded, beautiful, a little remote. Annelise had lucked out in the aunt department. Mac wasn't an official uncle yet, but really, it was pretty much only a matter of time.

Eden had never stopped to wonder whether she was living *her* dream. She'd been just too busy living, period. She'd never dreamed, for instance, that Annelise would be a part of her life. But she was practically Eden's very definition of happiness.

"They're out by Uncle Mac's goats, Leesy. Let's go find her."

They skipped up the flagstone path to the side road leading up to the Devil's Leap swimming hole. The metal-barred gate separating the walkway from the road was swung open wide. From a distance they could hear the steady, primal rhythm of someone chopping wood. She was glad for the sound of an ax. The scream of chain saws might have felt like a desecration up here.

Avalon appeared to be waiting for them by the gate. But she wasn't looking toward them.

A few seconds later it became clear she was watching whoever was wielding the ax.

So Eden looked in the direction, too.

And then all at once her head sort of floated over her body.

Her senses flooded as though she'd inhaled a particularly beautiful drug. She couldn't quite feel her limbs. Other parts of her, however, were on red alert.

"Mom, that's Mr. Caldera! Without his shirt!" Annelise added.

When Eden didn't say anything.

No shit, kid.

Improbably, like something out of a dream, Gabe Caldera was shirtless and swinging an ax against a stump of wood. Levering it up in the air, hurtling it down, in a steady, primal rhythm that was so fundamentally, unexpectedly hot Eden's lungs finally seized.

Muscles shifted and slid beneath glossy, bronzed skin as the ax came up.

Then down again.

It was hands down the most mesmerizing thing she'd ever witnessed.

She went as motionless as a hunter in a blind.

She only hoped she literally wasn't slack jawed.

"I honestly didn't know this would be happening," Avalon said on an apologetic hush, as if this was a trauma only the strong of constitution could endure. "Do you need smelling salts?"

"Smelling salts?" Eden repeated. Or thought she did. Unbeknownst to her, what she'd really said was something like "Mahumuh?"

Avalon stared at her.

WHAM! Down came the ax again.

He swung it up overhead again. Muscles slid and shimmered in slow-motion elegance. Hands down the most beautiful machine she'd ever seen.

WHAM! Down it came again. The three of them, Eden and Avalon and Annelise, gave a little jump. Chips flew; the trunk cleaved halfway.

And up it rose again.

"It's like porn, isn't it?" Avalon whispered into her ear. "Or like one of those Zen sand gardens. But an erotic kind."

"Mom, can I have an ax?" Annelise asked.

"Sure, after dinner, maybe," Eden said absently.

"Cool," Annelise beamed.

The ax came up again; muscles rippled and shimmered beneath that hard, glistening satin surface.

BAM, down it came again.

Avalon murmured right next to her ear, "Bet you'd like him to split *you* in two."

Eden's head whipped around. "AVALON. HARWOOD."

Avalon's face had gone a sort of fuchsia shade with the effort to keep from laughing. But she was playing a risky game. Annelise's ears were a little too sharp, and she was fond enough of drama to ask, "What does it mean when someone wants to split you in two?" in the middle of company.

"Just checking to see if you were listening, Edie. Maybe I ought to check your pulse, too. I bet it's doing at least sixty miles per hour."

She grabbed for Eden's hand. Eden snatched it out of reach.

That was another sisterly inside joke. They liked to give their brother Jude fits by feigning rank ignorance about biology. Heartbeats were measured in miles per hour; lungs were called "those pumpy things"; they insisted actual drums shaped like tiny bongos were situated inside their ears, and so forth.

"It really seems unnecessary for an elementary school principal to look like that," Eden said irritably.

"It certainly does," Avalon soothed. "It's very alarming. He has *some* nerve."

Eden scowled at her.

Truth be told, she *was* genuinely alarmed. She couldn't ever recall feeling literally dumbstruck by a man's beauty. Or awash in a riptide of what, let's face it, was probably lust.

"It's so cool! His stomach has squares. You could play checkers or tic-tac-toe on it!" Annelise observed cheerfully.

"He was a navy SEAL," Avalon explained. She made it sound as if the six-pack abs were military issued, along with the uniform. "Mac was in the National Guard. They have meetings once a week with local vets. That's how they became friends, apparently. I didn't know they knew each other, I swear it."

Eden didn't hear her. She was thinking, why play checkers, when you could just trace each square with your tongue, the way she used to savor the sections of a chocolate bar to make it last longer. Why do that, when you could even, say, gently nibble that firm, warm, smooth skin, then drag your fingers along those lovely trenches drawn by muscles. Why do that when you could—

"How do you get squares on your stomach, Mom?"

"By eating all of your vegetables."

Not even stomach squares interfered with the mom programming when it came to vegetables.

"Aw, man, it's *always* vegetables," Annelise said sadly.

"Yep, they are the key to pretty much everything," Eden confirmed cheerily.

And then Gabe finally noticed them—how could he not? They were lined up there at the rail like spectators cheering on a winning horse, and surely the beam of their collective admiration was as powerful as a set of klieg lights.

He slowly lowered the ax to his side. Shaded his eyes. Revealing fluffy armpits and another vista of expanse of muscle. He was literally shaped like a wedge.

And he had shaded his eyes to gaze in Eden's direction.

His spine abruptly straightened.

Instantly, something like invisible lightning snaked through the air between them.

It made Eden's breath stop and the back of her neck and arms prickle when all the little hairs went erect, the way they did when she heard or saw something particularly beautiful or profoundly true.

She couldn't move.

Then he unshaded his eyes and waved. Tentatively. She couldn't see his expression, but his smile flashed bright as an ax blade.

After a stupefied delay, she lifted her own arm in greeting. Avalon and Annelise were already cheerfully waving.

She could have sworn his smile got just a little bigger and just a little more amused. He rested a hand on his hip and let the ax casually swing from one hand, and he regarded her like a buccaneer on a ship's deck who'd fixed his sights on bounty.

Eden pivoted abruptly. "Leesy, let's go help Auntie Avalon get dinner on the table."

She had to make a conscious effort not to flick her hair as she walked away.

It felt a teensy regressive, the womenfolk bustling about the kitchen with tureens of steaming food, the men-folk, freshly showered and deodorized after a hard day's labor out in the fields, showing up at the table and rubbing their hands together exclaiming, "Smells good!"

If it was regressive, then so were Gabe's daydreams.

Not that they'd specifically involved the elusive-as-a-gazelle Eden Harwood fluffing plucked wildflowers she'd inserted into a vase then placing it in the middle of the table.

Then fetching a big ladle for the spaghetti.

Then prettily arranging bread in a basket.

It was just that literally everything she did was sexy.

And to think his subconscious had once gifted him with a dream involving Elizabeth Hurley and a vat of chocolate pudding. He'd revisited that one more than once when he was on active duty in the navy.

Times changed. Warmth and beauty and laughter

and a kitchen full of people he liked and a woman upon whom he had what could only be described as a painful crush, even at his advanced age of nearly forty, was apparently what got his motor running.

When they all sat down at the table, the clink of forks against plates was deafening, thanks to the fact that no one said a thing. The silence was as tense as a trampoline.

Mac was quiet because he'd just copped on to the source of tension at the table, and he was moving his eyes between Gabe and Eden with speculative surprise.

Avalon was quiet because she was captivated by the novelty of her cool, collected older sister's discomfiture, and she was witnessing it with a sort of rapt glee.

Eden was quiet, possibly because she'd been caught baldly ogling Gabe from across a field, and then they'd had what amounted to eye sex, a moment of zinging, unguarded eroticism that he hadn't been able to help and that had been better than actual sex with some women in his past, and it felt almost as though everyone here had watched them actually rut out there.

And Gabe was quiet because, absurdly, he felt almost . . . was the word *shy*? It couldn't be. He was *never* shy. It's not like he didn't encounter attractive women all the time, and it sure as hell wasn't as though he didn't know how to talk to them.

It was just that there had never really been . . . stakes . . . before. And somehow this kept him from opening his mouth.

Gabe and Eden were carefully not meeting each other's eyes now, because it was precisely what Avalon and Mac wanted them to do.

And the kid was probably quiet because she was at dinner with her elementary school principal, a generally surreal and not necessarily welcome experience for a ten-year-old. Also, her plate of spaghetti also featured a few florets of broccoli she'd promptly herded with her fork to what probably equated to Annelise Harwood's version of a leper colony. Far, far away from all the other food.

He'd watched Eden's jaw go tense when she'd seen Annelise do that.

And right after that Annelise coolly met her mom's eyes. And her own jaw gave a stubborn little jut.

A*ha*. Vegetable wars, if he had to guess.

It was so quiet, in fact, that when Mac leaped to his feet and said briskly, "Let's have some music!" everyone visibly gave a start. No one went so far as to clap a hand over their hearts, but Eden dropped her fork with a clatter on her plate.

Fleet Foxes filled the room with pretty, anodyne harmonies and Mac sat down again.

Enough was enough. Gabe took charge, because that's what he normally did. When in doubt, always start with the kid.

"Is it weird seeing your principal outside of school?" Gabe asked Annelise.

"Kinda," Annelise said shyly.

"A lot of kids seem to think principals live at school, the way Santa lives at the North Pole."

"Ha ha ha!" Annelise laughed, somewhat uncertainly.

Given her expression, odds were pretty good she'd at one time thought that was true.

"*Do* you live in a house?" Annelise asked a moment later.

"I live in the cafeteria. Carl the janitor is my roommate. We skate around in our socks when everyone goes home."

Annelise laughed so hard at that she spluttered, and Eden had to rub her back.

All the grown-ups laughed, too.

Ice broken, somewhat.

"That is hiLAR. You do not! I want to live in the cafeteria, too!"

"The cafeteria smells like feet and ammonia and hot dogs, Annelise. I don't think you want to live there."

She roared with laughter.

It was impossible not to laugh when she laughed. That was a big part of the reason he loved kids. Things were still so new to them, which made everything old new again. They were easy to surprise, and surprise was a big part of humor.

"Whoops, Leesy, honey, your hair is in your spaghetti," Eden said.

It was indeed.

Gabe kind of wished Eden would call him "honey" and rub his back.

Annelise pretended to insert the now sauced end of her hair into her mouth.

She froze—everyone did, such was its power—when Eden fired a glare-missile at her.

Annelise made a big show of using her paper napkin to carefully rub sauce from her hair.

"I actually live in a biiiig yellow house," Gabe said.

"Has a yard with a huuuuge oak tree and a tire swing hanging from it. And a porch like this one outside—wraps all around. And a pretty great view of my neighbor's front yard in the front and the mountains in the back."

He didn't spend a lot of time there. It mostly seemed for sleeping.

Annelise's eyes—same color as her mom's—went huge with yearning. "Oh, *man*. I wish we had a tired swing. We live over the flower shop, and we only have a little backyard, but it's really nice. It has roses and a hummingbird feeder and a birdbath. We have a really great cat, too. His name is Peace and Love."

"*That's* what I'm missing. A cat. And maybe a dog. I can get my donkey fix here with Mac and Avalon."

Annelise hesitated. "Do you have room for a pony?"

The look on Annelise's face told him that this would be the clincher. That this might just push her over the edge of unbearable yearning.

"I have room for a pony, sure."

She froze dramatically, mouth dropped open into an O.

"*Lucky,*" she breathed finally. "Mom, he can have a pony *and* a tired swing."

He shot a glance at Eden. He intercepted an expression on her face—fixed, rapt—that made his breath literally stop.

She dropped her eyes to her plate and determinedly wound some spaghetti on her fork.

"Auntie Avalon?" Annelise said idly after a moment.

"Yeah, sweetie?" The first words Avalon had said.

"Do you think it was your destiny to meet Uncle Mac?"

Everyone froze midchew.

"*What* the . . ." Mac was deeply suspicious of anything that smacked of gloppy romance. Which was pretty funny. "Why are you wondering about destiny?"

"Because I want to be a rock star like Glory Greenleaf. I think it's my destiny."

Annelise was now using the tine of her fork to scroll the word *destiny* in her spaghetti sauce.

And then she disdainfully shoved her broccoli all the way out to the borders of her plate. So far away the florets nearly tumbled onto the table.

"Maaaybe," Mac allowed, so cautiously that all the other adults at the table bit back smiles.

Eden's shoulders went back and she took a breath, as if she was bracing for impact. And then she cleared her throat. "Hey, Leesy? Do you think it's very important to fulfill your destiny?"

"Yes! Destiny is *everything*!" she declared with hammy melodrama.

Gabe wasn't certain he agreed with that. But he had a hunch Eden was leading up to something. Her mistake was in broadcasting it even a little, because kids could pick up on that stuff the way animals could sense an impending trip to the vet.

"So what do you think the new donkey's destiny is?" Eden asked. Casually but not casually enough.

"Um . . . to be cute and to help kids learn things," Annelise declared. As though it were a flash card quiz.

"What do you think Peace and Love's destiny is?"

"To be very soft and purr a lot and love me and you."

"What do you think broccoli's destiny is?"

The trap was laid.

Annelise and Eden eyed each other like a pair of gangsters, each aiming a pistol at each other's hearts.

"To smell like bad breath and farts," Annelise declared mutinously.

"ANNELISE HARWOOD." Eden issued this through gritted teeth.

Annelise sighed and looked down at her plate wretchedly.

Eden shot a glare at Mac when he snickered.

He blinked and clammed up instantly.

Judging from Eden's expression, this vegetable thing was a huge and ongoing source of anguish.

"You know what I think, Annelise?" Gabe said thoughtfully. "I kind of think it's your destiny to be brave."

She swung her head toward him. "You do?"

"Yeah. You know, I just get that feeling. And I've known a lot of brave people in my time, so I can tell. *Lots* when I was in the navy. Your Uncle Mac here knows a lot of brave people, too. But I'm not positive about you, yet."

"Why not?"

"Because, frankly, you have to be real brave when you first try broccoli—which is *delicious*, by the way. I heard Caitlynn Pennington tried some broccoli, but I don't think she actually ate it. Just put it in her mouth. But even that takes guts, boy. It takes *real* nerve to chew and swallow something for the first time. Think of all the people who had to try stuff for the first time. Chocolate. Cotton candy. Pepperoni. Someone had to be the first person to try all those delicious things. Someone had to be a pioneer."

Eden was absolutely motionless. She was staring at him, fascinated.

When he'd imagined Eden Harwood hanging on his every word, it hadn't been about broccoli.

But he'd take it.

Annelise stared at him with shrewd little blue eyes, looking for a way to poke a hole in that argument.

And he could see it was *killing* her, killing her that Caitlynn Pennington had done it first.

Gabe took a bite of broccoli and closed his eyes in bliss. "Wow. Just . . . *wow*. Am I right? Your mom doesn't want you to miss out on something wonderful, is all. Isn't that right?"

"He's right, Leesy." Eden swiftly took a bite of her own. Tipped back her head and closed her eyes. Gave her shoulders a little shimmy as she chewed. "Oh, *maaaaannn . . .*" she sighed. "So good."

Gabe's head went light. He carefully laid his fork gently beside his plate. He studied his own plate again, awash in an inconvenient tide of lust.

Pretty sure he was going to add that to his inventory of Eden moments.

Annelise's eyes remained narrowed, investigating all the adults for evidence of perfidy.

Avalon took a bite and chewed it happily. "You know, I never feel luckier than when I have a plate full of broccoli, Leesy."

Mac concurred somberly. "You know, it's the one food I'd take with me to a desert island. The last food in the world I'd ever eat."

All the adults were now busily chewing broccoli.

Annelise seized her fork with a certain resolve.

Clutched like Poseidon held a trident.

Everyone jumped when she stabbed a floret with her fork as if it were a mastodon needing killing.

She lifted it up and eyeballed it like Hamlet communing with a skull.

Brought it closer, and closer still, to her face.

Gazes ricocheted every which way around the table.

"Don't move," Eden whispered to her sister. They were seconds away from gripping hands, like people in an aircraft going down.

Then Annelise levered it up to her mouth and whispered something that sounded like an incantation.

She opened her mouth.

Eden's brow appeared to be sweating.

And Annelise thrust the broccoli inside her mouth.

Screwed her eyes closed.

Clapped her mouth shut.

Experimentally moved her jaw.

Once.

Twice.

Three, four, five times.

The chewing accelerated.

And, for the denouement . . .

. . . her throat moved in a swallow.

Not one adult in that room was breathing.

"It's good," Leesy said mildly, finally, as if the tectonic plates of her life and her mother's hadn't just shifted. "I like it."

And then she . . . *voluntarily took another bite.*

Silence, of the ringing awestruck sort, ensued. The

kind of silence often punctuated by chanting medieval monks and celestial music. A hushed and holy silence.

Eden looked drained and pale and wearily happy. As if it was the aftermath of childbirth.

"What did you whisper, Annelise?" Gabe asked.

"Promise you won't get mad?" Annelise said to her mom.

Eden sighed. "Sure."

"Up yours, Caitlynn."

Eden closed her eyes, shook her head slowly to and fro.

"That's how I say grace, too," Mac said happily.

CHAPTER 4

Immediately after dinner, Avalon said, "Hey, Eden, would you do me a favor?"

"Sure, babe."

"Could you go check on that hanging ivy you gave me? The one out on the porch? I think it has brown spots on the leaves. Gabe can reach up there and get it down for you, right Gabe? Leesy, come with me and Mac upstairs to get that trifold paper. It's in the turret!"

"The *turret*!" Annelise needed no persuading. The turret was magical, as far as she was concerned.

Eden knew *exactly* what Avalon was up to.

"Um . . . Leesy and I kind of need to get going, Avalon . . . We have to get that Aztec project—"

"Hey, we can pretend to be horses on the way upstairs, Leesy!" Avalon interjected, ignoring Eden. "Let's *canter*."

"YAY!" Annelise exulted.

That was a dirty, dirty trick. Annelise would never miss an opportunity to pretend to be a horse.

Avalon pawed the ground and tossed her head. "C'mon, Mac, let's go!"

"We're *all* going to the turret?" Mac was confused. "I'm not sure I understand this game."

Eden mouthed a furious *you're dead* at her sister. "Annelise, we're leaving here at seven on the dot. Avalon, make sure she's back down here at seven!"

Avalon batted her eyes at her, then darted up the stairs, dragging Mac by one hand. "C'mon Mac, gallop," she said. "And don't forget to neigh."

"*What* the—?" Poor Mac still hadn't copped on to Avalon's little machinations.

Avalon was already galloping up the stairs, and Annelise was loping after them, tossing her head and whickering. And so Mac went, because frankly he liked to be wherever Avalon was.

And so Eden went out onto the porch.

And Gabe went out on the porch.

And they stood there.

Eden wondered if this was how endangered rhinos felt when someone shoved another random rhino into their enclosure and expected them to mate.

And they stood there in silence, as the lowering sun painted long shadows across them.

"There's nothing wrong with that ivy," Eden said finally. Dryly.

"Yeah, I know."

"They're real sly."

He laughed softly and leaned against one pillar and faced her. "You sorry?"

She turned and leaned against the other pillar. She didn't answer that.

She gave him a crooked, speculative smile.

No one said anything for an awkward few seconds.

But they also did nothing but look at each other.

"That was some fine broccoli balderdash at the dinner table tonight by the way," she said finally. "Thank you. That moment in there was practically as profound as her first step. Annelise's war on vegetables is the only reason I actually drink the cheap wine at the Chamber of Commerce mixers."

He grinned and shrugged one shoulder. "She's got a vivid imagination, and she's a tough kid with a lot of pride in her work and a competitive streak. If there's anything I've learned over the years, it's that someone's strengths can be weaponized and used against them."

She laughed. "Did they teach you that strategy in the SEALs?"

"Hey, I'm the principal. Which means to Annelise I have pull and a certain mystique, in school and out. So don't give me too much credit. Unless she keeps eating broccoli at home, well, then . . . I'm going to insist on a commemorative plaque, to hang alongside my other diplomas on my office wall. I have a *lot* of them. Diplomas and certificates."

"You don't say."

"I was trying to impress you just then."

"I know. Mystique, huh?"

He gave a one-shouldered shrug again. "What can I say? One of the perks of the job."

Eden darted a glance toward the double doors. Naturally, no sign of any members of her family.

She was going to kill her sister.

She snuggled deeper against the porch pillar. It still held some of the day's heat.

"You and your sister are pretty close, huh?" Gabe offered.

"Yeah. And it's great to see Avalon so happy. I'm thrilled to have her living in town again. Not the least of which is because she's now become an integral part of my whiteboard."

"Whiteboard?"

"My kitchen calendar. I consider it my masterwork. Like the Sistine Chapel, only with scented erasable markers."

"Oh, gotcha. Yeah, Mac is the best guy in the world. But he's not the easiest guy in the world, believe me, so, you know, hats off to her."

"Avalon isn't exactly a walk in the park herself. I'm having fun watching the fireworks."

They smiled in a certain solidarity.

The next silence got a little long.

And a little tense.

She kind of knew what was next.

"Ever been married?" he asked finally. Quickly.

"Nope. You?"

"Nope."

"Single?"

"Yep. You?"

"Yep."

There ensued the kind of relieved silence that often followed ripping off a Band-Aid fast.

"Like to keep your options open, huh?" She sounded chirpy and insincere and even a little mean in her own ears.

He looked startled and maybe even ever-so-faintly offended. "No."

Eden sighed.

She felt like the old rototiller her dad would whip out every spring in order to get the garden ready. It would cough and sputter and shudder when he tried to start it, then speed away from him, then abruptly stall, nearly sending him ass over teakettle.

Her flirting carburetor was clogged.

"Sorry," she said. Glumly. "I was just . . . saying things."

He laughed. "Boy, this is some scintillating banter, Harwood."

"Hey!" she said with feigned indignation. "I haven't learned to 'weaponize' my 'strengths' the way you have." She heartily air-quoted the words.

"But I was including myself in my own sarcasm!"

"Courtly of you, but . . . well, let's put it this way. If PTA moms are cobras in baskets, then you're the guy with the flute."

"I swear to God, it's different when it's someone who I . . . Someone who's . . . I mean, when I . . ."

He stopped.

Took a breath.

Exhaled, with a sort of resignation, and the exhale turned into a short laugh.

And something like lovely spangles raced along her skin. A fierce sort of tenderness that robbed her of breath.

"Okay, so you *can* do awkward with the best of them," she teased gently.

He quirked his mouth wryly.

Honestly, had she *ever* known how to talk to a man

when she wasn't trying to sell him flowers? It seemed like a skill belonging to the distant past. It felt awkward. Like that time she'd seen her grandmother attempt to break-dance.

"Um, you ever look at those dating apps?" he asked, after another of their now patented Awkward Silences™.

"You know . . ." she said, haltingly. "I looked at Tinder, but only once. I just wanted to tell all those boys to put their shirts back on, for God's sake. Do they really think that's what a woman is looking for? I look at every girl making a kissy duck face and I think, what if that were *my* daughter? I'm barely thirty, and I see everything through a mom filter now. And . . . maybe an experience filter. It's just . . . so much *posturing*. It seems dishonest and needlessly difficult. It's hard to conceive at this point in my life of having time for that sort of thing. I want to tell them, c'mon, cut to the chase, kids."

She felt like she'd said too much, but he listened to this with the sort of somber, flattering intensity one listened to his commanding officer's orders.

"Ah. So you're saying I should keep my shirt on in my photos if I give Tinder a shot?"

"For you, I'd make an exception."

Those words had just popped out, special delivery straight from her id, utterly, frighteningly sincere.

It shocked both of them into momentary speechlessness.

And he smiled.

It started with one corner of his mouth. And then it spread to the other. Slowly, the way a fire took over a coal. Until it was a wicked little curve. Above it his eyes kindled in a way that ought to come with a mature content warning attached.

Hoooolly *shit*, was that ever sexy.

She wasn't viewing *that* through a mom filter.

She turned away swiftly and pretended to critically inspect the perfectly healthy hanging plant, which she'd sold to Avalon at a family discount.

She reached up and fingered a leaf, which was basically the equivalent of tucking a strand of hair behind her ear or flicking it.

She didn't know where a conversation could possibly go now. She needed a cigarette after a smile like that, and she didn't even smoke. She had no idea what to say next, and it was both unnerving and delicious. She wasn't at *all* accustomed to feeling uncertain of herself; surprises really had their work cut out for them if they wanted to sneak through her airtight schedule.

"You know how they have those free buffets on cruise ships?" he said suddenly. "Just heaps and heaps of food, chocolate fountains and prawns and things on sticks?"

"If you're still hungry, I think there's some broccoli left."

"Ha. I'm good. What I'm trying to say is that after a while you don't want any of it because it all looks the same and there's just too much of it and . . . that's kind of how Tinder—well, all sites like that—feel like to me."

"Mmm. So do you think 'hard to get' inherently adds value to something?"

His eyebrow shot up. He heard the faint challenge in the question.

"I know the difference between 'hard to get' and 'worth the effort to get.' I'm hardly a kid anymore—I'm pushing forty. I guess I see things through an experience filter, too. Life is short and time is scarce, and all the guessing surrounding dating feels like . . . I dunno, been there, done that. I don't need to graze at the buffet. I'm all right with waiting until I see something that feels right. And when I see what I want, it's hard not to just cut to the chase. Like you said."

Damn, but he'd just accomplished a lot with a few sentences.

He was telling her he wasn't a pushover.

That he'd probably known some loss.

And, if she was not mistaken . . . that he'd seen something he wanted.

And she was standing right in front of him.

She turned her face away from him a little too swiftly again. Her heart was doing a sort of fox-trot.

"Yeah, I don't really have time for . . . Tinder and dating and stuff like . . . like that, anyway."

She'd said that like a falling person scrambling for a handhold.

And regretted it instantly.

It was a reflex born of nerves and newness, and it just seemed easier not to do . . . whatever this was.

This time instead of fondling the plant she looked up pensively, as if captivated by the stars, the same ones that winked on every night in Hellcat Canyon. *What use are you, stars*, she thought, *if you can't perform*

*as a sort of celestial teleprompter and tell me what I
should say or think.*

Gabe didn't say a word.

She imagined, however, she could *feel* him silently
x-raying her words for evidence he'd been blown off.

"It's just . . ." she began. And stopped.

"Just?" he prompted. Voice quiet, soft as a pillow.

"It's just that between Annelise and my business,
someone needs to know where I am and what I'm doing
and how to reach me pretty much every single hour of
the day, and nearly every minute of my day is filled.
It's actually kind of exhilarating—like *American
Ninja Warrior* and Tetris and Whack-a-Mole all in
one."

He gave a soft laugh.

She rushed on.

"But whole weeks go by in a heartbeat, and I don't
want to miss a single second of Annelise's childhood
and it's just . . . easy to forget I'm a person apart from
my kid. And the awareness that I might be missing out
on something is kind of this . . . background noise, I
guess. Like the whir of a fan, or something. You can
kind of tune it out, until . . ."

She left that word hanging there, which lent it a melodrama she hadn't quite intended.

She didn't know how to finish that sentence.

She kind of wanted him to finish it himself, in his
head.

She immediately felt peculiarly raw, again, like she'd
said too much.

But he took all this in with that same flattering interest.

"Oh yeah, believe me, I completely get it," he said easily. He curled one hand around the post. "I'm on about four nonprofit boards locally, I'm in a softball league, I run a sort of informal group for veterans, I'm helping Mac and Avalon get their programs for at-risk kids and veterans up and running, I pinch-hit as soccer or basketball coach as needed, and next week I'm even standing in for a couple of days for Ray—"

"Ray, the guy who directs the kid pickup after school? Parking-monitor Ray? What's going on with Ray?" Her mom usually picked up Annelise after school, but Eden did occasionally, too. Everyone knew Ray.

"Gallbladder. I'll get a sub in by the end of next week. Mrs. Maker is circulating a card if you want to get in on that."

"I'll add it to my whiteboard."

He flashed a grin. "I guess what I'm saying is I swear sometimes I forget what the inside of my house looks like, because I come home and I'm out like a light the minute I hit the bed, then I get up and do it some more. And I love my job—I love making sure kids have what they need to thrive and shine, helping the teachers get it . . . I mean, one kid is like a whole *world*—often they're enchanting and other times they bore or madden the crap out of you, but it's all a piece of the puzzle. It's impossible not to give yourself over to that. They deserve everything we can give them."

But as she listened to this, she had a hunch there was a *reason* he didn't want to be home at his presumably empty-apart-from-him house.

She in fact had a million questions, all jostling for

the exits. But once she started, she didn't know if she could stop.

And who had time for that?

So she just smiled. Wistfully.

He stirred, restlessly, almost as if she'd stroked her hand slowly along his arm.

"Yeah," she agreed softly, finally. "That's my life in a nutshell."

"Guess it's next to impossible for busy adults like us to date." He shrugged.

"Guess so," she said after a moment.

She was fully aware that it was ridiculous to feel a little put out that he didn't sound more regretful.

Because *she* was relieved. Right? She was off the hook! She wouldn't have to relearn another person from the ground up, or shave her thighs, or buy better bras, or worry about yet another human's feelings.

Funny how *relief* suddenly felt like a synonym for *disappointment.*

It was possible the two feelings had arrived swirled together, like the vanilla and chocolate frosty cones Annelise loved. Reliefappointment?

And then . . . he actually *glanced at his phone.* Then turned it around to show her: Six fifty-nine. She'd told Annelise they had to get going by seven at the latest.

"I bet you get chatted up a lot at the flower shop, though," he teased suddenly.

"Oh, sure," Eden said. "Often by guys buying flowers because they did something to piss off their wives."

He laughed. "Have pity on us poor fools. Maybe the 2.0 version of men will have a bug fix. Now, if *I* was going to attempt to fascinate a woman like you—"

They whipped their heads around at a muffled thundering sound and saw Annelise skipping down the stairs and barreling toward the door, followed by Avalon and Mac. Avalon, good girl, was yelling, "Annelise Harwood, don't run on the stairs!"

At seven on the dot, Annelise burst through the doors exuberantly. "Uncle Mac gave me some broccoli to go!"

"Wow, that is *awfully* generous of him."

But her sister Avalon was behind Annelise, carrying the trifold paper, her face a gleaming question mark, and it was seven o'clock, and they had to get going, and Avalon was going to have to keep wondering about their conversation.

Gabe was already in the house, talking to Mac.

But damned if Eden wasn't *dying* to hear the end of his sentence.

CHAPTER 5

On the way home, Annelise said suddenly, "Once I saw Caitlynn Pennington's dad carry her on his shoulders. At a picnic."

They were all the way down River Road now and just about to head down Main Street. Back home to finish the Aztec report.

"Yeah?" Eden said brightly. Instantly guarded and alert again.

This *could* be about picnics, or shoulders, or about a rivalry with Caitlynn. Not another little delicate sideways attempt to find out about her dad.

"If I had a dad, we could go on a picnic, and maybe he'd carry me on his shoulders."

Annelise took notions as she tried to figure out the world. Once Eden had asked her why all but one of her Barbies were arrayed in a circle in front of a TV Annelise had made from the lid of an earring box.

The last Barbie was standing in a tall old necklace box, naked.

"I'm playing grown-ups," she'd explained. "They're

drinking coffee and watching CNN and Winter is taking a shower."

Apparently, Annelise had decided grown-ups didn't take baths. Grown-ups didn't have the time.

And here she was, trying to piece together what a dad was, what a dad did, what she might be missing. Ironically, one of the things she'd learned from Annelise's real dad that night was that he'd never known his own dad.

Eden's breathing went a little shallow. She'd done triple time as a mom since Annelise was born. And yet, she was beginning to feel cornered by the encroaching sense that it still might not be enough.

She turned onto Main Street now, where the familiar Gold Rush–era buildings painted muted shades of yellow, pink, and blue snuggled side by side like a little family. Over the flower store was their own beloved, cozy old apartment. It did indeed have a little backyard, not much bigger than a couple of tablecloths. Pretty and precious and theirs. Well, mostly theirs. The bank had the mortgage.

"I bet Mr. Caldera can carry even *you* on his shoulders," Annelise said, when they were a block from home.

Wow.

Just his name caused one of those thrilling jabs in the area of Eden's heart. Her mind's eye filled with huge gleaming shoulders, tree trunks cleaving in a spray of bark shrapnel—

She reached over to turn on the car's air conditioner, even though it was March.

That instantaneous weakness that swept through her

was both delicious and unnerving. And she wondered if that softening, that helpless fascination was some sort of programming built into the species designed to prepare a female for surrender in the face of brute male beauty.

Or if it was just that his strength reminded her that maybe she wasn't a fortress after all. That maybe doing it all, all by herself, all the time, wasn't a sustainable model for life.

That was a hell of a notion to attempt to accommodate right before they had to finish a report on the Aztecs.

"Wait—what do you mean he can carry *even* me?" she teased Annelise finally. "Because I'm as big as an elephant?"

"No, you're only as big as a yak!"

"No, I'm as big as a *wallaby*," Eden countered.

"No, you're as big as a pickle!"

"A pickle's not an *animal*!" Eden's outrage made Annelise roar with laughter. "What sound do you think a yak makes, Leesy?"

"Owwwwwoooooga!"

"Hey—that's the same sound Lloyd Sunnergren's old truck horn makes." Lloyd Sunnergren had a 1940s Ford in pristine condition, and Annelise was fascinated by it and by his big furry dog, Hamburger, who could soak her entire face with one giant slurp of his tongue.

"It's the sound a yak makes, too," Annelise insisted.

"Okay, I guess I'll have to take your word for it, since I don't know much about yaks."

"That's okay, Mom. We can Google them when we get home."

It was always pretty hilarious when she heard her own words coming out of Annelise's mouth.

And during the next few moments of silence, words flooded into her mind, like the refrain of a song: *If I was going to try to fascinate a woman like you . . .*

If only she could Google the end of that sentence.

How did he see her? How long had it been since she'd thought of herself as a Woman, not just a Mom, possessed of qualities unique only to her? What made Gabe Caldera *look* at her the way he did—like he was literally dazzled—and smile the way he did? Like he'd like to remove her clothes, slowly, with his teeth?

Because she couldn't imagine the next time she'd run into him. Might be weeks from now. And if Avalon tried to cleverly engineer anything, well, tough. She and Mr. Caldera (Gabe? Your Excellency?) had already established there wasn't time for any of that: for dating, or for "fascinating," or for hearing the ends of sentences that could only lead to other similar sentences that she didn't have time for.

So be it.

She'd likely forget all about it by morning, anyway.

When they got home, Eden cracked Annelise up by drawing a little smiling broccoli on the white-board on the day's date.

Then Annelise was dispatched to her room to finish her Aztec project, while Eden set about getting the house tidied and locked down for the night and began her preparations for tomorrow: she packed Leesy's lunch for school, loaded the dishwasher, tossed in one small, final load of laundry (because Annelise would want to wear her pink sweater tomorrow, and it was looking a little grubby), then went into their computer room—a little bigger than a closet, with a comfy old beat-up olive-colored love seat and a full-length mirror, and one of Peace and Love's two cat trees perched in front of a window that got a lot of sun—to power down the old desktop computer.

She sat down hard when she saw what was typed in the search engine bar.

Who is Annelise Harwood's dad?

Eden made a soft, stunned sound. Half laugh, half whimper of pain.

She sighed and pushed her fingers up through her hair. Dropped her head into her hands for a second. Oh, her baby. Trying to find things out in her way.

"I'm done with my report, Mom," Annelise called. "Can I play guitar for a little while?"

"Um, sure," Eden called absently.

Crap.

Seconds later, Annelise was playing that song again. "Invisible Dad."

Eden stood up slowly, then went to stand in Annelise's doorway and listen. Annelise was perched on the end of her bed. Her voice was pure, supple, naturally emotive, yet still sweetly childlike. She reached notes easily. And God only knew, genetically the kid probably got more than her fair share of confidence. And the talent sure hadn't come from Eden.

Invisible dad
The only dad I ever had
He knows what to say when I am sad
Invisible dad
Invisible dad
I wonder if his name is Brad or Chad?
If I knew that sure would be rad
Invisible dad

"Sweetie . . . that's . . . a . . . um . . . lovely song."

"Thanks!" she said cheerfully. "A minor goes good with C major." Annelise strummed and the wistful gloom of A minor filled the room.

"A rather mournful chord, isn't it?"

"What's mournful?"

"Sad. M-o-u-r-n-f-u-l."

Annelise mouthed the letters along with her. She'd have that word down, and it would likely get a starring role in quite a few of her sentences over the next few weeks.

"I know!" Annelise said with gleeful relish. "It *is* mournful!"

Eden sat down next to her on the bed. The coverlet was a retina-searing pink quilted job with pink bobbles on the hem. Annelise had insisted. Peace and Love was curled up on one of the pillows. He was a music fan.

The mermaid night-light was also pink, as was the little kid-sized guitar that Annelise set aside, resting its headstock on her pillow next to Peace and Love gently. She *loved* that thing.

Eden reflexively checked, and she saw that the tri-fold poster board, colorfully illustrated with information about human sacrifice and the Aztec language, calendar, education, and food stuffs, occupied a corner. Annelise would ace her presentation. The topic was a juicy one.

"Can I ask you something, Leesy?"

"Shoot."

Annelise had learned "shoot" from her grandpa.

"Do you think about your real dad very much? We haven't talked about that in a while."

Annelise searched her mom's face for some clue as to how she should answer.

Eden kept her expression open and cheerful.

"Mmm . . . just sometimes."

Eden's heart squeezed. In Annelise's rare thoughtful silences—for instance, when they were in the car together driving to Hummingbirds, or when Annelise was about to drift off to sleep—what did her baby think about?

"*Does* it make you sad that you don't know your dad?"

"Mmm . . . I don't think so. Maybe not *sad*. It's just . . . Caitlynn said he could be anybody. He could be the guy who sleeps in front of the courthouse. It could be Truck Donegal or Giorgio."

ARRRGH! Fucking Jan Pennington!

Because little Caitlynn was likely quoting her mom, who usually had the good sense not to say that stuff in front of her child, but give her a glass of Chardonnay, and she'd yammer on about anything. She'd probably said that to her husband, and Caitlynn overheard. Truck Donegal was an occasional bouncer at the Misty Cat, a reformed lunkhead of sorts, and Giorgio was their swarthy taciturn grill savant.

The only reason Eden cared at all was that it would send ripples of uncertainty and discontent across Annelise's world.

"I promise you, honey, your dad isn't anyone you've met or that even Mrs. Pennington has met. He doesn't live in our town. Caitlynn shouldn't say those kinds of things to you. It's a matter between you and your own family, and it's very impolite. If she says anything like that again, all you need to tell her is that it's private and you won't talk about it."

Easier said than done, that was for sure, given that her daughter was quite the gregarious talker. But she also had a good deal of pride and was no pushover.

"I told her he could be the president," Annelise said defiantly.

"Um—"

"Or maybe Nigel Lythgoe."

They religiously watched *So You Think You Can Dance*, and Annelise was very impressed by the strict, compassionate, knowledgeable Nigel.

"Well—"

"Or Han Solo."

"Han Solo is a fictional character, honey. And he seems lovely, but I've never met Nigel Lythgoe."

"Is it Principal Caldera?"

She was startled by another of those washes of weakness and that thrilling little heart jab. Just at the sound of his name.

"Mr. Caldera hasn't been in our town that long, sweets. C'mon, you're ten years old, Annelise. You have to get up close and personal to make a baby, and it takes nine months for a baby to get here. You know that."

"*So* gross," Leesy said placidly.

Songs about boys appealed to Annelise's sense of drama. The kissing part of boys and girls and whatnot still heebed her out a little. Thank God.

"Caitlynn's dad is on the city council," she said, with an offhandedness that fooled Eden not one bit. "That's pretty important."

So it was down to the competitive thing.

"Well, let's talk about what makes a person important and what makes a *thing* important. Who's the most important person in your daily life?"

"Um . . . you?"

Eden stifled a laugh. It was a pretty low-risk guess. "Good answer, kiddo. You are the most important person in the world to *me*. But you are also the most important person *you* know. And the *most* important *thing* to know is always be kind and sensible, right, because kindness comes back to us?"

"Right," Annelise agreed cheerily.

Eden reminded herself daily to savor these years where her daughter took her wisdom as gospel, and didn't know enough yet to ask questions like, "If you were so sensible, how did you get knocked up with me and wind up a single mom?" Those questions were a few years down the road yet, God willing.

"Baby, I can assure you that your father is talented and successful and cute, but nowhere near as cute as . . . *you!*" She lunged in for a tickle.

Annelise squealed in delighted outrage and dove right back at her for tickling.

Then Eden remembered she better not get her worked up before sleep.

"Okay, go brush your teeth and get into your jammies."

"Okeydoke!" Annelise half danced, half skipped off to the bathroom. She never simply walked if she could get there in a fancier way.

It often seemed to Eden like morning arrived as soon as her head hit the pillow, and she was looking forward to it, though she had a lot to think about tonight.

She turned around to leave Annelise's bedroom and then halted.

And slowly walked over to the Barbie Tableau.

The little doll she'd named Chrissie was perched atop Scrotal Ken's shoulders, and Scrotal Ken and Winter were holding hands.

And from a scrunchie and a length of yarn tie, Annelise had fashioned what looked like a tire swing.

CHAPTER 6

"You're awfully quiet, Lieutenant. You eat something wrong at Pasquale's?"

Gabe and his softball team had gone from practice at the high school field out to pizza, then back to the Veteran's Hall near city hall to work on a few repairs—wheelchairs, a tractor, a lawn mower, manly soothing activities requiring brute strength, grunting, and metallic clanks and clunks. With him tonight were Lloyd Sunnergren, who owned the feed store; Bud Wallace, who was seventy-two and tough and stringy as a guy thirty years younger and who had a sort of reserved dignity; Louis Hurlbutt, smart-ass ex-army; Mike Wade, also ex-army, a good guy with a mouth on him; Jordie Tahira, ex-marine, best wheelchair basketball forward in the league and had a killer arm. No one made it every week, but everyone made it most weeks.

Usually Mac joined them, too. He was busy with the donkey barn tonight, though.

"Everything is wrong at Pasquale's," Gabe said with

a little grunt as he attempted to wrench a rusted screw loose. "That's why we like it."

"Usually you're in full lecture mode right about now about how we did at practice."

This was true. Lecturing: a principal's habit. Kind of a lieutenant habit, too.

"Just thinking about my game. Deciding if I have any anymore."

"What are you talking about? You scored at least half the points last game." Bud's voice was a little muffled. He was upside down under a tractor.

"He's talking about women, nimrod," Mike said placidly.

"That's hilarious!" Louis crowed. "Who's the lucky girl who has you doubting yourself like you're some ordinary schmuck?"

This was what passed for sympathy among his friends.

"If I tell you, I'll never hear the end of it, and God knows you talk more than any of us want to hear, Louis."

"You're a catch, Caldera. Probably the most eligible bachelor in Hellcat Canyon. Since I was taken out of circulation, that is." This was Bud.

"Yeah, that's a dubious distinction. Who would be in the bachelor pageant? Me, Truck Donegal, Giorgio the grill cook at the Misty Cat?"

"We *should* have a bachelor pageant!" Louis announced.

"*What?* No, we shouldn't." Gabe was alarmed. "You've been breathing a little too much paint thinner, dude."

The conversation lulled, filled with clinking sounds and "Pass me that Phillips head" and the like.

"It's just . . . she's a little . . . squirrelly," Gabe ventured.

He knew it was risky talking about her. But the fact was, if he didn't talk about her, he might go mad.

"You're not talking about an actual squirrel, are you?" Mike wanted to know.

"What the hell is wrong with you? No. Pass me the torque wrench."

"I'm just saying you've been single for a while. No one would blame you if you wanted to get a squirrel for company. They're personable pets."

Gabe lifted his head to stare at him for a long time. "Okay."

"She pretty?" Bud wanted to know. Maybe it was his age, but Bud used words like *pretty* instead of *hot*, which Gabe kind of appreciated.

Gabe opened his mouth to answer.

Then closed it again.

And said nothing.

Because he felt like *pretty* did a disservice to Eden. The problem was that he couldn't really think of her in terms of simple adjectives. He thought of her more in terms of how she made him feel, like *want* and *soft* and *smile* and *like*, the kinds of words Koko the gorilla would sign to indicate her needs. He experienced her on a *very* basic, very fundamental level.

"Ooooh, he's got it bad," Jordie crowed.

He scowled at them and twisted a screw on Jordie's wheelchair. "I don't know why I say anything to you people."

"Listen, whoever she is, if she's single . . . you got nothing to worry about," Jordie soothed.

That was kind of sweet, actually.

"Of course she's single. I'm not *that* kind of guy. Not gonna moon after another man's woman."

"Then the only kind of guy who could give you a run for your money is someone like . . . oh, someone like Jasper Townes." Louis pointed at the flyer for Townes's side project, Black & Blue, on the bulletin board for an upcoming Misty Cat gig. Those flyers were all over town. "Man, I'd even do Jasper Townes."

"That guy from that stupid meme?" Lloyd scoffed. "Puhl*ease*."

Jasper Townes had indeed starred in a meme a couple of years ago. Something to do with John Mayer and an airport? Gabe couldn't quite remember now.

There ensued a noisy verbal division between jeering, mock horror, and a rumble of assent.

Gabe didn't think he'd be willing to do Jasper Townes, who admittedly did have something. But he *did* like Townes's band, Blue Room, kind of a lot.

"He's got that snaky-hipped thing going. Kinda like Jim Morrison or Jagger or Axl Rose. Like he's not a man or a woman but a . . . *sex* creature," Jordie claimed.

Gabe snorted. "What the hell is a 'sex creature'?"

Much spirited discussion of what a sex creature might be ensued.

Eventually it tapered off into a companionable silence.

"Or, you know, I'd do Sting," Bud Wallace said suddenly.

They all froze mid screw-twist and pivoted to stare at him, jaws unanimously dropped.

The silence stretched.

"He's into that tantric whatnot," Bud said with great dignity. "If this were a football pool, we'd want our guys to have *skills*. You want to have a deep bench."

Not a thing interrupted the total silence or dumb-struck stares.

Until: "Then you'll want to include a guy with a very long willy," Louis said thoughtfully, finally.

"And who was that movie star fella who put a hamster up his rear?" This was from Mike.

"That's an urban legend."

"And I don't know if that's a *skill*."

"Yeah, but he's a risk taker. You'll want one of those on your team."

Gabe rolled his eyes. They were, to a man, unasham-edly profane right down to the marrow, and not even a little bit prejudiced about anything, really. It was rather refreshing to listen to it now and again, given how tightly reined he kept his own id thanks to the require-ments of his job. Cathartic in the way that cranking the occasional death-metal tune in his car was.

He cleared his throat. "Hey, you guys . . . so, I'm really sorry about this, I can't make this week's game. I have to stop into the Chamber of Commerce mixer at the Misty Cat."

A stunned, frozen silence followed.

"*What?* You hate that kind of thing. You can drink bad wine any day of the week. We need you, man! You're our power hitter!" Louis was distraught.

Gabe wasn't taking it lightly, either.

He took softball just as seriously as they did, because if he was going to do something, he was going to go all in.

Which was exactly why he was going to the Chamber of Commerce mixer.

"It's just that I feel like I haven't been doing my duty as a representative of the school district."

The quality of the following silence told him that not one of them believed him.

"She's going to be there. That mystery woman." Mike blurted it like a *Jeopardy* contestant.

"It's Eden Harwood!" Louis guessed.

Gabe glared at him and resisted an impulse to look over his shoulder to see if Eden had appeared.

"Look at your face!" he crowed. "It is her, isn't it? What do I win?"

Gabe slowly straightened to his full height and aimed his best stone face—and it was a real Medusa-quality stone face—at them.

Which effectively subdued them.

For a few seconds.

"C'mon, Gabe. You don't have to worry about having game. Your résumé alone speaks for itself. It would wow anyone." It was pretty funny when Lloyd tried to soothe him.

"This isn't LinkedIn, Lloyd. She's not hiring a vice president of sales. This is about that intangible stuff. Chemistry. All that . . ." He sighed. "All that crap's sort of out of anyone's control."

"Oh, God. I know, right? Who knows what women want?" Louis complained.

"Obviously not you," Mike said, because someone had to say it and it was too easy.

Much laughter.

"Oh, man," Bud sighed. "Eden Harwood is so pretty.

If I haven't been married for a thousand years . . . but she's kind of a wild card. Enigmatic women scare me a little. Beware of the enigmatic woman, Gabe."

"Oh, *brother*, Bud," Gabe said. Albeit kindly.

He wanted to say, *She's not enigmatic. She's self-protective. I know her. I can feel her.*

The sort of woo-woo stuff that would almost definitely get him laughed at and might not even be true. The combination of infatuation and lust could do the same kinds of things to a man's brain as too much tequila did. That much he knew.

But he was older and wiser now. And he'd never felt this way before.

That alone was enough to try to see this thing through.

"You got this, Gabe," Mike said, and thumped him on the back heartily. As if he was part of a SEAL team going in to rescue hostages. "You don't need to worry about a plan."

Gabe treated him to a faint scowl, albeit one without rancor. These scoundrels still treated him with a certain tenderness around the subject of women. Which was touching and kind of funny, but also irritating because it only reminded him of *why* they treated him with a certain tenderness about women. He was tougher than that, for Christ's sake. Tough as a catcher's mitt, as nails, tough as the outside of the Joe DiMaggio baseball his dad had given him just before he died eons ago and which lived on his desk now, tough as Bud's ugly old toenail they all saw when he wore flip-flops.

"Oh, I have a plan," Gabe said, and gave the screw

one final, satisfying, decisive twist with the wrench, as he was locking it all into place even now. "I always have a plan."

The plan was, in fact, already underway.

He'd launched it at 6:59 p.m. at Devil's Leap yesterday.

Eden was shocked to find that she had to actually squeeze her way into the Misty Cat for the Chamber of Commerce mixer, but maybe she shouldn't have been. The previous winter had worked over everyone's nerves but good, what with Jamboree Street flooding into the music store, a giant redwood taking out Casey Carson's chimney during a storm (she claimed skillful Feng Shui saved it from smashing the roof), and the short-lived threat of a nearby dam bursting and washing away neighboring towns.

Getting accidentally-on-purpose a little drunk at the mixer and calling it networking was the only logical response to all of that.

Eden always found the mixer worth her while—it was a great way to learn who was getting married or buried or having a Quinceañera or a Bat Mitzvah or was in the doghouse with a spouse, all traditional flower occasions—even if she had to pay Danny twenty bucks to hang with Annelise for a couple of hours while she socialized and did her homework about all of this stuff.

She maneuvered in past Dion Gomez from Allegro Music who was deep in avid conversation with Greta from the New Age Store, and waved to her dad, who was selling beer to the folks who just couldn't bear to drink the wine. He was also managing the sound system, currently playing The Baby Owls, the band that had inadvertently given Glory Greenleaf a great big leg up in her career.

She arrived at the food table, helped herself to wine and one of the brownies stacked on the plate, and paused to admire a striking flyer taped to the wall above it—the paper divided into two rectangles, one black, one blue, the words *Black & Blue* in white across the middle. Beneath that was a date about a month from now. How dramatic. The Misty Cat hosted acoustic sets for a lot of rising bands on their way through from Oregon to the Bay Area.

At one time she would have known all of them. This band rang no bells at all. And that was life as a single mom.

Wine in one hand, brownie in the other, she turned around.

Her heart did a backflip so hard she nearly coughed. ("Hearts don't *backflip*, Eden."—Dr. Jude Harwood.)

Gabe Caldera was in the room.

Not only that, but he was wearing a *suit and tie*.

The impact was absurdly devastating. Maybe not better than a stripped-to-the-waist Gabe, but equivalently interesting.

He'd been principal at Hellcat Canyon Elementary for a few years, but she had literally never seen him at one of these events before.

She watched him weave through the crowd, smiling, lifting a hand in greeting at intervals—practically everyone had a kid or a grandkid in Hellcat Canyon Elementary—shaking hands, receiving and administering chummy back pats.

He was turning his head this way, scanning the place. Possibly looking, like all the reasonable adults present, for the wine.

Possibly looking for her.

Hope swept in like a riptide.

And it wasn't until that very moment that she realized how desperately she'd feared, on a subterranean level, that she'd never get a chance to hear the end of a sentence begun two days ago at Devil's Leap.

And how very, very much she wanted to hear it.

She'd had only two sips of wine, but as she watched him, she imagined him hurling aside all the people in his path like a linebacker to get to where she was faster. He probably totally could.

When he saw her, their eyes practically clinked together like wineglasses.

He made a beeline toward her, gracefully enough, not mowing anyone down.

She was pretty sure she didn't breathe the entire twenty seconds.

He arrived in front of her and stood smiling.

And she was smiling.

They both seemed to need a second to adjust to each other's presence.

". . . a woman like me . . ." she prompted finally.

". . . tough, but not as tough as she thinks she is. A little reserved, but that's because the waters run deep, and she protects those waters fiercely. Passionate. Graceful."

She stared at him, as dumbstruck as if he'd reached over and unhooked her bra.

He hadn't missed a beat.

"But I'm only guessing." His tiny, tilted smile was literally as sexy as a finger dragged slowly along the short hairs at her nape.

And from that particular recollection, memory spread like dawn over the land that her body was, in fact, a veritable map of pleasure. With little territories unexplored in what seemed like eons that could yield seismic jolts and electric currents of pleasure.

"Damn, Your Excellency, you don't mess around," she said finally.

His words were still kind of reverberating across her nerves. Shocking and delicious, like a strummed power chord. And just as invigorating.

She regarded him speculatively.

"I thought I'd cut to the chase," he said, "as we both claimed to prefer it."

"I guess I did say that."

"And?"

She thought for a second.

"I guess I do like it."

He smiled at that, slowly. The smile of a man whose risk had paid off in precisely the way he'd thought it would.

The crowd surged and heaved like a ball pit, and up popped the cheery face and body of Rhonda Grellman. "Hello, Eden! Oh, Gabe Caldera! Where have you been, you naughty man? It's about time you showed your face at one of these events again. Come talk with us about the Hellcat Habitats fund-raiser. We have some amazing ideas."

By "us" she meant her husband and a couple of the other board members.

Rhonda gave Gabe an encouraging tug, and off he went.

Eden would have watched him walk away just to savor that view, too, but she pivoted to a touch on her arm and found a smiling Ernie Digiulio, the best mechanic in Hellcat Canyon. "Eden, my wife and I want to talk to you about doing the flowers for my daughter's wedding."

Yay! A happy occasion. And lots more money!

"Oh, that's fantastic, Ernie! Congratulations! Is it Paula or Emmy?"

Ernie had five daughters. This was the reason, he liked to declare, he'd never be able to retire: all those daughters, all those college educations, all those weddings. Eden was pretty sure Ernie never actually wanted to retire. Not as long as he was still able to hoist the hood of a car, rub his hands together and say, "What seems to be the problem?"

So Ernie plucked her from the crowd like a flower from a bouquet and delivered her to where his wife was standing, over by the front window, and soon she was lost in her favorite kind of conversation, one about flowers and celebration. She didn't think about Gabe Caldera at all.

Except for wondering whether he was watching the back of her.

Or maybe her profile.

The entire back of her felt almost fuzzy with heat, as if she'd activated a heretofore unknown Gabe-sensing laser in her very cells.

About ten minutes—hereinafter her definition of

eternity—they moved past each other on the way to the wine table.

And stopped in front of each other.

He said, "Forgot also insightful. Smart. Warm. Funny. Beautiful . . . scared yet?"

She looked up into his face searchingly.

His eyes glinted a wicked dare.

"You know that roller coaster at Frontier World that has a ninety-five-degree drop, and three loops?" she said.

"Yeah?"

"I rode that thirteen times one summer."

"Wow."

"Got my name in the paper and everything."

"That confirms practically everything I just said."

"Didn't scream or throw up even once."

"You really can't ask for anything more than that from a woman."

She would have laughed, but the oxygen in the room had gone 100 proof, and she was kind of breathless. She knew for damn sure she couldn't blame the wine.

And for about two seconds they stood, an island in the crowd, sort of smiling at each other, sort of basking in each other's presence, and didn't speak while a lot of invisible things seemed to be taking place between them. Conversation had reached shouting volumes, as it invariably did about an hour into these things. Eden could hear Casey Carson laughing uproariously over the murmur of the crowd. Glass of wine number three usually made Casey laugh that way. She deserved it tonight. She'd set the hair for twelve bridesmaids in a raucous octogenarian wedding today while Eden had done the flowers: calla lilies. Simple and beautiful, white as the bride's hair.

Badfinger's "Day After Day" suddenly erupted from the speakers.

"Oh!" Eden said. It was an involuntary expulsion of delight. Her hand flew up to her heart and covered it.

"What's the 'oh' for? Please say it's because you just noticed and love my aftershave."

"This song. I love this song," she confessed. "It just gets me right here." Which was similar to where Gabe "got" her, but with him points south, so to speak, were also engaged. "Dorky, maybe, but man."

"Oh, *yeah*," he agreed, loudly, given that was how anyone could be heard at the moment in the Misty Cat. "This one and 'Baby Blue' are a couple of the tunes I sing in the—"

"Gabe Caldera!" Meredith Blevins, head of the Hellcat Canyon Planning Commission, do-si-doed a few people to get to Gabe and lassoed him with a chummy hand through the elbow. "Come talk to Paul Stansfield. He's thinking of running for school board next fall."

He was steered away, and because that's what people did at these things, he went, casting a wry glance over his shoulder.

Eden remained standing still.

Thoughtfully.

While all around her neighbors and friends milled.

She gave a start when her wineglass was gently removed from her hand by Casey.

"I hope you plan to replace that with a more interesting drink, Casey Carson. Otherwise you're just stealing, and that's not nice."

Sometimes she forgot to use grown-up words when talking to adults.

"How many of those have you had?" Casey asked suspiciously. On a semishout. Pretty close to her ear.

"You know I can't do more than one on a school night. Why?"

"Because you're just kind of standing there by yourself staring into space with a sort of loopy smile on your face. I've never seen you stand still for longer than a second during one of these events. I was beginning to wonder whether Greta laced the brownies with pot again."

Eden gave a guilty start. Where *was* Greta? She owned the New Age Store, which was thriving in this era of uncertainty for bookstores, which Eden thought must be due to some kind of magic spell and also because people will never *not* be willing to pay for a shot at hearing their futures predicted. But Greta had a way of reading auras at inconvenient times. She was a little worried hers might be pulsing red and pink, sporting long, vaporous cartoon arms looped around Gabe Caldera.

Her phone vibrated, saving her from making something up to tell Casey. Eden might be good at secret keeping, but she was bad at lies.

It was Annelise. Her heart gave a little jump, half fear, half joy, like it always did, and probably would for the rest of her life when her daughter called or texted her.

Mom, I can't find the glue stick!

This was followed by an emoji of a cat with wide, horrified eyes.

Uh-oh. Tonight's homework was doomed without the glue stick.

P.S. I even looked under the fridge!

Peace and Love had once stolen the glue stick and batted it all over the house, finally deliberately whapping it under the fridge like a fuzzy, dickhead David Beckham.

"Glue stick emergency!" She flashed her cell phone at Casey like an FBI badge. "Gotta run."

And while Gabe's head was bent attentively to listen to Meredith Blevins and her husband, she made a break for it, like Cinderella.

Because like she'd said that day in the hallway at school, she was onto him.

And if he knew how to fascinate a woman like her . . . she was pretty sure she knew how to fascinate a man like him.

If that was something she wanted to do, that was.

Because she didn't have time for that sort of thing, after all.

Cinderella stopped off on the way home from the ball at the all-night Walgreens in search of a glue stick.

When her head finally hit the pillow that night, instead of counting sheep or listening to some soothing, tweedly, New Age–bird song hybrid music, which she actually often did and quite enjoyed, a different refrain ran through Eden's head.

. . . *sing in the* . . .

She was pretty certain that last word was *shower.*

But it could be *car*. Or it could be *backyard* or *bathtub* or *key of G* or *Mormon Tabernacle Choir*.

But just as though it were a particularly fabulous book, the notion of missing the ending suddenly seemed untenable.

She had a hunch Gabe's strategy was to administer himself in potent little doses that released, stealthily, throughout her days. So that their conversation never really ended. So that in some way, he was always subliminally on her mind.

Which likely also meant she was always on his mind.

Diabolical man. She smiled to herself.

It was working like freaking gangbusters, if that was it.

But to figure out a strategy like that . . . damn. He must *really* want her. Not only that, but he seemed to *get* her. And while every woman wanted to hear she's beautiful in a man's eyes, true seduction was all about making it clear that he saw her for who she truly was. That maybe he saw things that no one else saw. And liked them all. And wanted them all.

His intuition about who she was under the mom clothes, the sexual tension between them she could literally slice and serve like birthday cake, but which he patiently held in check, which made it all that much hotter—Gabe Caldera was playing a long game.

And she couldn't remember the last time she'd felt so breathlessly, thrillingly uncertain.

Maybe when she was thirteen. She didn't know how on earth she could afford to apportion any of her life over to being uncertain, when the most precious person in the world to her was sleeping in the next room, still clutching the stuffed cat her Uncle Jesse had bought her when she was three.

Eden rolled over.

She picked up her phone.

She sat there in the dark, clutching it, heart picking up a beat ("Oh, brother. Hearts don't pick up a beat unless there's a *problem*, Eden."—Dr. Jude Harwood), suspended in indecision.

If she did what she was awfully tempted to do right now, it was tantamount to telling Gabe that not only was his plan working, but that she was officially participating. She was buying in.

But was it *really* as profound as all that? It was just one day in her schedule, right? One teeny tiny change. It didn't have to signify any kind of commitment.

She took a breath and dashed off the text to her mom.

Mom, I'll pick up Annelise from school tomorrow on the way to some deliveries. Danny's been dying to hold down the fort on his own and I'm going to give him a shot!

This wasn't *untrue.* Danny was dying to try everything in the world.

Eden would send Ray the parking monitor some flowers with a card that said, "Get well," but might as well read "Thank you."

Because she remembered *full well* who'd stepped into Ray's shoes while he was recovering from gallbladder surgery.

Her mom, who ought to be asleep by now because her day started incredibly early but who was probably awake reading the latest un-put-downable Susan Elizabeth Phillips novel, immediately texted back a thumbs-up and a half dozen kisses and hugs. Three each for her and Annelise.

CHAPTER 7

At ten minutes to three, Gabe posted himself in front of the school in Ray's absurd-but-deemed-necessary reflective vest and watched as mom after mom in car after car pulled up in front of the school—Suburbans, Explorers, Outbacks, sturdy, well-used, dust-powdered Hellcat Canyon SUVs. Most of the parents knew the pickup drill—where to line up in front of the school, how to enter the parking lot and circle out of it once their kids were safely collected and strapped in—but Ray's job was to make sure no one went rogue and took cuts or got confused or ran over a little person.

Despite Eden's speedy departure the other night, Gabe was feeling—possibly unreasonably—confident. All day.

At five minutes to three, just the slightest amount of doubt began to kick in.

So when the little white delivery van painted with a veritable garden of flowers pulled into the parking lot, it was all he could do not to fist pump.

He waited until Eden dutifully took her place in the queue.

She was the seventh car.

And then he strolled casually over and leaned down like he was about to issue a ticket.

Her window slid down.

She was wearing a green cardigan over a T-shirt that, if he was not mistaken, had a big cat face on it.

". . . sing in the . . ." was how she greeted him.

". . . shower."

Delight and hilarity, and something more intense and abstracted, like she was picturing him doing it, slowly suffused her face. "You sing in the shower?"

"Like a canary with bronchitis."

She laughed. Ye Gods, what a great, great laugh she had. Throaty and musical. Abandoned. The kind of laugh that made him want to pick her up and twirl her.

"Usually classic rock. And grunge is considered classic rock now, right? Soundgarden. A few selections from musicals."

"Aha. Like *Man of La Mancha*, for instance."

"Maybe so, maybe so. All right, Ms. Harwood. What are your guilty pleasure songs?"

"Oh, let's see . . . well, there's 'Nights in White Satin.' You know, that old song by the Moody Blues."

"Oh, yeah. Classic. I don't think you need to be embarrassed about that one."

"And 'Wichita Lineman.'"

"Another respectable choice."

"I've heard it about a million times over the years, and I confess I still get goose bumps from those very first notes."

"Do you often get goose bumps?" This was adorable.

He would, frankly, love to give her goose bumps. Maybe by applying his tongue to that little hollow beneath her ear where her heart would be thundering because she was wildly turned on.

"Mmm. Sure. Well, sometimes. Usually when I see or hear something that feels, oh . . ." She shrugged a little self-consciously. ". . . particularly beautiful and true."

He couldn't think of what to say, because what she'd just said was beautiful and true, as far as he was concerned, and she'd said it offhandedly, as though it was just one of the thousands of everyday thoughts she had.

So he just smiled.

Something about his smile made her tuck a strand of hair behind her ear and pink rush into her cheeks.

More cars pulled into the parking lot, and he stepped away to eyeball to make sure no one took cuts, double-parked, ran over an errant child or squirrel.

"Ray says to tell you thanks for the flowers, by the way," he said.

"Oh. Of course he's welcome. Okay. So what about you . . . what are your other guilty pleasure songs, Principal Gabe?"

"Oh, let's see . . . Okay, there's 'First Time Ever I Saw Your Face.' Roberta Flack."

"Oh." Her eyes were huge.

"What? Too gloppy?"

"No. It's perfect. That bass line. You know, like a heartbeat." She tapped her sternum with her hand. "Thump thump. Thump thump."

"Like a couple of lovers laying there after, you know."

"Yeah," she said slowly, teasing him for the euphemism in a way that made, if not goose bumps, then something similarly tingly, trace his spine and tighten his stomach muscles. "After 'you know.'"

"I have to use euphemisms on school grounds. And especially when I'm in uniform." He gestured to his glowing vest. "I do actually know all the grown-up words for 'you know.'"

He was dying to say, "And I'd happily whisper them in your ear in the supply closet right now, if you'd like," but he knew he was going to need to calibrate with Eden Harwood.

They smiled at each other, and hers was tilted, ever so slightly wry and rakish. But a little uncertain.

"It's kind of a cut to the chase song," he added thoughtfully. "Topic wise."

"It is," she agreed.

"Whenever I hear it, I stop what I'm doing and gaze mistily into the middle distance."

"You *do*?"

"I don't know. I'm just assuming. Based on the way your face looked when you heard 'Day After Day.'"

She laughed again, delightedly. "Okay, what else?"

"Um . . . okay, you know what gets me? That Blue Room song that was everywhere a few years ago?" He crooned, "'Hey, Lily Anne, I've never been so glad to be a man' . . . what? What's wrong?"

Eden's face had gone as blank as a jukebox with the cord yanked. It was the expression of someone who patently does not want someone else to know what they're actually thinking.

"What is it? Is my singing *that* bad? Not a Jasper Townes fan? Or is it because I can't hit the high notes the way he can?"

"No," she said, after a little hesitation. "I actually like your interpretation better than his."

"No accounting for taste, I guess."

She laughed at that, and light and expression flooded her face again, as if someone had flipped a switch. That was a relief.

"I'd probably get booed offstage at open mic nights at the Misty Cat, wouldn't I?" he said, faux glumly.

The clock on her dash showed two minutes to three. Gabe pivoted a quarter turn. The big double doors of the main school building had just been thrown open by Carl the janitor.

And then the final school bell rang. A sound that punctuated his days.

Whoosh! The colorful tide of kids began pouring out and running toward the cars parked for their moms or dads to ferry them home again. He could see Annelise in the crowd. Her goldy blond, pink-streaked hair flashing.

"Well, as you said, there's no accounting for taste," Eden said. "But my dad might give you the hook. He's a man of strong, distinctive opinions when it comes to music, and he has great taste."

"Yeah, I've met Glenn. A straight shooter, your dad. He's not stingy with opinions. So are you more like your—"

And just like that, Annelise was running up to the car, face lit up with the sheer pleasure of seeing her mom, backpack thumping on her narrow back, two pigtails flying.

"Hi, Mr. Caldera. Why are you here? Am I in trouble?" She sounded more curious than concerned. She was a pip, Annelise Harwood.

"Did you eat your leftover broccoli that your Uncle Mac gave you?"

"I totally did!"

"Then not today."

Annelise fell all over herself with giggles as she hurled herself into the car.

"Give me a smooch," Eden ordered.

Gabe actually took a half step forward before it fully registered that she was talking to her daughter.

Annelise pulled herself forward from the backseat and kissed her mom noisily on the cheek, then sank backward again.

"Mom, we're doing a report on ecosystems! Do you know what an ecosystem is?"

"I'm familiar with the concept, yes, child."

"We're gonna need some glitter."

"Glitter? Where is this ecosystem, the Land of Oz?"

"Noooooo!" This was hilarious, apparently. "I just wanted the flowers to be really shiny! Flowers are important!"

"Word, girlfriend." Eden held her hand back to be high-fived by Annelise. "She likes everything to be shinier," Eden explained to Gabe.

"It's a good life philosophy," he concurred.

Nothing was shinier than their two faces now. Glowing like a couple of little suns, happy to be in each other's company again.

He could all too easily imagine them being the sun in his ecosystem.

Behind them a car containing a mom and child gave an impatient tap on the horn.

He stepped away reluctantly. Eden gifted him with a smile, then lowered her shades.

"Okay, buttercup, let's roll."

"Bye, Mr. Caldera!" Annelise leaned out the window to wave. He waved at them.

Which made him feel obliged to wave at every mom and child leaving as they all departed the parking lot, like some kind of town eccentric.

If that was the toll for talking to Eden for a few minutes, he'd happily pay.

And it was actually kind of fun.

Even though he of course had to get to a board meeting.

The next day Eden said to her assistant, "Hey, Danny, I'm going to pick up Annelise and leave a little earlier today than yesterday. How do you feel about holding down the fort about ten minutes longer than usual?"

"I'm down with that, Ms. H. I can totally do that! You can count on me!"

She was blessed that she'd found an assistant who was such a nice person and who was ready to seize life by the throat, balls, nape, whatever portion of it he grabbed on to.

She only realized how embarrassingly, transparently early she was to pick up Annelise when she barely recognized the virtually empty school parking lot. She'd never seen it when it wasn't crowded with harried parents in revving vehicles. It was empty, apart from a couple of blue jays hopping around on the sidewalk.

And Gabe. Standing there in Ray's reflective vest.

She could see his grin from the entrance.

She pulled up right next to him and rolled down the window.

"You came first," Gabe said.

He froze in place when he realized how that sounded.

So did she.

Behind him a blue jay hop hop hopped, comically, in the fraught silence.

She slowly dragged her sunglasses away from her face.

"You don't *mind* if I come first, do you?" She furrowed her brow ever so slightly.

"I'm all about whatever you need," he said instantly, with such quiet, staggeringly thrilling conviction her breath stopped.

YOW!

Her nether regions flared with heat as though a match had been tossed down there.

She was reminded in that moment that this was a capital "M" man. Whatever they were doing, he meant business. What he'd just said confirmed for her everything she suspected he held in check.

He was waiting for cues from her.

She didn't know what to say.

Her mind had blanked. Part of her floated overhead, watching herself in her L.L. Bean button-down mom shirt (albeit a flattering one) in her flowery mom van, trading sizzling sexual innuendos with an elementary school principal whose green eyes were now just a little crinkled at the corners.

He knew exactly what he'd just done to her.

And he probably knew that she'd shocked herself.

Where on earth could their conversation *go* when it had started with an innuendo about orgasms? She should just start the car, back up, and pull quietly out of the parking lot and never return.

Instead, she folded her hands primly in her lap as if tucking in wayward wantonness.

"Are you more like . . ." she prompted. Somewhat subdued.

". . . your mom or dad," he completed easily. His eyes were still full of those wicked lights. Amused. But no less serious.

Her breath hadn't yet returned to normal cadences.

And might never.

"I'm going to go with . . . well, I love them both madly. But I'm more like my dad."

"Your dad, huh? Yeah, I think I see the resemblance around your fluffy mustache."

He was laughing now.

"Hey! I'll have you know Casey Carson prides herself in ripping every single hair off my face in exchange for really creative bouquets for her salon waiting area."

He winced. "I'm not sure that's a fair exchange. But why do you think you're more like your dad?"

She hesitated. "Well, my dad's a little less effusive, a little more guarded than my mom. Ferociously loving and protective, in his own growly way. Thinks my mom hung the moon, even after forty some-odd years of marriage."

"Yeah?" he said softly. "Why do you think you're guarded?"

It was a friendly, conversational question. But it was also a dare, in a way. And if she took it, it was another step down the ladder into the deep end of the pool.

Then again, every question between them was like this.

And she excelled at swimming.

And she couldn't resist a dare.

But the deeper they got in, the harder it would be to just zip right back out to the safety of certainty.

It had been a pretty long time since she'd answered these kinds of questions about herself. Who was she, apart from Annelise's mom? When was the last time someone wanted to know?

"Mmm . . . maybe I was born that way? But sometimes I think it's because every family is dealt a sort of quotient of emotions to be distributed among the members, you know, like cell phone plans dole out minutes. My sister Avalon was always so very heart-on-her-sleeve, playing St. Francis to all these animals and I . . . I kept mine under wraps because I thought everyone would be surprised by how . . . *powerfully* . . . I felt things. I think pride was sort of wrapped up in it, too. And then I kind of liked being hard to read. I have never said that to anyone in my life. Certainly not in a drive-by situation."

Her cheeks were warm. It was something of a warning. To tread delicately. Saying these things out loud made her feel a little raw.

"It must be the persuasive authority of my uniform." He gestured to the neon vest. "But thank you for being honest."

"Natch," she said.

That made him grin.

"It's why I have only one cat, by the way," she added.

"How's that again?"

"Because I feel like I can love him really well and really personally, rather than being profligate with my affections."

That was a warning.

And a reassurance.

And an explanation.

Gabe's head went back a little. Came down in a little nod of comprehension. As if filing this away, adding it to his impressions of her.

"You know, I once put my hand against the smooth wall of this locked room and discovered it was hot," he said casually after a moment. "Turns out it was because the room was on fire."

"Mmm. Boy, that is one subtle metaphor, Mr. Caldera. Do you race into burning rooms, or away from them?"

"What do *you* think?"

"I think it depends . . . on who might be in there."

Their eyes met again.

And in the quiet, the opening crystalline notes of Blue Room's "Lily Anne" chimed from the car radio.

Eden reflexively slapped the radio off like it was an insect needing killing.

She left her hand there, as if covering it would prevent the song from escaping. Her heart was pounding.

"Hey," Gabe said, startled. "Wasn't that—"

He pivoted as a big Chevy Suburban pulled into the parking lot, screeched to a halt behind Eden. The mom whipped out some knitting. Moms everywhere, stealing minutes here and there for something other than momming.

Eden glanced at the clock on her dash. Two minutes and counting.

"Are you more like your mom or dad?" she said in a rush.

"Oh, definitely my dad. Smart guy. Taciturn. He had this very distinct sense of right and wrong. Kinda saw things in black and white, and I think I have a tendency to do that, too. Affectionate in mostly an arm-punch kind of way. Boy, did he love us, though. And once he loved something, *anything*, it was for keeps, hell or high water. Career army, which was tougher on my mom, but they were rock solid. Had really strong convictions about all kinds of things. I wanted to be like him. And I really wanted to make him proud. But he died when I was sixteen. Bum ticker."

This recitation was pretty casual, but every word of it practically glowed with affection. Eden just sat for a moment, enjoying the warmth he gave off.

"He's the one who gave you that baseball on your desk," she guessed.

His face blanked in astonishment. "How did you . . ."

"You sort of seemed to commune with it the other day when I was in there with Jan Pennington."

"*Commune?* Maybe I picked it up, but—"

"Communed," she said firmly, laughing quietly. "Like

you're checking in with your dad when you give your sage Principal Gabe advice."

He was clearly nonplussed, which was both funny and touching. This guy had a bone-deep confidence, built like strata in rocks through testing himself again and again.

And she realized the soft places on his inside might be just as enthralling as the hard places on his outside.

"I'm a grown man. I was a freaking lieutenant! I don't need to commune with my dad to make decisions."

He still sounded amused, but a little adamant. And just a little bit like he was trying to convince himself of this.

She tipped her head and studied him. "Maybe none of us ever grow out of needing . . ." She faltered, as she realized what she was about to say. ". . . needing a dad."

Damn.

She bit her lip.

The double doors burst open to the school then, and Carl the janitor locked them into place. In a minute or so, the first kids would begin to trickle out, and then it would become a colorful, frisking tide.

"That's what I'd rescue from a burning building, by the way. That baseball. What about you? House is on fire, you have two seconds, you grab . . ."

"Let's see. Well, Annelise isn't technically a possession . . . because I can't sell her on eBay, though pre-broccoli-eating days, I've been tempted to do that once or twice. And Peace and Love isn't a possession, he just kind of *lets* us take care of him . . ."

"Peace and Love is your well-loved cat, right?"

"Mmm-hmm. Daughter, cat. As long as we get out together, we're good."

"That's all you need, huh?"

The question was light. But it fell on her ears a little bit like a test she wasn't certain she'd crammed for yet.

Crap.

And then all at once she remembered Gabe snatching that kid out of harm's way, and suddenly she knew the right thing to say. The thing he needed to hear. The thing she wanted him to know.

"If you're the person standing outside the burning room, we'll have nothing to worry about. We'll get out okay."

He said nothing. Leaned back from the car.

Just looked at her as if maybe seeing her for the first time, and his expression, the sort of amused wonder in it, made her heart skip.

"He's proud of you, Gabe," she said suddenly. "Your dad."

"How do you know?"

"I'm a mom now. It confers certain superpowers. So I know."

He quirked the corner of his mouth.

They both looked at the door of the school.

Ten, nine, eight, seven . . .

Suddenly Gabe said, "So do you consider yourself com—"

FOOSH! An explosion of life and energy as kids began pouring out of the school, and Gabe took a step toward the kids and back from the car, and Eden could already see Annelise, her colty-legged darling, the pink streak in her hair glowing, racing toward them. She popped the locks as Annelise hopped in.

Gabe stepped back from the car to make sure everyone and everything was in his view and safe, and as she pulled away before the moms could start honking at her, she had no doubt that it was.

CHAPTER 8

Jan Pennington was startled but pleased to get a call from Principal Gabe Caldera two days later, on the day after a substitute was found for Ray the parking monitor.

"Well, certainly, Gabe, we can always use another hand on the carnival decorating committee, if you'd like to stop in, or if you'd just like to see how things are going. We start at around six. We'll be in the cafeteria for a couple of hours. You can find us there."

He could *just* about fit a few minutes of that in if he grabbed a sandwich and ate at his desk. And maybe showed up at tonight's board meeting at the first break, instead of right when it started.

When he arrived at the cafeteria about a quarter after six, about a dozen women were arrayed around big slabs of poster board and sheets of butcher paper spread out in the middle of the cafeteria floor.

Over in the corner, a few little girls, Annelise Harwood and Caitlynn Pennington among them, were sitting at a lunch table pulled out for the occasion, mounds of backpacks flung about the floor and what looked like a selection of dolls in the middle of the table. Much giggling was going on.

He didn't know what it said about him that he spotted Eden pretty much immediately, even though he couldn't see her face: on her hands and knees, butt up in the air, from the looks of things meticulously stenciling a big "F" in metallic gold.

It was worth blowing a hole in his schedule for that charming view alone.

He was a mature adult, but he was a man, and he forgave himself for standing there, kind of mentally measuring each of her cheeks and comparing it to the span of his hands. By his calculations, if he pulled her body into his and slid his palms down to cup it, the fit would be about flawless.

He gave a start when Jan rushed forward to thrust a paintbrush into his hand. "Welcome, Gabe! We can use you on the dunking booth sign. I hope you brought your smock."

"Oh, I never go anywhere without my smock, Jan," he said gravely. He patted his jeans pocket. She glanced at his pocket, puzzled. He shouldn't tease her. Jan clearly took smocks seriously. "I think I'm just going to stroll through and check out what everyone is doing first."

"Wonderful," she enthused, then zipped off again, to micromanage someone's sign painting.

Eden was now sitting back on her heels, critically assessing her handiwork.

When he arrived next to her—he didn't quite make a beeline, maybe more like a "C" line or an "S" line—

she looked up slowly, her eyes traveling along his shins and torso all the way up to his face. The smile that spread all over her face was a little cocky, wildly amused, and—maybe this was wishful thinking, but he didn't think so—relieved.

Eden was invested.

That was a thrill that rendered him momentarily speechless.

"Your Excellency," she said by way of greeting.

After they'd spent a moment basking in each other's presence.

He nodded once. Absurdly, he couldn't speak yet. Her hair was piled on top of her head, exposing her long neck, and she was wearing a big blue man's shirt, which immediately made him wonder about, and feel a twinge of jealousy about its provenance.

And also gave him an opportunity to imagine her wearing one of his after a particularly lusty evening.

She rose to her feet slowly. "So do you consider yourself com—"

They both gave a start when seemingly out of nowhere Jan Pennington appeared next to them, practically vibrating like a dart hurled into a bull's-eye. It was pure indignation.

"Look at this, Gabe. Just look at it!" she hissed.

To his amazement, she shook a doll at him like a voodoo rattle.

"Jan," he said evenly. "Please don't shake a doll at me."

Which was something he'd never thought he'd need to say to anyone, really.

"But look at *this*."

She shoved what appeared to be a pantless Ken doll into his hand.

He had no choice but to grasp it.

"Seems this thing belongs to Annelise Harwood," Jan said. "All those little girls were over there playing with it. LOOK. AT. HIM."

Gabe fixed Jan with a long, quelling stare. "Jan, we teach our children to use the word 'please' in front of any request. Don't you think we ought to model the behavior?"

"Please," she said. In an anguish of outrage.

He stifled the mother of all sighs. And then uncurled his palm and peered down at the doll lying in it.

The Ken doll gazed mutely up at them, his brown eyes poignantly blank. His painted-on crew cut was circa late sixties. He was wearing a little striped jacket with wide lapels.

And nothing else.

Between his legs someone had drawn a really explicit, textbook-quality member. Meticulously rendered in ink, it rested atop a plump healthy scrotum, all of which was nestled into hair depicted by generous pen curlicues.

They all stared wordlessly down at him, like CSI detectives gathered around a victim on a slab.

No one moved.

Until—cautiously—Gabe tweezed up Ken's little striped jacket with his fingers. Why, he didn't know. Checking for tattoos or scars or other identifying marks? Isn't that what they did on *CSI*?

"Nice . . . um, pancreas?" he hazarded finally.

He cautiously lifted his eyes.

Eden's mouth was trembling like a dam about to burst. Her eyes were turning pink. Could someone expire from holding in a laugh?

"Obviously, it's not the *pancreas* I'm concerned about!" Jan hissed.

Annelise skipped over. "Mama, what's wrong? Am I in trouble? I was changing Ken into his shorts!"

"You're not in trouble, sweetie. It seems Mrs. Pennington is a little startled by the illustrations on your Ken doll here." Eden sounded a trifle strangled.

"But it's only a penis, Mom, right? Nothing to get worked up about? Isn't that what you said?" Annelise's hands clasped worriedly.

Gabe slowly levered his head to stare at Eden.

The laugh he couldn't release filled him like helium. It was almost an out-of-body experience. He could practically feel himself hovering somewhere around the cafeteria ceiling.

But Eden was looking at Annelise, who was looking up at Eden with innocence and trust and absolute conviction in her mother's sovereign knowledge and judgment.

"Yes, sweetheart, you're exactly right. All boys have them, and private parts are private," she said calmly.

Eden turned to Jan and said, "There's an anatomically correct heart on there, too, Jan. And about three-quarters of a pancreas. And part of the circulatory system. Did you bother looking under his shirt, too, or were you just determined to see what he had in his pants?"

Damn. High-fiving her was probably inadvisable, though it was all he could do to keep his hand at his side. For some reason, he was still clutching the half-dressed Ken.

Jan's cheeks flashed red, then white, then red again.

Gabe was a little worried that if Eden and Jan were about to throw down, he wouldn't stop them.

At least immediately.

"Some would argue that a man's heart is just as important as his penis," Eden added. With a certain quiet, grave reproach. "Maybe Caitlynn would benefit from learning that."

Gabe wasn't fooled. Eden was *furious.*

But she'd skillfully rendered Jan absolutely speechless, and surely this ought to rank among superpowers.

And just when he thought she couldn't get any sexier.

"Mama?" Annelise was still uncertain.

"Annelise, honey, everything's okay. Mrs. Pennington was just surprised, that's all, because he doesn't look like the other Kens. Why don't you go finish your homework? I'll bring Ken back to you."

"Okay," she said trustingly. Rightness restored to her world by a word from an adult.

She skipped off.

"Jan," Gabe said patiently, instantly, "the kids have had sex ed classes this quarter. Surely Caitlynn knows boys have different private parts? She has a brother. She's such a smart, intuitive kid. I know you're startled, and I sympathize, but maybe you can use it as a teaching moment. About the circulatory system, if nothing else."

"It's just that it's a little wearing to be so consistently

startled by Ms. Harwood and her offspring," Jan said icily.

"Jan, I'm going to confide something to you," Eden said, all low-voiced, apologetic confidence. That soothing, talking-someone-from-a-ledge voice again. "This Ken is a hand-me-down. He's a couple of decades old. I couldn't afford to get new Barbies for Annelise at that time, so she played with the ones we had as a kid. And my brother, Jude? He's a cardiac surgeon now." Eden paused to let Jan absorb this, and watched, predictably, as her face transformed. Jan was *all* about rank and perceived status. "Even back then, Jude was a stickler for accuracy. I screamed bloody murder when my brother did this to my Ken, but I wasn't really in a position to buy new dolls. And I *so* wanted her to have some to play with. And you know what that's like, right? How hard it is to deny your kids anything?"

It was positively *masterful*.

There was really almost nothing Jan could say that wouldn't make her sound like a heartless bitch.

"I understand," Jan said finally, her voice a little creaky. "I was just, um, surprised, as you said."

"Naturally," Eden soothed.

Gabe finally extended the Ken doll to Jan, who took it gingerly. "I'll just go take this back to Annelise now," she said almost meekly.

"Thank you," Eden said magnanimously.

She watched Jan go. And then she drew in a long, long breath and exhaled.

Gabe was regarding her as though she was a miracle.

"Nothing to get worked up over, huh?" he said.

"Well, it all depends, of course." She said this mildly.

He stood, utterly arrested by the lingering flush of anger in her cheeks and that wicked glint in her eyes.

A half dozen wicked optional responses flitted through his mind: "I bet I can give you something to get worked up about, given a few minutes alone in the supply closet." Or, "Did you know I rechristened my penis 'Your Excellency'? I'd be happy to demonstrate why."

He was pretty certain his eyes got that point across. Because her own went rather dark. And she tucked a stray hair behind her ear.

What he said out loud, though, was, "I think I'm going to have 'some people think a man's heart is just as important as his penis' embroidered on a pillow."

"Or you could have it engraved on your car's license plate frame."

He laughed. A little too loudly, apparently.

Heads swiveled toward them, including Jan's. He clapped his mouth shut guiltily. Gabe understood that they were here to get the school's business accomplished, and the school's business was his business.

So like kids caught passing a note in class, they both dropped to their knees.

". . . complicated or . . ." Eden prompted. She gestured at the "E." At the opposite end of the sign, room enough so that they wouldn't accidentally paint each other.

He dunked his brush in shiny, gloppy gold.

". . . simple? You can only choose one."

"Complicated," Eden said instantly.

"Complicated like a labyrinth, or complicated like an . . . ecosystem?" He meticulously stroked one arm of his assigned "E" full of gold paint. And paused to admire it.

"Mmm . . . I'm gonna go with complicated like an ecosystem, but aren't they elegantly simple when you understand them?" She was already done with the "F" and moving on to the "O." Which brought her just a little closer to him.

"So I guess you're more *intricate*, as it were, than complicated. Although I'll accept the word 'elegant' when it comes to you," he allowed.

"I guess I am. And I'll accept the flattery. My life has a lot of different moving parts that may not seem at all related but which are, in fact, interconnected and necessary to each other's mutual survival."

"*All* of the parts are necessary?"

She paused. Sat back on her heels. Held her brush thoughtfully aloft, like a conductor with a baton.

"Mostly. For a visual representation, you should see my whiteboard, man. I am the Bobby Fisher of whiteboards."

He stopped, too. Sat back on his own heels, next to her.

"Well, you know, sometimes ecosystems are missing the one very important thing. You know what happened when they reintroduced wolves to Yellowstone after seventy years after the deer had grazed it down to nothing? It changed the behavior of the deer. They didn't chomp on the vegetation so much. The trees and vegetation grew back, all kinds of wildlife thrived again and moved into the region. It even changed the course of rivers. It was restored to its original natural . . . wild . . . beauty."

Their gazes collided with such force.

"Wolves are kinda hot," she said offhandedly.

"Ecosystems, too."

"If only Red Riding Hood had known. Her story could have had a whole different ending."

He grinned. A little wolfishly, as it so happened.

She took what looked like a sustaining breath, which made him hope that she'd momentarily lost hers.

She turned her gaze away with apparent reluctance. Dipped her brush in paint again and applied herself to the "O."

"Now you," she said softly. "Complicated or simple?"

"Simple," he said instantly.

"Simple like Lloyd Sunnergren's dog, Hamburger, or simple like a . . . mountain?"

"Wow, that's practically like a Zen koan, that choice."

"You have to pick one."

"Mountain. Big and basic," he said decisively.

"Did you know mountains are created over millennia due to violent underground activity, Gabe? They're strong and peaceful, but it's a hard-won peace."

He went still.

"Damn, woman," he said finally. Weakly.

If he wasn't already on his knees he'd be tempted to fall to them in supplication, only half in jest.

She smiled, gave a little shrug. "Annelise had to do a diorama of mountains. Not that I was entirely without knowledge of mountains and how they got there before we did that project."

"Mountains support ecosystems, too. They have ecosystems all *over* them."

She laughed at that, that amazing, musical, throaty laugh.

"Okay, so who was your last serious—"

The timer on his phone dinged and he lunged for it. "Oops, gotta get to the board meeting. They need me for a vote."

He sprang to his feet. "And would you believe it? I'm back on parking monitor duty tomorrow after school. Just for a day."

There was some solace in the flicker of regret and amused knowing in her eyes, the rueful tilt of the corner of her mouth.

He'd see her tomorrow in the school parking lot. He would wager just about anything on it.

Still. As hard as it was to leave her now, he knew it was only going to get harder.

"Make sure everyone here knows that I painted that beautiful 'E,'" he added over his shoulder, when he'd gone five steps.

Just for the opportunity to see her one more time.

And to see if she was watching him leave.

She was.

Which made leaving just a little more bearable.

The next day . . .

"**. . . m**y last serious . . . ?" Gabe was back in the green reflective vest. Eden was about ten minutes early this time, as they both knew she would be.

"Girlfriend. Who was your last serious girlfriend?"

She almost didn't want to hear the answer. But surely it was a fair question, in their series of questions? Who was the last person who knew all the answers to the questions she wanted to ask him?

"Ahhh, let's see. Last *serious* girlfriend was actually my fiancée, Lisa Mazzoni. It's been about seven years."

She froze. The word *fiancée* was a sudden dart to the heart.

She froze, as shocked by the piercing pain of it, as by the news. Which shocked the dickens out of her. It took her a full precious two seconds to reassemble her thoughts. To get a grip.

"What happened? Twenty-five words or less."

His hesitation registered on all of her senses as a warning.

"She died. Car accident."

The words drove the air from her lungs.

A strange sweep of vertigo, as if she'd sustained an actual blow, made her fingers curl into a tight grip on her steering wheel. As if she could imagine that moment. And what it had done to Gabe's life.

He didn't say anything.

And she couldn't yet speak.

And she couldn't just leave him standing alone with those words ringing in the air. "God, Gabe. I . . . I'm sorry . . . I didn't mean to be so . . ."

He gave a "what can you do" shoulder shift. "No worries, Eden. Our deal is we answer each other's questions, and it was a perfectly reasonable question. You didn't know, and I'm okay with talking about it. Some drunk asshole running a red hit her."

"Horrible." Her voice was arid.

"Yeah."

A big mom van zoomed into the parking lot, then slowed. The face behind the wheel was clearly craning to see where she ought to park.

Gabe stepped backward away from Eden, gestured the mom into line with a wave.

An oddly personal hurt, very close to fury, simmered around her heart. Like he'd always been hers to protect, and she should have been there for him. How had life *dared* to be so cruel to him?

But within all of that was a tiny grain of pure, breath-stealing jealousy: he'd once offered forever to another woman.

The way she felt about that could rightly be called an epiphany.

Gabe returned. "Sorry. I don't like to talk about it mainly because I'm aware that it's hard for people to hear. Sorry to lay it on you like that."

"You didn't lay it on me," she said instantly. "I asked because I wanted to know. It's not a burden, and I'm not as delicate as all that. Thank you for telling me."

He smiled faintly.

"I'm only just . . . incredibly sorry that happened to you. I just . . ."

Wish it hadn't happened? Wish you hadn't suffered?

She wished all of those things and more.

"I've dated since then, of course," he said. "It's been quite a while."

"Still," she said.

"Yeah."

A big old Toyota Highlander cruised into the parking lot. Emily's mom. Both Eden and Gabe turned to watch her, and to raise hands in greeting.

And for a few moments they didn't speak. She was glad of the silence, as all of the things she'd just learned sifted together with all of the things she felt. And then suddenly something else was clear.

"Is that how you got simple?" she asked. "Because of Lisa?"

He took a quick reflexive little step backward. As if she'd just swung a flashlight into his face.

He assessed her almost warily.

And then a smile, a small, slow one. In it was something like surprise. And surrender.

"Yeah," he admitted.

Interesting. He could suss her out pretty well, but it was clear he wasn't used to being as accurately read. He was a guy who was used to being in control.

"It's just . . . I have a feeling birth and death are like laser beams that slice through and sort the daily bullshit," she explained. "When I found out I was pregnant with Annelise, it was funny . . . it should have been chaos, but everything just instantly got crystal clear. Everything in my life suddenly sorted itself into categories—into important or not. And it was quite the epiphany what made the cut and what didn't."

They said nothing for a moment.

"I guess that's how you become a member of the 'cut to the chase' club," he said wryly. "Birth or death."

He was looking away from her.

"Guess so," she said.

She wished he was close enough for her to touch his arm. The conversation was delicate, but the silences weren't awkward. They felt like the essential moments of quiet, the rests in a piece of music.

"You know . . ." he said finally, hesitantly, "when I was a SEAL, potential death was always part of the job description. But we were highly trained, and even if something went wrong, we couldn't say we hadn't done our best or at least had a plan. But when Lisa was killed, I realized what a cocky fucker I'd been all along to think I had any real control over *anything*. It was awful, but it was humbling, too. Life got real complicated while I kind of held everything I thought I knew up into this new light. And then it got real simple. And stayed that way." A beat of silence. "Mostly."

That beat of silence, she was fairly certain, contained *her*.

And whatever it was they were doing here.

The word *mostly* was nestled in warmth and wry. And was followed by the faintest hint of a question.

Awful, he'd called it. How like a man, to encapsulate total devastation into one word. And yet it was this quality, this clear-eyed simplicity, that made him feel like oxygen.

She wished she could give him something more than silence right now. His news was old to him, but it was new to her, and her heart wasn't a trampoline. It wasn't bouncing right off.

"Just to make this clear, Eden, that isn't—Lisa, I mean—isn't the reason I've been single."

"But it's the reason you've stayed busy," she said at once, albeit gently.

He went still. And then he made a little stunned sound, almost a laugh. But not quite. He swiped a hand through his hair, then seemed to realize he was doing it and dropped it.

He turned away again.

Interesting. He didn't want her to see his expression.

She had a feeling she'd led him up to an epiphany of his own. Gabe had a few places he kept protected. Which made her feel that much more protective of him.

"So how long have *you* been single?" He'd recovered his aplomb.

"Ten years."

She never hedged when she was asked that question. If it freaked anybody out, so be it.

"And Annelise's dad—"

"Wait. You're not going to whistle long and low and say, 'ten years! Boy that's a long dry spell' and stuff like that?"

"Nope. Ten years is like an eyeblink, especially when you're a single mom and your whiteboard is full. Don't worry. You'd be amazed at the kinds of things that are just like riding a bike."

Her jaw dropped open wide.

For several seconds.

It took that long for the little outraged squeak to emerge.

His face was pure deviltry. He was *very* pleased with himself.

She *would* have laughed.

But then it hit her with the force of a blow: this was it.

She couldn't dodge the question, because he'd recognize the dodge for what it was, and call her on it. And she couldn't hesitate, because he would read—and rightly so—something into any undue pause before answering.

Hours of angst-filled, delicate consideration would need to be condensed in a few seconds.

And the kids heading toward them told her she had about a second or two to decide whether the time to divulge something she'd never told another human was now, to Gabe Caldera while he stood outside her daughter's elementary school in a neon vest. It wasn't fair.

And in the end, a few seconds just wasn't enough.

"One-night stand. He's out of the picture." Her stock answer, when anyone got bold enough to ask that question. Vague, wry, good-humored, accompanied by a shrug. "Annelise and I are great."

When he quirked the corner of his mouth ruefully, she felt as guilty and sullied as if she'd cheated on him.

Damn. She'd wanted him to know only her truest self more than she'd wanted that from anyone before. She wanted to live her whole life from that place. Because of him.

And she may have just ruined it all.

Maybe not. Maybe, if and when the time came to tell him the whole truth, he'd understand. Maybe.

Still, she felt rattled and subdued. And just the way he had a moment ago, she was tempted to turn her face away.

But the colorful little torrent of kids was pouring toward them now, and among them the gold and pink flash that was her very heart.

"Out of the picture, huh?" he said. "So when was the last time your heart was bro—"

"Mom, I got an A + on my math test! A PLUS! Right after the A! Check. it. OUT."

She presented Eden with the evidence. Fluttering a paper into the front seat.

Emotional 180-degree turns were par for the course when you were a mom. Eden often felt as though she'd faceted into parts that could work and think and feel independently of each other. One part of her remained simmering in angst.

She gave her best enthusiasm to Annelise right now.

"All right! Baby, that's *fabulous*. I know how hard you worked on that."

Annelise gave Eden a noisy smacker right on her forehead before hurling herself into the backseat, wearing a smug smile.

"Hey, good job, Annelise," Gabe said. "I know Mrs. Murphy is tough, but tough teachers are often the best."

Annelise squinted up a little skeptically about the last part of the sentence. "Okay. Thank you, Mr. Caldera."

"You're very polite, Annelise," he said somberly.

"Thank you, I know," Annelise said in all seriousness. "My mom taught me."

"Hear that? I taught her," Eden said.

The convoy of moms and dads were starting their engines, and one mom cheerily called out the window to

Gabe, and so, with evident reluctance, he headed in her direction.

And Eden ferried Annelise home. Her eye on the rearview mirror, watching him walk away, and she realized that as pleasant as the back of him was to look at, watching him leave her at all, for any reason, was never going to be easy.

CHAPTER 9

Eden was studying her whiteboard as if it were a sudoku.

And gradually, that tricky little band of muscle between her shoulder blades tightened like a vise. At about three thirty today she'd gotten a call about a last-minute wedding—this weekend, that's how last minute, and who was she to question the judgment of two twenty-year-olds in love?—and could she provide some simple flowers? She could, as it so happened. For a premium, she explained nicely. But they will be *beautiful*.

And that wedding would push her nicely into the black when it came to monthly earnings, and she'd be that much closer to paying off the shop mortgage and maybe, just maybe, dropping a dollar or two into Annelise's college fund.

But! And wasn't there always a "but"? Where was a dentist appointment (Annelise's), an annual gyno appointment (hers), a day off (Danny's), a sleepover (Annelise's at Chloe's house) to be skillfully rearranged without the whole thing toppling?

Behind her at the kitchen table Annelise had bitten one-half of her grilled cheese sandwich into the shape of a lion and was pretending her bowl of tomato soup was a watering hole and the steamed zucchini on her plate was lion poop.

Eden didn't have the energy—or the heart—to tell her to stop playing with her food. Frankly, the minute she was able to sit down she might bite her sandwich into the shape of a gazelle just to make things even more interesting. She'd learned to pick her battles. If some zucchini ever made it into Annelise's mouth, even accidentally, even under gross pretenses, she'd declare victory.

Zucchini made her think of Gabe.

Would the broccoli stratagem work with zucchini? Would Annelise get wise to that?

Or did it have to be Gabe doing the persuading?

Lately all of her thoughts were fringed with addendum and footnotes just like that: what would Gabe think? Would Gabe like this? Today she'd looked at a flower arrangement and thought, *These would look great with Gabe's eyes*. Which was patently ridiculous. They were *flowers. Orange* flowers. It was like six degrees of Gabe Caldera. She could make literally anything—a crack in the sidewalk (don't step on a crack/you'll break your mother's back, Gabe must have a strong back, remember when Annelise thought she could ride on Gabe's shoulders?) lead back to him within just a few thoughts.

Funny. She did the same thing with Annelise. All roads led to her.

The last time your heart was bro—

She wasn't certain her heart had in fact been broken. Not by a man, anyway. Which seemed almost like a character flaw—had she not loved enough? Gabe had about ten years of life on her.

Still. Her last ten years had been, in many ways, about nothing else but love, thanks to Annelise.

But her heart did feel bruised and a little heavy and peculiarly thwarted all afternoon, like a bird futilely throwing itself at a windowpane. As though she'd been too late to protect him from hurt, from the grave injustice of his loss. Which made no sense, really. But then, ambiguous new emotions flapped into her life like unidentifiable butterflies a few times a day lately, thanks to Gabe. She allowed them to circulate rather than trying to pin them to a board.

She wondered if even Gabe truly understood how much he didn't like being alone. She had a hunch that, just as her whiteboard gave her the illusion that the vicissitudes of life could be shuffled and sorted and managed like squares of a quilt, he was trying to drown out being alone with board meetings and hacking trunks out of pastures.

Although, who knew. Men often just liked to hack things.

Someone really ought to bear a burden or two for him.

How she longed to carve a place for them outside of time, just a small space. Maybe about the size of a phone booth, or a closet.

She indulged in a little fantasy now. Her and Gabe, alone, together, in this little space she'd just carved.

Wait. Something was wrong with this picture.

She mentally removed all of his clothes.

That was better.

And then hers.

Even better.

Just for fun she vajazzled herself.

No, no, that was alarming.

She restored her standard fluffy wedge.

Then she mentally pushed those two people up against each other's bodies.

Wrapped them together.

Whoa.

Lust skewered her, and the breath-stealing spiky rush of heat skittering over her skin was delicious, but she didn't have the luxury of standing there in front of the whiteboard, frivolously savoring it. She banished it. She ought not to have even summoned it.

It was right about then that Annelise had gotten awfully quiet behind her. No spoon clinking against the soup bowl.

"Are you ever going to eat that lion, Leesy?" she said absently.

"Mama?"

"Yeah, sweet thing?"

"I don't feel good."

Eden whirled, the marker held aloft like a saber, ready to rush into mom battle. "In what way?"

"My throat hurts."

Annelise put the grilled cheese lion down and propped her cheek on her hand.

Eden all but lunged for her and lay the back of her

hand against Annelise's forehead. Her heart gave a little lurch.

"Oh, honey. You're warm. Who in your class is sick?"

"Emily, Tobin, and Braden."

"*All* of them? Cheezus!"

"It's hard to tell. Tobin kind of always has some snot on him, but he stayed home yesterday."

"How's your tummy?"

"Kinda weird."

Eden closed her eyes. She might as well take a rifle, throw the whiteboard up like skeet, and shoot it into smithereens.

And after she took Annelise's temperature, she picked up the eraser and with one mighty swipe, the drawing of the tooth, the cat, the flowers became a big gray smudge.

None of that mattered when her baby was sick.

Two weeks later . . .

The Wasteland.

That's what Gabe mordantly christened the period between the last time he talked to Eden to the next. Oh, sure, his schedule was full that entire time. Even lively. Meetings with the vets, softball games, various board meetings. Hearty laughter. Beer.

His big empty house.

His vast white ceiling.

It was like functioning in a world suddenly stripped of birdsong or music. As if the colors had desaturated. Or if all the windows were sealed shut and no fresh air could get in.

And no one looking at him would have noticed a damn thing. Gabe had learned long ago how not to visibly wear suffering.

He knew all about Annelise being out of school, because that cold cut a swath through the fifth grade, and all those parents called the office. Annelise also missed soccer practice, and Eden missed a decorating committee meeting, and Jan roped him into helping, which was how he wound up painting the words *Dunking Booth*.

He considered texting her. To commiserate. To check in. To see if she needed anything. But would that be an intrusion? Did he have the right? She hadn't given him her phone number; it was part of the school records.

No, he decided, this was a long game. It hadn't played itself out yet.

And boy was this ever a test.

She might not even be thinking about him at all. She might have decided that in light of the chaos life could dish up without warning, a courtship conducted in the chinks of their schedules was pointless. Even foolish.

He would just have to wait.

The Tornado.

That's how Eden thought of those two weeks. Because tornadoes were seasonal (though of course not really in California), and this one wasn't unprecedented. They came along now and again and sent her best-laid plans twirling into the next county. Like that scene in *The Wizard of Oz*, when Dorothy had looked out of the window of her flying house and saw her wicked neighbor peddling on by through the sky—that's how she imagined all those little drawings on her whiteboard.

Mostly because, boy, the store-brand cold medicine was potent stuff.

Annelise got better pretty fast.

But Eden caught Annelise's cold. And it went nice and bronchial on her.

And then Danny caught her cold.

And he was out for a couple of days.

And then her mom and dad spent some time with the cold.

And then Avalon somehow got it.

And it was a mad scramble to keep her life running for those two weeks—to make sure orders at the store were fulfilled and food entered the house and the bills were paid and Annelise got to where she needed to go. Eden was on the phone constantly, sniffling and croaking, planning, rearranging, negotiating favor trades like that crazy agent Ari Gold on *Entourage.*

And yet through it all some vein of grace ran. Something that during previous tornadoes hadn't been there at all. Something that felt like hope or peace, maybe? The cold medicine was awfully good; it blurred access to sophisticated thinking, and she could probably lay a lot of the inner calm at its door. But she was pretty sure she could also call that inner calm "Gabe."

The epiphany was that she'd all along thought she hadn't room in her life for him. But you didn't make room in your life for a beautiful song or the weather. It just was there, making things better.

"The last time your heart was bro—" She knew, too,

by the end of those two weeks, how she was going to answer his question.

Gabe went still when he saw Eden in the hall, zipping out of Annelise's classroom into a crowd of kids moving toward their next class.

He had a hunch someone had forgotten her lunch again.

He half smiled. *Wow*, she looked like hell.

And like an oasis in the desert.

Also: like the very essence of beauty, as far as he was concerned.

A bulky blue sweater worn over a blue-collared shirt that was slipping out of the back of her jeans, like she'd thrown all of it on in a second to get here. She saw him. Froze. Then drifted toward him. There were mauve shadows under her eyes. Her hair was tied up in a ponytail and she'd missed a few strands and they were fluttering alongside her chin. The mauve shadows made her eyes look even bluer.

And for a moment they said nothing at all. Just gazed.

He wondered if he looked the same as he had two weeks ago, or if he looked haunted from missing her.

"Give me back my fidget spinner, you big turd, Todd!" some kid hollered behind them.

Gabe whirled around and barked, "HEY."

The kids yelped and gave a start, and Todd immediately thrust the purloined fidget spinner at the other kid.

Gabe adroitly intercepted it and shoved it in his pocket. "You can pick it up in the office after school," he said sternly. "Now get to class."

The kids glumly shuffled off to class.

He turned back to Eden.

Who was biting her lip to keep from laughing.

". . . ken?" he said tenderly. Tentatively. Like a tourist in a foreign land revisiting a language he'd learned in high school.

She drew in a long breath. Exhaled. "When this great guy I know told me how he lost his fiancée. That's the last time my heart felt broken."

He gave a soft, stunned laugh.

Together they stood absolutely wordlessly in the hall as kids swirled around them.

Two minutes until the bell.

He struggled to recover his aplomb, then gave up. What use was it to him?

"Truthfully," she said, a little more conversationally, "you really made me think hard about it. Because I don't think a man has broken my heart before. But I've realized it breaks a little all the time. In a sweet way. You know how sometimes there are swarms of little quakes along the minor faults in California? When Annelise says something amazing . . . a little while ago, and this is going to sound dumb, but I caught her talking to a caterpillar outside near our roses, explaining that it was about to become a butterfly, which might feel funny, but she was reassuring it, telling it not to be afraid. It's something I told her about. My heart is broken and rearranged all the time, feels like, but it's stronger along the broken parts. The whole landscape of my life changes all the time."

That funny pain in his chest was like that jerk after

you yanked your parachute rip cord, and it unfurled to catch the wind.

"Not dumb at all," he said, when he could finally speak.

He didn't really want to speak, actually. He just wanted to stand there and look at her and listen to her, as if she was music. And touch her poor beautiful tired face, which, if he was not mistaken, was sporting a teeny booger in the left nostril. It was pretty clear she'd had Annelise's cold, too.

He really just wanted to make her life easier and better. To buy them name-brand Barbies if that's what they wanted. To take care of them when they were sick.

Their bodies were suspended in that push-pull tension, leaning ever so slightly toward each other while being tugged at by their days and their duties.

Mrs. Pfingsten called to him from the hall, "Oh, Mr. Caldera, I wanted to talk to you about the sixth-grade field trip. Got a minute?"

"Sure, Peggy, why don't you meet me in my office."

He smiled at Eden. "All those earthquakes sound kinda like the making of an ecosystem, in fact," he said over his shoulder, as he headed back to his office.

There was some consolation in walking away to the sound of her great laugh. Rightness was restored to his world once more.

And with the sound of the class bell ringing came the conviction they were headed toward that moment where a rogue breeze either knocked him and his parachute off course face-first into a cliff . . . or whether he would waft gently down into a smooth green meadow toward her smiling face and open arms.

And . . . maybe she would be naked, too, in the meadow.

Because what the hell. Even lyrical fantasies could be improved with a little nudity.

Four days later . . .

Eden's dad usually did soccer game duty for Annelise because Eden needed to mind the store, but Eden didn't even have to have an angsty heart-to-heart with herself before she sent Glenn the text that morning.

> Hey pop—it's a beautiful day and Danny's minding the store. I thought I'd take Annelise to her soccer game. You could probably use the break!

Her dad texted back:

> I do have to go to Home Depot. Water heater at Misty Cat is acting up. Thanks pumpkin. Tell Leesy knock 'em dead. xoxox

She'd brought a folding chair and sunglasses. Puffy white clouds scudded across a sky so blue it dizzied. The pesky cough that had hung on for weeks was just about gone. She no longer felt like a convalescent. Especially when Gabe was standing next to her in jeans and a polo shirt, hands on his hips, squinting out at the field, silver whistle glistening from the chain around his neck.

Sex on two legs with a whistle, she thought.

There truly could not be two more different men than Gabe and Annelise's father. Who, ironically, was also considered an actual sex bomb by a large portion of the population.

"Why flowers?" Gabe said. Still watching the field.

She knew what he meant. "Mmm . . . because when I found out I was pregnant, suddenly I was fitted with these like—don't laugh—new goggles. The metaphorical kind. I'd been gung ho on this . . . GO LEESY GO! GO GO GO GO!" She leaped to her feet.

Annelise was a pink and blond and peachy blur driving the ball toward the net.

"KICK IT!" Gabe bellowed. "NOW! NAIL THAT BABY! YOU CAN DO IT!"

BAM!

The Acorn goalie leaped heroically, pigtails flopping, but came down hard with an armful of air and THWACK! The ball slammed into the net.

Much enthusiastic shrieking and pogoing ensued among the Hellcat Canyon Wildcats.

"Atta girl, Annelise!" Eden hollered. "*Beautiful* goal!"

Annelise raced and bounced a horizontal path along the sidelines to high-five Gabe, Eden, and anyone else who had their hand stuck out, just like a pro boxer before a big match.

"Her first goal this season," Gabe said proudly.

"And about her seventy-second try."

They both smiled. Annelise *always* went for the goal, whether it made sense to do it or not. She was crushed every time she missed one. Once she'd slipped and accidentally kicked her own butt, landing hard in the mud. Eden wouldn't admit it out loud, but sometimes watching fifth grade soccer was as much fun as watching a Warner Bros. cartoon.

Gabe was working hard on helping Annelise to choose her moments.

"And that was a bull's-eye, too," he said with relish. "A real beaut of a goal. GIRLS, GATHER ROUND."

He trotted off to talk to his team full of colty-legged little girls possessed of endless supplies of energy, not all of it juice box–fueled.

And while he was gone Eden contented herself with watching him: the way he moved, his confidence, his easiness with who he was, his good-humored authority with the team. All of it was downright erotic, as far as she was concerned.

He strolled back up the line, shared a few words with some other parents swigging from thermoses, then returned to his spot next to her.

Hand shading his eyes, looking toward the field, he said, ". . . you were gung ho on this . . ."

". . . this really proscribed career path—I was going to be an attorney and live in a big city. I decided—and suddenly all I wanted was a . . . nest. Near my family. And near all the familiar things I'd always loved so I could share them with my baby while at the same time being completely independent."

He turned toward her. "Complete—"

"Mr. Caldera! Mr. Caldera!" Their goalie, Michelle, clearly had some urgent business, which may be a bathroom break. He trotted off to have a word with her.

Then trotted back.

". . . completely independent . . ." he prompted when he returned.

"Yep. And as for flowers . . . when I was pregnant I was just so much more emotional, and when I saw the shop for sale . . . Well, flowers require tender care and creativity and they make people happy and everything else just a little more beautiful, and suddenly the idea of being a purveyor of beauty and happiness, of being a little part of other people's life events around here made me feel part of something bigger, and I wanted that. Like I was creating this lovely net below a high wire or something like . . . What?"

He'd turned to stare at her. Taking his eyes from the field. Entirely. His expression was almost . . . awestruck.

"Nothing," he said lightly. After a delay.

His voice was a little gravelly.

Suddenly she felt a little shy. "Anyway, so the shop was for sale, and it just seemed like serendipity. I decided to spend the money I'd saved for tuition and buy it. It's cozy and it sustains us. You?"

"SEAL or principal?"

"Start with SEAL."

"Because I wanted to join the military like my dad and always like to be the best at whatever I do. Back then, I was happiest when I was striving, or so I thought. Challenging myself all the time. And when I want something, I set out to get it. And I always did."

Her eyebrows shot up.

"What?" He was amused. "Was that too alpha?"

"I don't know if it was *too* alpha, but it certainly was *very* alpha."

"It's true, though," he said, a faint smile still playing

around his lips. "And I was like that until—" He raced up the sidelines. "C'mon MARTINEZ, SNAG THAT BALL FROM HER! YOU CAN DO IT! YES! GO GO GO! YOU CAN—"

He sighed. The Acorn defender nutmegged the ball right through Chrissy Martinez's legs.

She bent over in surprise to watch it roll away from her, only to be briskly captured by another Black Oak Acorns defender, who scurried off dribbling it.

"THAT'S OKAY, CHRISSY, GOOD HUSTLE. JUST REMEMBER THE DRILLS WE prac . . . oh for the love of . . . DON'T CRY. I KNOW YOU'LL GET THIS."

Gabe exhaled in a great, long-suffering gust and propped his hands on top of his head.

"Sorry, Caldera," Chrissy's beleaguered dad, standing next to him who also loved to win, said. "We've been working on it at home, but she chokes with an audience."

"Ah, no worries, she's doing a lot better this year than last, Doug. We'll keep working on it."

Doug Martinez took a swig out of his thermos and winced with great satisfaction. Eden was pretty sure he'd spiked his coffee with whiskey, which was a perfectly reasonable way to get through a soccer game.

Gabe paced back to Eden.

"Boy, coaching fifth grade soccer must be killing you if you like to win," she said.

"By a thousand cuts," he confirmed with cheerful resignation.

". . . until?" she prompted.

"Ah, yes. Until . . . I figured out winning was about

proving something to myself. Still like to win. I just know the difference now between fighting to win just to *win*, because my ego craves it, and doing my best to win something because I know it's . . . absolutely right."

The collision of their gazes just then by rights ought to have struck sparks like an axle hitting a roadway. The kind of sparks that lit countrysides on fire.

And that telltale tingle along her spine, her nape, her arms.

She dropped her eyes and surreptitiously inspected her arm: Goose bumps.

She slowly lifted her eyes again.

His smile, tilted, almost rueful; his eyes, unreadable. He gave a one-shouldered shrug.

He saw the goose bumps, too.

And of course he remembered what she'd said: that she got them whenever she heard something particularly beautiful and true.

The way they both remembered, despite their busy lives, every single damn thing the other said.

"Oh, Eden! I'm so glad to have caught you!"

They both gave a start, as though they'd actually been caught in the middle of something other than goose bump perusal.

Jan Pennington, looking like a stinging insect in her bright yellow cardigan, was bearing down on them.

Gabe was off like a shot, perfidious man, to confer with a member of his staff, and Annelise was already skipping her way over to her mom and reflexively Eden reached out to scoop her into her body for a hug. "Good game, sweetie."

"Since you missed the decorating committee meetings," Jan said, with faint reproach, "I was hoping you could sign up the volunteers to man or woman our game and dunking booth."

Jan thrust what appeared to be about ten sign-up sheets into Eden's hands. Eden really didn't have the right to say no to either: she knew it was all part of doing her share. All parents did, sick, well, busy, no matter what.

"Of course, Jan."

But Jan was already zipping off again.

And Gabe had disappeared.

CHAPTER 10

Four nights later . . .

"**. . .a**nd then, if you can believe, they raised my flood insurance rates!"

"WHAT?" Gabe shouted.

"FLOOD INSURANCE!" Dion Gomez from the music store bellowed at him. Beaming.

Gabe just nodded sympathetically. He'd missed the entire first part of that sentence and had only caught a word here and there of the entire conversation, but he'd had about five shouted, tipsy conversations since he'd arrived at the Misty Cat for the Chamber of Commerce mixer an hour and a half ago, and his mood was rapidly abrading. Blue Room's greatest hits were for some reason being played on an endless loop, and sometimes Gabe was in the mood for Jasper Townes's uber-soulful rasp punctuated by the otherworldly howls. Other times he yearned for the days of LPs so he could take and smash it over one knee. Or hurl it like a discus.

He was three beers in because he couldn't bring

himself to drink the wine, and he'd started to feel them, which made him feel his age. And he was missing another softball game for this. Right about now he would love to take a hard swing at something, hear that SMACKing sound, and watch it soar to unfettered freedom.

No sign of Eden.

See, if she was here, no amount of shouted conversations or howling Jasper Townes would have made a difference.

She wasn't here. And yet, after that soccer game moment, he'd been so sure they were reaching a sort of tipping point. After all, tonight was their cut-to-the-chase-aversary.

Greta from the New Age Store maneuvered through the crowd, then stopped and stared at him wide-eyed.

"What?" he said, this time a little churlishly.

"Gabe, your aura is really . . . well, you ought to have brought a fire extinguisher with you this evening, that's all I can say, because *that* thing is . . ." Greta fanned herself with a hand and rolled her eyes in an ay-yi-yi fashion.

He scowled at her.

Greta just batted her eyes knowingly, smirked, amused, and took herself off to unnerve somebody else sufficiently enough to persuade them to buy a tarot reading in the back of her store.

Gabe took another few ill-advised steps toward the bar. Glenn was doing a booming business. He really liked all of Eden's relatives, the ones he'd met anyway. He saw Glenn when he had lunch at the Misty Cat or drank after a game, at shows, at Annelise's soccer games . . . if only Eden was as ubiquitous in his life as her dad was.

And there was *still* no sign of her.

Had she chickened out?

He was beginning to feel like he'd rearranged his schedule on a *hope*. Like a lovesick teenager. Not like a man who was patiently following a plan through to its conclusion.

What on earth was he doing? What were *they* doing? He'd been playing the long game, but the long game had begun to feel like a rubber band drawn way, way, way back, and everyone knew that hurt like a bitch when it finally snapped. Was her very elusiveness the attraction? Yet how was it that she didn't feel elusive— she always seemed to reverberate through him even when she was nowhere near. But every little hit he took of her made him yearn for the next. He wanted her with a ferocity that made the sheets of his bed feel woven of burrs and thistles. That's how much he tossed and turned at night lately. And he knew she wanted him, too. He'd never experienced anything like their chemistry. But, you know, life. It was what it was. Just because it felt meant to be didn't mean it would, in fact, be. It seemed, however, inconceivable.

And then after all of that, when he turned around, there she was.

She was wearing a black dress. He'd never seen her in a dress. It hugged her slim curves and her knees were exposed, and a sweep of pale collarbone glowed and her hair was up and her neck was long and slim and pale.

It was hardly the uniform of a siren.

But he knew it was, so to speak, an anniversary present for him.

But all he could think of was pressing his lips to that place just above her heartbeat. Trailing his mouth down, down, down, closing his mouth on her nipple, hearing her gasp. Pressing her body against his.

He couldn't say a damn thing. He stared, silent and hungry, mute with gratitude and relief, irritable that he should feel all of these things that made him feel as though he had no control at all. Understanding that things might be beyond one's control didn't stop him from wanting it.

She looked up at him, and he could have sworn it was like looking in a mirror. Her expression, that was.

And she made a beeline for him. Or, rather, she wove through the crowd, ninjalike in her black dress, and arrived before him, almost momentously.

She deserved a compliment, something gracious, eloquent, subtle.

She deserved to be maneuvered out into the moonlight and kissed like she was precious, made of blown glass.

She deserved a question, crafted in sweetness and subtlety, that would bookend the first part of this courtship.

What emerged from his mouth was: "What's the best sex you ever had?"

What happened was her jaw dropped.

She stared at him in pure astonishment.

And then she yanked her phone from her purse and stared at it.

"Something's come up, Gabe. I gotta run."

She spun around and made a break for it just as fast as she'd arrived.

The next day . . .

Gabe grasped the sides of his skull gingerly. His brain was pulsing in there like a subwoofer. How much *did* he actually drink last night? It was a bad sign that he couldn't remember. Cheap wine plus good beer plus . . . did he actually stay and do a shot after Eden took off like a . . . shot?

It was the first time he'd ever gone to school with a hangover, and he felt like a real sleaze. Even though he could cope, hands down. It wasn't going to happen again.

That's what enigmatic women would do to you.

Mrs. Maker peered in. "Mr. Caldera, I'm about to go pick up lunch. What can I get for you?"

"Oh, anything, Donna," he said. "As long as it's tuna on rye."

Tuna was his preferred hangover food. Which seemed counterintuitive. Maybe it was a sort of punishment for overindulging.

She beamed. "I know just the thing! Oh, here's Ms. Harwood. Thank you for the flowers, Eden, dear. They're so lovely. I think he may have a minute or two before his next meeting, so don't keep him long. I'll be right back."

And there she was in his doorway. Wearing jeans and a slim-fitting pale green ribbed turtleneck.

"Eden," he said. Stunned.

"Annelise forgot her lunch—again—so I brought it to her. And I thought I'd bring this in here."

She came around to his side of the desk to slide something in front of him.

"Here's the sign-up sheet for the dunking booth. Annelise thinks we'll make the most money when you're sitting up there, so we're hoping you'll take this shift."

She leaned over to point at something, and when she did a long strand of hair she'd tucked behind her ear swung down and brushed against his jaw. It smelled like coconut and flowers. It was like a magic wand—it banished his hangover and filled his brain with what felt like helium and his blood with what felt like lava.

He was a man in quiet torment.

He stared down at it and said nothing.

For a long time.

Neither did she.

And then he finally looked up.

"Listen, Eden, I'm sorry about what I said last night. I was out of line."

"Well, I did show you my clavicle. You were overcome. I get it. I didn't run away because of that, Gabe. Sheesh. Sorry I did that."

"Are you sure? Because it was practically like watching the roadrunner flee the coyote. Like a vrooming sound and cloud of dust."

"You thought *that* question scared me?"

"Didn't it?"

She didn't answer for a few seconds. She tucked the hair back.

Damn.

"I thought about it all night, as a matter of fact," she said.

He almost closed his eyes at the notion of her thinking about sex all night long.

He did and didn't want to know the answer, he realized.

He wasn't going to press the point.

"So why'd you split like that?" he asked.

"Mmm . . . well, Annelise texted that Danny—that's my assistant and babysitter—had accidentally locked himself out of the house on the roof when he went up there to get Peace and Love down. Peace and Love can get his own sweet self down, but Danny is quite a Boy Scout and saw the need to do the rescue and . . ."

"Everything turn out okay?"

"Oh, yeah. Yeah. I got the ladder out, and Danny used it to get down and Peace and Love came down over the fence."

"Oh good. Because I was on pins and needles there for a moment." His voice had gotten softer. A little drowsier.

Somehow he—they—were closer now.

"Welcome to my life," she murmured. "Thrills, chills, spills, never a dull mo—"

He stopped her sentence with his lips.

Why then? He didn't know. It just seemed like the only reasonable thing to do. When you touch something hot, you jerk your hand away; when something you want overwhelmingly is *right there*, you take it.

His defenses were shattered by the hangover and the coconut hair.

After a millisecond of frozen astonishment, he could feel her go soft as smoke, yielding, which made him nearly savage with want in a very primal way.

But they ended that kiss.

Tacitly.

He sat back a little.

Closed his eyes. Sighed.

Opened them.

They remained motionless, their faces still a mere few inches apart. He could feel her breath, faster now, against his chin.

"God, Eden, it was . . . I'm sorry . . . your face was right there and . . . I couldn't . . ."

What? Bear it any longer? Wait for one more millisecond?

He could see a faint old scar on her chin, probably from a childhood bout of chicken pox or some such. He was instantly ridiculously jealous of anyone who knew how it had gotten there. He wanted to know her life story. He wanted to protect her from future scars and heal all the old ones. It struck him distantly that these were somewhat feverish and irrational thoughts to be having three minutes before the class bell was due to ring, with the blinds slitted a little so that any determined person could peek in if they bent just so. Mrs. Maker couldn't; sciatica was her besetting plague. Thank goodness for such mercies.

The second hand of the clock ticked forward.

"The stapler's right there, too," Eden whispered finally. "Are you going to kiss the stapler?"

She was a devil woman.

"I'll kiss anything you want me to." He made it sound like a blood vow.

Her pupils flared like black fireworks.

Above them, the skinny hand swept past another second.

She gasped when he slid his hand up through her hair and held her fast. This time he went in for a take-no-prisoners kiss, designed to melt bones, stop time, erase the memories of all kisses that had come before, what-the-fuck-did-they-have-to-lose kind of kiss. Molten, savage, skillful. They were on the clock.

He was a guy who knew how to make a point, and he never half-assed anything. Clearly, neither did she. Silk, heat, tongue, lips—the taste of her roared through his bloodstream, tightened all his muscles, sent red alerts to his groin. He curled one hand into the edge of his desk, a reflex against floating up to the ceiling, because suddenly whatever boundaries he'd once had melted away. And damn, she gave as good as she got. It was a hot, deep, dangerous tangle of tongues, the slide of lips. Nearly as carnal as fucking. Sweet. Jesus.

When she moaned softly, low in the back of her throat, guttural, helpless pleasure, he slipped his hand from her hair and sank backward into his chair.

One second before the bell rang.

Eden staggered back a few feet as if she'd just gone a few rounds on the roundabout out in the playground.

Classroom doors banged open. Rustling, the thunder of feet, shouts and laughter and the metal clang of lockers.

He closed his eyes briefly against the spin of the room.

He opened them again and turned his face up to hers.

If he'd had to assign a word to her expression, it would have been *amazed*. A little more nuanced than that, but still.

Her face was pink. Her eyes were hazy and hot.

He thought, *I bet that's what she looks like when she wakes up.*

He thought right then he would literally die if he didn't learn soon how she looked when she woke up.

There was a lot he could say right now: apologies and so forth. All of that would have been superfluous. She got the gist.

His fate was in her hands.

He didn't regret it.

In fact, he was pretty sure he hadn't so much taken a risk as issued a dare.

"Well, um, I've got to . . . I've got to get . . . get to . . ." Eden's pitch, at least, was cheery. But her voice a husk. "See you tonight at the carnival, I suppose."

She waved her arm vaguely at the hall outside his office.

"Of course." His own voice had taken on a phone-sex timbre. He cleared his throat. It wouldn't do for Mrs. Maker to think he was trying to seduce her when she delivered his lunch.

He would have stood up, like a gentleman, but he wasn't eager to show off his erection to anyone else who might happen to walk in. "You know where to find me if you want me."

He didn't think he could make that any clearer.

She pressed her lips together. Then touched her fingers to them.

She turned and wobbled just a bit when she left, and he thought it was only right that a woman who had altered his own center of gravity to experience a little axis-tilt of her own.

It wasn't easy to drive from the school parking lot back to Eden's Garden while the dirtiest, hottest, sweetest kiss she'd ever participated in reverberated in her cells like a million dramatic little cymbal clashes, especially since she hadn't scheduled "Get a grip" into her calendar that day. She didn't even know how she'd draw that on her whiteboard.

Gabe Caldera should be a controlled substance. There was no way on earth anyone could kiss him and not want to do that again.

And again.

And again and again and again.

Such that logic and reason, when they finally ventured back into her awareness at around the third stop sign from home, felt like intrusions into reality, not a restoration of it.

But ultimately they infiltrated her giddiness ("Dear Diary—Gabe Caldera kissed me!") and a rather aggressive, almost punitive, sobriety set in.

Making out with the principal in the middle of the day when Mrs. Maker could unexpectedly pop in to ask, "Was that tuna or turkey?" wasn't something any responsible mother should be doing.

But where did she *think* this was headed all along?

She'd been following a fascinating bread-crumb trail of questions right into the gingerbread house of sex. That's what she'd been doing.

Maybe Jan Pennington had seen something in her all along. Some feral quality she'd managed to keep metaphorically trapped like a spider under a coffee cup, something she'd once done at the Misty Cat Tavern when she worked there as a teenager and completely forgot about, until it made a break for it the minute an unsuspecting customer lifted it. Whereupon said customer released a scream so blood-curdling another diner fainted face-first into her scrambled eggs. Boy, was her mom pissed at her.

So maybe this was who she was: tightly wound Eden unwound with a violent suddenness, usually with someone slightly scandalous, at least once a decade or so, the way a Corpse flower is said to bloom.

The last time she'd ended up with a pink plus sign on a stick.

And it felt like dangerous sacrilege that for the seconds she was kissing him . . . nothing else existed. There had been only her, only him, only need.

She had never felt that way before with any man.

And surely it was a perilous way for a mother of a ten-year-old to feel.

The carnival was clearly a roaring success, in part because it's what happened in a town where the highlight of a given week was bingo at St. Ann's, and in part because it was a chance for adults to mingle and have adult conversations with other adults while their kids ran happily amuck. There was a sort of tacit agreement that they had free rein to keep each other's kids in line.

The grounds of the school field were studded with rented popcorn and cotton candy machines and carefully built game booths painted in blindingly cheerful primary colors, striped and polka-dotted and scrolled and labeled with suitably festive fonts, shiny, heavily glittered. Gabe paused to admire the "Fortunes Told Here!" sign and admired the "E" he'd painted.

Slightly distorted calliope music echoed from the loudspeakers, just to maximize that fever-dream effect.

Most of the games involved shooting or hurling things at other things—balloon, bottles, hoops, clown mouths—for the kinds of prizes one or two degrees superior to the ones usually found in Cracker Jacks. But the spirit of competition reigned in Hellcat Canyon. A prize was a prize.

Gabe's buddy Bud Wallace strolled by. A fluffy pink unicorn tucked under his arm.

"That's right, I shot that clown in the mouth with the water gun," he said to Gabe, with great dignity, in passing. "I shot it real good."

And all at once there was Eden, flanked by Annelise and her friend Emily, both of whom were rocking near horizontal ponytails.

He paused.

And as usual, it took a moment for the adults to say anything, such was the impact upon their hormones of each other's presence.

"Hi, Mr. Caldera!" the girls said.

"Hi, girls. Having fun?"

They nodded so vigorously their ponytails whipped about.

Annelise plucked at her mom's shirt. "Mom, can we do the ring toss and then get our faces painted?"

"Sure." Eden handed over a wad of tickets, and they scampered off again.

"I hate to say it," Eden said, "but I think Jan Pennington deserves some kind of crown. Maybe even a parade."

"She'd have to organize her own parade. No one else could pull it off."

Eden laughed. "I think you need to give yourself some credit, too. Everyone wants to help the school because you've made it such a great place."

He gave an aw-shucks one-shouldered shrug, which made her smile.

"Yeah, so great that I'm staying late tonight doing the accounting so I can report to the board tomorrow."

She smiled at that, almost sadly.

He took a little step closer. He couldn't help it. Once he'd touched her, every moment not touching her seemed wasted.

She didn't back away. She tilted her head up to look into his eyes.

And there were her lips . . . *right there.*

Speaking of ring toss, all he had to do was loop an arm around her and tug, and she'd be snug up against his body. Talk about winning the prize.

"Gabe . . . Okay . . . I have something to say."

"Okay," he said softly. The tone instantly made him a little wary.

"While that . . ." She lowered her voice, even though the sound around them was akin to gulls dive-bombing carrion at the beach, and yet somehow he heard her clearly. ". . . kiss was really . . . very nice . . ."

"Nice?"

He said that a little too loudly. Heads whipped around. Hands shot up and waved gaily when they heard his voice.

"Okay. While it was . . . mind-blowing . . ."

A smile started a slow migration across his lips.

"You're the principal of my daughter's school. It just seems too risky to . . ." She stopped. Flared her fingers.

"Embark on a passionate sexual affair . . . at the very least?"

Her blue eyes practically went black again with that pupil flare.

So, he assumed, did his.

A couple of people strolling by jerked their heads in their direction, as if they, too, recognized something about their stillness. Like two predators about to pounce and filet each other with their claws and teeth, or maybe leap to that other thing nature channels were so known for.

Fucking, in other words. That was the other thing nature channels were known for.

"Gabe, I mean . . . your standing in the community and mine, if someone finds out we're—"

"You're not Hester Prynne. I'm not Dimmesdale."

This made her smile. Albeit somewhat tautly. They were straight up a couple of nerds to pull out that reference during a sexual negotiation. They were perfect for each other.

"Or if it doesn't work out with us . . . it's not like there's another school in Hellcat Canyon . . ."

"Eden . . ." He struggled to keep his tone patient.

". . . we've both survived awkward situations. I'm a professional. You're a professional. People might talk. But people will always talk about stuff. What else is there to *do* but talk and butt into everybody's business in Hellcat Canyon?"

Never mind that all around them people were competing for stuffed animals and candy at various booths like it was the Hunger Games. There was *plenty* to do in Hellcat Canyon. There was bingo at St. Ann's, and the annual landscaping contest between Heavenly Acres and Elysian Shores mobile home communities, and then there was always softball and open mic night at the Misty Cat. Hellcat Canyon was *hopping.*

"And there's just . . . finding the time . . . with Annelise . . . my work . . . it's just . . . it'll be hard on you, and I don't want you to resent me for dashing out at odd hours, or abandoning you thanks to work or Annelise's needs. Gabe . . . I don't think I can give you what you deserve."

He drew in a breath. He was tense with frustration.

He knew what he wanted to give *her.*

The moon. His name. Everything he owned or ever would.

He was pretty sure those were the perfect things to say out loud if he wanted to hear an actual vrooming sound and see her disappear in a cloud of dust.

He could say: *Anything precious to you, Eden, is precious to me, and that means Annelise, too.* Who, frankly, he liked for her own goofy, lovely, unique self.

And Eden stood there, on the precipice of ending all of this between them. Her mouth was saying one thing but everything else—the slight cant of her body toward him, the pulse in her throat, the soft, unguarded *want* in her eyes—said something else altogether.

Underlying her words was a sort of coded desperation: *save me from myself.*

And then he got it: she was scared.

She wanted him, all right. But panic was a perfectly viable response when facing a gigantic unknown, even a sexy one. Ten years was a long time to be single. And in that time she'd become more accustomed to giving than taking. To living for her daughter and assuming that was what it meant to live for herself.

But she wasn't going to admit that to herself or to him, because, like Annelise, she was proud, and she claimed to not be afraid of a damn thing.

He just didn't know what the hell to say that wouldn't make him feel like a creep trying to talk her into the sack.

He could have said, *What about that roller coaster you rode thirteen times? Where's that girl who isn't afraid of a damn thing?* But that wouldn't have been fair. He could have said, *Where there's a will, there's* always *a way.* But she also knew that.

"I understand," he said finally. And he did. He didn't like it at all, but he understood. His heart was sinking through his body like an anchor flung from a ship, but he understood.

"Maybe when Annelise can drive."

"Ha." He managed a smile, for the benefit of the people strolling by, many of whom were women, many of whom whipped their heads around to get a better look at him, as if he was a magnificent tree planted there for tourists to admire.

"I'm sorry, Gabe. I'm *really* sorry. Please don't hate me."

"Eden," he said this weakly, almost impatiently, "for fuck's sake . . . that's . . . an impossibility. You know that, right?"

That might be the first time he'd said the "F" word out loud on school grounds.

She didn't say anything. It seemed ridiculous that the two people who were looking at each other right now could even be contemplating walking away from each other.

Thundering little feet came at them, and Annelise and Emily were pogoing with excitement.

"Mom, Principal Caldera, I won a whole elephant!" Annelise hoisted it aloft.

"A whole *elephant*! Not just the trunk where he keeps his stuff?"

"Ha ha ha ha! Mr. Caldera! You're so funny! We're going to go get our faces painted now, okay?"

"Sure! And if you lay off the popcorn and candy, I'll take you for sundaes after."

"Thanks! Love you!"

They ran off again, tagging Eden like little pinballs, and left him alone with her.

Gabe rifled through his years of experience for something useful here. Like he'd once said, everyone's strengths could be weaponized and used against them . . . and like the broccoli, everyone would be a winner.

Or he'd just really piss her off.

It was a risk, but he didn't have much to lose at this point.

So he said it.

"Ten years *is* kind of a long time," he said sympathetically. "But I guess I didn't take you for a chicken."

And Gabe went off to do his time in the dunking booth. To literally drown his sorrows, and cool down the rest of his body, and he was glad none of the carnival games nearby featured actual darts, because he was pretty sure one would be twanging between his shoulder blades right now.

CHAPTER 11

Eden watched him go, her jaw dropped for so
long it was a wonder someone strolling by didn't
take her for a coin-operated game and drop a
quarter in.

A *chicken*!

He had a lot of fucking nerve!

A lot of fucking nerve to pinpoint the teeny tiny
kernel of doubt about that very thing at the very center
of her entire rationale!

It wasn't as simple as that, was it?

That this was new, she didn't know how to do it, she
was *scared*, and so she was walking away.

When she lost sight of him in the crowd, panic flurried
in the pit of her stomach like the little popcorn cyclones
in the rented machines studding the walkways.

"Hey, Eden, come on in here."

She gave a start.

Greta was standing in the doorway of the little
fortune-telling tent, beckoning with a sweep of a hand,
her spirally black curls leaping gaily in a breeze.

"Hey, Greta! How are things going?"

"I'm making bank reading tarot cards, that's how things are going. Sent some people out glowing, some crying, you know how it goes."

Eden didn't, really, but apparently Greta was accustomed to making people cry or exult.

"I have a lull," Greta said. "Let me do yours."

"Um, yeah, I don't know about that." She didn't need the tarot cards ringing in on her future. Her life was complicated enough at the moment. And as much as she adored Greta—and she did—her own innate self-protection didn't want yet another person privy to her angst.

"It won't hurt, Eden. Lord, girl, what are you, chick—"

"I'M NOT CHICKEN."

Greta blinked.

But apparently not much fazed her. "Then come on in," she said mildly.

She sighed and followed Greta into the tent, which was moodily lit with glowing amber lamps, because apparently the future could only be told in dark places, not, for instance, in the fluorescent glow of a school gym.

Or maybe it was because the future was so bright you needed protection from the glare. Heh.

"Hold these and think about your question. Then shuffle them. And cut them," Greta ordered.

She did. She took the sturdy, clearly well-used cards in her palm and held them, feeling a little foolish as she shuffled them, and into them soaked all of her angst about Gabe and life in general.

Greta pulled a card from the top.

"Ah, here we have Death," she said cheerily.

Eden's blood literally went cold. She swore she could feel it momentarily stop moving in her veins.

"For crying out *loud*, Greta," she said faintly.

"Calm your tits. It's not what you think. It's just the absolute end of the way of life. Transformation. Change. Something isn't working for you anymore. It must end in total."

"Oh, is *that* all."

"Life is a cycle, sweetheart. I've seen it all come through. Some things need to end completely in order for new and better things to begin. Your reading might be a little more circumspect if you chose the ten-card spread, but the three card gives you a sort of distilled answer."

"It's a kind of cut to the chase kind of spread is what you're saying."

"That's exactly how I'd put it."

Imagine that.

"Okay, choose your second card."

Eden flipped over another card from the top of the deck.

"Hmm. The Hanged Man, reversed." Greta tapped her chin thoughtfully with one finger.

"Death *and* hanging? I'm amazed people didn't run out of your tent screaming." She was going for flippant, but her voice had gained a half octave and was a trifle squeaky.

"He's hanging by his foot, not by a noose, silly. Look closely." She pointed with a scarlet, flawlessly manicured nail that could probably easily slit an envelope or possibly a throat. "When he's upright—turned in the other direction—he represents a sort of stasis . . . a willingness to give up temptation and instant gratification for a higher purpose. He puts his own personal needs aside. To wait for a long time for what he wants. He's a martyr."

Eden had never been less happy to hear her own decisions affirmed so succinctly.

"My goodness, look at your face. You look stricken! I wonder why." Greta sounded a little gleeful, as if she knew precisely why. "Let's find out. Let's turn over your next card."

She flipped it over. And there they were, a naked man and woman against the backdrop of some kind of radiant arch. All pulsing red and golds. It said THE LOVERS across the top, as if that wasn't already perfectly obvious.

"The Lovers. Well, well, well. Well, well, well, well, *well*."

Greta sat back and beamed at the spread, and then at Eden.

Eden was irritated that that tarot deck appeared to be patting down her soul like a cop and emerging with her secrets as though they were switchblades tucked into her boot. "What does *that* mean? A hideous death by guillotine?"

"It means exactly what it looks like. Red hot love, baby. This is the outcome."

Heat raced across the surface of her skin. Joining the anger and irritation in the panoply of things she was feeling.

"See, this is the thing. When the Hanged Man is *reversed*, it actually means you need to look at your situation from a completely different perspective. That maybe something in your outlook needs to change. And see all these vines and leaves around the hanging fella? That's about abundance. It means whatever situation you're asking about will be fruitful and *luscious* when you give up the impulse to martyr yourself. When you give up your fear of change."

Eden stared at her almost accusingly.

For a long time.

Greta just gave her a sympathetic smile. Nothing she wasn't used to, clearly.

"So if I were to sum this up . . . if you want this red hot love . . ." Greta tapped a nail to the card. " . . . a certain way of being and thinking has to end for you."

Eden sat for a moment and let that conclusion simmer for a moment.

"And then what?" She heard the words all but creak out of her mouth against her will.

"Well, let's see . . ." Greta laughed softly and peeled up the corner on another card. Eden glimpsed what looked like a black tower, with a sky full of lightning and plummeting bodies, which probably meant she'd adopt a cuddly kitten. But Greta slapped it back down again. "Oops, I've got a paying customer. See you in the hood, Eden."

Someone's shy little face was indeed peeping into the tent.

Merchants in Hellcat Canyon had each other's backs. A customer was a customer.

Greta collected those cards with the brisk profession-
alism of a Vegas blackjack dealer and Eden walked out,
feeling both fascinated and a little violated. Those tarot
cards took some liberties, boy.

The only person she'd felt comfortable yielding her
deepest secrets to was . . . was Gabe.

She stopped short.

How could she walk away from that?

When Eden emerged from the tent, the grounds
seemed thronged with kids hopped up on cotton
candy, bouncing like rubber balls from booth to booth
and shrieking with glee, a jarring contrast to having her
soul quietly excavated by Greta.

She strolled casually up a few booths and surreptitiously peered in at Annelise and Emily, who were both
being painted to look like butterflies. Neither of them
were clutching anything sugary.

She smiled.

She figured they'd get some actual nutrition in the
nuts and the cherry on top in a sundae. Right? Technically a cherry was a fruit?

And then she made a beeline for the dunking booth.
One of the advantages of being the person who roped
in the volunteers was that she knew exactly who was
scheduled to be sitting up there right now.

What passed for an enormous crowd in Hellcat
Canyon was clustered around it. And Gabe sat up there
on the platform like a king on a throne in a T-shirt and
shorts, the late-afternoon sun picking glints from his
hair and the hair on his shins.

He was heckling the poor woman who'd just whiffed her second toss.

"Aw, c'mon. It's like this is *literally* the first time you've ever thrown a ball."

The audience was disproportionately women. Which served to remind Eden that there was no reason on earth Gabe Caldera needed to be alone for a single second if he didn't want to be alone.

And Gabe wanted her.

Lowering her voice to a faux baritone, she shouted, "He's a *witch*!" à la Monty Python. "Sink him!"

He grinned, craned his head, looking for the source.

She ducked behind the crowd.

She had to wait through five truly terrible throwers before she got her turn.

To be fair, those women might have been able to throw Nolan Ryan fastballs in their spare time, but Gabe had smiled at each of them as they cocked their arms back, and clearly their arms turned to butter. Weaponizing his strengths, as it were.

Finally it was her turn.

She paid her ticket to the volunteer she'd roped into running the booth. Emily's mom, as it so happened.

Eden hefted the ball thoughtfully in her hand.

"Hello, Ms. Harwood," Gabe said finally.

"Your Excellency," she said pleasantly.

They locked eyes for a long, speaking moment.

He tilted his head and said, with more of that faux sympathy, "You sure you're not scared to throw that—"

BAM!

She hurled that sucker like a freaking missile. The

bull's-eye target whipped around, Gabe's arms shot straight up in the air and his eyes and mouth made "O"s and KERSPLASH! Down he went, for the first time that night. Vanishing into the water.

A delighted roar went up.

"WOOOOOOO! Eden!"

She thrust both arms in the air like a champion and took a bow in every direction.

While Gabe hauled himself back up on the platform and gave his head a shake, flicking the hair from his eyes.

"What do I win?" she asked him.

As if in answer to her question, he slowly, deliberately drew off his soaking shirt and shook his wet hair out of his eyes.

The crowd went stone silent.

And then there was a soughing sound, like a breeze through a stand of birches, which was essentially a dozen women exhaling in wonder and something close to pain.

Emily's harried mom thrust a pink teddy bear into Eden's hand. "Thank you for convincing me to volunteer for this booth," she whispered fervently. "Thank you."

"Who's next?" Gabe called cheerfully.

When the crowd surged forward, tickets in hand, Eden hung back. Way back.

Far enough so that from up on his perch, his eyes met hers, and she could have sworn they flashed like smugglers signaling the coast. Defiance, and a dare.

Oh, anyone could go next as far as she was concerned.

But she was the only one who was going to claim a prize.

About an hour later, as the sun was lowering, the crowds were thinning, and only a few cars were left in the parking lot, she came across her parents, strolling hand in hand. Tucked under her mom's arm was a big blue stuffed pig sporting fluffy eyelashes and a smile.

"Won it for her," her dad said. Smugly. "Shot a clown."

"Never let it be said romance dies," her mom said.

Her parents had always been unabashedly, frankly in love.

She had a hunch they wouldn't disapprove of what she was about to do.

"Hey, you guys? I promised Emily and Annelise I'd take them for ice cream, but I forgot something inside school. And then I need to swing by the all-night market and get some breakfast stuff. Do you mind taking them? Promise I'll be home in an hour, hour and a half on the outside. In time to put them to bed."

They both lit up as if they'd won another blue stuffed pig. "We'd *love* to, honey," her mom said.

Gabe swiped a hand through his still-damp hair and heaved a sigh that fluttered the little flag planted on his desk. He picked up his baseball, hefted its smooth, soothing weight in both hands for a second. "Commun-ing," he snorted.

It was, however, undeniably, a touchstone of someone he'd loved.

He liked the school at night. Silence and shadows didn't bother him. He knew all the ambient sounds, and the quality of the light through the various windows as the sun went down. He knew where Carl the janitor was in his rounds—clear on the other side of the school. The very last thing he'd do would be to lock up. But Gabe had keys, too. They didn't have security cameras. They were probably a fund-raiser or two in the future.

He sighed and put the ball back on its stand and pressed his palms over his eyes. When he pulled them away again, Eden was standing in the doorway.

He stopped breathing.

He didn't dare blink.

Because this was hands down the best damn game of peekaboo he'd ever played.

She was so precisely what he wanted to see that he wasn't confident he wasn't hallucinating, or dreaming, and either way, he wanted it to last as long as possible.

Behind her the hall was dark, apart from the dim glow of the intermittent sconces that did more to create eerie shadows than to illuminate anything.

He held his breath when she stepped across the threshold of his office.

She paused.

He rose slowly to his feet.

She turned her back to him.

His heart skipped. *No, don't go, please . . . even if I'm hallucinating from all the water inhalation . . .*

But it was only so she could pull the door closed.

He took another step forward.

She turned the lock on his door.

His heart literally forgot to beat.

And then she turned around to face him again, leaned against the door as if by pressing her back against it, none of her doubts or the demands on their time could possibly get in.

"You said I knew where to find you if I wanted you."

He took another step.

Then another.

He was midstep when suddenly everything went black.

"What the—"

He misjudged his next step, drove his thigh into the corner of his desk, dodged backward hissing and swearing, collided with his guest chair and landed hard on the seat, whereupon it promptly went gliding gently across the pitch-black room as if he'd just boarded the teacup ride at Disneyland.

Eden yelped as he crashed into her. He grunted as his face was instantly filled with her silky hair and her knee just barely missed his groin and her hands flew off in the darkness beyond his shoulder.

He caught her before they both toppled. With some deft maneuvering, the two of them got her turned around and her limbs all going the right way, so that he was cradling her after the fashion of a ventriloquist's dummy.

And as *he* wasn't a dummy, he wrapped his arms around her.

And held on.

He could feel her breathing—the rapid rise and fall—beneath his arms. She smelled like flowers and coconut. Still.

A silence, rather stunned in quality, ensued.

"I must have leaned against the light switch," she offered on a whisper, finally.

He didn't laugh. He didn't yet want to besmirch the glory of holding this woman with unnecessary conversation. Fate was on his side: he'd only gotten to her faster in a rolling chair.

"So thoughtful of you to pick me up at the door," she whispered.

He found his voice. "Yeah, well, I'm a gentleman . . . at first. That's how I hook you. And then I do things like this . . ."

He touched his tongue to her lips, coaxing them open. And what ensued was so scorching, so slow and claiming and carnal, that by rights the metal girders holding up the school ought to have melted.

Everything else on him was hard as a girder.

Falling or flying? He couldn't tell in the middle of that kiss. Both.

He lifted his lips from hers. Just a very little. He could still feel her breath against them.

But he could feel her body swaying as her breath came faster.

He brushed her hair back with his other hand, an excuse to touch the satiny skin of her throat; her heart was pounding.

"We have about thirty minutes," she whispered against his lips. "They think I went to pick up milk and orange juice."

"That's the hottest thing anyone has ever said to me."

"Is there anyone else left in the building, do you think?"

"Just Carl."

"Do you think he can hear us?"

"Why, do you plan to be loud?" he said with great interest.

"Maybe, if you do your job right."

In truth, that was more bravado than she actually felt. She was nervous as hell, and so turned on she could hardly bear it.

"We're good. Carl's way across the school cleaning the boys' locker room bathrooms right . . . *now*. And his hearing isn't what it used to be."

"You know such sexy things. You're like an omniscient James Bond."

To reward her for her banter, he slipped his hand up under her shirt and snicked open the latch on her bra so easily it was like he'd previously sent in a practice reconnaissance team.

Maybe he'd gotten that deft by defusing bombs.

Wow, this was happening fast.

For one thing—it had to happen fast, if it happened at all.

And she supposed they'd essentially engaged in foreplay for weeks now.

His thumb slid across her bare, already bead-hard nipple. A current of pleasure ricocheted between all of her erogenous zones like lightning in Tesla's lab. She gasped.

Dear God. How had she forgotten how good this was?

Gabe had the ergonomic advantage—hands free and within touching distance of all of the parts of her that were throbbing with anticipation—and he wasted no time exploiting it. He slid a hand, followed her thighs—no delicious dallying on the tender, wildly sensitive inner part, time was of the essence—and slipped a finger beneath the elastic of her underwear and commenced the sort of deliberate rhythmic stroking a flamenco guitarist would envy.

And each stroke sent pleasure rippling and shimmering over her nerves. Again and again.

"Oh God . . . Oh Jesus . . . God . . ." She wasn't certain why she'd launched into a roll call of deities. The pure surprise in her own voice was nearly comical.

Gabe embarked on a wildly effective three-step campaign: kisses that made her senses spiral, one hand stroking and teasing her breasts, the other at work farther south. She wanted to pitch in, but she was at a disadvantage when it came to reaching or stroking the parts of him that would make him call upon various deities, but she discovered that skillfully applied breath and a tongue tracing the whorls of his ear could make him shudder, then duck his head against her throat for more.

She shifted in his lap deliberately to hear his sucked-in breath, and to feel the hard poke of his erection. He hissed in a breath.

And then gave a short, wondering laugh.

"Eden . . ." His voice was low and prayerful. It cracked on that last syllable.

Her heart tipped over hard in her chest in supplication, the way Peace and Love did when he wanted a belly scratch.

She was grateful her expression was cloaked by the dark. She wasn't certain what Gabe would see in it.

"Gabe . . . Gabe, I think I'm going to . . . Oh God, any second now."

He heard her. He scraped his heels on the floor to get the chair in motion and they sailed over to his settee. If this had been one of the rides at the carnival, they would have made a mint.

The teeny red number of the digital clock on the shelf behind his desk read nine thirty-six.

"Hang on," he said, and she reflexively obeyed.

She locked her arms around his neck.

And he actually managed to *stand up*.

With all five foot nine of her in his *arms*.

As if he was rescuing her from a *burning building*.

He must have thighs like pile drivers. If she wasn't half unconscious from lust before, that realization would have pushed her over the edge.

She was going to get to touch them. She was going to touch everything she possibly could while the little red numbers scrolled away the half hour she'd stolen.

The next breath she drew in was ragged and literally hot. As if the two of them had turned the room into a furnace with a surfeit of lust.

He stood like that with her in his arms for a millisecond longer than he needed to. To prove that he could, perhaps. To turn her on just that unbearable bit more.

"I just assumed you wouldn't be able to stand by now," whispered the wicked, cocky man.

He lowered her to the settee, and she landed with a soft whup.

He reached over and slid out his desk top drawer, rummaged for a second and retrieved exactly what she thought he'd been looking for. "Kid brought them to school to use as water balloons. Expensive ones, too. Boy, was his dad *pissed*. And mortified."

The crackling of that package. The erotic, portentous clink of a belt unbuckling.

The rustle as she peeled off her own underwear and bunched it in a fist.

So romantic.

And yet.

He joined her there, his shadowy bulk hovering for a moment, then looping his arms around her and rolling her into his arms on the narrow expanse as if he were MacGyvering her out of the way of an explosion. The only way they'd fit properly on the settee was if they were locked together. Which of course was the plan.

She wrapped her legs around his waist and arched up against his hard cock, begging for release that was a mere few seconds of just ". . . please . . . Gabe . . . hurry . . . I . . ."

And as soon as he guided himself into her, she came apart. Her body arching like a cut wire. Her cells seemingly cast into the ether like flaming glitter. She stuffed her own fist in her mouth to keep the scream from escaping, and the sound she made was his name, and the bliss was nearly intolerable.

And he was moving now.

She slid her hands up under his shirt, against his hot, smooth skin and found his heartbeat thundering, and then slid them up to hold on to his shoulders. She locked her legs around his back to pull him deeper and closer. And her head went back hard when he thrust in deeply.

And the settee thudded softly against the floor like a goat trying to kick down a stall as he drove into her swiftly.

The dark room and the confines of the time and the space. The rushed, desperate, illicit hunger, the tacit understanding of their lives' constraints—all of it was ridiculous and shockingly hot.

And underlying it was something scary—something beautiful and new and so dangerous they might as well have been making love in a hammock suspended between two stars.

"Eden . . . God . . ." His voice was a wondering rasp.

His breath was ragged against her throat, as she clung to bare hot skin, and in her ear as she tucked his head there, bracing himself, and her eyes stung from some powerful emotion.

And then he went still, and his body jerked beneath her hands and his head fell against her chest.

She held him while he shook like a rag.

The clock ticked over to ten p.m.

"Gotta go," she whispered.

He sat up, and they reassembled themselves as efficiently as if they were getting ready for work. Her underwear had wound up behind his head. He held it out to her, dangling from one finger.

Practical cotton numbers. Six to a pack at Target. She was some vixen, boy.

She shimmied into them and then went to stand up.

He pulled her gently back by the arm.

They sat side by side a moment.

And then he leaned in and kissed her lingeringly.

They smiled against each other's lips for a moment.

"I'll walk you out."

"You'd better not."

He thought for a second. "You sit here, and I'll go do parking lot reconnaissance. And then I'll walk you out if the coast is clear."

And so he walked her out to the car, under the moonlight, and kissed her again, quickly and illicitly.

And she went off to buy milk and juice.

CHAPTER 12

Two weddings, a funeral, and a fiftieth anniversary party, a Hummingbird meeting (at Avalon's house up at Devil's Leap—and Avalon had volunteered to run it) and a report on Egyptians, various other to-ings and fro-ings—while the next week wasn't a tornado, every minute of it, from its start at four a.m. on Monday on through its conclusion on Sunday, was packed to the brim.

And while Eden was indeed joyously grateful for the business, it was a struggle not to pause in midsentence when she was talking to a potential client on the phone and indulge in a misty reminiscence about an orgasm that could have registered on the Richter scale. Or to interrupt a future bride endlessly hand-wringing about lilies versus roses by grasping her wrist, gazing earnestly into her eyes and saying, *Yes, yes, but let me tell you about the best sex I've ever had.*

Not that she'd had all that much sex in her life. It was just that she felt she could retire her nether parts, now that they'd partaken of Gabe Caldera.

As it was, she didn't tell a soul. It was still too new.
She wasn't a guy, to announce a conquest to his friends
over beers with high fives and a *yeah, I banged 'im!*
spirit of joie de vivre. And she definitely didn't tell
Avalon, from a typically siblingesque complicated
mishmash of reasons, including that she didn't want
Avalon to be right, and she didn't want Avalon to be
disappointed if it didn't work out, and she didn't want
Avalon to gush.

Throughout the week, just the very thought of him
created its own ecosystem: whenever the word *Gabe*
would float through her mind—and she summoned it
rather a lot—she went hot and weak and motionless, as
if she'd suddenly stepped through the door of her nicely
air-conditioned flower shop into some sultry jungle.
(Which, coincidentally, was an awful lot like how her
mom described menopause. Her mom spared no one
the details of . . . well, anything, really.)

She could see what was in the next square on her
whiteboard, but Gabe was a question mark. They didn't
text each other. That wasn't what they did. Yet, anyway.
She didn't have his phone number. She didn't know
when she'd see him next.

But now she knew that her schedule was full of hair-
line fissures through which light and air shone, and surprising nooks into which intimacy of all kinds could
be shoehorned. And instead of worrying about what
would happen next, she was, for the first time in eons,
willing to be surprised.

* * *

On Saturday afternoon, Eden raced up to Avalon's at Devil's Leap to drop off Annelise for a Hummingbirds meeting—they were going to learn all about chickens today, courtesy of Mac, and Avalon said she'd bring Annelise home later that evening.

And after she kissed Leesy goodbye and returned to her car, whom should she encounter beeping open his truck in the driveway but Gabe Caldera. Looking a little sweaty.

"Hi," he said. His voice a husk. Devouring her with his eyes.

"Hi." The word left her in an expulsion of breath.

"How are you, Eden?"

"Never better. Really busy. You?"

"Oh yeah. Just helped Mac renovate the chicken coop."

And apparently that was the end of verbal conversation. A lot of other silent things were being said, however. The air practically shimmered with heat.

Finally he said, almost idly, "You on your way out?"

"Yeah. I left Danny in charge of the shop. I have a mother of a bride and the bride coming in to go over some floral options in about an hour."

"You going out via River Road?"

"Yeah." Was there another way?

"You know . . . that unpaved bit before you hit River Road? It can be tricky. I got a flat tire out there one day. Down by that lookout. Off River Road. You know how there's an overlook well off the road? I was down there."

This seemed like quite a detailed narrative for a story

about a flat tire. Not that she was unsympathetic. "Oh yeah?"

"Yeah. A flat tire. In a secluded spot. A flat tire can really hold a person up." He said all of this slowly and carefully. "You could even be loud and no one would hear it," he prompted.

Realization and lust whooshed through her with such tidal force she dropped her keys.

Gentleman that he was, he stooped to pick them up.

He placed them into her outstretched palm, and his fingers lingered there for a millisecond, transferring about three billion kilowatts of desire along with it. ("Lust isn't measured in kilowatts. For Christ's sake, Eden."—Dr. Jude Harwood.)

And held her gaze.

"About how long does it take to change a flat again?" Her voice was a little shaky.

"Oh, twenty minutes or so, give or take. If you're really slowing down and doing the job right . . . thirty, even."

Her head went light. "Well, that's very interesting."

"Isn't it? Well, I've got to get going." He opened his truck door.

"I'll be leaving in a few minutes, too. Right behind you."

Behind you . . . behind you . . . behind you . . . echoed in her head.

She could just picture him behind her a little too well.

What felt like a veritable carpet of heat unfurled across the back of her body.

"Bye!" she bellowed at Avalon, who had peeked out

the window at the sound of their voices, and leaped into her car.

And peeled out of there so fast gravel spit.

Heart pounding, she slowed her car as she approached that River Road overlook. Hands already trembling. She braked to send a text to Danny.

> Danny, I think I have a flat. I can fix it. But I might be just about fifteen minutes later than I anticipated. Sorry!

She coasted forward around fifty gently curving feet until she was just off the road.

And pulled up alongside Gabe's truck.

Clever spot. They weren't visible at all from the road.

She opened the car door with trembling hands. Climbed out and stood against her car for a moment.

Gabe rolled down the window of his truck. "Trouble, miss? Need a . . . ride?"

"Wow. Cheesy *and* hot . . . two of my favorite things."

He pushed open the door to the truck and tilted his head, beckoning her inside.

She gave her van door a hip bump to close it.

She climbed into Gabe's truck and pulled the door closed behind her. It smelled like leather and Armor All and a little bit like sweaty man.

From now on, lust would smell like leather and Armor All and sweaty man to her.

There was a condom on the dash. Ready and waiting.

It was almost funny. Never had efficiency been so erotic.

They smiled at each other.

Something joyous bloomed inside that little cabin. Funny how it was so like the space she'd imagined carving for them.

"I texted my assistant," she said. Already going breathless, thanks to her heart rate. "I bought about thirty min—"

He looped a hand around her neck and kissed her.

The kiss was leisurely, but the hand clambering down the buttons of her shirt was patently not.

In seconds flat, daylight and cool air touched her skin. And then his hot hands were skating over her skin and up over her back, because, silly her, she'd worn a bra that clipped behind and not in front. Such was her impatience she would happily burn all the ones that clipped in the back. What a waste of time!

He got it unclipped. She shrugged out of it with practically unseemly eagerness.

She snaked one arm around his neck to pull him closer, and the kiss got deep and hot and dirty as his hands closed over her breasts and he stroked. No subtlety, just fingers heading straight for the nipples and making her wild within seconds.

"Oh God. Gabe . . . holy *wow* . . ."

He ducked his head and drew her nipple into his mouth and sucked.

She thought she might actually faint from the rush of pleasure.

Her hand fell upon the top button of her jeans, but her fingers scrabbled there futilely, like a spider on ice. ". . . stupid . . . effing . . . *pants* . . ."

He reached over and tugged, and the buttons gave way as if they were serrated like a paper towel.

"My superpower," he said modestly.

She thrashed her way out of them in about a split second while he was unfastening his jeans and yanking them down, along with his boxers. She slithered out of her underwear and parked them on the dash.

And then she closed her hand around his cock in a way that meant business.

And dragged it up hard.

"Ohmygod," he said in an amazed, choked rasp.

"It's only a penis," she murmured in his ear, right before she dipped her tongue onto it. "Nothing to get worked up about."

His laugh became a ragged groan of pleasure, and she felt like she had superpowers of her own as he thickened and hardened and arched into her relentlessly stroking fist.

It really was like riding a bike. A girl just didn't forget.

And for a time it was quiet apart from his gasps for breath, his moans, this hiss of pleasure as his hips arched up into her hand. She savored watching him attempt to withstand that pleasure as he swelled into her hand, his breath coming in gusts, his eyes closing and his head whipping back.

He was half laughing, half moaning.

"Eden. Christ . . . come here . . . now . . ."

She straddled him. Rose over him so that her nipples were just about level with his eyes.

"Wow, look at me," she murmured. "I have aaaall

the control. You're going to have to *ask* for what you want."

She went for his shirt buttons. She wanted to feel her bare skin against his.

"That's what you think," he said, as he drew his hand up between her thighs, delicately but deliberately, and the vulnerable skin there shivered with pleasure and anticipation as his fingers dipped into where she was wet.

"Gabe," she rasped. "Dear God."

"You're going to want to beg *me* in a second . . ." he murmured.

He did it again, but no one begged anyone. Suddenly it was too serious.

They got the condom on him in seconds, and she rose up so he could guide her down onto his cock. Glorious.

He sighed, muttered an oath of pleasure.

She closed her eyes, savoring the feel of him inside her.

She rose up, his hands sliding over her butt. Slowly, they moved, at first, and he began murmuring, the low velvet of his voice nearly as erotic as a stroking hand. "Yes," he sighed. "God. Picture it . . . we're fully dressed . . . we have hours and hours and hours . . . I'm undressing you slowly . . . button by button."

He was trailing hot kisses over her throat as he said that, and the "b"s made little puffs of air. Surprisingly erotic.

"Yes," she urged, on a groan.

"You are *aching* for it, begging . . . so I make you wait."

He arched up into her, but she kept it slow, torturously, blissfully slow.

She closed her eyes, drunk with sensation, and tipped her head so he could reach her ear with his tongue and send those quicksilver shimmers of sensation fanning out to the nether reaches of her body. "More," she demanded breathlessly. "Tell me more . . ."

She rose, slowly, her nipples chafing against his chest, maddening both of them.

". . . and then I'm peeling your clothes away slowly like . . . like you're a . . . you're a . . . delicious fruit . . ."

He dragged his fingers delicately over the seam of her butt. Oh wow. Oh lovely shivering nuance of pleasure.

"A *fruit*?" she whispered hoarsely.

"Forgive me . . . I'm not . . . Omar Khayyam . . ."

Pizza would have worked as well as fruit.

The fact that he knew Omar Khayyam well enough to reference him during sex was nearly as hot as his tongue in her ear.

"And then . . ." she urged breathlessly. Rising up. Sliding down. Filling herself deeply with him. Watching herself in his eyes. Lingering at the tip of his cock. Teasing him. Teasing them both. Sinking down again.

"And then . . . I just . . . I just . . . Oh God. Oh God . . . Eden . . ."

Their rhythm was almost wave-like now. Languid, steady, maddening each of them. Eden rose along his lift and plunge, her breath mingling with his. She could watch his gaze go black. The cords of his neck go taut.

". . . and then . . ." she all but whimpered. When it came, this orgasm might just kill her with its intensity.

"I lay you out flat . . . savor you with my eyes . . .

because damn you're so hot . . ." His words were a staccato rhythm against her collarbone, against her lips, against her nipple, as she rose and sank onto him, the blood pounding in her ear . . . "I lick every part of you . . . every hollow . . . every sexy angle . . . I take my, sweet . . . sweet *time* . . ."

"*Yes* . . ." she moaned. "*Yes*. Time . . ."

This was what her life had come to: the notion of great expanses of time was basically their version of dirty talk.

"And you are just writhing . . . moaning from . . . the licking . . ." He was losing the thread.

His face was sheened in sweat.

He seized her hips and urged her faster. "Eden, baby, I can't . . . I'm going to . . . I need you to . . ."

He didn't have to ask twice.

She needed it, too.

They were colliding together now. She rode him fast, his hips bucking up into her, her body crashing down onto him almost painfully, chasing the insane quotient that would be theirs in seconds. She could feel it pulling back and back like a tsunami, and it was going to break, and she was going to scream.

She did.

His name.

Her consciousness was whipped into the stratosphere while pleasure all but took over with a near violent, indescribable bliss. It racked her body. And seconds later he went still, with a choked roar against her clavicle. She could feel him shuddering beneath her. They clung to each other.

She tipped her head against his. He kissed her. Drew her hair back with shaking fingers.

Their bodies heaved together, still.

"No one has ever called me 'baby,'" she murmured. Bemused.

He laughed. Breathlessly. "It just slipped out. I was channeling a swinger. Sammy Davis Jr., maybe."

"Or Sonny Bono."

"Or Dean Martin."

"Or Bob Newhart."

He stared at her, openmouthed, aghast. "Bob Newhart was not a *swinger*."

They both laughed absurdly hard at this.

"Casey Carson once told me that one of her friends yelled 'ride me, you lop-eared son of a bitch!' in the throes of sex."

He stared at her. "Why'd you have to tell me that? Now I have to top it."

She laughed. "Am I squishing you?"

"I really want to say no, but in about two seconds I won't be able to feel my thighs."

She shifted from him and reached immediately for her pants and her underwear.

There was no time to linger, to savor every last particle of the feel of him inside her, on her skin, or her lips. It felt wasteful, ungrateful, almost criminal, to partake like that and just leave.

Suddenly they were both somber; it was silent. She was getting good at wriggling back into her clothes in enclosed spaces.

He was busy putting himself back together. There

was something so frank about the undressing and re-dressing in front of each other.

They sat together in silence for a time, staring out through the windshield.

"This is madness, you know," he said thoughtfully.

She knew he meant the Furtive Speed Sex they'd been enjoying.

"I know."

She put her hand on the door handle. Then took it away.

They had two minutes. She was going to take both of them.

Three, because she could break the speed limit with relative impunity on this road; it was isolated enough and she knew it well. It would be irresponsible and reckless and apparently that's what she was now.

Oh, God, she was someone's mother. What the hell was she doing?

Having the best time of her whole life, pretty much.

"Eden . . ."

She loved the way his voice emerged from the silence; she loved the way her own name practically caressed her eardrums. In that instant she didn't want to leave this truck ever again.

"Yeah?"

"I like you. A lot."

She turned to him and her breath actually hitched, such was the impact when she looked at him after even a short period of not looking at him. Even sweaty, with his hair rumpled from her rifling hands.

"I like you, too."

Honestly. This was the kind of conversation first graders might have while they toed the ground. She felt shy as a first grader. There was some comfort in the fact that he didn't look much more certain about things than she felt. Simple words, jokey ones, were safer. They buffered the danger of bigger, more adult feelings. The word *like* was a disguise, a button-down L.L. Bean shirt pulled over the pulsing, secret, sweet terror of that other "L" word.

"I really want to spend more time with you. And that's not a euphemism for I want to do you again. Though, you know, that stands to reason."

She flashed a smile. "Natch."

But then he said nothing else. He was waiting.

She took a breath. "That would be nice. I would like that. More time, that is. I can . . . I can make that work."

Funny how halting and inarticulate two intelligent, glib, wildly capable people could suddenly get when it came to asking for things that could get them hurt if it didn't turn out the way they'd wanted.

"It's . . . you know . . . scheduling . . ."

They both turned to the clock on his dash. And as per their conditioned response, the sex-blurred thoughts sprang to their feet crisped up again, and they began to disperse, to take up their usual burdens of worrying and planning.

"I'd like to take you to dinner. Dinner at, you know, a restaurant with white tablecloths."

She furrowed her brow. "A restaurant . . . with white tablecloths?" she repeated slowly, with faux wonderment, like someone just discovering fire.

"Oh, the most amazing thing, Eden. We dress up in clothes we don't wear every day, and sit across from each other in a restaurant that not only has white tablecloths and lit candles and prix fixe menus and sometimes unpronounceable yet delicious food . . . but . . . here's the best part . . . someone else cooks the food and brings it *to* you. Someone you're not even *related* to."

"No! You can't be serious!"

"Scout's honor. And if you can believe it, they don't even have a *kid's* menu."

She clapped a hand to her heart. "I swan!" Which was what her great-grandma used to say.

"And . . . you might want to brace yourself . . . they serve really . . . good . . . wine."

She tipped her head and eyed him with great, great skepticism. "Are you sure you aren't making this up?"

"I would never lie to you."

It was funny, but that last bit emerged sounding a little less like a joke and more like a vow.

And Eden knew at once it was true. Guilt pinpricked her. Even though she hadn't precisely ever lied to him about Annelise's dad, she was more and more certain Gabe might not see it that way.

There was a little silence.

"You know . . . maybe we could go on a picnic?" she suggested, almost shyly.

Suddenly it seemed like a way to give the arc of their relationship a more gradual rise. Though on the line graph of dating, sex was usually pretty close to the top.

She wanted to be outside in the wild with him, completely alone apart from squirrels and deer and any other critters that might want to spy on them.

He was quiet, mulling. "I know this beautiful spot up above Firelight Falls . . . you get a view of the canyon, the falls are close enough to see. We could spend two, three hours? Maybe?"

She drew in a sharp breath. Of all the half dozen or so lovely falls in Hellcat Canyon, Firelight Falls was her favorite. Not as dramatic as Full Moon Falls, perhaps, what with its proximity to the Eternity Oak, and all. It was a little hidden, more subtle and elegant. The long, long narrow cascade that glowed a deep fiery gold when the sun lowered in the afternoon at a certain time of year—hence its name. She'd always thought it was the most romantic place for a date, and yet no man had ever taken her there. She hadn't been in years, in fact.

And . . . oh, wow. Two, three, hours. They could talk. About whatever. Anything they wanted. Anything and nothing. Oh, the untold luxury of goofing off with a gorgeous, funny man, of an hour purposeless apart from impressing and savoring each other.

They could even . . . oh, maybe hold hands on the way there.

She'd just ridden him hard and egged on his dirty Time Porn talk, but it was the notion of holding his hand that made her blush.

She looked at him, and even though his polished leather seats were firm beneath her backside (but not as firm as his thighs), she experienced a peculiar vertigo. That sense of walking along a cliff's edge, where the view was giddy and vast and the view was of the entire world, and the drop perilously infinite.

Rediscovering herself as a person distinct from Annelise was messing with her equilibrium in unexpected ways. It was a bit like relearning a skill, like . . . like riding a bike.

"I think I know the spot. I can ask if Avalon and Mac can hang out with Annelise . . ." Her heart was pounding now. "Are you free next Saturday between, say, twelve and three?"

Arranging a babysitter was tantamount to a formal engraved announcement that they were embarking on a *relationship*. Not only that, but it was inviting the merciless teasing and probing from siblings and family members and then, of course, everyone else in Hellcat Canyon who caught wind of it.

One didn't endure that sort of thing frivolously.

"That sounds perfect," he said.

She smiled at him.

"You're sure about this?" he said.

"Yeah," she said lightly.

"Great. I'll text you."

She reached for the door handle and popped the door open.

She leaned forward and kissed him, with just enough tongue to keep his lust on parboil for possibly the rest of the day and maybe into the night, when he could take matters into his own hands, literally. As long as he was dreaming of her.

Just so the last view of him when she walked away was his expression of dazed appreciation and something more thrilling and resolute.

She'd better know what she was doing. Because she knew she couldn't dip a toe in with this guy. It would be all in, or nothing.

"**O**kay, guys, I know you're counting on me this Saturday at the game . . ." he said casually, as he twisted the wrench.

Everyone froze.

"Are you about to blow us off again?" Louis demanded.

"I'm not dating all of you, Louis. Keep dreaming."

"But *Gabe* does have a date," Bud guessed. Slyly.

"Awww," they all said. Various kissy noises ensued.

"Fuck you," he said grumpily.

They all just laughed.

"Go get her, tiger. If we lose, though, you have to buy us dinner for a month."

He scowled at them.

"Deal," he finally agreed.

Pasquale's was cheap. And frankly, he'd pay just about any price for time alone with Eden.

There was a long, long silence after Eden told Avalon over the phone about why she needed a babysitter for Saturday.

"Avalon? You still there?"

"I'm just so *happy*," Avalon said on a dumbstruck hush. Sounding genuinely overjoyed and more than a little wickedly gleeful.

"Knock it off. Knock off the gloppiness right now. It's one date."

"It was the abs that made you cave, right? Those squares?"

Eden gritted her teeth. "He's nice."

Avalon was laughing so hard now Eden had to pull the phone a little bit away from her ear. "How did he ask you out?"

"Very nicely," Eden retorted tersely.

Avalon snorted. "Yeah, you guys have been on simmer for a while, I'm thinking."

If only she knew.

"Mac and I will take Annelise all night if you want," Avalon added. "We love having her here. If you want to . . . you know."

Oh, the unimaginable luxury of having Gabe all to herself for one entire night. They could be noisy and dirty and use more than three square feet of any given surface to have sex, in every position she could get into.

No. She wanted to take this part of their relationship gradually. She needed to take this gradually. Because the next part would include Annelise.

"We're just going on a picnic," she said firmly. "I'll pick Annelise up around dinnertime."

"Are you going to that Black & Blue show at the Misty Cat Friday? Do you know who they are? I've never heard of them."

"Isn't that weird? Once upon a time we would have known every band that came through here. I have no idea who they are and Annelise has another report due and I'm going to get my beauty sleep."

"Yeah, you're going to want to rest up for you know."

Eden sighed and clicked the call to an end to the sound of Avalon laughing.

CHAPTER 13

Saturday, day of the picnic . . .

Apart from some slight sleep deprivation—apparently Black & Blue had some pretty ardent fans, and they noisily filled the streets with drunken "Wooos!" as they spilled out of the Misty Cat last night, tempting Eden to slide open a window and dump buckets of water on their heads, but she didn't. Her mom had picked up Annelise from school yesterday, and Annelise had met one of the guys from Black & Blue at their sound check at the Misty Cat. She said he was really, really nice and had taught her to play another mournful chord. So since the guy from Black & Blue was nice and generous to her daughter, Eden decided she'd be nice to his fans, even if his fans were obnoxious.

All in all, however, Eden felt *amazing*. As though she were wearing clouds for shoes.

Avalon had already picked up Annelise, who only knew she was going to be spending a delightful day with her aunt and uncle and the goats and the donkey. It was too soon to tell her about Gabe.

Today, for the first time, Eden was going to have hours and hours with Gabe, and hopefully a lot of those hours would be spent at least seminude out in the wild.

She was just getting ready to load the day's deliveries into the van for Danny to handle, after which she'd hang the "Closed" sign on the door a little earlier than usual, when the door jingled.

And in walked a god.

Not the Michelangelo-Statue-of-David-aquiline-nose sort. Maybe less a god than a faun. The rakish kind that lived in the forest, slept on beds of moss under blankets of leaves, and captured and humped nymphs, not necessarily with their express permission.

He wasn't classically handsome. His jaw was a little too square, his lips a little too pillowy, his nose too big, his eyes maybe a little too narrow. They were shiny and mischievous as a bird's. It was all topped by a pile of dark curls, so loose and unruly one would need a compass and a machete to untangle them.

Things seldom turned out well for the various nymphs these kinds of gods pursued, regardless of whether they were willing. They were turned into trees or spirited off to Hades for months at a time.

In Eden's case, she'd been quite willing. And she'd wound up knocked up.

And yet it had taken her a split second to recognize Jasper Townes, because he was literally the last person she expected to see in her shop, though maybe that

shouldn't have been true. She now thought she understood what it truly meant to have the living daylights
shocked out of her.

She froze in place behind the counter, three-quarters
of her turned toward the door, one hand reaching for a
shelf, as she'd turned herself into a tree, already out of
self-defense. Which would not look out of place in her
shop.

Jasper Townes was Sexy. Capital "S," land *hard* on
the "X," sexy. But it was more a result of some aura,
something he was born with, rather than the net effect
of a series of qualities, such as reliability and foresight
and protectiveness or those other Boy Scout (or navy
SEAL, if she was getting specific) type things that got
her motor running these days.

Being lead singer of a now very popular band called
Blue Room was all part and parcel of Jasper's sexiness.

"Eden?" His low, raspy voice was sure familiar.

"Yes?" she said pleasantly in her shopkeeper voice,
although thanks to nerves she'd acquired kind of a dry-
mouth click. "And you are?"

He actually laughed at that, quite genuinely.

Because, ha ha ha, wasn't it funny that everybody in
the whole freaking world knew who he was.

He had a pleasant laugh, he really did. It was just that
suddenly the world was an echo chamber, and everything, even the poor baby roses in the courtyard, looked
sinister in light of the moment she'd been sort of dread-
ing for the last decade.

His band had a drummer who played a double bass
drum.

It had nothing on the beat of her heart right now, though.

"Wow, you look pretty much the same as I remember," he said. Admiringly.

She didn't say anything. She just stared. Was that . . . was that a feather dangling from his hair? Did a bird crash into him or did he deliberately install a feather into his hair? Maybe it was a remnant from a down pillow.

"From the front, anyway," he added excruciatingly.

And very, very wickedly.

Oh, God.

He'd been like a freaking Chinese acrobat that night. She'd been wheelbarrowed and scissored and flipped like a pancake inside of an hour. For a laconic poet type, he'd sure had a lot to prove about his prowess.

She'd been more bemused than anything about the whole thing, though it had been interesting the way trying all the rides in the carnival was interesting. A one and done. That had been her plan, anyway.

She stared him down until the roguish, pleased-with-himself twinkle vanished from his eyes.

"I bet you get away with saying anything you want these days, huh, Jasper?"

"Sorry. Maybe that was a little, um, graceless."

"Um, yeah. A little." Tersely as a nun with a ruler about to smack his hand.

"I was trying to lighten the mood."

"I was unaware we had established a mood."

A little silence.

Became a long silence.

"I never forgot that night with you, you know. Thought about it quite a bit over the years," he tried carefully.

"I always think it's funny when men say things like that. Like they should get a medal for bothering to remember boinking someone."

He looked faintly surprised. "I never thought of it that way."

There was, in truth, no reason she should be rude to him. Apart from nerves and guilt that she didn't really deserve, because she *had* tried to get in touch with him.

Was *that* why he was here? Oh God.

She steeled her nerve. "What brings you to town, Jasper?"

He looked surprised again. "I thought you'd know. I'm the 'Blue' part of Black & Blue, my side project with Renfro Black from Powder Keg. We played a set at the Misty Cat last night. Then I'm off to Europe with Blue Room after a few NorCal gigs."

Oh, God. Jasper's band was *Blue* Room, after the lyric in that David Bowie song, "Sound and Vision." Black & Blue!

Oh, shit shit shit. How had *that* escaped her?

Oh right: she'd been riding Principal Gabe.

The hypervigilant part of her brain had kind of been anesthetized by fantastic sex and giddy infatuation.

And she'd been busy being a mom.

And then the last part of what he'd just said registered:

He'd been at the Misty Cat for sound check.

Which was when Annelise was there yesterday.

And he was the guy who'd taught Annelise a new chord.

And just like that, her heart was in her throat.

Honestly. Did the universe have to pack two moments of truth into one weekend?

"You own this place now?" He looked around, wonderingly, frowning faintly, as if he was puzzling out what a flower shop precisely was.

"Forgive me, Jasper, I'm afraid you caught me at a bad time. It's nice to see you again, but I have to get these arrangements out to the van for delivery. So . . ."

Now that was purely chicken-shit, and she disliked herself for it, because it spoke to who she was when backed into a corner. Apparently she was willing to just attempt a dodge on the off chance she got away with it.

She couldn't imagine Gabe ever doing that, but then, Gabe was six foot a jillion, and he'd never gotten knocked up by a rock star.

Or had a daughter all to himself for ten years.

She desperately wanted Jasper to leave. *Leave us the way we are*, she urged him, as if he were a tarot deck she was clutching. Willing her question into him.

And yet she'd never forgive herself if he did leave.

He just smiled, a bemused little smile. "Literally no one has ever told me to go away in at least a decade."

"I'll give you a second to Google what those words mean, if that helps."

He glanced over his shoulder, as if he was reflexively looking around for an assistant to do the Googling for him before he caught himself.

And then suddenly, something about his posture signaled . . . intent. He was here for a very specific reason.

He drew in a deep breath. Like he was steeling his nerve.

Portent gusted through her soul and her stomach turned like a chicken on a spit.

"Okay. Listen. I didn't just come in for old times' sake."

He stepped forward and slowly laid something on the counter. Like he was playing a card.

It looked like a scrap of paper. A dollar bill? A *coupon* for a bouquet? Good Lord, wasn't he making good money by now?

She peered closer.

All the little hairs stood up on the back of her neck.

It was a faded Polaroid.

Of Annelise.

Her baby. Eden's lungs seized up. All skinny colty legs and long shining hair to her waist, standing in front of what looked like a suburban house, her eyes squinted closed, smiling that adorable gap-toothed smile.

"Where the hell did you get this picture of Annel . . ."

And then she stopped.

Because she somehow understood before he even confirmed it aloud.

"It's a photo of my mom when she was eleven," Jasper said.

It was like a trapdoor had opened beneath her feet. Eden pressed her fingers against the counter to steady herself against a swoop of vertigo.

She didn't look up.

She couldn't yet.

The longer she looked down the longer she could pretend he wasn't standing here in her shop.

Her breathing was rough in her own ears now, though.

"I met Annelise at the Misty Cat during sound check. She's a sweetheart. Told me she could play guitar, too. She actually told me a lot of things." He smiled faintly. A little nervously.

He was nervous.

"Yeah. She takes lessons," she said faintly. "And she's . . . she's a gregarious kid."

"She's a charmer. She told me she was ten years old. She showed me her new favorite chord. It's—"

"A minor."

She and Jasper said it at the same time.

There was a little silence.

He breathed in. Exhaled at a steady length. He was gathering courage for something.

"She told me she used a lot of A minor to write a song called 'Invisible Dad,'" he added.

Fuck fuck fuck triple fuck.

"She said she doesn't know who her dad is, but he had to leave town for an appointment. She says she's pretty sure he has big shoulders."

Bless Leesy's friendly, talkative little heart and her dreams of a certain kind of dad.

Eden had nothing to say to this. All she could think of was Gabe, and his shoulders, and his warm eyes, receding like a dream. Like he was standing on the opposite shore and she hit a sandbar just as she was about to walk off the boat into his arms.

"She has one of these, too." Jasper pointed to the dent in his chin.

Eden had nothing to say to that.

"I connected the dots," he concluded.

Yep. Jasper was no dummy. She remembered that well.

She slowly leveled her head up and stared at him. She caught a glimpse of her own face in the mirror up in the corner of the store: pale, eyes big and hunted. She herself looked like a shoplifter who'd just gotten caught.

Annelise not only had the chin dent. Annelise had his eyebrows, the way they sort of winged up at the end. And probably a thousand other subtle little things.

She said nothing, as the full import of all of this washed over her. As if she'd gone down in a dunking booth.

"So, I'm just going to come right out and ask. Eden . . . am I that kid's father?"

She was pretty sure her expression already answered that question.

"Yes."

Absolute and total silence reigned for a few seconds.

Then he pushed his hands back through his hair and sucked in a long, long breath.

She was surprised things didn't fall out. A dime, or a gum wrapper. The kinds of things one found in sofa cushions. Because he still looked like a guy who'd partied hard the night before and fell asleep on the couch.

"Huh. Wow. Well."

A long silence ensued while Jasper looked off into the middle distance pensively. He swallowed. Then he pressed his lips together.

"Do you need to sit down?" she asked solicitously. With her foot, she nudged a chair over toward him.

He shook his head.

"Do you need a . . . drink? I only have water," she added hurriedly.

When she'd learned she was pregnant, it was also about the time Jasper was in the news for dating a British supermodel with whom he subsequently loudly, publicly, and drunkenly argued in an airport lounge, about, bystanders said, the fact that she preferred John Mayer's last record to his.

"*THAT* PRAT?" he'd shouted, waving his arms in an outraged inebriated fashion, like those inflatable men outside car dealerships.

It had become a meme.

He'd in fact been girlfriend-free for all of about five minutes after he left Hellcat Canyon.

Shortly after that he'd gone to rehab for some unspecified "dependency."

His unspecified dependencies were something else she ought to learn about. For Annelise's sake.

He shook his head again.

"Jasper . . ." she said carefully. "I still have to get these flowers in the van or they'll wilt. This is my livelihood."

"Eden . . . it's just . . . why didn't you *tell* . . ." he began. His volume escalated a little.

He caught himself.

"I did tell you," she said instantly, evenly, with as little emotion as she could muster. "Or at least I did try to tell you. Multiple times. I managed to get through to your agent. Or one of them. You seem to have a slew of agents and managers of various kinds running interference for you. I was told very kindly that approximately twenty-five women a day claimed to be pregnant with your child. I left a message for you. When I didn't hear back, I figured you just didn't want to know. Which was actually fine with me. I was only fulfilling what I thought was my moral obligation. I couldn't imagine the news would thrill you at that point in your career."

Jasper was white about the mouth now. He didn't dispute that last part.

"I swear to you I never got any of your messages. I did have a phalanx of people protecting me from other people back then. I guess I still do."

The thought popped into her head: how Annelise would love the word *phalanx*.

Because all thoughts led to Annelise. She was her very heart; the world was like the circulatory system.

And yet Jasper was part of Annelise, too. And Annelise was part of him.

The push-pull of that thought was a sort of sweet anguish.

"By the way, that was right about the time you fought with the supermodel and went into rehab and then after that dated another supermodel."

"Which one was that? Annika or Marie Hele—"

"Are you kidding me right now?"

"Right. Right. Sorry. Just thinking out loud. Kind of . . . kind of thrown."

"Okay. Well, that makes both of us. Maybe you can get a song out of it."

He remained quiet.

Perversely she liked him for not blathering something insincere, or defensive, or self-righteous.

Something terrified and tense in her was easing: she'd liked him back then for a reason, not just because, well, he was sexy and a musician. Apparently he wasn't a bullshitter. He was, in fact, an actual person. Her judgment wasn't entirely awful.

The news of children pretty much sobered everyone in a damn hurry. Shock was great for burning off the mists of bullshit.

"I *would* have gotten in touch," he said quietly, finally.

She wasn't positive she believed that.

His tone suggested he wasn't even certain he believed it.

The guy he was back then might not have.

The guy he was today apparently believed he would have. He was here, anyway. And that took some nerve.

She let it lie.

They stared at each other in the hush of her little store. So precious to her, like Annelise, like her mostly predictable life in Hellcat Canyon.

"You never got married, huh?" he said next.

She sighed. "C'mon, Jasper. I'm barely thirty, and you're not much older than me. And I've been kind of busy raising a child and running a business."

"Sorry. I meant . . . It's just that . . . so it's not like you were . . . um, waiting for . . ."

When his meaning dawned on her, she coughed a laugh so incredulous it fluttered the leaves on her floral arrangement. "For *you*?"

She said it with such genuine, scorching amazement color actually rose in his cheeks.

She was also amazed anything could still make him blush.

"I'm sorry, I'm a little thrown, too, and I default to snarky when I'm thrown. I don't mean to be unkind, Jasper, but, uh, no. I had no interest in a relationship with you. Now, or then. I wanted what you wanted that night, and that's all." She tried to say this a little more gently. "It was fun, though. It was memorable. And I guess I don't regret it."

That was hardly flattering.

He accepted this with a wry twist of his mouth.

He looked so stunned and so oddly stranded in her store, like a creature abandoned by his mothership. He had always had that quality of otherness about him, that charisma that rock stars exuded, that drew the world in and kept it at a remove.

She tried her soothing voice, the same voice Lloyd Sunnergren had used that time a coyote had wandered into the feed store a few years back.

"Jasper . . . just so you know . . . in case you were worried . . . we never needed or wanted anything from you. And we still don't. Not money, not time, certainly not publicity. We are really, really great. Annelise has dozens of people in her life who adore her and will always be there for her, and we have a really great, happy, full life. So you have absolutely nothing to worry about."

She stopped just short of saying, *So you can walk out guilt free right now if you want.* She knew he was smart enough to recognize what she'd just said for what it was: the ladder dangling from the rescue copter for the guy who'd tumbled into a ravine. And if he latched on to that ladder, it would be an out for her, too.

"I'd like to talk more with you about this. Can we? I'm here for the next two days. Staying in J. T. Mc-Cord's house while he's in Los Angeles filming some spots with Franco Francone. Then I'm off to Sacramento, and from there San Francisco, then Europe. Here's my number."

A collection of bracelets jingled on his wrist and seemed to collectively act as a fan that sent a little waft of patchouli toward her when he held out his card.

What adult male had *time* to dab on patchouli? None of the men in or on the periphery of her life were scented by anything other than deodorant soap and deodorant and sweat and in the case of Giorgio the grill cook, hamburger grease. Gabe always smelled clean in a way that immediately made her picture him nude in the shower.

When she didn't immediately take the card, he placed it on the counter and slid it over to her.

And slid the photo back into his own hands.

"I don't have too many photos of her. I carry this one around with me. Prop it up on hotel room nightstands when I'm on tour."

He carried a photo of his mom and parked it on his hotel nightstand like an anchor, she supposed. Because he was a rootless guy. She remembered that about him. "I flow like a river, baby," he'd told her then, and that had struck her as profound right before she slept with him, and a month later when that pink plus sign showed up it seemed like possibly the most dangerous thing a man could say.

And now she understood him a little more.

Why *now*, was the question?

She asked it. "Why now, Jasper?"

He hesitated. "Eden . . . I swear I don't have an agenda. I don't want to disrupt her life or yours. I just . . . happen to know what it's like not to know who your dad is. I still wonder about mine. And even if Annelise doesn't pester you about it, I'd bet my left nut that she wonders about it. And my left nut is my favorite."

He waited for the laugh, which of course wasn't coming. Not today.

"I didn't know my dad. And you know what? After a while I stopped asking about him, because I didn't want to hurt my mom's feelings, because I didn't want her to think she wasn't enough."

She couldn't say a word, because he'd just voiced precisely everything she'd been thinking for going on two months.

"Anyway. Good seeing you. Call me or text me if you want to have dinner to talk about it tonight. I'll let you get back to . . ."

He waved his hand vaguely, puzzled, to indicate the shop, her life. Her ordinary, extraordinary life that had just shifted to allow in the possibility of an extraordinary man. Gabe Caldera.

She was no stranger to sacrifice, but what she had to do next seemed so wildly unfair she was arrested in a moment—just a tick of the clock—of grinding self-pity at the injustice and gracelessness of the universe's timing.

And then, because she always had, she did what she had to do.

CHAPTER 14

Gabe stared at the text for so long his stillness drew the attention of all his friends.

> I apologize profusely, Gabe, but I can't make it to Firelight Falls today. Something has suddenly come up.

He now held in his hand what felt like a grenade, but which could be a perfectly innocuous text.

What did it actually *mean*?

And to think, just an hour before he'd been standing in the shower singing an homage to one of Eden's guilty pleasure songs: "The first time . . . ever at Firelight Falls . . . ba da da daaa . . . dum de da da da da daaaaaa . . ."

Eat your heart out Roberta Flack, he'd thought.

That mood suddenly seemed eons ago.

Did she need help? Did she have cold feet? Had she changed her mind about the two of them? Did he have the right to press the issue? *Should* he press for answers?

Some premonition slowly iced his stomach. But

surely it was just another blip in their schedule challenges, not a definitive blow off?

Finally, he texted back:

> If I can help with anything let me know. I'll be there in a flash.

He meant it when he'd said he hated games.

But he'd also just put the burden of asking for help on her. Which he also hated.

Suddenly he realized what was really bothering him about that text she'd sent: the two of them established a sort of radical, good-humored directness. And that text was oblique as hell. All apology, no humor, no real . . . intimacy.

Another text dinged in.

> Thanks for understanding, Gabe.

And that was all.

Not even an emoji, for crying out loud. Not a heart or a smile or a cat.

He would have loved an emoji from her. And emojis got on his nerves.

He looked up when he realized it had gone silent. All of his friends were staring at him.

He cleared his throat. "Hey, looks like I can make the game after all."

There was a long silence.

"Yaaay," Louis said weakly. Finally.

* * *

"**N**ice, um, restaurant."

Jasper seemed uncertain as to whether this was the appropriate word to use. A little wonderingly, a little amused.

She'd chosen Pasquale's Pizza specifically for its unique qualities: it was way, way off the beaten path of downtown Hellcat Canyon, at the south end of town two streets behind the high school, where the buildings grew gradually more and more faded, drab and disreputable, as if the town was running out of toner by the time it got to them. And she was very unlikely to see anyone she knew there.

Its other unique qualities included a facade of dirty, chipping beige stucco; a no-frills rectangular marquee announcing PAS UALE'S PIZZER A; grubby, fissured beige linoleum that curled at its outer edges like potato chips; and battered and wobbly Formica tables crowned with glass shaker jars of cheese that had probably been powdered around 1977.

The pizza wasn't horrible, which was perhaps the kindest thing that could be said about it.

"We're not liable to run into anyone we know here, is the main thing. The pitchers are cheap. Free refills on iced tea, too." She rattled her glass. Someone, somewhere, a few decades ago, might have passed a tea bag over the water, enough to give it its color. If she really gave her imagination a workout, she could almost taste tea.

One ordered at a glassed-in counter, behind which were the pizza oven and a trio of surly employees. They stared at Eden when she strolled in with Jasper, not so much in recognition of either of them but with vague hostility, as if customers were merely an inconvenient byproduct of running a business.

She'd taken a table way, way against the back wall, near a silent jukebox. She'd tied three knots in her straw wrapper so far. Three little knots to represent the great big knot in her gut.

Jasper had ordered a bottle of Michelob and wasn't drinking it. He was percussing it with his fingers. Annelise did that, too: jauntily tapped things.

Eden inhaled. "Soooo . . ." she said on the exhale. "What did you want to talk about?"

"Soooo . . . well, I guess it's that I'd like to get to know, um, our daughter."

"The word *our* implies a *we*, and as I established, there is *definitely* no *we*," she said instantly and reflexively.

This was not off to a great start.

"Okay," he said carefully. "I'd like to get to know the fruit of my loins?"

She closed her eyes. "So. Much. Worse."

"'Fruit of My Loins' is the name of my next record, as it so happens."

Incredulity made her eyes snap open again.

"Kidding," he said shortly, probably lest she actually fire the blue daggers she could feel glinting in her eyes into his heart. "Funny, I remember you had a pretty good sense of humor. Which was part of what made you so hot."

"I *would* have laughed, except, you know, my daughter's life is no laughing matter to me." She landed just a little harder on "my" in that sentence than necessary.

Given that she'd already made her point. "Why don't you just call her Annelise."

Another little silence.

"Okay. Sorry. It's just I don't know how to talk to you about this. But I want to. What do you need to hear from me so that you're convinced I'm sincere?"

He sounded quite reasonable. Not angry, not defensive.

He sounded perfectly normal, in fact. Although she knew this could not ever be entirely true.

"I don't know. I'm having a hard time with this. It's just . . . I mean, Jasper . . . you have a pet *jaguar*."

"But Annelise likes cats. She told me."

"And don't you have a python?"

"Used to." But he sounded somewhat wistful. Which made her wonder whether the python had made a break for it, and whether one of his neighbors was destined to find it emerging from their plumbing or cuddling them in their bed in the dead of night.

"I could get a koala, instead, if she likes animals. It's safer." He paused and tipped his head back as if remembering something. "Well, marginally."

"You can't just go to the store and buy a freaking koala!"

He looked at her with something like tender pity for the Muggle she was. He could probably get his hands on anything—and anyone—he wanted.

"Listen to me, Jasper. Annelise is not something new to add to your menagerie, or some item your PR people can use to keep your name in the news, or something that you try on like . . . like . . . *Kabbalah*, to see if it fixes your life. No."

"I was never into Kabbalah. You're thinking of Madonna. I did have a guru living with me for a while. Maybe that's what you're thinking of."

"Oh. Right. Silly mistake."

"He slept with my girlfriend. Had to kick him out."

She closed her eyes again. "Jesus, Jasper."

"Jesus Jasper is the name of my *next* next record."

That almost made her laugh.

Although the hysteria might be doing that, too.

His life was both kind of magnificent and sad. He was the Parthenon, a glorious wreck.

"I'm not a bad person. Sometimes I'm even boring."

"Do you mean boring, or bored?" she said tersely.

He went silent.

"*You're* not boring," he concluded finally. He didn't sound altogether pleased about this.

"True," she agreed tautly. "When it comes to my daughter, I'm not boring the way a Tasmanian devil isn't boring."

"You really are beautiful, though."

The "though" was almost funny. As if one could be "not boring" or beautiful, but not both.

She supposed this was his go-to compliment when it came to disarming women.

"Well, I must be, right? I'm sure you never boink ugly women."

He smiled. "None that I recall, anyway. They all seem beautiful at the time."

Dear God.

"Jasper, that's . . . that's not how you . . . look, maybe this is a mistake. Maybe I should get going."

"Eden," he said firmly and evenly, "I just want her to like me. And I wouldn't hate it if *you* liked me. Believe it or not, I'm *nervous* about this."

She eyed him suspiciously.

"I like kids, I really do—I'm the godfather to John's kid. Travels with us. He's still little. His name is Milo. Want to see pics?"

He whipped out his phone and showed her his screen saver: a photo of him crouching next to a diminutive plump toddler with big dark eyes. It was pretty stinking cute. They were both making peace signs.

"John is . . . ?" Eden said absently. Studying that picture. Adorable as that kid was, she was really glad Annelise wasn't the kind of kid subject to the vicissitudes of life on the road with a band.

"John's my drummer. And if I'm partly responsible for Annelise being in the world, I want to be part of her life. At least a *little* part of her life. It literally kept me awake last night thinking a kid of mine is growing up not knowing who her dad is. I mean that. I mean, I know *your* dad. Cool guy. You had that growing up."

She was going to have to tell her parents about Jasper, and she had a hunch Glenn would *not* be a cool guy when he heard the news.

"Yeah. I have a great dad. Annelise has plenty of positive male influences in her life."

She landed on "positive" a little too hard.

She forgave herself.

She was all for making Jasper work for this.

"You know, speaking for myself, when you don't know your dad, there's this . . . you're always just kind of aware that something's missing. No matter what. Even if you don't really *lack* anything. For me, it added this level of restlessness, I think . . . maybe that's why I have a jaguar."

She smiled a little at that. But he was serious.

"And yeah, I've tried a few ways of, um, thinking and being. Who doesn't do that? It's just that the things I've tried are on a slightly, um, epic scale, and make it into the news."

This did sound like a reasonable explanation.

"She's a little girl. Not a supermodel. You're a rock star who possesses a certain amount of charm—"

"As much as that, huh?"

"—and you're intelligent, and odds are good you're not a sociopath."

"Now you're just trying to turn me on."

"She's a delightful, funny, blazingly smart, sunny-natured easy child, and I lucked out with that, I really did. I'm totally aware that it could be so different. So it's not that hard for *anyone* to make her *like* them, Jasper. She's trusting and openhearted and . . ." She stopped, freshly breathless with trepidation, suddenly, at the idea of exposing Annelise's tender, trusting, open heart to the relative wild card that was Jasper Townes.

But she was the one who'd slept with this man and created Annelise, the heretofore fatherless child. The onus was on her to manage this and make it right for Annelise. Because like it or not, this guy was her father. And it was either now, or maybe never. This moment, this opportunity, might not ever come again.

". . . and . . ." he pressed.

"I meant to say, the idea of *you* being her father? She's been wondering more about who her dad is lately. And you may not be what she has in mind. And she does have a mind of her own."

"That's odd, considering her mother is so easygoing and mild-mannered."

"Ha ha. Anyway . . . you're going to just have to be yourself and let the chips fall where they may."

"Okay."

A little silence.

"I think I'd like another beer," he said suddenly.

"Didn't you go to rehab? I mean, if you have any dependencies, congenital diseases, it'd be good to know."

"I didn't go to rehab. I went to Cozumel."

She stared at him. "Come again?"

"My manager at the time thought rehab sounded more glamorous than the fact that I'm afraid to fly so I get drunk first. I hardly ever drink because it makes me fat. I hate to fly, and I don't like working out. So I watch my weight like an old fart, and I'm only thirty-five. I do get stage fright, believe it or not. I sometimes get a little drunk before I go onstage. I smoke a little weed."

"And that's all?"

"These days," he said. After a moment of what appeared to be genuine brain-racking reflection.

She wasn't certain she believed him. Rock stars usually only truly repented all their bad habits right about the time they got their second liver.

He stuck his tongue out, folded neatly in half. "And I can do that."

She smiled at that, somewhat reluctantly. "Annelise can do that. I can't."

"Dominant and recessive traits. See, I'm no dummy."

"Never thought you were, Jasper. Not now, not then."

"I'm not a saint, either. If you have any cute friends, I'll probably hit on them a little. It's a reflex. In the spirit of full disclosure."

She sighed. "If you could refrain from ever doing it in front of Annelise . . ."

He went still.

"Does that mean . . ."

She paused. "Let's . . . let's talk some more."

Gabe had bashed the crap out of the ball every time it was pitched to him, sending the outfielders scrambling and alternately fuming or whimpering.

They won by three points.

It wasn't a pretty win, but somehow that made it even more satisfying. He was in the mood to fight to win something. A win was a very decisive thing: You either won or you lost. No guessing, reading between the lines, no wondering or worrying or waiting.

Still, the restlessness set in once he wasn't playing anymore.

As per usual, they all repaired to Pasquale's for cheap pizza and pitchers, because it was nearest the high school field where they played, and because the hardcore no-frills atmosphere perversely appealed to all of them. That, and the cheap pizza and pitchers.

"Hey, Wade, where's your ten bucks? Wade!" Gabe bellowed from the order window while the surly employees glared at him.

He glanced over his shoulder.

Wade was frozen and staring straight at the back of the restaurant, and muttering wonderingly to himself. "What the ever loving . . ."

"Wade, didn't I tell you not to stare at women with your mouth open? It creeps them out."

"Dude, it's not a woman," Mike said sotto voce. "I'm looking at Jasper Townes." He held a ten-dollar bill out to Gabe without turning his head away.

"Didn't you have him in your pervert pool, or whatever you want to call it?" Bud reminded him.

They all laughed. Gabe held up three fingers to the guy behind the counter for how many pitchers they wanted to get started with.

"Hey, Caldera, you spike the Gatorade? Wade's hallucinating," Louis chimed in.

"Nice try, trying to blame your inability to hit a damn thing on the Gatorade. Why would Townes be anywhere near here?" Gabe collected one of the pitchers.

And then suddenly Wade was half indignant, half vibrating with the thrill of certainty. "No, man, I swear, that really is Jasper Townes! And check it out! He's with a wo—"

Suddenly Mike grabbed Gabe's elbow and pivoted him up against the counter like a cop about to tell him to spread his legs.

"Hey, I think I might want something different this time. Or maybe we should get Chinese instead of pizza. And . . . and . . . German beer. Let's just stand here and read the menu for a while. They might have added something new. We don't do that often enough."

"Get off me, man." Gabe extricated himself. "What

the hell are you doing? *German* beer? Did you get hit in the head? You don't like change. Of any kind."

"I'm just not in the mood, suddenly. And . . . oh wait . . . I think I left my wallet at the high school. We have to go back right now!"

Gabe frowned at him.

Suddenly all of the guys were still, forming a little phalanx between him and whoever was in the back of the restaurant.

Something was up.

He deliberately sidestepped Mike and stared toward the back of the restaurant.

He went motionless.

Mike saw this, closed his eyes, and swore softly.

The rest of the guys went still and stone silent.

The rest of his team hovered behind him, and three of them reflexively, absently, removed their hats and covered their hearts, as if they were at a funeral for Gabe's love life.

Or perhaps saluting Jasper Townes, the way one stands for the national anthem.

No one said a damn thing. Nothing snarky, nothing profane.

Which made it even more horrible. Because that alone confirmed it was indeed as bad as it looked.

He felt himself moving before he was aware he'd given that command to his feet.

"Gabe. No, Gabe. Stay, buddy."

Lloyd said this as if he was talking to his dog, Hamburger.

But Gabe didn't hear him over the strange roaring

sound in his ears, which he supposed was the beat of blood. He couldn't stop moving if he tried, anyway. He moved as if he was mounted on a dolly, tugged forward by a hideous fascination, like peering over to get a close-up view of a cobra even if you knew it would bite you.

He had to see it up close because he was no fucking coward.

He had to see it with his own eyes.

He knew it was going to hurt; it already hurt.

His gut was wall-to-wall ice.

Eden was pale. She fidgeted with the wrapper of her straw. She'd already tied three knots into it.

Townes looked up. He didn't even give a start.

"Oh, hey, dude. Sorry, man, I don't have a pen on me. But I can sign with a french fry and ketchup if you have any."

He cheerfully, resolutely wiped his hands on a paper napkin.

CHAPTER 15

Color fled Eden's face and left her as white as the napkin.

"Gabe."

"Yeah," he said with great irony. "Hi, Eden."

"I didn't . . . I didn't know you'd be . . ."

He watched color rush into her cheeks as she realized there was no way she could end that sentence that wasn't incriminating or insulting.

Townes was watching all of this alertly.

"I guess it must be your lucky day, then," Gabe said evenly. "Or mine."

"Did I get in the middle of something here?" Jasper said in that distinctive raspy speaking voice so many of the best singers seemed to have, in Gabe's experience. He sounded amused.

"Did he get in the middle of something?" Gabe delivered those words to Eden like little bundles of silk-wrapped ice.

It was a truly shitty thing to do to her. It put her on the spot to define something they hadn't yet defined.

Some part of him was aware that he was being a jerk. A part of him that had bypassed his usual reason and control. He didn't care.

Eden's jaw took on that hard set, and her eyes flashed hot as the blue center of a flame.

Wow. Was she *pissed*.

It was gorgeous to witness.

Also a little scary.

But he was fine with that.

Ultimately, she ignored the question. "Forgive me," she said evenly. "Where are my manners? Jasper Townes, this is . . . my friend . . . Gabe Caldera. He's the principal of Annelise's school."

Townes leaned back and studied Gabe with shiny dark eyes. "That's not the expression of someone who's just a friend, man. He hasn't blinked once since he got here."

Gabe turned his head slowly and aimed an expression of pure incredulity at Eden as if to say, This *guy? Really?*

"Jasper . . . says things." Eden was aiming that flame-thrower glare at Jasper now.

"Children say things, too," Gabe said with a deceptively offhanded bonhomie. "It stops being cute around the age of twelve, though."

He'd sounded so pleasant that the insult worked on a time release. Townes's friendly smile vanished as if it was on a dimmer switch.

"How do you know Eden?" Gabe said this pleasantly, too, though it was absolutely none of his business. All's fair, however.

"We go way back, me and Eden. Way in the back of my tour bus, that—"

She slapped her hand down on the table. Jasper jumped. "Are. You. Out. Of. *Yourfreakingmind*."

The whispered words hissed from her like launched missiles.

Townes's eyes widened and he put up his hands as if she were mugging him at gunpoint, then brought them down again.

Gabe stared down at Jasper's long-fingered, narrow, nimble hands. Three chunky rings glittered from them. A collection of bracelets. It seemed odd that a guitarist would want to weigh his hands down that way, but maybe he liked to look down at glittery things when he played.

Was he strumming Eden with those hands?

The thought was literally agony, and nothing relieved that sort of agony—temporarily, anyway—except acting like a dick.

"Look, I think I get what's going on here," Jasper said soothingly, as if he was in the business of humoring plebeians like Gabe all the time, "beautiful women have a way of getting under a guy's skin, brother. You didn't expect to find her here with *me*, of all people. I know people like me can be pretty intimidating. Sorry if I wandered into your territory, but you know how it goes."

This was many things: hilarious, insulting, condescending, annoying (*brother*?), and so wrong Gabe was very nearly tempted to laugh.

The "me of all people" was nearly farcical; it ground

against his nerves, because (let's face it), Gabe was already kind of thinking that: Jasper Townes, of all people.

Eden listened to this with her jaw dropped.

Then she clapped it shut again.

"I'm not *anyone's* 'territory.'" Eden was getting more and more furious by the minute. Her jaw was white with tension.

Gabe, at the mercy of testosterone at the moment, longed to beg to differ regarding the territory bit, though he was pretty positive she wouldn't enjoy that argument, and he knew in his rational mind that it wasn't remotely true.

"Nice necklace," he said instead, and pointed at the leather thong around Townes's neck.

"Thanks, man," Jasper said kindly.

"When I was a navy SEAL I learned not to wear the kind of jewelry the enemy could use as a garrote."

Townes's magnanimous plebeian-humoring expression froze.

And then gradually, his eyes got hard and speculative.

"Good word, *garrote*," Gabe mused. "Maybe you should use it in a song. Rhymes with throat, bloat, high note, turncoat, showboat—"

BAM. Eden thumped her iced-tea glass on the table hard. "Gabriel. A word, if I may."

"Wow, you used every syllable in my name. You sure we have time for that, Eden? Isn't 'brief' what we do?"

He seemed to be channeling some glib macho monster. Every word that exited was both delicious and painful, as if he had a gut full of them, all icy and jagged, and saying them out loud brought a momentary relief.

Both Gabe and Jasper gave a start when Eden leaped from her chair, seized Gabe by the bicep with a surprisingly strong grip that owed some of its persuasion to fingernails, and frog marched him over to the corner by the currently silent jukebox. Frog-marching Gabe anywhere was not an easy feat.

She had the element of surprise on her side.

"I would ask you why you're being such a dick, but we probably don't have time for the answer."

He stared at her, stunned.

"Damn," he said, finally, impressed. That was some opener.

Despite himself he ferociously admired it. He admired fighters. And it was all the worse, because it just, perverse fool that he was, made him like her even more.

She barreled into that moment of stunned silence. "Gabe, I'm genuinely sorry I had to cancel on you and *meant* it. And I'm sorry you had to run into me here with all your buddies, and for however you're feeling now. I have a very good reason and I will explain it to you. But I'm not going to explain it to you now. I can't."

Her words were rushed and terse, only very faintly placating. She was furious and tense and on edge. Was it just about being caught with Townes?

Their gazes locked. He had a million questions, it felt like.

Suddenly he knew the right ones to ask.

"Would you have 'explained it to me' if you hadn't run into me today?"

It was both the right question.

And the wrong one.

Because he could see that it got to the crux of the matter pretty quickly.

She hesitated.

"I . . ."

The following little pause was like a spear in the gut. Something about Townes was a secret she'd been keeping.

Never fall for an enigmatic woman, his friends had warned.

"Yes," she said finally. "I would have told you. Probably. Eventually."

"So he's not your cousin or a dear friend of the family, and he's not your invisible brother Jesse?"

She drew in a breath. Like she was siphoning up courage. Sighed it out. "No. He is exactly who he looks like. He is Jasper Townes." She said this reluctantly, as though she were up on the witness stand testifying against herself with painful but necessary words.

"And you do have a previous acquaintance similar in nature to the one he so charmingly described."

She was within rights to say, *I don't owe you any information at all.*

And he didn't have the right to ask that question while they were standing just a few feet away from the guy. The knowledge that he had no actual defined rights did nothing to assuage the sensation that his guts were in a vise.

But after another little hesitation: "Yes."

Oh, fuck me, Gabe thought. Why had he even asked

that question? No part of her answer made him feel better. It didn't illuminate much of anything. And asking made him feel like even more of a jerk.

"It's okay," he said softly, reasonably. "I get it, Eden. Who wouldn't cancel a date for a chance to sit across from the guy who dressed up as a warlock in his last video?"

She stared at him, jaw set.

He stared back at her. There was no way she saw anything yielding in his face.

Her cheekbones had gone dark red.

"You *don't* get it. It isn't what you think it is, and my word on that matter should be enough for you."

It really should be.

Shouldn't it?

Were they *there* yet—relationship wise?

Were they even in a "relationship"?

Maybe they have been there from the very beginning? Because wasn't that the premise of their whole relationship? Radical honesty? Cutting to the chase?

But he'd heard it—the faintest bit of doubt in her voice. As if she suspected that the blind acceptance she was asking of him wasn't *entirely* reasonable, but she was throwing a Hail Mary. Hoping he'd be noble and just let her slide.

He honestly didn't know what to say.

All he knew was that he wasn't feeling noble, or selfless, or magnanimous.

Finally he just turned around and examined the dusty jukebox. He fished through his pocket, dropped a quarter in the slot, and punched in a song.

Then he fished out another quarter and punched in another song.

In the reflection of the glass he saw that Eden was standing motionless behind him. He couldn't see her expression.

He put another quarter in the jukebox and punched in a song.

He emptied his pocket of quarters and punched buttons five times.

He could see her standing behind him for the first three.

And when he heard her chair scrape back again, he went back to his buddies, whose heads all swiveled in tandem toward the wall-mounted muted television to pretend they weren't watching him with the same avidity they watched any sporting event.

He went back to them without another word.

"I was saying hello to Eden. She was having lunch with Mr. Jasper Townes, who is apparently an old friend in town for only a short time."

He reached for the pitcher and tipped it.

Beer glugged out into his glass to the sound of near total silence.

Apart, that was, from the John Mayer song on the jukebox.

The song he'd chosen.

Five times in a row.

He hoped Jasper Townes *thoroughly* enjoyed that.

His body was jangling with a cacophony of emotions. He couldn't isolate any of them for inspection. The net result was a sort of numbness that seemed to result from all emotions, the way all noise was white noise.

He finally looked up.

He'd never seen so many subtle variations of the Pitying Gaze before. All limpid-eyed, fidgety, sympathy from *this* grizzled, disreputable bunch. And they weren't even drunk enough to be sentimental yet.

He supposed he could add "moved" to the variety of very complicated things he was feeling.

"To Bud getting lucky and accidentally getting that home run."

"Luck, my ass! I hit that thing on purpose."

Eden sat back down across from Jasper. She felt like a cat who'd been vigorously rubbed backward until all of her fur was erect and shooting sparks. She'd once rescued a saucer-eyed, patient yet astounded Peace and Love from the loving ministrations of four-year-old Annelise, who knew she was supposed to only pet him forward.

"But Mommy, I love him so much I wanted to pet both sides of him."

A lesson in compromise for Annelise, that moment, and in love and power dynamics: always default to kindness when something is smaller than you are and dependent upon you. Sometimes what *you* want means less than what someone you love wants.

Did she want to pet both sides of Gabe?

Her heart was slamming so hard, she was a little nauseous and her mouth was arid from nerves.

His face. Implacable, stunned, and behind that, something much worse: a hard resignation. He'd already indicted her and she hadn't done anything wrong.

Or had she?

She *sat* in reeling silence a moment. The way she felt now told her that it wasn't about who did or didn't have rights. She just never wanted to betray Gabe.

"What the hell is wrong with you?" she said finally to Jasper, and so suddenly he gave a start.

He shrugged. "That dude rubbed me the wrong way."

"*So?*"

"I have a feeling he's been rubbing you the right way. Am I right? Which is a good thing. I mean, *someone* should rub you the right way," he said charitably.

She stared at him in livid amazement.

She lunged forward until her face was so close to his she could count his stubble and get a bit of grip on his T-shirt collar.

"You listen to me, Jasper Townes. I know you think you're being cute and clever and flippant is your schtick now and you get away with that crap. But we are not a *thing*, you and I. We happened exactly once. I don't like the macho posturing, and I don't like you to joke about anyone *rubbing* me. And I really, truly don't care if you don't like me for being a hard-ass about it. But if you want to think you're worthy of spending one particle of time in the company of *my* daughter, if you want me to think you're a grown-up? Go apologize right now to Mr. Caldera. Tell him you were out of line and give him an appropriate excuse that in no way mentions me. Make it believable. I'll wait right here."

She released him and sat back in her chair hard.

He stared at her in openmouthed, unadulterated amazement for at least half a verse of John Mayer.

"You're fucking with me," he concluded.

She rolled her eyes so hard she nearly sprained them. "Believe me, I am in no way . . ." She dropped her voice to a mocking, raspy baritone. ". . . 'fucking with you.'" She air-quoted that.

He stared, apparently had no idea what to do with an angry redheaded mom who was clearly immune to his charm.

"He was a dick to me, too," he offered finally.

Those words were just a hairbreadth away from a whine. He smoothed his leather necklace back into place.

She closed her eyes.

Why the hell did *anyone* have anything to do with men? She suddenly yearned for a can of Ego-Off to spray all over the room. Testosterone-B-Gone.

"Yep. He was. And I bet you get some kind of apology from him, too, because he's a fucking adult, not a petulant child."

Jasper's eyes flared at once to the size of beer coasters. Then narrowed into little glittery outraged slits. His impressive jaw clenched and jutted stubbornly.

It was actually a good look for him. He ought to use it in his next publicity photos.

"Aw, did I piss you off, Jasper?" she crooned. "I don't care. *You* need to prove yourself to *me*. So suck it up. Make it good, make it graceful, make it sound sincere. I've seen you in interviews. I know you can do it. And believe me, whatever you say will get back to me, because this is a really small town. I don't care whether you *feel* sorry or not. You can either apologize to him now or walk out of here for good. That way I'll know how serious you are about all of this. About Annelise. About forging some kind of civil, respectful relationship with me. Because Annelise and I are a package, and our life is here in Hellcat Canyon, and Gabe Caldera is the principal of her school. He's someone she admires and respects, an important part of her life and the community here."

And then, perversely, all at once, she was grateful for all of Gabe's metaphorical chest-thumping. Because if Jasper passed this test, she'd know he was serious about getting to know Annelise. Posturing was one thing.

Voluntarily groveling to a guy who had two inches on him in height and who had arguably bested him in an ego-off over a woman was another thing altogether, and she was pretty sure it was not something Jasper Townes had ever had to do.

He held that outraged expression for a few moments longer.

And then Jasper pushed his chair back so abruptly the legs squealed on the tile.

He stared down at her, lips pressed hard together.

She stared right back up at him. And arched an eyebrow.

He turned his back on her and moved at a leisurely swagger across the checkerboard floor. Which may or may not be how he actually walked and not something cultivated for show; one never knew.

She watched his progress. What a teeny, tiny butt

he had. Annelise didn't have a prayer of having hips, unless some wayward gene conferred her grandmother's figure upon her.

Keep walking, a guilty, dark corner of her heart urged. Walk. Walk past Gabe right on out that door, out of our lives.

It would be a relief, right?

And then, some years down the road, she could say to Annelise with a certain conviction: *I knew your dad was as stable as a leaf floating on the breeze, and I didn't want him to break your heart when your heart was still so innocent. I couldn't have borne that. I was responsible for your happiness and for making you feel safe in the world, for giving you that foundation of courage and faith in life that comes from being loved, so that you feel clear and brave enough to discover whether my truths are also yours. And that's why he wasn't in our lives when you were a child.*

And she could tell Gabe about Jasper. And this anger and sense of overwhelm, this chafing sense of injustice—shouldn't he just *trust* her?—a niggling fear that they were on the precipice of disaster would fade.

And years from now she could tell Annelise *this* very story—of that time her father appeared out of the blue, and then walked out at the slightest whiff of challenge.

A story Annelise would be able to receive, hopefully, with a certain amount of pragmatism, when she was an adult.

Four tables remained between Jasper and Gabe's table.

Suspense slowed and stretched time as she watched him walk up the aisle.

Even as her heart sped.

Because now some deeper truth was asserting itself.

Something she'd overlooked in all the hazy sex and rushed, intense intimacy was the possibility that Gabe might not know himself as well as he thought he did. That maybe some corners of his heart remained raw and wounded, that maybe he'd only put up hazard tape around his losses and heartbreaks. That the two of them together hadn't been tested. That his pride might do him in. That his tendency to see things as black and white or right or wrong would tempt him to shut her out forever. What would be would be.

And yet none of that mattered right now. Because every snarky word out of Jasper's mouth had scored her own heart with little paper-fine cuts.

And this was the other reason she'd sent him to apologize. She would be damned if anyone spoke to Gabe Caldera with anything other than utter respect. She couldn't bear to see him hurt.

Two tables left . . .

Eden applied such force to the napkin in her fist that it was nearly spitball size.

One table . . .

She curled her nails into her palm.

And then he stopped next to Gabe.

Eden released a breath that nearly deflated her two sizes.

And then she breathed in a shuddery draft of pizza-flavored air to compensate for the fact that she'd stopped breathing.

Because she also knew then, definitively, that she

didn't want Annelise to have a wuss for a biological father. She wanted her to have a father who knew when to make a sacrifice, even if it was only of his own ego. Who maybe wouldn't even see it as a sacrifice, because it was for *Annelise*.

And when she looked at Gabe, she realized it might mean losing everything else she wanted.

John Mayer crooned for the second time from the jukebox when Jasper Townes arrived at Gabe's table.

Gabe had been aware of his approach in his peripheral vision, and he was prepared to handle it in any necessary way.

He looked up.

The skin of Jasper's face looked stretched rather tight. As if he was struggling to hold at bay a thousand emotions eager to reveal themselves via his mouth and eyes and cheeks.

He looked, in fact, a bit like someone being forced at knifepoint to rob his own ATM.

Gabe's own face felt like it had petrified over a series of a thousand years. Stone hard and implacable. As though he couldn't move it if he tried. Like the hardness was starting at the surface of his skin and working its way down through all the layers, would eventually reach his heart, turn it into a stone, and he'd finally have a little respite from this torment that was, admittedly, only about ten minutes in duration.

His friends, who by rights ought to be exclaiming over Townes's appearance, had clammed up tight.

"Hey, um, Gabe, right?" Townes said.

"Right. Jasper Townes, right?"

A muscle in Jasper's cheek twitched.

And then Townes drew in a long, long breath. Almost as if he was going to release one of his famous high notes. Maybe he wanted to shatter the glass on the jukebox to shut John Mayer up.

"I wanted to apologize if I came off a little . . . flippant . . . a minute ago. Sometimes my sense of humor doesn't translate the way I want it to."

Huh.

Gabe's friends' heads whipped toward him with such speed the paper napkins took flight. The sympathetic doe eyes were now blazing headlights of curiosity.

Gabe studied Townes.

He thought: Annelise Harwood would sure like the word *flippant*.

It was a funny thought to have right in that moment, but it was a reflex. The people he cared about automatically congregated at a sort of hub in his heart, and thoughts fanned out from there.

As much as he longed to write Townes off as one-dimensional, he knew, of course, he was more than that.

Which of course made all of this so much worse.

He also had kind of a hunch Eden had forced the guy to apologize. And if she could make him do that, their relationship was not a casual one.

All of these thoughts transmuted into feelings that basically turned his stomach into a roiling snake pit while his face showed not a damn thing.

Gabe was, at his core, a gentleman, caveman instincts

notwithstanding. The apology on its surface was gracious. And so he really had no choice.

"Apology accepted, Townes. And you have my apologies, too."

He didn't specify for what.

Jasper Townes extended his hand, and Gabe cleaned his own hand thoroughly, a little sardonically, on a napkin before inserting it in the other man's. They both gripped each other a little too hard, and Gabe indulged in a teensy fantasy about the satisfying crunch those long, nimble beringed fingers would make, fingers that he suspected had touched Eden and maybe heard that little sigh she made when the pleasure became too much to bear.

And a teeny part of him, a part that he thought couldn't possibly make itself known, was awed that he was shaking hands with *the* Jasper Townes, who made the kind of music Gabe sang badly in the shower. If he crunched those fingers, he'd never hear "Lily Anne" live again, and goddamn but he loved that song.

He wondered if any of his songs were about Eden. Jesus, what if Lily Anne was about Eden?

A fresh stab of pain greeted that thought.

He took some minute consolation in the fact that this apology was clearly making Jasper miserable.

He let go of his hand.

John Mayer was still singing.

His friends were still silent.

But they were looking to him for cues.

Gabe sighed. "Go ahead."

Instantly they all clustered about Jasper, filings to a magnet, cell phones in hand.

"Mr. Townes . . . would you mind terribly?"

And the flurry of autographs and photos ensued, all of which Townes was gracious about.

Jasper finally returned and sat down with Eden in silence.

He drummed his fingers a little on the table.

"Sorry," he said after a moment. "About all of that." Sounding a little more subdued.

She just nodded.

It took all of her pride and willpower not to turn her head. She wanted to be with Gabe, looking at Gabe, touching Gabe, laughing with Gabe, feeling his arms around her.

A loud laugh rose from their table. Hopefully it wasn't about her.

Jasper had plucked up a coaster and was now tossing it from hand to hand like a Vegas dealer with only one card. He stopped at a look from her. He fidgeted the way Annelise did.

"Boy, you really are a mom. You kinda reminded me of my own for a second there." The clouds were already lifting from his mood. He quirked the corner of his mouth ruefully.

It occurred to her then that Annelise's sunny resilience might not be down to just being lavishly loved by her crazy family. Maybe it was a DNA gift straight from her dad. God knew her mom was hardly laissez-faire.

In fact, every single one of her mom's nerves were still buzzing and squealing as if they'd been plugged in to a Marshall Stack and strummed, hard, à la Jasper Townes.

A whole treasure chest (Pandora's box?) of discoveries like that awaited if Jasper became a part of their lives. Things that could deepen even her relationship with Annelise, make it even richer. Things she might even look forward to.

And there was a raw place in the center of her chest, as if someone had taken a peeler to her heart and shaved off a curl.

She yearned to turn her head to look at Gabe.

"So what do you think? Shall we tell her I'm her dad?" Jasper asked. Carefully. Reasonably.

How did anyone make this kind of decision? In a perfect world she'd have *weeks* to mull. But her life, once again, was condensed into hours and minutes.

Maybe she'd only been stealing time with Gabe, anyway. Kidding herself all along.

Why, then, did she feel like she was being robbed of destiny?

"Yeah. Let's do it," she said.

Jasper's face lit up charmingly.

And then she finally got over her pride and fully turned, took one gulping, hungry look at the crowd at that table.

Gabe was gone.

CHAPTER 16

How innocent her whiteboard had looked Monday morning. The poor thing didn't know Eden's life was literally a giant snarl at the moment.

Eden was tempted to take the marker and scrawl tornadoes, barbed wire, arrowed hearts, exclamation points, and question marks in the next few squares, just to illustrate her internal weather.

Danny arrived at the shop just in time for Eden to take Annelise to school. She had to get to Gabe first thing.

So she kissed Leesy goodbye, and with her heart pounding like jackboots coming down, she headed for Gabe's office.

"Good morning, Mrs. Maker. How do you feel about baby roses today?"

She settled the little pot of roses on her desk.

"Oh, Eden, honey, you're just the sweetest. Did you know Mrs. Pennington brings cookies when she wants to get in to see Mr. Caldera?"

"Um . . ."

"Oh, I know the roses are not a bribe, dear. I was just mentioning it."

"Well, that's interesting, thank you for sharing. Is Mr. Caldera in?"

"He is, and he has about fifteen minutes until his next meeting. Why don't you just knock?"

So she did.

Hard enough for the sound to drown out the sound of her pounding heart, hopefully.

Gabe looked up at her from his desk, and his heart leaped in reflexive joy before his thoughts yanked it back down.

"Good morning, Ms. Harwood. What can I do for you?"

This was hearty pleasantry for Mrs. Maker's benefit.

Eden stepped inside. She closed the door gently.

And then she gingerly sat in the guest chair they'd commuted in together to the sex couch.

In total silence, they regarded each other.

She was pale, and she looked like she hadn't slept.

Then Gabe looked away, flipping a pen idly. Thump. Thump. Thump. Against his blotter.

"I think Mrs. Maker might be shaking down the PTA moms for cookies in order to get access to you," she began. Lightly enough.

Her hands were knotted, however. Like that straw wrapper on the table between her and Jasper Townes.

"I'm going to look the other way," Gabe said. "She doesn't make all that much money. She has a killer pension, though. All school district employees do." He said this pleasantly, too.

And yet everything seemed heightened. Sound. Sight. The air of the room almost hurt his skin.

He waited.

"Jasper Townes is Annelise's father."

The words basically blanked his mind.

He wasn't entirely certain how many seconds passed before he spoke.

"Are you . . ." His voice was sandpaper raw.

"Sure? Yeah. Kidding? No."

He was happy he had a baseball to squeeze. He wasn't going to do that in front of her, however. She knew too much about him. He was suddenly furious at this fact.

"Did you want me to soft-pedal that, Gabe? Direct is what we do." She didn't sound conciliatory. Her words were all still taut.

Taut as guitar strings. Heh.

He shook his head, as this information sifted down through his awareness like a rain of shrapnel.

"You're the first person I've told," she continued. "Haven't told my family. Haven't even told Annelise yet. We're telling her tonight."

He breathed in.

Breathed out.

"We're . . ."

"Me and Jasper."

"Ah. You," he said slowly. "And Jasper." He made a sound. A humorless almost-laugh. "Sounds cozy."

"It's not even a little bit cozy. Ten years ago he was

passing through just as his career was really taking off. He did an acoustic set at the Misty Cat. I was in town on Christmas break from school. I worked the show to help out my parents. We got to talking. One thing led to another. I slept with him."

"As one does."

"Yeah. Just once. But you know how that goes. That's all it ta—"

"Thanks, I took sex ed, too, Eden."

A silence. Their words, this exchange: all of it clipped, glib, ironic, almost playful.

A silence. But an invisible presence was crouching in the corner of the room. Something big and dangerous. The silent, seething mass of all not yet spoken.

"The back of the bus?" he said distractedly, casually, tap tapping his pen.

"Does the geographic location of conception matter?"

"Nah. Just checking to see if he's a liar as well as a jerk."

"He's not a total jerk."

"Some people say that about me, too."

There was a pause.

"Is that your way of apologizing for being a . . ."

". . . dick, I think is how you put it Saturday? No. I have to ask—what made you think I was a saint? The roadside orgasms?"

"I never thought you were a saint. I guess I've been laboring under the impression that you're *mature*," she said evenly.

"Well, you're the one who canceled our first date with a cryptic text. So, you know, pot, kettle."

Another long silence.

Two clocks ticked off precious seconds.

He didn't know what to feel. Only that every question he asked would likely uncover a new layer of hurt, a new reality to accommodate, navigate. And as he wasn't a coward, he had no choice but to keep courting pain and asking them.

"So . . . have you been in touch with him all this time?"

"Saturday was the first time I'd talked to him at all in ten years. I did try to tell him about Annelise after I found out I was pregnant, but only out of a sense of moral obligation—a man should know he has a child in the world. I didn't want anything from him.

"He said he never got the message. I believe him. He kind of sussed it out on his own when he met Annelise at the Misty Cat when he was doing sound check . . . apparently Annelise looks just like his mom at that age."

Gabe just absorbed this silently. And now that he thought about it, he could see echoes of Annelise in Jasper Townes and vice versa . . . their eyebrows. The cant of their eyes. Even though Annelise, lucky kid, looked more like her mom, for sure.

"He's only going to be here for a few days, and so I had to make some huge decisions fast. Which is why I had to cancel. When you saw us at Pasquale's was the first time we ever talked about it."

This was reasonable. He knew it was.

And yet nothing about it was making him feel reasonable.

"When I asked about Annelise's dad, you said, and I quote, he was 'out of the picture.'"

"He was. And now he's back in it."

That did it. The thing in the corner pounced.

"Knock it off. That's disingenuous and you know it. You could have said to me, 'it's complicated.' When I told you my favorite guilty pleasure song was that gloppy Jasper Townes song 'Lily Anne,' you could have said, 'hey, funny story . . .' You could have said something, *anything* else that indicated that somewhere down the line something huge might . . . blow up in my face. I feel like an idiot, Eden. Is he the reason you didn't want to get involved?" He wasn't even trying to disguise the emotion now.

"No, Gabe. I swear to you. He's just a *guy*. He represents *one night* of my past."

"He is patently *not* just a guy. You know it and I know it. He's the guy who's dated supermodels, presented Grammys, and so sexy even Louis down at the Veteran's Hall said he'd be willing to, and I quote, 'do him.' How do you think that felt, Eden, to walk in there and see you with him? How much do you think I enjoy being pitied by my friends?"

"So your feelings of what . . . ego? Pride? Embarrassment? *That's* what's important here?"

"They're not *un*important. Do you think how I feel doesn't signify at all?"

There ensued another silence, as soothing as those intervals between sets of car alarm wails.

For the first time in his life emotion was running away from him, drowning out reason.

"What did you tell your friends, Gabe?"

"What do you think I told them? I said that Townes

is an old friend of yours, and you were just catching up because he was in town for only a little while. I can tell you right now not one of them believed me. But while they would follow me into battle, I don't think any of them blamed *you* for ditching me, either, because, you know, sexy, sexy Townes, blah blah blah. And that's . . . while on the one hand, that's kind of funny, on the other hand, it really, really isn't."

"Gabe . . ." She exhaled an exasperated breath. "Do you even *own* a mirror?"

"But I'm not Townes," he said flatly.

She didn't deny this.

She pushed her hands through her hair. "I'm not interested in him in a roadside way! AT. ALL. I don't *care* what Louis thinks. Jasper represents *one night* from my past."

"Eden," he said slowly, with exaggerated patience, "he's *not* in your past. He is now a part of your present and your future. Pretty much forever. If your plan is to introduce him to Annelise."

She went still.

The truth of this fully settled in and altered everything they'd begun to think the future might look like.

"Gabe. Do you not *get* how *huge* this is for me?" Her voice cracked. "For Annelise? Do you not understand that I don't have a road map for this?"

Her voice climbed in pitch all the way to the end of that sentence.

He closed his eyes briefly. He drew in a breath. "Do you think there's a chance in hell I don't genuinely understand how big it is that Annelise is going to get to know her father? I hope he understands how lucky he is. And I'm actually *thrilled* she's going to get to know her father—that's important. Even if—maybe especially if—it's a guy like Townes. It will be . . ." And suddenly the fury sputtered, and his tone flatlined into a punishing, dull resignation. ". . . life transforming. And not just for her."

Silence.

"Yeah," she said finally. Her voice was frayed.

They both knew where this particular rolling chair was headed. Right off a cliff. They seemed to be deliberately steering it there. Neither one of them seemed able to stop it.

"The thing is," he said slowly, "I think you didn't tell me about Townes because it was just easier not to. And if I hadn't seen you in Pasquale's, you may or may not have told me even as he was sitting up there in your apartment talking to Annelise. Because it was easier not to. And that . . . that makes me feel like shit, Eden. It makes me feel like maybe you're not the person I thought you were. And makes me question . . . *everything* . . . between us."

She went motionless.

And then hot color rushed her skin and her eyes narrowed to glinty sapphires.

"*How* could you . . . how *dare* you . . . I just . . . why *can't* you . . ."

She stood up so abruptly the chair wobbled to and fro like a drunk. It didn't topple.

"I can't deal with this right now, Gabe. With *you*."

He said nothing. Some perverse part of him was

savoring both her anger and his own. It was anesthetizing. Even as a tiny voice of reason was making
what sounded like a faint air-raid-siren sound in his
mind.

"And I guess . . . that's what I basically came here
to say," she added slowly. As if deciding that, then and
there.

They stared each other down.

He didn't know what his expression revealed to
her. If it was anything like hers, it didn't look like a
person who had won an important point or gained
the upper hand or come to a comfortable decision. It
looked like the face of a person being prepped for the
guillotine.

"Well, I guess it *is* impossible for busy adults to date."
His tone was richly laced with irony.

He stood up, too. Reflexes. Manners. Slowly. Just to
make the point that he still had a certain amount of
control. And because whatever else he was, he was a
gentleman.

Even if he was a dick.

Apparently the two weren't mutually exclusive.

"So I guess this is it, then," she said. She tried for
insouciance. Her voice was shaking.

"Guess so," he managed neutrally enough.

Though his voice had gone arid as the Sahara.

She hovered in place. There was a split second where
he contemplated reaching across to touch her. She
might have decked him. Or maybe that awful, cold, furious pain in her expression would dissolve and she'd
crumple into his arms and he would say *I don't know*

what the hell I'm doing or why, but something in me hurts so savagely all I want to do, all I know how to do, is defend defend defend and I can't stop it. Even if it drives you away. Stay. Stay. Stay.

She spun on her heel, flung open his door, and vroom.

She was out of there, hair sailing out behind her.

Because everything in her life was scheduled down to the minute, she used her time in the car between leaving Gabe's office to the time she made it home again for racking, noisy rage sobs, growling and taking the name of Gabe Caldera in vain.

"What an asshole! I can't believe he would . . . GAH! He has no right!"

At another stop light, she bellowed, "You are hands down the sexiest human I have ever touched or tasted, Gabe Caldera. How could you think otherwise? I was in love with you!"

Why hadn't she said that?

Was she in love with him?

Was she *still* in love with him?

"No! I'm the one who's right here!" she blustered at another stoplight.

The man in the car next to her gave a start. And quietly rolled his window all the way up.

If only she were more *certain* that she was right.

If only she had time to think.

But there was no time. There never was. Onto the next thing, the next emotion.

*   *   *

She'd texted her entire family, even Jude, Dr. Jude, who was always, *always* busy, but did make it into town now and again on weekends to see his parents, and Jesse, who was in the Himalayas or Machu Pichu or camping on a glacier or some such nonsense on assignment for Redmond Worldwide.

> THIS IS URGENT. I need a family meeting. 7 o'clock tonight. It'll only take a few minutes.
> P.S. Nobody's dying. xoxo

That ought to intrigue them.

Home to everyone meant the Harwood family homestead, the comfortable old 1940s farmhouse shaped like an L, perched on a slight rise between Devil's Leap and Main Street at the end of town. It was painted a soft periwinkle-blue, which blended in with soft summer days and clear winter twilights.

At seven o'clock Avalon and her mom and dad were cheek to cheek on the squishy old olive-colored sofa that never relinquished anyone willingly—you always had to kind of fight to stand up from it. Jude, handsome devil, her much-loved, pedantic, witty, pain-in-the ass brother who was fond of fast cars, inappropriately fast women, and saving lives, was slouched in the old armchair they used to fight over. Jiggling one foot. His face was alight with anticipation.

Jesse was on Skype on a laptop screen on the desk, over in some corner of the Himalayas, if she recalled correctly, on some adventure travel assignment for Redmond Worldwide. He was rocking quite a bushy beard. Through which they could see his bright smile.

Eden stood in the middle of the circle braid carpet, feeling like an idiot child about to do a tap-dance routine for company.

Her mom darted a surreptitious glance at Eden's belly.

"No, Mom," Eden said tersely. "Don't worry. I'm not quite that careless."

Though that sure didn't feel precisely true anymore.

"All babies are welcome, honey," her mom said. Which was easy for her to say now that she knew there wasn't going to be a baby.

Eden drew in a long, long breath for courage. And then exhaled.

"Okay, first of all. Forgive me for the sudden drama. It had to be suddenly. I have something to tell you. I'm going to say this quickly, before Skype locks up. Annelise's father is Jasper Townes. From Blue Room and Black & Blue."

This was greeted by resounding silence.

She scanned their faces. They might as well have been mannequins. Not a dropped jaw among them. Not a twitched finger.

Nobody moved a hair.

And then there was a little sound. Like a breeze rustling the leaves.

She realized, after a moment, that it was the sound of pockets expanding as hands plunged into them, and butts brushing across upholstery. Fabric swishing as everyone moved, subtly and at once, to dig through their wallets, retrieve cash . . .

. . . and hand it to Avalon.

Eden glowered at her family. "What the—did you guys have some kind of *pool*?"

"No, we just thought we'd order takeout," Jude said innocently. "What do you want? Mushu?"

"You had a pool!" she accused vehemently.

Guilty silence.

Limpid stares.

"Yes," Avalon said gravely. Resignedly. "We had a pool."

She goggled at them, livid with indignation. "But—you—I—"

"Honey," her mom said gently. "It wasn't as though there weren't clues. Avalon arrived at the logical conclusion by doing the Eden calculus."

"The *Eden* calculus?" Her voice climbed into a squeaky register. "You got a C in calculus, Avalon! You never freaking studied!"

"Hey!" Avalon sounded wounded. But unsurprised.

"Well, the *name* of the formula was my idea," Jude said modestly. "And I got an A in calc—"

"YES, WE KNOW, JUDE," everyone said at once, even Jesse, from his screen.

"So what was in this formula?" she said more evenly. Still, her jaw was pretty taut.

Avalon began ticking it off on her fingers. "Annelise is ten years old. Jasper Townes was last in Hellcat Canyon ten years ago. You were at that show, and at least one person remembers you having what looked like a long, soulful conversation with him, your heads very close together across one of the tables. Annelise is a music nut. She's always making up songs. She took to the guitar like a fish to water."

"And she looks like him, honey," her mom said gently. "Maybe in as many ways as she looks like you.

Subtle ones. And then when we watched them together at sound check the other day . . . well, we know you like we know our own hearts, Eden, and we know Leesy, too, and it was, I have to tell you . . . eerie."

Her father didn't ring in on this assessment. His expression was interesting. Rather abstracted.

Rather, in fact, thunderously absorbed.

"You can send me your cash later, Jess," Avalon said.

The Skype image of Jesse had frozen on an image of him with his mouth wide open, so it was difficult to know if he was shocked or laughing uproariously. Eden was deeply envious. He was far, far away. He wasn't sitting in *this* room having *this* conversation.

"It was also pretty clear Jasper had no clue about Annelise," her mom continued. "Does he know now? Is that why you're telling us?"

"He came into my shop. He figured it out, believe it or not. He's not stupid. We talked about it. We decided to tell her."

For some reason she was feeling like defending him a little, if only so they wouldn't think she'd slept with a total idiot.

"How do you feel about it?" Avalon ventured. "You're not going to, um . . . and what about Ga . . ." She trailed off at a warning glare from Eden.

"Jasper's not husband material, if that's what any of you are thinking," Eden said hurriedly. "And he's not even boyfriend material. I'm not thinking along those lines at all, and neither is he. His life is kind of a circus, and I really want to keep this news on the down-low and so does he. But it's been pretty clear to me for a while that Annelise has been curious about her dad, and I would need to do something about it. And when he showed up, well . . ."

"We were so worried, sweetie, that you were nursing a broken heart all these years and being very noble and, you know, Elinor Dashwooding it," her mom said soothingly.

"Did you just turn the heroine of my favorite book and movie into a *verb*?" *Sense and Sensibility* was a big family favorite.

"And you're so very fond of your dignity and privacy . . . you were so very adamant than no one should know," her mom added.

"Quite the tight-ass," Jude said wickedly.

Which was a grave injustice, as this was very much the pot calling the kettle black.

"I'm not *fond* of my . . . it's who I . . . tight? *Argh!*"

This was excruciating. The part of her that kept her emotions so under wraps did not enjoy the fact that her family had been peeking under those wraps all these years and coming away with fairly accurate perceptions, or at least interpretations based on their own understanding of the world.

Only Gabe truly *got* her. She knew that with a resounding, punishing clarity as she stood in a room full of people she loved.

"Why the hell hasn't he—" Her dad stopped abruptly.

Everyone swiveled toward him.

She realized, then, that these were the first words her dad had said since her announcement.

Which made everyone eye him a little uneasily.

It was pretty clear that he wasn't taking this particularly well. His eyes were burning in a rather portentous way above his magnificent silver mustache, and she was pretty sure his spine wasn't touching the sofa back.

"I tried to get in touch with him, Dad, when I first found out about Annelise, but he says he never got the messages from his management. And you know what? I think I believe him. It was a crazy time in his career. He came to me about it Saturday, and he didn't have to do that. And because Annelise has been wondering about her dad for a while, I decided it was now or never. I needed you guys to know in case she brings it up or asks you questions."

Her dad wasn't mollified. "I mean, The Baby Owls came through here and wanted Glenlivet, and I thought *that* was unreasonable. Shtupping my *daughter* is beyond the pale."

"It's what they do," her mom said, with a certain amount of philosophical resignation, patting his knee. "Rock stars. And she was a grown woman even then."

Her dad darted her mom a look that warned her mom not to get too explicit.

A rogue impulse to shock both of them rose in Eden.

"I was delighted he was here, Dad. It was thrilling for me. We flirted, we drank. It was quite mutual, only a little drunken, and I had a *great*—"

Her dad launched to his feet, clapped his hands over his ears, and staggered from the room as if suddenly assaulted by squealing guitar feedback.

They all watched him go.

"Give him a second," her mom said, more or less peacefully, in a stage whisper.

Her poor dad had a much lower embarrassment threshold than her mother's. Her mother didn't so much have a threshold as a sieve. "Edie, honey, isn't it time for a *real bra*?" she'd once bellowed to her clear across a crowded Macy's department store when she was a teenager. "They have these adorable teeny tiny A cups on sale!"

"So what happens now?" Jude wanted to know. He was probably figuring someone ought to be practical. Like Eden, Jude liked to know what the plan was.

Her dad returned to the room and sat down as though he'd never left.

"Well, I'm going to have him over to my place this evening and . . . he and I are going to tell her. And I'd like him to meet all of you, and you him, so you can get a sense of him . . . so if we can have dinner together tomorrow? Would that work? Have him over to this house?"

"Yeah . . ." her dad mused. "*Let's* have him for dinner."

His tone suggested her dad was picturing Jasper trussed and browned like a roasted chicken while he stood over him scraping two big carving knives together.

Eden left them to go home to relieve Danny of baby-sitting duties.

On the way, she had a text from Jesse. It said:

THAT PRAT?

Followed by a whole row of emojis guffawing tears.

CHAPTER 17

Jasper had suggested he emerge from another room in her apartment, maybe to the sound of one of his songs playing on the iPod, maybe from behind her folding screen.

She stared at him in wonderment.

"It's not *American Idol*, for fuck's sake, Jasper. It's not The Big Reveal. She's ten. I think finding out you're her father will be dramatic enough."

Although a tiny part of her thought that Annelise might actually enjoy a little fanfare. She did have a flair for the dramatic. Apple, tree, etc.

"Sorry, just . . . trying to make it memorable. I'm at a loss."

"Well, follow my lead. We'll have no idea how she's going to feel about the news, so you're going to have to play it by ear. There's no need to be anything but yourself." But she said this a little more gently.

She didn't add: *and it might not be a walk in the park. It might not be as fun as your little chat with her at the Misty Cat sound check was.* He was going to have to get through this and see for himself.

"Why don't you have a seat right there. I'll go get her."

Annelise was playing with her Barbies—the Ken doll was seated on a plastic horse, and he seemed to be carrying Winter off over his shoulder—and Winter was going reluctantly, judging from the way her arms were stretched straight out beseechingly behind her.

Eden sat down on her bed. "Sweetie, come sit by me for a second."

Annelise bounced over and plopped down next to her mom.

Eden inhaled. "Annelise, there's something I want to tell you. It's kind of a big deal, and it's kind of a surprise, and I hope you think it's a good one."

"We're going to get a horse?" she guessed, clasping her hands together.

"Um . . . well, noooo . . ."

"A tired swing, like at Mr. Caldera's house?"

"I think you mean tire swing. Nope."

"We're going over to his *house* and ride on his tire swing? We're going to live with Mr. Caldera?"

Jesus, how long had *these* particular dreams been gestating?

This could go on for a while, and Eden didn't think her nerves, let alone her heart, would hold out, if the word *Caldera* entered the room one more time.

"It's something else you've been wondering about. Do you remember when you met Mr. Jasper Townes at the Misty Cat?"

"Oh, that's right, I did. He's super nice! He showed me how to play E minor. Now I have two mournful chords."

"Well, he's here for a visit. You want to come say hello?"

Annelise went still and studied her mom. She was no fool.

She'd picked up a vibe.

"Okay," she said finally. Sweetly enough.

But with a certain amount of suspicion.

Little did she know her life was about to change.

She followed her mom—skipping, of course—into the living room.

"Hey, Annelise, sweetie. Good to see you again." Jasper was sitting on the sofa. He held out his fist to be bumped, and Annelise obliged him. Somewhat warily.

Eden sat down a more than polite distance away from Jasper on the sofa.

Annelise perched on the edge of the chair across from them. Then folded her hands. It reminded Eden of how Peace and Love curled his tail around his feet when he was feeling a little uncertain.

"Okay, Leesy, sweetie, you know you've been wondering a lot about who your dad might be? And you even wrote a song about it?"

She nodded mutely.

"Well . . ." Eden drew in a deep breath. "Jasper is your real father."

Nobody said a word for a long, long time.

Annelise's face was almost immobile. "Really?" The word was said in an astonished hush.

Eden nodded.

Annelise's eyes darted between Eden and Jasper, then settled on Eden, almost pleadingly.

"You're not teasing?"

"Oh, honey, I would never ever tease you about something like this. I didn't know he'd be in town, but he came into the shop and we had a nice chat. We decided that since you've been so curious about it lately, we should tell you that he is your father. Is that okay?"

Eden was desperate to know if she'd done the right thing. Desperate for someone solid to be standing behind her while she changed her daughter's life forever.

After a second, Annelise nodded mutely. She was staring at Jasper's face like a traveler inspecting the Flight Arrivals board at an airport and not seeing the flight she was supposed to catch.

"You're my *dad*?"

Also, she sounded deeply puzzled.

"I am."

Another silence.

"*You're* my dad?"

Jasper nodded. Two spots of color were in his cheeks. Eden appreciated those. It was indeed an excruciating moment.

Annelise clammed up again.

She blinked rapidly.

"Honey . . ." Eden said tenderly. ". . . do you want to tell me what you're thinking?"

"But . . ." Annelise folded her hands on her lap, and her gaze moved from Jasper's face to her mom's and back again. It wasn't skepticism, precisely. But you could see that her mom + Jasper wasn't a formula she'd entertained.

"Are you *sure* about this, Mom?" It was practically a whisper. Awestruck. Tremulous.

It was almost funny.

Her hands were curling and uncurling in her skirt. Which happened when Annelise was nervous and uncertain—which she rarely was.

Oh, her baby. Was she doing the right thing?

Sometimes she thought she'd trade five years of her life for a manual that had all the answers to all of her decisions.

"Do Grandma and Grandpa know?"

That was a little funny. Because in Annelise's mind, their knowledge of it would legitimize it, maybe.

"They sure do, baby. I knew you would want them to know. And I know what a grown-up, thoughtful girl you are, and I know you've been thinking about it a lot even if you don't tell me all the time. Isn't that right?"

Annelise nodded.

Taking in the info, like a little accountant, reconciling it against her previous guesses and conjectures.

Oh, for a glimpse into her mind now.

Jasper cleared his throat. "You see," he began, "your mom and I met quite a few years ago, before you were born. I've been traveling a lot for work for years now, so it was really hard for your mom to get a message through to me about you. But when I stopped into your town and saw you, well, I just *knew* when I saw you. Do you know, you look a lot like my mom? She'd be your grandma. I thought you were just the nicest kid, so interesting and funny. I'm proud to have a daughter like you. And I'm very, very sorry I haven't had a chance to meet you until now."

These were the absolute perfect things to say. Eden was astounded and grateful and she held her breath and didn't so much as twitch an eyelash.

Annelise bit her lip.

Color flooded her cheeks until she was as pink as the streak in her hair.

Her eyes glimmered, then welled, then . . .

Annelise's face slowly, slowly crumpled, and she dropped her face into her hands.

Bawling like her heart was breaking.

Yikes!

"Oh, baby. Oh, honey. It's okay. It's a big thing. I know it's a big thing."

"I don't know why I'm crying." Annelise sniffed, sounding genuinely astonished and not at all grief-stricken. She pulled her head up out of her hands. "I really don't know why, Mom. It just happened! It's j-j-just surprising, that's all. It's just big. And it's cool! I always wanted to know!"

They were all crying, actually.

Jasper knelt on the rug. "Hey, c'mere," he said softly, jocularly. He tipped his head, beckoning. "It's big for me, too."

And opened up his arms.

Annelise went into his hug. Sedately, almost ceremonially. With, Eden thought, a certain noble resignation and drama that cut Eden through while at the same time almost made her want to laugh. He may not be the father of her dreams, but a famous musician dad wasn't bad as dads went. The hug looked genuine, and painfully sweet, and maybe this would be all right, maybe this would work.

She remembered just in time to take a photo of that moment with the phone in her hip pocket.

And she did it right when Jasper looked over Annelise's shoulder at Eden wearing perhaps the most complicated expression she'd ever before seen on another human. Raw and unguarded, moved and gratified, surprised and worried, a little beseeching. The very picture of a man who was all emotion and no preparation, because how on earth could he have prepared? He'd probably winged a lot in his life. You couldn't really wing being a dad convincingly.

The beseeching part was because he was looking for approval, or maybe help. This grown man who was five years older than she was.

And while she was glad he wanted that, and he cared what she thought, and cared about doing the right things, the weight of that look settled on Eden like a lead shawl.

She was accustomed to that sort of inner wriggle and shrug required to shift a new responsibility into place, to move through her days with a new burden, that would hopefully feel like less of one as time went on. She'd adjusted to countless things since she'd become a mom. For Annelise, she could do this.

And yet she couldn't imagine Gabe turning that beseeching look on her. His instinct was to help and protect, to shoulder what he could. Not beg. Life had carved him out good and deep, like a well or—like Hellcat Canyon itself. He had vast stores to call upon: of patience, of passion, of compassion, of awareness.

Of smoking hotness.

He was entitled to expect, even demand, the same in return, she supposed.

Why the *hell* couldn't he understand her position here? Her breathing went shallow again.

It had never occurred to her that he would shut her down so swiftly and even coldly, as though he savored meting punishment. Leaving her flailing to refind her balance. She was furious at the injustice, furious at him for showing her what life could be like with him, just a little hint, and then taking it all away in a heartbeat.

Like Annelise, Eden curled her fingers into her own skirt as if seeking a hand to hold as family history was made in her living room.

Eden had decided ahead of time that it was best to keep Jasper's visit to just an hour and a half.

During that time, Annelise almost never took a breath as she dragged Jasper from room to room and narrated her life for him.

It went a little something like this:

"Who's your best friend? Mine is Emily. She's in Hummingbirds with me. The Hummingbirds went over to my Uncle Mac and Auntie Avalon's and they have goats and a donkey and we helped find worms in the garden. Do you have a garden?" She turned hopeful eyes upon him.

"Um. You have to stay in one place for a long time to have a garden, sweetie. But I have, um . . . a Bentley!"

Eden tried not to laugh.

"Is Bentley your best friend?"

"Bentley is a car," he said kindly.

"Oh, you named your car Bentley?"

"Sure," he said after a moment. A little desperately.

"Mr. Caldera was there in the garden at their house

chopping a stump with an ax and he has muscle squares on his stomach."

"Shocking," Jasper said grimly.

And, "This is my cat, Peace and Love." She smoothed a gentle hand down Peace and Love's side. Peace and Love was trying to sleep on the kitty tower in the computer room, but he obligingly rolled over and trilled, then sighed deeply. "He's called that because he has a paisley on his side. See?"

"That's a great name." Jasper reached over to pet him. Peace and Love opened one golden eye and fixed it on those dangling bracelets with great interest.

"Be careful how you pet him, though. If he's scared, he scratches!"

Jasper's hand froze cautiously in place over Peace and Love's head, as though he were bestowing a blessing.

Fortunately Peace and Love was more of a lover than a fighter and bumped his head up against it.

"But he hardly ever gets scared," Annelise claimed.

And, "I'm good at spelling. Check this out—m-o-u-r-n-f-u-l. Like A minor."

"Oooooh, good one!" he agreed.

She clasped her hands together. "Oh, how I love words."

Jasper grinned at this. "You know what? I love words, too. Check *this* one out—phalanx. Do you know it?"

Annelise was clearly torn between longing to know and a little jealousy that she didn't already know the word. "Did you make that up?"

"No, I swear it's a real word."

"Spell it," she demanded, like a prosecuting attorney.

"P-h-a-l-a-n-x."

She mouthed it along with him. "It sounds like a Dr. Seuss word! Or like those things grown-up ladies wear to keep their bellies smushed in that Kayla sells in her store."

"*What* the . . . do you mean Spanx?" Eden guessed, stifling a burst of laughter. Proof positive right there that little kids were sponges and overheard *everything*.

"Yeah. Those! What's a phalanx?"

"It means a row of soldiers, a line of defense," Jasper told her. "Phalanx."

"Ohhhhh." She silently mouthed the word again. "Mr. Caldera was a soldier, did you know?"

A beat of silence.

"Uh, yeah. It might have come up." Jasper shot Eden a baleful look.

"I wonder if he was a phalanx, too."

"Well, it's more something you're a *part* of, rather than something you are," Jasper tried.

"Were *you* ever a soldier?"

Dead silence for a good two seconds.

"Er, no. But I did sell out Madison Square Garden." He rummaged in his pocket. "Here, here's a guitar pick for you. It has my name right on it!"

"But I thought you didn't have a garden."

"Um . . . it's a different kind of garden. Instead of flowers it's a stadium with screaming, adoring people in it who came to hear me sing and play music."

Eden fixed him with a meaningful stare in the hopes he'd get his bristly ego smoothed down.

Throughout all of this, Annelise was doing a lot of

staring, fascinated and bright-eyed and a little bemused, not entirely flattering. The kind of staring she often did right before she announced something like, "Mom, do you know you have a hair growing out of your chin?"

Jasper, who one would think would be accustomed to being stared at, seemed a little disconcerted by the perusal.

But Gabe *was* coming up a little more than Eden preferred, or expected. And she had a hunch Gabe wasn't just under her skin, he'd lodged under Jasper's, too.

And it was pretty clear that Annelise had someone like Gabe in mind when it came to a father type, and she was trying to reconcile the two men in her head, like a little accountant.

And Jasper was clearly trying to impress a ten-year-old, something he'd likely never had to deliberately do in his whole life.

"Ooooh," Annelise crowed delightedly. "Screaming fans!" She was authentically wowed by the idea of an audience, because she frankly loved an audience. Jasper smiled, mollified and relieved.

"Okay. Well, we can play Phalanx with my Barbies, and your Ken doll can pretend they're all soldiers. And *then* we can play your thing. Your Madison Garden thing. And these are my Barbies! This one is named Coconut and this is Judith and this little one is Ariel, this is Winter, this is Ken, but today I call him Phil. Here, you be Phil."

She pressed the half-dressed Ken doll into Jasper's hand. Jasper gave a start.

"Whoa! This dude has quite a package."

"Don't be scared! It's easy to make him modest. Here are his favorite pants." Annelise handed him a pair of brown pants. "They're brown because he works for UPS, like Jeffrey who comes into my mom's store and hangs out longer than he should."

Jasper clutched the Ken doll and darted a look at Eden that was reminiscent of a guy tied to a post in a basement that was rapidly filling with water.

Eden was conscious that she'd been standing back like Jane Goodall observing the interactions of primates. And part of that was to make a possibly unworthy-of-her point: children are dazzling, and children are effort, and sometimes children are boring. But they're always worth it.

Just exactly what Gabe had said.

"Annelise, why don't you show Jasper your guitar. I'm not sure he's in the mood to play Barbies. You probably got your own musical talent from him."

"Okay!" Annelise said brightly. "This is my guitar." She retrieved her three-quarter kid-sized guitar from its stand.

He cradled it respectfully in his long hands, with a reverence that Annelise clearly relished and that Eden appreciated.

"Wow, she's really pretty," he told her.

"My guitar is a *girl*?" Annelise breathed. "How do you know?"

"I can just tell. I know a lot about girls."

He shot a mischievous look in Eden's direction. Which she didn't reward with anything like a smile. He didn't need the encouragement.

"I write all my songs on this guitar," Annelise pronounced as grandly as if she were Adele. "I wrote 'Invisible Dad' on this guitar. I know Glory Greenleaf. She's super great. She taught me to play C and G and then she went away to be famous. Play A minor now, okay?"

Jasper obligingly strummed an A minor chord, and then, thrillingly, sang.

"Annelise . . . oh Annelise . . .
The wind in the trees whispers sweet Annelise . . .
The trees
say to the bees
have you seen Annelise?
She's as pretty as the spring
And she'll make you want to sing
. . . Annelise . . ."

Eden and Annelise listened, motionless, utterly enchanted.

That was Jasper's power. He could whip out a silly song just like that and sing it with enormous soul and have a stadium eating out of his hand.

He smiled at Annelise, pleased with himself, charmed by, and probably relieved by, Annelise's rapt silence and glowing eyes.

"Maybe something about breeze next," she suggested shyly. "Or grilled cheese. And maybe you could really whisper one of the sentences."

"Those are all excellent suggestions. I'll work on it. Did you name her?" He gestured with the guitar.

"Guitars have *names*?" Annelise was fascinated.

"Oh, yeah. For example, the two guitars I play the most are named Arrow and, um, Veronica."

"How come those names?"

He hesitated again.

Eden was pretty sure there was some prurient reason for both of them.

"They just seemed to fit," he said diplomatically, apparently catching on how easy it was to get lost in a conversational labyrinth with a ten-year-old, where one question never led out of it; it just led to another and another and another.

"Maybe you should name a guitar Annelise."

"Maybe I should."

"It would be so cool if you could sing at my school," Annelise said with great wistfulness.

"Why, does Principal Caldera sing?" he asked, with startling, almost comical bitterness. "I could totally sing at your school."

Eden shot him a warning look.

"Oh, could you?" Annelise clasped her hands again. "We're having a raffle and everything to raise money for a new baseball field. Mom is donating flowers. But Caitlynn Pennington's mom is donating a whole fancy dinner and a getaway at a hotel in Black Oak."

"Not in Black Oak!" Jasper gasped.

Annelise nodded dismally.

"I can do better than that. I can give you a signed *guitar* to raffle."

Annelise froze.

Then she sucked in a dramatic, long breath. "Seriously?" she said in that squeaky register only ten-year-olds seemed able to achieve.

Jasper didn't even flinch. His hearing probably wasn't

what it used to be, anyway, from proximity to all those
Marshall Stacks.

"NO. WAY." Annelise gripped his wrist and gazed
earnestly into his face like she'd just had a religious
conversion.

"WAY."

They froze that way in a moment of communion.

Annelise was clearly thunderstruck by her luck.

"It's in two whole weeks. On a Friday night! We're
going to have a table and Mom is doing the flowers
and it's going to be so much fun! You can maybe even
sit with us!"

"Maybe so," he said, rather noncommittally, and with
an eye dart that made Eden's radar ping with alarm.

"Mom, did you hear?"

"I heard," Eden said rather grimly.

Then a ding on his phone made Jasper spring up.
He'd probably set a timer.

"Well, lovely girl, I've *loved* spending time with you,
but I have to get going. Can I have a hug?"

He knelt again. Annelise hugged him goodbye with
something a little closer to her usual abandon.

This time, Eden couldn't see his expression.

He stood up so fast his bracelets jingled frantically.
"We'll talk again soon, okay? Fist bump, daughter of
mine?"

Annelise put out her fist to be bumped.

They smiled at each other.

And then Jasper didn't quite bolt for the door, but he
sure got there in a hurry.

"Honey, why don't you play A minor while I talk to
Jasper?" Eden said to Annelise, and followed Jasper.

He paused there. "Thanks, Eden," he said. "For . . . all of this."

His eyes were glazed. She could have sworn he'd even aged ever so slightly.

"You did great for a first go-round. You look a little shell-shocked, though."

"Yeah?" he said distractedly. "Wow, she's just . . . it's just . . . wow."

He pushed his hands through his hair.

"Yep," Eden agreed cautiously.

"Is it always like that? Um, dizzying? *And* dazzling?" he added hurriedly.

"No."

Something like a smile began to curve his mouth.

"Not when she's sleeping," she added.

The smile dropped off.

She was tempted to laugh, but she took pity. "She *is* a little keyed up. Naturally. She's sharing things about herself and kind of showing off, too. Kids have insane amounts of energy."

He took this in with silence. And then he smiled a sort of wistful smile. "She's . . . amazing."

"She is." She already knew this, but she couldn't help but feel gratified that Jasper recognized it, too.

Though the word *amazing* had quite a number of facets and dimension, the way he said it.

"Can I hug *you* goodbye?" he said, almost diffidently.

She eyed him skeptically. "As long as your hands stay far, far away from my ass."

"Deal."

She hesitated, and then thought, oh, what the hell. He *was* family.

He smelled like patchouli and was pleasantly lean. But the way he clung for a desperate moment made her think that he'd asked for the hug because he'd needed reassurance and not a grope, which made her feel about a thousand years old and like his mother, which wasn't sexy in the least.

He left her with the scent of his patchouli and doubt adhering to her.

She supposed they were only at the beginning of this. They would just have to feel their way through. Maybe set up regular visits via Skype with Annelise, if that's what they both wanted.

She stared at the closed door, and thought of what Gabe had said about a smooth, white wall with fire behind it, and her emotions ricocheted between fury and ferocious yearning and settled into something like stillness and numbness because that was the only safe place for them.

She felt a nudge at her calf. It was Peace and Love, winding through her legs.

She knelt to give him a thorough petting.

And then she went still. What was it that Annelise had said? That Peace and Love scratched when he got scared?

And that was it. That was the thing she'd been trying to sort from the snarl and pain and anger in his office.

Maybe Gabe was scared.

"Boy, late night, huh? You gonna be much longer, Mr. Caldera?"

Carl the janitor was paused in the doorway, hands folded over the handle of his mop, which he'd soundlessly glided down the hall. If Carl was in the hall, it must be about eight o'clock. He had the nightly cleanup routine down to a soothing, ammonia-scented ballet.

"Yeah, I just have to finish up paperwork."

Carl gave a shudder at the word *paperwork*. He wouldn't want Gabe's job for the world.

At five o'clock, Gabe had been reviewing and signing various invoices for the big Fund-raising Raffle about a week away. He'd fully expected to be home by six.

But then he'd come to the one for Eden's Garden, and stopped.

He hadn't done much but sit in the semidark and think ever since.

"You okay?" Carl added. "Boy, you sure look like you could use some sleep."

Gabe snorted. "Hey. This isn't the most flattering lighting."

Carl grinned and moseyed off, whistling what sounded like, for Christ's sake, "Lily Anne" by Blue Room. The universe was a bastard, sometimes.

Gabe blew out a long breath. He reached for his baseball. Hefted it once, twice.

He realized what he was doing and swore and put it back again immediately.

Goddammit.

Just because she was right about *that* didn't mean she was right about everything.

He sighed, surrendered, picked up the ball and tossed it thoughtfully.

He realized what he'd been trying to do here in the semidark of his office: listen. Because the sort of odd ringing, wired numbness that usually followed a disaster—

an earthquake, an explosion, a crash, a shattering breakup, for instance—was ebbing from his body. He still felt like shit, but various realizations were beginning to sift down like ash.

And he knew from experience the quality of the silence that followed a disaster was a hint as to what, if anything, remained.

He knew exactly what it felt like to lose someone or something. In his experience, when a person was gone, boy, they sure *felt* gone. Greta at the New Age Store downtown might beg to differ, but even though all of the things one said in the wake of a loss—that someone will live on in your heart and memories, and so forth— were technically true, the absence was still resounding. Gone was *gone*. As though a lovely song that had been playing all your life had been . . . slapped off.

The way Eden had slapped that Jasper Townes's song off the radio.

So he listened.

She was here. Eden was. In that chair across from him, where she'd toppled into his arms for the first time. In the way his skin hummed when he so much as brushed up against the memory of how it felt to touch her; his fingers curled hard when he recalled her fingers clinging to his shoulders as he plunged into her when they made love on that sofa.

And she was in the doorway, too, her pale face as they shredded each other's hearts, each of them wielding pride as a battering ram.

Ironic to discover that deep down inside there was a little bit left of that cocky fucker who thought he had control over anything. He was darkly amused by this. He'd had a damned plan, for God's sake! What could possibly go wrong? Literally the last thing he'd ever imagined, that's what had gone wrong. Jasper Townes waltzing into town to claim paternity was, in its way, pretty damn funny. *Surreal* funny, like those dreams you had after eating Pasquale's pizza too late at night.

Joke was on him, though.

Townes would be meeting Annelise tonight. The restless, territorial, subterranean misery of knowing another man—a man like Jasper Townes—was in Eden's apartment right now was part of the reason Gabe was sitting in the dark.

But he knew instinctively that wasn't the only reason he was still sitting here.

And that's when he admitted to himself that he was sort of keeping vigil. The same way you would if you were waiting for a loved one to get home on a stormy night or out of surgery. Maybe not as dire. As if you were waiting to hear an award announced. As if somehow his vigilance could keep Eden and Annelise safe, make that meeting go well, make it everything Annelise hoped it would be, help Eden feel peaceful about it.

What had Eden said about Gabe waiting outside the burning building? That they'd be fine if he was the one waiting out there. That's what she thought. He believed it himself.

Ah, but she "couldn't deal with him right now."

She had pushed him away, hard.

He gave a short laugh. Then sighed.

Fuck it.

He signed the invoice and turned off his desk lamp.

Carl was right: he needed to sleep.

But that was the other reason he was hanging out here.

He wasn't looking forward to his empty house. And somehow his big yellow house felt even emptier than before.

CHAPTER 18

"Well, what do you think of today, Annelise? What do you think of Jasper?"

They'd gotten Annelise into her pajamas, and Eden was perched on her bed.

"He's really cool." Her face was still alight with a sort of wondering abstraction, but her cheeks were flushed, and her eyes had a sort of hectic brightness she got when she was exhausted but still hopped up on emotion in a night-after-the-day-at-an-amusement-park kind of way.

And that wondering abstracted expression reminded Eden of the time Annelise had wanted a Sunshine Sandy doll for Christmas and had gotten a Patty Peaches doll instead because Sunshine Sandy was sold out.

And as it turned out, Annelise ended up loving Patty Peaches.

But not right away.

"I'm going to keep this forever!" She held out the tortoiseshell guitar pick that said, "Jasper Townes" on it. They were probably chucked by handfuls into audiences at his shows. At least it wasn't a koala. "I'm going to take it with me everywhere!"

"It's lovely," Eden agreed. "So are you glad to know who your dad is?"

Leesy nodded. "It's like . . ." She sighed theatrically. "The suspense was *killing* me. But I thought he would feel more like . . ."

She glanced up guiltily.

"More like . . ." Eden prompted gently.

"More like . . . mine." And she folded her hands over her heart. "You know, like, the way you're mine, and Grandma and Grandpa are mine. Like I thought I'd feel him right here right away. Because he's my dad."

Eden was speechless.

And it was darling and hilarious and gratifying and deeply painful and beautiful that her daughter was probably, right now, trying to be delicate with her mom's feelings.

"Well, right now you're getting to know each other. Maybe someday he'll feel like yours. How *does* he feel to you right now?"

"Mmm . . . well, he's funny and nice. He doesn't really feel like a dad, though, if that's okay. He's maybe too thin? Dads are usually a little thicker and wider, seems like. And he smells like Greta's store, kind of. Is it okay if I don't think he feels like a *dad* dad?"

That smell would be the patchouli he dabbed on. Greta at the New Age Store sold every imaginable oil and incense.

"Sure. I think being a father and being a dad are a little bit different. Being a father is a result of biology—

you know what that means, right? It takes a lady and a man to make a baby." Annelise scrunched her nose here and waved her arms as if her mom had just farted by way of discouraging her from expounding on that. "And being a dad is something you kind of become as a result of being there every day and being involved in everything you do, and taking care of you the way a mom does."

"Like carrying you on shoulders at picnics and fixing stuff and coaching your soccer team and stuff like that?"

"Yeah, stuff like that. And making sure you're safe and happy and eat your vegetables and clean your room and learn how to build stuff and teaching you to drive when the time comes . . ."

She stopped when guilt swooped in: *she'd* had a great dad, who was part of nearly everything she was and said and did, the same as her mom was. She'd known the luxury of waking up with Glenn's comforting, gruff, hilarious presence in the house every day.

And here she was expounding on the idea of a great father to a kid who had . . . Jasper Townes. More an exotic pet than a dad.

She was desperate to ask Annelise: *Do you feel safe here with me? Do you feel loved enough? Are you conscious of missing something in your life, like Jasper said he was? Was it like a house with a drafty window or a gap where your baby tooth fell out, and now everything is whole again, now that the mystery is solved?*

Questions she of course couldn't ask a ten-year-old.

She was going to have to keep doing the best she could and take it with a heaping dose of faith, the way she'd taken everything so far.

"So . . . like Grandpa is a *dad*?"

"Right. Your grandpa is a great, great dad for me and a great granddad to you."

"And some people are naturally kind of dads even if they don't have kids, like Principal Caldera?"

Damn.

That was as painful and shocking as stepping on a Lego in bare feet in the dead of night.

She couldn't speak for a full two seconds.

"Maybe so," she said breathlessly. Her voice hoarse.

And there followed a little pinprick of fury, like a lit cigarette brushed against her skin: how could he just *bail* on her like that? When the notion of him had reached little tendril-like roots into her dreams and plans for the future, and she hadn't realized how deep they'd gone until they'd been yanked out.

Maybe he'd been *looking* for an out.

No. She didn't believe it. When she'd walked out of his office, his face was as white and stunned as Jude's was that time he broke his collarbone.

"Is my dad Jasper *your* destiny, Mom?"

She took a cleansing breath.

"Well . . . it's not like with Auntie Avalon and Uncle Mac, if that's what you're thinking. It was my destiny to be your mom, baby girl, and he was . . . he . . . kind of helped me along the way."

"Like how broccoli's destiny is to be nutritious, and the cow poop Uncle Mac puts on it helps it grow?"

"Um—"

"Or like how when Auntie Avalon bought the big house and Uncle Mac was already living there so they had to get together? Because of the house?"

That was a pretty amusing interpretation of events. She'd have to remember to tell Avalon.

"I'd say Jasper's role in my life has been somewhere in between cow poop and the house and Devil's Leap."

They sat side by side in silence on Annelise's eye-searing counterpane, her arm looped around Annelise, who cuddled up against her, burrowing her head in a bit. They were both a little drained. Eden had to admit that in exchange for a whole raft of potential complications she'd won a certain peace she didn't know she'd been craving.

Why, then, despite the newness, did her life feel like it had constricted instead of expanded?

Annelise put a hand on Eden's knee and looked earnestly into her face. "My dad Jasper is famous, Mom," she said somberly and sleepily, as if breaking the news to her. "Really famous."

"He is, indeed."

"So, Jasper . . . where did you grow up?" Her mom began the friendly questioning.

The old Harwood dining room—the heavy old round oak table that had belonged to their great-grandmother was set with a platter of roast beef, tureens of mashed potatoes and gravy and steamed broccoli, a typical Sunday dinner, even if it wasn't Sunday. Hearty and basic.

The only exotic thing was their guest. Jasper had politely taken a big helping of everything on the table and made yummy noises when he tasted the roast under the watchful eyes of her mom and dad, Annelise, Avalon, and Jude. Her dad had taken an inordinate amount of time carving the roast at the table with a big glinting knife while everyone silently watched. For the first time it occurred to Eden that Jude's surgical skills might have been passed onto him by their dad.

"Well, I was born in upstate New York. Small town. Moved around a lot with my mom, though. Arkansas, Alabama, Texas, Reno, San Francisco. I grew up on the road, I guess," Jasper told her.

"Some of those are cities," Annelise pointed out. "And some of those are states."

"That's true. You're pretty smart, Annelise."

"Yep," she said easily. No one in the Harwood family had much patience for stating the obvious.

He grinned at her.

She smiled back. Pleased. But it was pretty clear Annelise was comparing and contrasting Jasper with the rest of her family. Working things out in her head in her way.

"Went to Los Angeles when I was eighteen to get into the music business, and that's been home ever since. I don't know who my dad was. And look at me now!"

Everybody was already looking at him, so his point was a bit unclear.

"You can be anything you want, Annelise, no matter how many parents you have," he explained.

"Ah," said Jude, nodding, sagely, but with great irony,

when it seemed as though no one else would say anything.

"Jude here is a heart surgeon. He can cut your heart right out," her dad volunteered suddenly.

Eden was tempted to kick her dad, though she kinda understood where he was coming from.

"Well, usually we're trying for a little more accuracy in the operating room, but I suppose in a pinch I could certainly do that," Jude agreed.

Jude, the smart-ass, was enjoying himself a little too much. Eden longed to kick him, too. She was only within kicking distance of Avalon, who hadn't done anything yet to warrant it.

"Is your real name Jasper?" Avalon wanted to know. She sounded very polite and even a little awestruck, uncharacteristically abstracted. Which was funny, given that this was Avalon. Probably she was storing up all kinds of teasing fodder to unleash on Eden later.

Then Jasper grinned at her, and Avalon went a little misty-eyed. "Yep. But you can all call me Jazz if you want. That was my childhood nickname."

"Yeah, I'm not gonna do that," said her dad.

This statement launched a tense wordless interval that was almost long enough to convince Eden this dinner was a terrible idea.

But in some fashion, just like Annelise had asked whether her grandma and grandpa knew about Jasper, Eden had wanted this to happen in order to sort of officialize Jasper's role. She wanted her parents to experience him, to have opinions, to know him for Annelise's sake, to be able to field questions.

She wanted to live from a place of open honesty from now on.

Because not doing that may have cost her Gabe.

Annelise finally broke the silence.

"Why does your hair look like that?" Annelise wanted to know.

Eden had a hunch this was the question that Annelise had on low simmer for the past couple of days.

He chewed and swallowed. "Freedom," he said finally.

Avalon's and Jude's heads popped up like prairie dogs, and their eyes were suspiciously bright. As if this answer was too good to be true.

Her dad muttered, "Oh, for the love of—"

A grunt signaled the fact that her mom had kicked her dad under the table.

"A grown man can wear his hair any way he likes in a free country, Annelise. And so I like to express my freedom in ways that sometimes surprise people, because it's fun to see what people do or think. Like your pink streak. It's pretty and surprising."

Annelise mulled this somberly while Eden clamped her teeth together at the tone with which he delivered the wisdom. And maybe this was what he thought dads did. Imparted wisdom. He'd never had an example of his own, after all.

And yet it wasn't a *terribly* wrong thing to say.

"I could loan you my brush," Annelise offered shyly.

Oh, her precious girl. Annelise was born with a built-in bullshit detector and a heart like a satellite dish. Color was one thing; unruliness was quite another.

She was both her mother's and her father's daughter.

Everyone waited, breath bated, in the short fraught silence that followed.

"That would be great," Jasper said kindly. "Thanks."

Annelise smiled at him, and he grinned back.

"So Jasper, how long are you in town?" Jude wanted to know.

"I'm off tomorrow. Gotta bunch of tour dates up and down the West Coast. Interview, live spots on radio, stuff like that."

No one at the table had any idea what would comprise "stuff like that."

"Did you know a jasper is a kind of rock?" Annelise told him. "We learned about geology and geography and stuff in school. Isn't that funny? Because you're a *rock* star!"

Everyone laughed. Jasper lit up with surprise and delight in her cleverness.

"And we learned in geography about volcanos and stuff. And my principal's name is Caldera. A caldera is like a steaming hot thing."

"Boy, I'll say," Avalon said under her breath.

Finally providing an excuse for Eden to kick her.

And Jasper's face, quite ironically given his namesake, turned to stone.

"So what happened?"

Mac and Gabe were sitting in the Misty Cat, as they often did after Veteran's Hall meetings on Tuesday nights, in large part because open mic night was every Tuesday, and it was often inadvertently entertaining. Given the Misty Cat's associations, Gabe would prefer another bar at the moment, but really, it was the cleanest and it had the best beer, and apart from Jasper making love to Eden right there on the stage, not much would make him more miserable than he was now.

Mac Coltrane was probably the only person in the world who knew how deep the thing with Eden went. This was the first chance he'd had to talk to Mac about it.

Gabe took a sip of his beer. "Jasper Townes happened."

"Brutal."

Gabe looked at him, dryly amused. "You're not going to butter me up and tell me what a great guy I am and how I'm so much better than he is and I was a SEAL, for God's sake, and just look at me?"

"No, man," Mac said in all seriousness. "It's Jasper Townes."

That actually made Gabe laugh. Just one short "Ha!" however, because now that the initial anesthetizing numbness had worn off, everything really hurt. As if he'd been dropped from an airplane and his chute hadn't opened, only instead of smashing his bones and organs it had smashed all of his emotions and his hopes and dreams.

There also remained the possibility that he had deliberately left the cord unpulled. As if he'd been trying to protect himself from something.

"So, um, how do you feel, exactly?" Mac was tentative.

"I feel," Gabe said thoughtfully, "as if, maybe . . . I've had an organ removed, an important one. Did you know that all of your organs can function as a sort of kill switch, and when they malfunction they can stop your heart? I feel like my kill switch has been activated. Kind of like that."

There was a beat of silence.

"Holy shit," Mac breathed. Alarmed and impressed.

"But I'm sure I'll feel better after a couple of beers," Gabe said with mordant cheeriness. He raised his beer bottle in a sardonic toast.

"She's not dating Townes? Or sleeping with him?"

He stifled a wince. *Dating* and *sleeping*. Both words were horrible. "She says no," he said shortly.

"Then why wouldn't you believe her?"

"Why, indeed? Why indeed?"

He in fact did believe her. That was part of the problem. He still couldn't quite locate the source of the misery he was experiencing, and he was pretty certain a lot of it was self-authored.

Although it was possible he'd been a big enough dick that he'd driven her right into Townes's arms for some patchouli-scented comfort.

His fingers clamped around the bottle.

But Eden was nothing like impulsive.

Then again, she'd done it in the truck cabin with the principal.

Which sounded like a pornographic game of Clue.

"Eden is a good person, Gabe," Mac said cautiously. "Just a really lovely nice person."

Gabe glared at him. "You better have a point."

"I would say she's on the level. I'll admit the Townes thing is kind of a wild card, though."

"You know what Bud said? Beware of enigmatic women."

"Bud Wallace? Like he's Yoda."

Gabe snorted at that.

"She's really not all that mysterious, Gabe. One big secret notwithstanding, and knowing Eden, you can kind of get why she wouldn't want to trumpet that."

It was true. She was that smooth cool surface over brilliant fire, sweetness and warmth. She wasn't a grandstander.

"Avalon says she met Townes, and there was zero chemistry between them. Like she was barely tolerating him for Annelise's sake."

Gabe went still. "When did Avalon meet him?" he demanded.

Mac hesitated. "At a family dinner last night," he admitted. "I couldn't make it. Couldn't reschedule a meeting with a contractor."

Gabe was silent, astonished at how much weightier his heart managed to get at the news. But of course. Townes was part of their family now, the Harwoods. He had more of a right to be there than he did, at this point.

And he thought about that cozy night up at Devil's Leap sitting around the dinner table, and it was pretty much what he wanted from life.

"She could have told me that Townes was Annelise's father. I mean, I get that it's awkward and improbable, but I thought we were straight up honest with each other. There were even a couple of moments where she could have told me. Aaaaaand . . . she didn't. I felt like a complete and total ass in that pizza joint when she was there, sitting with him. It sucked for so many reasons."

"I agree she could have done that better. Which part of you is hurting the most? Stop me when you feel a twinge. Your pride? Your ego? Your, um, heart?"

"I get a ping off all of them."

This wasn't Mac's comfort zone. Providing comfort, that was. Then again, Avalon was doing wonders with his emotional vocabulary.

"You know, Gabe, this isn't a foxhole. I mean, she didn't train for how to integrate a rock star into her life and yours. Maybe you can cut her some slack. Maybe she was afraid of losing you, and she chickened out when she had those chances to tell you about him. Not everyone is Joe Courage like you are."

"Joe *Courage*?" Gabe snorted, incredulous.

But a second later, something Mac had just said settled on him and in sank a sort of uncomfortable truth: *afraid of losing you.*

He went quiet.

"Maybe she knows *you* better than you think. And she anticipated all of . . ." Mac gestured to Miserable Gabe and the beer. ". . . all of this. You acting like this. All broody and self-righteous."

Of his friends, only Mac would get away with assessing him that way.

And frankly he didn't think anyone knew him as well as Eden did. Some of it she'd learned, and sometimes it seemed she'd been born knowing him. Which was not just a luxury. It was a freaking miracle.

"The problem is," Gabe said slowly, "and this is what kills me . . . is that she might have been right to end our whatever it was before we both got too deep in.

Because who knows where this Townes thing is going. I mean, maybe she needs to get Annelise and her whole family accustomed to Townes being a part of her life. And that part of it doesn't really include me at all. And maybe it shouldn't. And maybe . . ." He drained his beer. ". . . I don't want to sit by and watch that happen like . . . Brother Teresa."

And that would have been pretty funny, if it wasn't so tragic.

Mac laughed anyway.

Gabe shot him a baleful look.

"Huh. Do you think any of that is true?"

He took a sip of beer. He mulled that over.

"Nope," Gabe said finally, with a ghost of a smile.

Mac gave a short laugh, more sympathy than humor. "So tell me, Gabe, do you think she's your destiny?"

He gave the word *destiny* the sort of melodramatic flourish that would warm Annelise's heart.

Gabe was saved from answering that question when Glenn leaped to the stage, seized the microphone, and announced, "Everyone give it up for Mikey McShane!"

Mikey's songs tended to be heartfelt and literal, and Gabe and Mac often enjoyed them, not always for the reasons Mikey intended.

"Thank you," Mikey, whose hair was dyed black and whose nose piercing looked as though it might be a little infected, said to the smattering of applause. "This song is called, 'The Polar Bears Are Dying.'"

Mikey settled himself on the stool onstage, stuck his tongue between his teeth, and painstakingly went about tuning his guitar down a half step, as befitted a dirge.

"What do you think this song is about, Mac?" Gabe wondered dryly.

"I'm gonna guess it's about dying polar bears, Gabe."

What would he do if he was afraid of losing? What would a polar bear do if it was cornered and afraid?

Fight back.

Lash out.

"So what are you going to do?" Mac broke into what was turning into an epiphany.

He didn't have to say "about Eden." The subject of all the sentences in Gabe's life right now was Eden.

It was a fair question. Mac had known him long enough to expect Gabe to know. To have a plan. When didn't he?

"He's floating on a glacier all alooone . . ."

Mikey sang.

Which felt a little uncomfortably on the nose, at the moment.

"Finish this beer," he told Mac finally. "And survive this song."

CHAPTER 19

Eden spread her fingers apart and pressed them to her forehead as she sat at the kitchen table and reviewed the printed directions to her new all-in-one printer. Maybe Greta at the New Age Store would have some magic reflexology tips. Greta, whom she was tempted to blame for the upheaval in her life, thanks to the stupid tarot cards. Several nights of fitful sleep with too much caffeine and not enough water and too much Gabe angst was enough to give anyone a headache. At least Jasper had left town. Her whiteboard might start to look accurate again.

"Mom?" Annelise called from the computer room.

"Yeah, honey?"

"What's r-e-h-a-b?"

"It's a place you go if you want to break a bad habit. You pay money and helpful people help you to learn better habits," she replied.

"Oh!" Annelise shouted cheerily. "Okay. Thanks."

Seconds later, comprehension set in.

And Eden broke land speed records dashing across

the carpet to the computer room. She wouldn't have been surprised if she'd left a narrow flaming trail of fire behind her.

She positioned herself casually in the doorway. Panting.

"Hey, Leesy. Whatcha looking at?"

"About a billion things come up when I Google my dad Jasper!" she said happily.

This was how she'd taken to referring to Jasper. As "my dad" didn't feel entirely right, and neither did "Jasper." Together they'd become a brand-new honorific.

"Honorific" made Eden immediately think of Gabe, which caused her heart to sort of clunk painfully in her chest. She shoved that thought away.

"Sweetie, I know you're really curious. How about we Google him together for about ten minutes or so a night whenever you get curious, so that when you have questions I can answer them for you."

Annelise was nobody's fool. She tipped her head and studied her mom.

Who was still rather incriminatingly breathing a little heavily from her mad dash.

"Okay," Annelise said. Brightly and a little too easily.

Eden sighed and plopped down on the old love seat across from the computer desk. If Annelise wanted to know something, there were ways to do that when her mom wasn't looking over her shoulder. Not all of her friends' moms policed the internet at their houses. She was a good kid, but she was also really resourceful and more than a teensy tenacious when it came to acquiring knowledge.

"Leesy, your dad Jasper has had a very colorful

life. Quite different from the lives we live in Hellcat Canyon. Not necessarily better or worse, just different, you know? We have our ways of doing things, and he has his ways. It's like that with a lot of people who are famous. If you hear something you think is weird or surprising about your dad Jasper . . . come right to me and we'll talk about it. You know how we talked about how some people are sort of naturally dads and others have to learn it? It's like that. He hasn't, um, behaved like a dad very often. I'm your mom, so I know what's best for you."

She'd decided it was best to start issuing disclaimers for Jasper now, to try to provide a buffer between Annelise and what she hoped was potential, but which she feared was inevitable, disappointment.

Maybe Jasper would surprise her.

More than he already had, that was.

Though Eden wasn't a cockeyed optimist, in general.

Annelise pointed at the computer screen. "It says here he went out with that girl who has her picture on a magazine I saw when Casey was getting the gum out of my hair that time. Katri . . . Katri . . . something."

It was useful to have a hairstylist right across the street from their apartment, that was for sure.

"He certainly did go out with her."

Annelise frowned. "But you're prettier than she is," she said stoutly.

"Well, that's very kind of you to say. But everyone has different tastes, and pretty is as pretty does, right?" Eden said. "I don't want to go on a date with your dad Jasper, and he doesn't want to go on a date with me."

Though Eden was uncertain this last part was true. She had a hunch that Jasper would go for the mile if given an inch. "I'm happy to be his friend, though! Everyone has different tastes, right? You like Braden in your class, but you don't like Tim because you saw him pick his nose once. But he's cute, and everyone picks their nose now and again. And tastes change as you get older."

"You mean he might not like the taste of boogers when he gets older?"

"Uh, no, not . . . well, yes. By tastes I mean as in your *preferences*. The things you like will change and grow the way you do. Like when you were little you used to hate it when your food was hot, and I had to blow on it before you'd eat it but now you don't mind if it's hot."

Annelise mulled this. "I've never seen you pick your nose."

"Because I'm setting a good example for you."

"Oh. Okay."

Usually Eden could keep on-mothering-point, but this was wobbling off the tracks. Boy, was she tired.

"Okay, computer time's over!" She clapped her hands briskly. "Let's tackle that math homework."

Annelise sighed prettily and slumped with great melodrama over the keyboard. "Can't I play my guitar for a few minutes? Pretty, pretty pleeeease? I could maybe write a song for Dad Jasper with A minor and G and he'd like it." She batted doe eyes at her mom from beneath her bent arm.

Annelise's guitar was leaning against the couch, as

it so happened. Because there was a full-length mirror in this room, and she could watch herself in it as she played.

She really *was* her father's daughter.

Eden wondered how many of these types of pleas she could expect in the future.

"A half hour of guitar. Then math."

"Okay."

She was scrutinizing Eden's face with the same bright-eyed, somewhat critical way she'd inspected Jasper. Trying to figure something out about her. Something she might just blurt in front of other people.

"Don't worry, Mom. I'm sure you'll find someone for your tastes one day," she said gently.

Eden stifled a laugh.

"Thank you, child," she said somberly.

Eden leaned back against the little old sofa and for a millisecond, imagined it was Gabe's chest, and then pushed herself away from it because imagining that kind of comfort was really just another way of courting pain.

A couple of days later . . .

"It wasn't my fault, I swear it. I truly meant to trim that tree branch."

Harvey Millwood was in the kind of bind that roses could get him out of, which was why he was standing in Eden's Garden, gazing at her imploringly.

"Well, it could happen to anyone," Eden soothed from behind the counter.

"Just because I *hated* that ridiculous birdbath fountain doesn't mean I would *deliberately* destroy it. My wife loved it."

"You don't strike me as a vandal, Mr. Millwood."

"I knew you'd understand, Miss Harwood. You have such sympathetic eyes. Has anyone ever told you that?"

"Well, that's thoughtful of you to say. And you know, nothing says I'm truly sorry like a dozen long-stem Ecuadorian roses . . . this color is called Movie Star, and you can tell her, 'you're the only star of my life.'"

"She would love that!" Harvey breathed, as if she was The Bard herself.

"Given that it's a rather urgent apology, I can let you have them for . . . thirty."

Which was their exact price. She was sympathetic. She wasn't a patsy.

Harvey was sorting through his wallet for cash when her cell phone rang.

He peered over the counter at her phone and read the incoming caller.

"Mrs. Maker, huh? I'm guessing your day is about to get even harder than mine."

Good Lord. Small towns. Everyone knew who Mrs. Maker was, and there were usually only two reasons she'd call, and both of them sent her adrenaline skyrocketing.

Eden leaned across the counter, snagged a twenty from Harvey's wallet, and mouthed, *take 'em*.

It might not be Eden's lucky day, but it was Harvey's.

He departed, beaming.

She crossed her fingers and muttered, "Please be a

butt dial please be a butt dial please be a butt dial . . ." and then answered the call.

She composed her voice. "This is Eden Harwood."

"Mrs. Maker, here, Ms. Harwood."

"Oh, shit. Oh God. Sorry, I didn't mean to say that out loud or mean it personally, Mrs. Maker. It's just you're so often a harbinger, as it were, of . . . of things . . ."

She closed her eyes and said a prayer.

"I know, dear. I can handle a little cursing. A harbinger and a humdinger, my husband always says. It seems Annelise has been in a fight." She delivered this very matter-of-factly.

Eden's heart stopped. "A fight? Like . . . an argument?" Even as she said it she knew it was just a hopeful guess. As if she could actually persuade Mrs. Maker to change history.

"Oh, yes, dear. But it was also a physical altercation."

Oh, God. Her heart thunked over like it had been thrown to the mat by a wrestler.

Probably one of the only kinds of teams Gabe hadn't been roped into substitute coaching.

"Is she . . . are they . . . okay?"

"Oh, absolutely. She has a bloody nose and grass stains, but is otherwise unharmed. The other girl has a bloody nose, too."

"The other girl is . . ." *Dear God, cut me some slack, please don't let her say . . .*

"Caitlynn Pennington."

God was clearly on a lunch break.

"But . . . *why?*" Although theories about the reason why were even now beginning to formulate, and she liked none of them.

"They're in Mr. Caldera's office right now. You or someone you designate will need to come to pick her up for a discussion, and I'm sure you'll hear the whole story then."

If only life followed a romantic comedy plot. It seemed needlessly awkward to have to see Gabe Caldera only a week after the snarly death of their romance. Like Lloyd Sunnergren's dog, who stuck his nose up people's hind ends and then stood back and smiled about it, the universe had no sense of timing or propriety.

"I'm on my way, Mrs. Maker. Thank you."

Mrs. Maker ushered Eden briskly through the office as if she was a paramedic en route to a crash. Mrs. Maker's guest chairs had been brought into Gabe's office so that the culprits, Annelise and Caitlynn, could be installed in them on either side of their mothers.

Gabe was sitting behind his desk looking big and delicious and somber.

Jan Pennington swung her head toward her and whipped off her sunglasses. Her eyes practically bulged with outrage.

"Eden," she said frigidly.

After she'd bulged at her for a telling moment.

"Hi, Jan," Eden said evenly. "Mr. Caldera," she said politely.

"Thank you for coming, Ms. Harwood."

A sizzling, frisson of tension arced between them for a silent second.

He had not gotten one particle uglier since she'd last seen him. Wearier, maybe.

And then she dropped to kneel next to Annelise and cupped her face in her hands. "First, honey, are you okay?"

Annelise glumly nodded. There was only a little blood on the front of her shirt, some around the rim of a nostril. Not her first bloody nose by far. Nothing looked swollen, askew, or scraped.

"Okay. Annelise, I need to tell you—I am so disappointed in you. *How* many times have I told you that violence is not the answer to anything?"

"Eden, why don't you have a seat." Gabe's voice, bass and smoke, reasonable, soothing, sexy as a pair of arms looped around her.

Fucker.

Eden took a seat in the chair they'd commuted to the sex couch in.

"I'm afraid your daughter started it, Eden," Jan said. Because naturally she had to take control.

"Mom, I did not! Caitlynn said *I* was a liar and my *mom* was a liar, and *no one* calls my mom a liar! She's *not* a liar! And what I said was true!" She thumped a furious little ankle against the chair leg. "It's *true*, right, Mom? He came over to our house and he had dinner with our family and everything."

Oh, shit, indeed. Eden was starting to get the gist.

"So Caitlynn said to you . . ."

"That you were lying about who my father is!"

"And *that's* when you hit her?"

"I told her she was a liar for calling my mom a liar. She got mad and pushed me a little."

"And *that's* when you hit her?"

"I didn't hit her!"

"But—why are we here?"

"I swept her legs," Annelise said with matter-of-fact resignation.

Caitlynn nodded confirmation of this.

A startled silence ensued.

Gabe pressed his lips together. "Your first move was to sweep her legs?" He actually sounded a little curious.

"Bam, down I went," Caitlynn added, just as matter-of-factly. Sounding, in truth, impressed.

Another silence ensued, involving the adults.

"Her . . . her Uncle Jesse taught her that last Christmas," Eden said. Somewhat apologetically.

Gabe looked at her. And regardless of all that had happened between them, she could tell he was struggling not to laugh.

"Useful to know in some circumstances," he said mildly enough. "We were taught how to do that sort of thing when I was a SEAL. But it's not a move typically used on school playgrounds by fifth grade girls. It seldom seems necessary."

That was so dry it almost made Eden laugh.

"Well, after that, Caitlynn jumped up again and pulled my hair. And then I think we hit each other but not on the face."

"Caitlynn could have been badly hurt!" Jan was practically quivering.

"Kids get hurt, Jan," Eden defended, irritably, though truthfully she was mortified. "They *play* rougher than this all the time with each other."

"But this was *combat*."

"Jan." Gabe's voice was a little bit too quiet, and the little hairs rose on the back of Eden's neck.

It got Jan's attention for sure. She went as still as if Gabe was a predator.

"You know I was actually in combat, right? Please. I understand your outrage, but let's try to keep to the facts. Hyperbole isn't useful."

Jan pressed her lips together, took in a long breath. Then gave a short nod.

Annelise's head shot up alertly, and she stared at Gabe. Then she ducked it again.

"H-y-p-e-r-b-o-l-e," Gabe repeated patiently. Because he knew exactly what she wanted.

Eden stared at him. An epiphany arrived with a throat lump, when she thought, *That's why I'm in love with you, you asshole. Right there.*

He knew her. He knew Annelise. And he gave Annelise the gift of a new word.

And he had taken himself away from them.

Eden's eyes began to sting.

She sucked in a sharp breath in an effort to get a grip.

"I'd like to speak to Annelise for a moment, if it's all right."

Eden turned to Annelise. "Okay, first, Leesy, I appreciate your loyalty and your defense of the truth, and it's a fine quality. But there are other ways of handling this situation, and you know it. I want you to apologize to Mr. Caldera and to Caitlynn and Caitlynn's mom for resorting to physically fighting right now."

"But—"

"*Right now.* Regardless of the provocation, violence is

not the answer. You know a lot of words and you know how to use them, so there is absolutely no reason to fight, unless you're actually defending yourself physically."

"She *start*—"

Eden fixed her with a glare that ought to have reduced her to sparkly pink ashes.

Annelise *immediately* said, "I'm sorry, Caitlynn, Mrs. Pennington. Mr. Caldera."

But her lip was quivering. From frustration as much as woe.

"Caitlynn? Is there anything you want to say?" This was Jan Pennington in mom mode. Bless her.

Caitlynn was now looking down at her lap. "Sorry," she muttered.

She showed no signs of wanting to look up ever again.

Another little silence fell. Eden looked around her again. At the couch, and the baseball, and the clock in the corner that had once been basically an orgasm countdown.

"You girls have so much in common," Gabe said in that soothing voice that made everyone in the room unclench just a little. "You're excellent students and charming, hardworking girls, and a little competition makes both of you better. Having a worthy opponent is something to be grateful for, because a worthy opponent in academics or sports make you try your best. There's a lot to like about each other. So let's talk about why you *don't* like—"

"We do like each other!" Caitlynn and Annelise burst out at the same time.

Astonished.

Which clearly astonished the adults.

"Like, a lot," Annelise reiterated, while Caitlynn nodded vigorously. And swiped her eyes with her hand.

Two bright little pair of eyes stared in puzzlement at Gabe.

A nonplussed silence fell upon the room.

Gabe said suddenly, almost sharply, as if he'd had an epiphany. "Caitlynn, what exactly did you say to Annelise?"

She ducked her head, embarrassed. "Her dad," she mumbled.

"Can you speak up please."

"I teased her about her dad."

Eden curled her fingers into the arm of her chair.

"*Why* did you do that?" Gabe kept his voice even. But she could see in the set of his shoulders how pissed he was.

"Because it's the only thing that gets her worked up! I didn't expect her to go *nuts*!" She looked at Annelise. Half in indignation, half in admiration.

"Caitlynn," Jan Pennington said with great, strained patience, "why on earth do you want to get Annelise worked up?"

A long silence ensued.

"Caitlynn . . ." Jan prompted. More sternly.

"Because . . . because she's so *good* at everything!" Caitlynn's lip was trembling now.

"But so are you!" Everyone in the room said that to Caitlynn. In genuine surprise.

"But I have to *try* really hard. She just . . . she just is *good*!"

And then to everyone's astonishment, Caitlynn burst into noisy gulping tears.

"Oh, honey," Eden and Jan said at the same time, to both girls, collectively.

Eden whipped out a wad of Kleenex, already primed at the top of her purse—she'd done that like a soldier loading a gun before she got here—and handed it to Jan, who handed it to Caitlynn, who snorkeled noisily into it while her mom circled her hand on her back.

"But I do have to try! And I have to try *hard* in math," Annelise said, and reached across her mom to gently pet Caitlynn's arm. "Sometimes my mom even has to make me."

Which was both funny and all too true.

"Is it all right if I say something? To both girls?" Gabe interjected.

Gabe's voice was balm. Sunshine after rain. Precisely the right tone.

"Please do."

"You two girls make your parents so proud. But that competitive streak—well, you know, it's a good thing in many ways. It'll help you excel, and I know you both want to excel. But you have to be in charge of it, and not let it be in charge of *you*. It's better to excel for your *own* sake. And remember, it takes real courage and maturity to be kind. You can still be a fierce competitor and a nice person. You can make each other better and stronger," Gabe reiterated.

"It's not always easy to be nice when you really want to win," Annelise said sadly.

"Tell me about it, kiddo," Eden said. "Trust me, it

gets easier with practice, and we're going to make sure you practice. You know how I know? I'm the same way. You're your mother's daughter, kid."

Annelise always loved being called her mother's daughter. Eden suspected this wouldn't always be true. But for now she basked in Annelise's breathtakingly sweet smile.

Which was part Jasper, that smile.

She wondered if Gabe noticed, too.

Jan cleared her throat. "I confess Caitlynn probably gets her competitive streak from me, too. Her dad is a little more laid-back, even though he's a successful city councilman."

Jan seldom missed an opportunity to slip that into conversation.

And yet it was clear that some of the tension was seeping out of her. She was a mom, after all. And while neurotic, she wasn't insane. Or a monster.

"And Caitlynn . . ." Gabe began, then paused. As if considering—or reconsidering—what he was about to say.

He thumped his pencil a couple of times. Everyone waited.

At last he breathed in what sounded like a steadying breath, then exhaled. "I know that sometimes when we're scared about losing something, or not being good enough, sometimes we lash out, but then we end up . . . end up feeling bad about it, and it's worse than before. If you feel that way, it's best to just be honest about it, rather than hurt someone . . . someone you . . . like."

Eden stared at him wonderingly.

Hope flared like the sunlight in her chest. Its sudden presence made her realize how dark and cramped her life had felt without it. Without him.

But Gabe was deliberately not looking at her.

"Okay, Mr. Caldera," Caitlynn said.

"One more thing," Eden said. "I'd like to know *exactly* just what Caitlynn said about your dad."

"Well, she said my dad could be *anyone*. Like she said before."

Spots of color rose in Jan's cheeks. Guilt spots, if Eden had to guess.

And Eden dug her nails into her palm. If only she could have spared her baby any of this. If only life was as sensible and orderly as she wanted it to be.

"And I said I *knew* who my dad was. My dad is Jasper Townes. And that I met him and talked to him and he's *great* and he gave me this." Annelise held up the guitar pick. "And he's going to donate a guitar to our raffle! He said! And he might even sing a song, too!"

Incredulity illuminated Jan's expression. And then she shot Gabe a speaking look, complete with a *can you believe this lunacy?* head tilt, which made Eden bite down so hard on her molars it was a wonder sparks didn't shoot from her ears.

Gabe was so still. Like an animal about to pounce.

"Annelise? Caitlynn?" He sounded very stern and official. "You'll of course both have detention after school for the rest of the week. For now, would you please have a seat out front with Mrs. Maker, and close the door as you leave? I'd like to have a word with your moms privately."

The subdued girls scooted out.

Jan pivoted toward him instantly.

"Gabe, do you think Eden ought to be . . . spreading that kind of fiction? I mean, while Eden either doesn't know or would prefer not to divulge her daughter's parentage, doesn't perpetuating nonsense make matters worse?"

"Mrs. Pennington, Eden is perfectly capable of answering your questions, and it's up to her to decide whether they're any of your business. She is not obligated to answer them. Please address them to her."

The tone was icily, dangerously remote.

Red flooded into Jan's cheeks.

But she was also intrepid. "But honestly, Eden, *Jasper Townes*?" Her voice was a little creaky. "The singer for Blue Room? I mean, if you're going to make something up out of thin air, make it believable. That poor child is going to get a complex, and you're opening her up to ridicule if you . . ."

Eden's steady, patient stare finally penetrated.

Jan went utterly motionless. And then a whole paradise of fascinating emotions chased themselves across her face.

"You're . . . *serious*, aren't you?" Jan breathed. "It's true?"

Eden gave her a rueful "what can ya do?" smile. And a little one-shouldered shrug.

Jan's eyes were enormous now.

"That show he did . . . ten years ago." She was nearly stammering. "At the Misty Cat. You were there . . . I remember seeing you . . . and you . . ."

"I remember seeing you, too," Eden said evenly.

Jan was studying Eden, her face so taut that Eden could practically see the dozens of questions working beneath its surface.

"Was he good?" Jan blurted finally. On a hush.

Boy, Eden wasn't expecting that one.

"He looks like he'd be really good in bed. Oh, God, sorry, sorry. That's awful. No, don't answer that. I'm just a little surprised by the news. Don't answer unless you want to. Ha ha. I mean, no, sorry. Oh, God, I'm sorry, it's . . . just Jasper *Townes*?"

It was fair to say that Jan was struggling to contain the impulse to indulge in a tizzy.

Eden met Gabe's eyes.

There ensued an outrageously intimate, complicated, silent exchange. Because she could tell that Gabe *wanted* her to fuck with Jan, even if he suffered pain in the process. And he *would* suffer pain.

Because the opportunity was just too good to pass up.

"He was . . . creative," she confided in Jan gravely.

Jan froze. And stared at her.

Then she made a tiny whimpering sound.

Gabe closed his eyes briefly. Gave his head a little shake.

God how she hated being a source of pain for him. And loved that he knew why this was unbelievably funny.

She sighed. How she longed for emotions that weren't hybrid: humor without anguish or guilt. Or love without longing.

"Look, Jan," she said, "it's been intense. Pretty good

so far, but intense. Annelise is more than a little keyed up from the news, as you can imagine, though she seems pleased to know the truth and we're all actually doing okay. We're still working our way through it, and that means Jasper, too. We'd rather not deliberately make it public, if we can help it, and I know Jasper is keeping it under wraps, too, for Annelise's sake. Maybe you can explain this gently to Caitlynn. Even so, I'll be able to handle whatever comes up, if it does become public knowledge. But this is such a delicate time in Annelise's life. I could use the support of someone as strong and smart as you. I would so appreciate it if you would keep all of this to yourself."

Gabe was watching this with an expression, if she had to give it a name, akin to something like pride. More rueful than that.

"Of course, Eden. You've got my support. Whatever I can do."

"Thank you."

She smiled so warmly at Jan that Jan's own face erupted into a sloppy, charming smile of bonhomie.

"Maybe we can get the girls together for a play date, just the two of them. Maybe take them up to Devil's Leap to visit with my sister's animals, or go swimming up there."

"And maybe have a glass of wine," Jan added.

"And definitely have a glass of wine."

They smiled at each other again.

Eden turned back to Gabe. "Sorry to take up more of your time, Mr. Caldera. And I apologize again for Annelise's behavior, no matter the circumstances. I'll have a long talk with her about it. And I'll do my best to make sure it never happens again."

"Yes, thank you, Gabe. And I'll make sure Caitlynn understands the consequences of her actions, as well," Jan said to both Gabe and Eden. "And now, I must be off."

She scooped up her sweater and her handbag.

Eden was about to follow her just as quickly.

"Eden," Gabe said gruffly.

She turned.

"Don't," he said simply.

"Don't . . ."

". . . feel guilty about Townes being Annelise's father and how it happened or Annelise getting into a fight. Because I know you're feeling guilty right now. None of us really gets much of a say in our parents."

She was dumbstruck.

"How'd you . . ."

She stopped.

They *got* each other. That was how he'd known to say that.

She hovered there, her entire being twisted like a rag over knowledge of what they could have had. They got each other, but fundamental things in their characters— pride and stubbornness and a need to win—had blown it apart.

Why didn't she know how to fix that?

Mrs. Maker appeared in the doorway. "Mr. Caldera, your next appointment is here," she said, and melted away.

"And thanks for coming in, Ms. Harwood." He dropped his eyes.

His voice had gone formal, pleasant, abstracted, a busy administrator politely dismissing an appointment and moving on to the next line on his calendar, ready to move on to whatever he had next on his plate.

He seemed to be looking at his iPad. His palm was resting on his baseball.

CHAPTER 20

Among the biggest of the veritable confetti storm of surprises lately was the fact that Jan Pennington seemed to have stuck to her word about keeping the news of Jasper Townes on the down-low. If she hadn't, the entire town would be showing up at Eden's Garden with questions like "I read he has a pierced willy. Does he?" and variations thereof. (His willy was unadorned back then. She couldn't speak for his willy decorations now, and didn't anticipate being able to do that any time in the future, either.)

But the final event of Hellcat Canyon Elementary's fund-raising month—the raffle, during which they usually netted the kinds of amounts that would help them replace old banks of lockers, for instance, or paint a few classrooms—was this weekend.

Annelise was so beside herself with the prospect of her dad Jasper showing up and bringing a guitar to raffle off that she enacted the event with her Barbies. Scrotal Ken played the part of Jasper; she'd created a wig for him out of the hair she'd scraped from her own hairbrush. She'd constructed a little guitar and a stage, complete with a curtain. Chrissie played the role of Annelise.

And Eden didn't know if this was about the Caitlynn rivalry, or finally having a dad, or having a particularly glamorous dad. Or whether the raffle fever had taken on a life of its own and was a fever for the sake of being worked up about something. Annelise loved a little drama.

"He might be so busy, Annelise, or in the middle of something that makes it hard for him to get here." Eden suggested this lightly. "We can still enjoy the raffle if that happens, though. They're going to have a DJ and we can dance!"

"He won't forget, Mom! He wants to do better than Caitlynn's mom, too! You heard what he said."

Leesy was so *certain*. She was accustomed to adults who had whiteboard calendars and muscular senses of responsibility, adults who would practically prefer to die rather than disappoint her. She wasn't a spoiled kid, but she trusted the world because grown-ups kept their word and kept her safe.

So no matter what Eden had already told her, she still couldn't conceptualize an adult who didn't quite act like one.

And Eden was left to wonder if perhaps she had done her daughter a disservice by making sure her life ran along a mostly smooth track, or by introducing the wild card of Jasper Townes into it.

All Eden knew was that if Jasper flaked, she would have to be the one to see Annelise's baffled, devastated face. The one who would have to teach Leesy how to accommodate shredded pride and a broken heart. Even as her own heart was still reeling from the battering she'd endured—or subjected it to—thanks to Gabe.

She kept replaying in her mind the advice he'd given Caitlynn Pennington: about how being afraid could lead to lashing out. Had it really been a coded message to her? Her heart lurched at the idea of Gabe being afraid. Once or twice she'd seized her phone intending to text him, but then her nerve had failed. What would she say? What would *he* say? Gabe was his father's son. He saw things in black and white, too.

She'd texted Jasper, though. Just once.

Because, so help her, this was a test, too. She reminded him of the date of the raffle once, but she could and would not be the person who nagged him like a mother.

And as of the morning of the raffle, she hadn't heard back from him.

But even if Jan hadn't added her two drops to the little river of gossip that flowed through Hellcat Canyon, it was the buzz in the hallways of school: that Annelise Harwood had a big surprise in store for the raffle. Theories ranged from a full-fledged concert by Blue Room with Annelise and Beyoncé singing backup and free guitars as party favors for everyone, to the notion that Annelise Harwood was making stuff up just to get attention.

Annelise didn't necessarily *object* to attention.

She *hated* being suspected of making stuff up just to make stuff up.

"When they bug you, Annelise, just smile like this . . ." Eden demonstrated a Cheshire cat smile. ". . . and say, '*you'll* see.'"

Annelise grimaced. "*You'll* see. Like that?"

Eden crossed her eyes and wrinkled her nose. "Like this. *You'll* see."

They stood in front of the bathroom mirror and practiced, and pretty soon wound up cracking up over it.

G abe was worried, too.

He wasn't cursed with an overactive imagination—imaginations were often instruments of torture, as far as he was concerned. But no matter how he looked at it, both eventualities—Jasper Townes showing up as a dazzling hero and star of the raffle, and a hero in Annelise's and therefore Eden's eyes, or Jasper Townes bailing entirely—the evening would be well nigh unbearable.

The night of the raffle . . .

E den was right, Gabe thought. Jan really did deserve a parade for all she accomplished. Damn her and bless her.

The auditorium was a festival of blue and gold streamers and balloons, and little round tables—draped in white tablecloths and dotted with miniature bouquets of geraniums courtesy of Eden's Garden—were arranged in clusters around a dance floor created just for the occasion. Every seat was filled, and everyone, judging from all the laughter, was having a wonderful time.

And Gabe hung back against the wall and observed as Mrs. Clapper, the gregarious sixth grade geometry teacher, strolled across the stage with a microphone. She was great at getting the crowd lathered up to buy raffle tickets, and it was usually pretty fun to watch, a bit like witnessing Ruth Bader Ginsburg doing Vanna White's job. Every donation featured a little display of some kind—a poster, a dressmaker's dummy, that sort of thing—for illustrative purposes, and because it was free advertising for local businesses.

She stopped in front of a glossy placard featuring a photo of laughing party guests pulling meat off skewers with their teeth.

"And from Truck Donegal, we have—a catered event for *twenty*! Wow, this is a deal! Whether it's a baby shower? Gender reveal? Funeral? You can count on Truck to be there!"

Laughter erupted from the audience.

Truck looked uncertain about why this was funny, but he decided to smile. It was pretty universally accepted in Hellcat Canyon that his chicken satay was indeed out of this world.

Mrs. Clapper next strolled over to a dress form bedecked in a beguiling, silky, flowing tent of a dress. She grasped one corner of it and swept it up and out with a flourish.

"Next we have—from Kayla Benoit of Kayla Benoit's Boutique—The Whatever Comes First Package—a wedding dress or a five-piece maternity wardrobe! I know a lot of mamas-to-be out there who would be absolutely lovely in both. If you have a mama or a bride-to-be in your life, you're going to want to buy a lot of tickets now, aren't you?"

Plenty of whoops for Kayla, who was sitting next to Truck, much to Casey Carson's angst. Casey was sitting with Eden and Annelise and Avalon and Mac.

Annelise Harwood, in a pink dress featuring sparkles at the sleeves for the occasion, was literally bouncing up and down on the edge of her seat, swinging her legs and scanning the stage, her face alight with joyous expectation. Eden sat next to her, a few strategic soft spirals spilling from her piled up hair, her spine rigid. Gabe went breathless. She looked beautiful. Also, tense as a board.

Mrs. Clapper strolled next to a lavishly floral trifold board with Eden's Garden logo across the top and a photo of a delighted woman, hands clapped to her face, mouth opened in an O, receiving a bouquet of flowers from a beaming delivery person.

"'From Eden's Garden,'" Mrs. Clapper read from her little cards. "'The I Love You–I'm Sorry–Congratulations! package—a dozen roses sent to three people of your choice!' You just have to use it inside a year! Holy smokes, Eden, that is one fantastic prize. Everyone wants to say those things to someone throughout the year, am I right? What a classy way to do it!"

Happy applause indicated approval, and Eden nodded in acknowledgment.

"Moving on—from the Misty Cat Tavern—a year's

free pass to all special events! And for those of you who attended the Jasper Townes Black & Blue show recently, you know how *amazing* this prize is! Thanks to Glenn and Sherrie Harwood, the two of you are fabulous."

Lot of hooting here, for Sherrie and Glenn and the Misty Cat and Blue Room equally, probably, which made Gabe grit his teeth.

Because there was an empty place on the stage where a prize should be.

And that empty spot might as well have been spotlighted. Because everyone who had bought a ticket knew that something *belonged* there, and something clearly *wasn't* there. And a lot of them knew that whatever belonged there was donated by Annelise Harwood.

And as Beth Clapper, geometry teacher extraordinaire, strolled down the line of raffle prizes, working her way skillfully and cheerfully through all of them, getting closer and closer to that empty spot, a little more of the bouncy exuberance and light went out of Annelise.

Until she was utterly still.

A condition completely unnatural for her.

Gabe swore viciously under his breath. He knew definitively that the promised guitar suddenly wasn't going to materialize on the stage. Showman or not, Townes wasn't going to burst through the double doors of the auditorium when he was due to go on-stage in about ten minutes at a stadium almost two hours away.

That fucker had welched.

Jasper Townes had flaked.

If it looked like a duck and walked like a duck, Gabe thought grimly, it would fuck you over like a duck.

He felt zero satisfaction. Something glacial and jagged seemed to have lodged itself in his sternum. He sicced his mind on the problem like a junkyard dog.

Gabe glanced at his phone. Five minutes to eight o'clock.

He silently consigned Jasper Townes to hell.

Although hell would have to wait. Right now Townes was probably getting a preshow massage, gargling with pearls and champagne or something.

Then he'd strut out onto a stage in front of a sea of ecstatic, screaming fans and make noise while his image was projected twenty feet high behind him in case someone at the tippy top of the stadium missed seeing the sweat beading on his lip as he sang.

While a bewildered little girl waited for him to show up with his guitar, and shrank in her seat, and the light in her dimmed, and bore the kind of humiliation she likely would never forget.

A desperate fury made him feel hollow.

And then Eden turned and said something to Annelise, draped her arm around her shoulders. The lights in the auditorium briefly revealed silvery tracks beneath Annelise's eyes. Annelise brushed at her face and smiled hugely, like a Cheshire cat.

But she'd been crying.

Gabe closed his eyes. Drew in a long, ragged breath.

Right now Eden was probably formulating the first of what would likely turn out to be a million excuses for Townes in order to forestall the inevitable crushing of trust. She was getting ready to withstand the sympathy and gloating and curiosity of everyone in her town. Based on a decision she'd had to make in a manner of minutes.

And with a blinding clarity he knew there was literally nothing he wouldn't do for her. No matter what. Nothing mattered, not his pride or his feelings, not who said what when. It all seemed patently ridiculous to care about these things when all he wanted out of life was to make things right for Eden.

And he knew exactly what to do now. It was his own sort of Hail Mary.

So basically Jasper Townes had given him a gift.

Mrs. Maker appeared at his elbow holding a clipboard. "All set to launch the raffle, Mr. Caldera?"

"Hey, Donna? Give me five minutes."

"Have to tinkle?" she whispered sympathetically.

"Just don't go anywhere until I get back." He inadvertently used his lieutenant voice. Which made her blink. "And please tell Mrs. Clapper she'll have to take over the prize calling duties. She's doing great."

"Yes, *sir.*"

"Mama . . . I don't see a guitar on the stage yet. Do you?"

"No, honey. Not yet, honey."

Eden felt as though a guitar pick were lodged in her throat. How could anyone look at Annelise, promise her something, and then *bail*? How could you not want to move heaven and earth to give her the moon? How the hell dare he insinuate himself into their lives, raise Annelise's hopes . . . and not say a damn thing about not showing up? How could he put her through this?

It had been a test, not just for him. And now Eden felt as though she'd failed it.

She was holding her body rigidly, as if to protect it from blows. Because it hurt. Every muscle in her body was locked thanks to a mix of rage and grief and impending heartbreak. Her daughter's, hers. It was all the same. She had anticipated this. It didn't mean she was ready for it.

She didn't see Gabe anywhere.

"Do you think maybe he'll appear on a platform on the back of the stage and there will be smoke and stuff and then he'll have the guitar?"

And finally Eden couldn't speak. She'd run out of things to say to reassure or deflect.

She wanted the moment of humiliation to be over, so she could get to the part where she searched out an excuse for Annelise, one that would take that worried expression from her face, restore some of her inherent faith in the trustworthiness of adults.

Eden knew it wouldn't be the last time in Annelise's life someone she'd decided to trust had let her down. No one got through life unscathed like that. But a little bit of innocence was lost the first time it happened, and it never returned, and it was too soon, too soon for her baby to become jaded.

Fuck.

Mrs. Clapper was talking. ". . . and last, but *definitely*, not least, the very, very special prize donated by Annelise Harwood herself . . ."

She glanced to the empty spot on the stage.

Which was where every eye in the place was fixed.

Until they all swiveled over to where Eden and Annelise were sitting.

Mrs. Clapper pushed her glasses up a little higher on her face and cleared her throat into the microphone.

Long, awkward silences were typically followed by a whole audience full of curious murmurs, Eden knew. It was only a matter of seconds before those started up.

". . . um, it seems we are miss . . ."

She trailed off at the sight of Mrs. Maker, breathing hard, bolting down the aisle with her skirt hiked a little to free her knees for running, her tethered glasses bouncing on her magnificent bosom. She bound like a gazelle up the little flight of stairs to the stage, a veritable advertisement for Hush Puppy pumps.

She tugged Mrs. Clapper's arm, and Mrs. Clapper's torso bent sideways so Mrs. Maker could whisper in her ear.

Then she handed the bemused but unruffled Mrs. Clapper a note card.

She frowned down at it, then pushed her reading glasses up higher on her face. And her face lit like a lamp as she read, "'. . . from Annelise Harwood, a baseball signed by none other than Joe DiMaggio! Joltin' Joe DiMaggio! The Yankee Clipper himself!'" She gave a little hop as she announced this. "Woo-hoo, that's a humdinger of a prize!"

A collective gasp seemed to rustle the streamers.

Eden's hands went up to her mouth. "Oh my God," she murmured, her eyes burning.

Gabe might have just handed over his heart to be raffled.

("He can't just *hand* over his heart, Eden. For God's sake."—Dr. Jude Harwood.)

The auditorium echoed with delighted WOOOOOOOs and thunderous applause. Maybe that prize wasn't what everyone had expected, but who the hell cared? It was a Joe DiMaggio baseball!

"That thing is worth at *least* a thousand bucks," a guy near Eden marveled over the sound of the crowd. "I want it!"

"You can buy five tickets," his wife said sternly but lovingly. "Only five."

"Awwww," he said sadly.

Grins and thumbs-ups were aimed at Eden and Annelise.

Eden looked up and caught Jan Pennington's eyes on her. Her expression was kind of hard to read. She didn't appear to be gloating, however. Eden was pretty sure she'd be able to spot a gloat from across the auditorium.

She tried to smile.

But she found herself turning to curl her arm around Annelise again. She tucked her head against hers and briefly buried her face in Leesy's hair, buying a moment alone with her joy. It was too overwhelming and too personal; she was not prepared for the whole auditorium to see the contents of her heart writ large on her face.

Gabe had done it because he was, indeed, his father's son. And what else had he said about his dad? "When he loved something it was for keeps. Hell or high water." An argument could be made that Jasper Townes was certainly both.

And Gabe had saved Jasper's ass for her sake and for Annelise's.

Eden saw Gabe nowhere in the crowd. She hadn't seen him all night.

Annelise's smile was uncertain, but the applause—damned if no matter what, she was her father's child, too—was making her smile. She waved, graciously.

Which almost made Eden laugh.

"I don't get it, Mama. Did my dad Jasper send a baseball instead of a guitar? And people like it?"

The truth was deceptively simple, but it had infinite strata. Now was not the time to attempt to explain strata. Yet she couldn't bring herself to lie to Annelise about something sacred.

All she said was, "Yes, people love it, honey."

"And the baseball is good, right?" Annelise heard the roars of approval.

Still, it wouldn't be official until her mom—the person she trusted more than any other person in the world—confirmed it.

"It's *wonderful*, honey. It's the best thing here, truly! People are going to want it, and you'll make a lot of money for the school and everyone will be so happy and proud and grateful to you, because it's because of you. The baseball is the kind of thing that people will cher . . ." She swallowed. Drew in a breath. ". . . cherish their whole lives."

"Yay!" Annelise brightened, her world restored to rightness. But her light dimmed a little when she turned to Eden and put a hand on her knee. "But Mama, why are you crying?"

"You silly, I'm not *crying*. I just got something in my eye."

The backstage area of the Glenco Arena was teeming with people coiling cords and pushing big containers this way and that, strolling past each other and saying things like "Great show, man," and "Hot solo on 'Old and Fucked Up,' Townes!"

"Great show, man," Gabe called to Jasper. Just to get his attention.

In truth, he'd just arrived about five minutes ago.

Jasper froze.

"Oh, shit," he said sincerely, by way of greeting.

"That's right," Gabe agreed.

They stared at each other.

Townes had a towel draped around his neck and his idiosyncratic hair was glued back from his face with sweat. He looked quite weary but still lit from within. It probably was a pretty transcendent show. No one could say the guy didn't work for his money.

"How did you get back here, Principal Gabe? Rappel down the stadium wall like G.I. Joe?"

"As it so happens, I served with the head of your security team in Afghanistan. He was happy to let me have a backstage pass. He knew me as Lieutenant Caldera back then."

He'd made that phone call about the backstage pass on the way to the stadium, and he'd condensed the long drive into about an hour, too.

Gabe knew the shortcuts.

And all the state troopers on the way, if it came to that.

Jasper gave a short, unamused laugh. "Did Eden put a hit out on me? Did they teach you to do the Vulcan pinch in the SEALs? If you saw my show, you know I'm a great screamer. I don't have time for whatever this is, Caldera. It's on to the next town, as usual."

He shot a desperate look at his tour bus.

Gabe stood between him and it.

"Eden doesn't know I'm here at all. But I think you know why I'm here. It's about an auditorium full of people who now think Annelise Harwood totally made you up. She only cried a little."

Jasper closed his eyes. He heaved a huge sigh. He opened his eyes again. He looked genuinely uncomfortable.

Gabe waited.

Jasper pressed his lips together. "Like I said, I was just getting ready to pack up—"

"You don't have a second to talk to a veteran?" Gabe raised his voice sonorously in hurt surprise.

A person with a press pass stopped so comically short his shoes made a screeching sound on the concrete.

Jasper sighed. "Oh, for fuck's . . . come with me." He strode over to the bus and yanked open the door. "Hey, everyone, can you clear out for a second? I want to have a chat with . . . an old friend."

A gaggle of women and men, all woolly head hair, exposed midriffs and tattoos, emerged on great plumes of weed-scented smoke and dutifully filed off.

The bus was luxurious, but not ostentatious. It smelled like pot and sweaty people.

"Want a beer?" Jasper yanked open a mini fridge.

"Sure."

Jasper flipped the beer out backward like he was pitching a fastball.

Gabe caught it with one hand.

Coors Light. Pretty funny choice. He hefted it, bemused.

"I grew up drinking these," Jasper explained. He took a seat on a plump padded sofa. Gabe sat opposite him on its twin.

"Me, too. Coors, that is. Not the light ones."

"It's weird, but I find it comforting when I'm traveling a lot. They keep wanting to foist Cristal on me. Yes, I hear how that sounds."

"No, I get it. Good beer tastes great, but cheap beer tastes like I'm about to lose my virginity to Deborah Bellacino at a kegger. And that's a damn good flavor."

Jasper gave a short, tense laugh. "I'm going to steal that line for a song, Caldera."

"Knock yourself out."

There was a little silence.

"You know what I'm doing here?" Gabe said idly after a moment.

Jasper didn't say anything for quite a long time.

That was fine. Gabe wasn't going anywhere. Besides, this was an unbelievably comfortable sofa.

Townes finally leaned toward him a little. "I once thought I was tough, Caldera. I mean, and sure, maybe I am tough. I mean, you batter pretty much anything enough and it gets a tough outer shell, right? Calluses? And so forth? I've stared down any number of tattoo needles."

"Heh. Yeah. I have the internet. I know your sad origin story."

"I can deal with bad reviews, hecklers, distorted stories in the press, angry women . . . I don't love it, but it comes with the territory, and I've learned how to deal with it."

"Your point?"

"Tough . . ." Jasper gulped some of the Coors. ". . . ain't the same as brave."

Gabe took this in. Jasper was clearly getting around to the point in the way of a storyteller.

"Oh, I don't know. I think standing in front of thousands of people in that getup is pretty brave."

"Hey, I'm working these pants, man." Jasper wasn't the least offended. His jeans looked as though they'd been dragged behind a semitruck on a bad highway for about forty miles. "But back to my point, Caldera, and I do realize I'm taking a while to get to it . . . you're a brave guy, right? I mean, you've been shot at. Probably. I'm guessing."

"Sure. I was doing my job."

Jasper gave an exasperated laugh and shook his head. "Oh, *c'mon*," Jasper said irritably, "cut the noble shit. That's how everyone defines 'brave.' Willingly getting shot or blown up. Defending people. Rushing into burning buildings. There has to be danger for someone to be brave, right? Doing the right thing, even when it's hard, even when you really don't want to or when you're afraid you're going to fuck it up. And so forth. That's what brave is. And I don't like knowing it, but I know definitively I am not that guy. I am not brave. Tonight was the culmination of me recognizing the magnitude of something I'd gotten myself into with Annelise and chickening out. She's going to want things from me. Like . . . consistency. And follow-through. I'm going to have to think about what I do and say because it'll get back to her, and I've never had to do that before. And I want her to *like* me. Even love me. Her family hates me. And I . . ." He sank back against the sofa and pressed his lips together again.

Gabe was familiar with the tactic of easily accepting blame. It could disarm an argument pretty fast.

Townes was not going to get off easy.

"First," Gabe said easily, "I meant what I said. It's a job. I was fit for it and I did it. Just like your job is to get up there and make people go 'woooooo!' and then go home and tattoo quotes from your songs on their bodies and regret it in a decade when they try to get grown-up jobs. Mine was to occasionally come close to getting killed. Also, to make sure no other members of my team were killed. An oversimplification, but when you have a job to do, and you have an affinity for it, you do it well. I was good at it. Just like I'm good at being a school principal now. I can manage and read circumstances and people. And . . . you do what you do. Extraordinarily well. Other things—things that have no precedent in your life, things that are entirely new—take practice."

"Okay, Caldera, I get what you're saying. Here's the problem with that. You know how when you were a kid, and you're mouthing off to your mom and you make a face and Mom would tell you your face would freeze that way?"

"Sure."

"Getting through my childhood—totally rootless, didn't have a dad, my mom wasn't cuddly—I had to be completely self-focused and you know what? I've mostly been great with it. I have no real ties holding me down. I've been pretty fucking awfully cavalier with the feelings of women and the excuse I always use is 'that's just how I am.'" He used air quotes and hunched, palms upward, parodying himself. "I've never been proud of that, but it's just kind of . . . the groove I've worn through life, and I keep sliding along in that groove. Or maybe it's a rut. Anyway. It's also not working for me anymore. Hasn't been for some time. I swear on . . ." He threw his arms out in a gesture like a conjurer, encompassing the trailer, the arena, the guitars, ostensibly, his entire life as a rock star. ". . . all of this that I do want to be part of Annelise's life. I want to be better. It just . . . it just started to snowball on me, man. I realized that this one little person is going to want me to do what I say I'm going to do, and . . . I promised something I realized I couldn't deliver and . . . I just . . ."

He lifted up both hands and splayed his fingers. "I freaked. I lost my nerve. I'm a balls-out coward."

Gabe nodded thoughtfully. Then leaned back. "Okay, Townes. Like I said, I know your life story. But here's the thing. When a kid—your kid—is involved, how you got the way you are doesn't factor. That's between you and your shrink. Right now you're not a rock god or some poor fatherless kid. Right now you're just the asshole who broke a little girl's heart when he could have so easily been a hero."

Jasper froze. His hand tightened on the can of beer.

"And to my knowledge it's never been broken before, so you know, there's a dubious milestone for you. She trusts adults. She's innocent that way. Annelise is the most precious thing in the world to Eden, and she took the risk of allowing you into her life because that's what you wanted. Do you have any idea how tough that decision was for her? For her to share her amazing little girl with you? Do you really get it? When you broke Annelise's heart, you broke her mother's heart. And I'll be *damned* if I let anything hurt her mother if I can do anything about it."

Gabe's voice sounded reasonable, but it gathered the tension and threat and the resonance of a vow.

Jasper pressed his lips together. He looked a little weary now; the adrenaline of a show wearing off. He did have a job. His responsibilities were vast, but less personal.

Outside a female keened drunkenly, "But I *looooove* him. I have to see Jasper. I saw him in a dreaammm—"

A scuffling sound ensued as security hauled the woman away.

Jasper didn't appear to even notice. This was the ambient noise of Jasper Townes's life, no doubt. The way crickets were the ambient sound of the woods. Recess bells and lockers slamming the sound of Gabe's.

Jasper remained motionless. His face unreadable. One hand gripping his Coors so hard it dented, the other pressed into the knee of his jeans.

"So," Gabe continued slowly, as though speaking to a child who was one transgression away from juvie, "I'm here because I'm going to offer you a chance to make it right with Annelise, and look like a big man who just made an innocent, rookie mistake. And that's all Eden or her daughter are going to know. Because I think the fact that you actually care enough to run away means you actually care enough to get your shit together around this. After that, you're on your own."

And so Gabe told Jasper his plan about how Jasper could make it right.

It was the weirdest sensation, feeling paternal toward a man not much younger than him, who was listening with all evidence of absorption. Especially a man who'd just been projected twenty feet high to a stadium of people so the ones in the cheap seats didn't miss out seeing all his sweat and contorted expressions when he launched into the solo on "Old and Fucked Up." A guy who probably had piles of money that somewhere down the road could impact Annelise's future. But not every aspect of our personalities mature all at once, Gabe knew. Something only matured once it's been tested and tempered.

For Eden and Annelise, he had to try to get the point across to Townes.

After another little silence he said, "Listen, Townes . . . the things that don't come naturally to you—like showing up for a small-town grade school raffle because you ran your mouth off and promised a little girl you would, because you were showing off or because you thought that's what you were supposed to do or you were just at a loss for conversation, who knows why you did it—that's going to take practice. You know how to practice. Let yourself off the hook for this one. It's a process. But . . . *calibrate* . . . going forward. Unless you enjoy feeling like an asshole."

Jasper's posture had eased. Gabe did not want to like the guy, but his instinct told him that, even if he failed, Jasper was sincere about wanting to try.

He was still pensive, though. He arpeggiated his fingers along the side of his beer can.

"I don't know if you're going to be in her life after this. Whatever, they'll go on. They have each other. You'll be lucky as hell to be a part of *that* family even if they kind of hate you right now. You're just going to have to try harder. But I hope one day you do love Annelise. Because if you want to be brave . . . *that's* how you get brave. You will be willing to fight ugly, and risk failure and embarrassment or anything else that makes you wake up sweating, heart racing in terror, in the middle of the night, to make sure someone you love is safe and happy. And you'll know it's love when you do it without even thinking."

Jasper reanimated then. Drained his beer in a few gulps, then meditatively, slowly crushed the can.

And sat back and regarded Gabe with his bright eyes.

"You mean you'll do stuff like showing up in the middle of the night and finagling a backstage pass and lecturing a rock star? That kind of stuff?"

Gabe stared at him.

"I guess I'm glad you're not stupid, Jasper."

Jasper's mouth curved ever so faintly. A funny smile. Achingly sad, yet pleased with himself.

Gabe stood and opened the door to the tour bus, and paused, and Jasper followed him there.

"But just so you know, Eden is not for you."

Jasper's grin grew crooked, cocky, ever so slightly jaded.

"But you haven't quite got that locked down yet, have you, brother?" He leaned indolently against the doorframe. The very picture of a rock god. "If I had to guess. And all's fair."

They stared each other down.

"Yeah, I'm not worried," Gabe said finally. With a smile cockier than any Townes could ever dream of issuing.

It might be the cruelest thing he'd said to Jasper Townes yet.

CHAPTER 21

Two days later . . .

Everyone looked up alertly when the old intercom system crackled in every classroom in session at Hellcat Canyon Elementary—teachers with a certain wariness—last time it had been employed it was because a snake had gotten loose in the biology lab and had last been seen lounging in a planter outside the library—the kids with gleeful anticipation.

Especially Annelise Harwood. Just because she'd studied for the math test didn't mean she was looking forward to it. She crossed her fingers in her lap.

Everyone knew better than to tease her about the Jasper Townes's no-show at the raffle—they didn't want their feet swept, after all. And they were all very impressed with the baseball donation. She'd accepted their congratulations regally and with the Cheshire-cat grin her mom had taught her.

Mr. Caldera's voice, soothing yet authoritative, nothing-can-possibly-go-wrong-on-my-watch voice emerged from the crackles.

"All classes report to the auditorium for a brief special assembly to begin at eleven o'clock. Please be in your seats in the auditorium at exactly five minutes to eleven o'clock. Thank you."

Principal Gabe signed off.

Teachers squelched the excited speculation, but even they yearned to text each other with speculations of their own, and mourned just a little that they were already adults and had to be reasonable and wait patiently.

At eleven o'clock sharp all butts from grades kindergarten through eight were in the auditorium chairs, wriggling and giggling.

Until Mr. Caldera strolled out onto the stage.

"Quiet please," he said into the mic.

Silence didn't so much descend as swoop. You could have heard an eyelash bat.

That's all he said.

A second later, the huge heavy old curtain, which they hoped to replace in the next fund-raiser, shimmied upward.

To reveal a thin man sitting on a stool, looking down at his lap. He was wearing jeans and boots and a bowler hat perched on a wild head of hair. A microphone was set up in front of him. He was cradling a guitar.

(The guitar was Veronica.)

The wondering murmurs started up again. And then the man took one finger and tipped the brim of his hat upward. "Better late than never, right?" he said into the mic.

With a rakish grin.

And then comprehension set in.

A gleeful pandemonium erupted. WOOOOOOOOOs and stomps and squeals. Annelise was practically doing jumping jacks.

This was exactly the kind of entrance Jasper loved.

He cleared his throat and like magic, everyone settled down and went silent.

"This song is a work in progress, but I'm calling it 'Annelise in A minor.'"

He strummed a wistful progression, lilting and arpeggiate.

And then he crooned over the chords.

"Annelise . . . oh Annelise . . .
The wind in the trees sings of sweet Annelise.
The bees hum to me have you seen Annelise . . .
And when I make a grilled cheese I woooooonder . . .
what Annelise . . .
is . . . doing . . . now."

He whispered that last sentence. Just like she'd suggested.

Annelise was hopping up and down in her chair in an absolute conniption of vindication and joy, that's what she was doing now.

For the rest of her life, she would never forget this moment or that song.

Jasper waited patiently, grinning while the auditorium screamed approval. He had another song up his sleeve.

"I guess today is a day for songs about girls."

And he strummed the first notes of "Lily Anne." And it was fair to say that the entire auditorium, from the kids to the teachers, freaked out.

"Hey, Lily Anne

I've never been so glad to be a man . . .
Let me show you that I understand
How to make you feel like a woman . . ."

Despite himself, Gabe was enthralled. He didn't care what anyone said, that was a freaking great song.

He wasn't going to forget this moment, either.

"Lily Anne" brought the Hellcat Elementary house down. A full two minutes worth of screaming and stomping and clapping ensued.

Then Jasper raised a hand in a wave and bent his long lanky body into a bow just as Mr. Caldera strolled onstage again and made a "cut it" gesture with his hand. Everyone went silent.

"Thank you all," Jasper said. "You're all beautiful, and so is Hellcat Canyon. Wish I could stay, but I've got to get onto the next show in the next town."

He stepped well aside when Gabe took over the mic.

"Let's all give Mr. Townes a huge hand and a thank-you. He just made a remarkably generous donation to our music department—we're going to have brand-new instruments. *And* he's going to stop by once a year to give us all a little music lesson."

Just like Gabe had kind of given Jasper a little lesson.

That was because Gabe drove a really hard bargain.

And Jasper Townes, who hated to fly . . . flew to his next gig.

Gabe returned to his office after that assembly feeling like he'd lived a month's worth of life in around two days. And really pretty grateful that he didn't have to see Jasper Townes for a while.

He sank into his chair, sighed, and found himself reaching reflexively for his baseball.

His hand landed on air.

Ah, hell.

Well, he supposed there was a certain poetry in the fact that Jan Pennington, of all people, had won the baseball in the raffle.

He blew out a long breath.

He felt a little raw. Exhilarated and a bit shaky. Like he'd stood up there in front of everyone in the town and declared his love for Eden right into the microphone. He'd never done anything like that in his life, he'd done it without thinking, and he didn't think he could have made a clearer statement.

Only a few people knew who really owned that ball.

Mrs. Maker knew. But she would never rat him out to anyone, however. She was old-school loyal, right down to the bone.

But Eden knew.

And right now she was the only one who mattered. The ball, as it were, was in her court. And just as he'd had a hunch a few weeks ago at 6:59 at Devil's Leap, he had a hunch about what would happen next.

"Mr. Caldera?"

Mrs. Maker was standing in the doorway, holding a little pink box. He eyed it hopefully. It looked like the sort that might contain pastry.

"Eden Harwood brought this by for you this morning." She thrust the box his hands.

He went still, but his heart gave a sharp little jounce. And as it took a moment to recover from the sudden mention of Eden's name, he didn't say anything.

He closed his fingers around the edge of the box, almost tenderly.

"Kind of looks like a corsage box. She's the flower lady, after all. Or maybe there's a little cake inside," Mrs. Maker suggested hopefully.

"Thanks, Donna," he said.

He finally felt able to look up at her.

She could peer limpidly at him through her bifocals all she wanted; he wasn't going to open it in front of her.

"You're welcome," she said finally. "Do you want me to . . ."

"Door. Yes. Close it. Thanks, if you would."

So she left the office and closed the door behind her.

His heart had started racing thanks to that bastard Hope.

Frankly, he wouldn't mind a small cake in the least, though. He used his letter opener to slice the neat Scotch tape closing it.

Then peeled up the lid.

He looked down into a little nest of raffia. He frowned faintly, puzzled.

Then he gently parted it. Aware his hands were actually shaking just a little.

His breath left him in a gust.

He reached in . . .

. . . and lifted out his Joe DiMaggio baseball.

He didn't even need to verify that it was the very same ball he'd given up at the auction. He was positive it was the moment he saw it. He had a hunch how she'd managed it, too, and it was pretty funny.

He hefted its comforting, familiar weight in his hand, then put it back on its little stand on his desk, leaned back, and crossed his arms behind his head.

And then a slow smile spread over his face.

He was feeling just a little cocky once more.

He reflexively glanced at the window. Funny. It felt as if the sun had just moved out from behind a cloud. Still a little overcast out there.

Suddenly a little strip of paper fluttered to the desk.

He plucked it up. It proved to be a note written in what he presumed was Eden's handwriting. Neat, forthright, only a little frilled. Rather like her.

Guess who's getting a free Jasper Townes mini concert?
Hint: she wanted to know if he was "good"
P.S. Have you ever fallen in—

It was the world's best fortune cookie.

Because he could now see how his future would unfurl, and like he'd told her in an alpha moment outside a soccer game: when he set out to get something he knew was right, he always got it.

He glanced down at his arm. How about that? Goose bumps.

And yep, suspicions confirmed on how she'd got that baseball. *That* was pretty funny.

He basked in the moment, but for only a second. Duty, as usual, called.

He reached for his phone and texted his team.

Can't make it to the game tonight. Got one more Chamber of Commerce mixer to go to.

He braced himself for the barrage of outraged emojis. Middle fingers, grumpy faces, maybe even a butt crack or two (he wouldn't put it past Louis to go there).

But all he got back was a lot of little hearts and "go get 'ers."

What a bunch of reprobates.

That night, at the Chamber of Commerce mixer . . .

It wasn't like Eden was *riveted* by the door of the Misty Cat, or anything.

Occasionally her eyes moved an inch or two to the left or right of it, for variety's sake. The restaurant was her home away from home; she knew every inch of the place.

She'd taken up a viewing spot near the food table—tonight, Rice Krispies treats were heaped on a plate. Whoever was on snack duty this week must be double-tasking a third-grade class party.

Then again, Rice Krispies treats were *delicious*.

She gripped one with a white napkin to keep the marshmallow from gluing her fingers together and bit the corner of it. Then decided she couldn't eat it. It was against her nature to waste food. She folded it up and put it in her purse for later.

Above the table she fancied she could still see the ghost of Scotch tape marks from the old Black & Blue flyer that was up there. Would things have been different if she'd had a clue about that?

She was learning to quite like how things had turned out.

Annelise had been almost incoherently ebullient about the Jasper Townes mini assembly. Eden knew without being told that this improbable event was somehow related to Gabe's mysterious absence from the raffle, and that he had engineered it.

Whereupon Eden had eloquently essentially torn Jasper a new one over that sacrificed baseball, via text.

She'd spackled on the guilt so heavily—and he was surprisingly susceptible to guilt, at least when she was wielding it, which was useful to know—that she was able to broker a trade deal.

Eden kind of wished she could be in Jan Pennington's living room when she made him sing "Lily Anne" five times in a row.

The door opened and Eden's heart lunged ("Hearts can't *lunge*, Eden. Get a grip."—Dr. Jude Harwood) like a half-starved junkyard dog smelling steak.

It snapped back again when it proved to be just Truck Donegal.

Although some would argue Truck was prime beef (Casey Carson, for instance), she wasn't among them.

The place wasn't quite as teeming as the last few events, since the raffle had provided a quotient of excitement and it was as usual low-lit. The comforting pop and hiss of her dad flicking the lids off beers for everyone who didn't want the cheap wine and a soundtrack of strummy, moody Nick Drake tunes, which meant you could actually hear yourself think and you could shout to each other in a slightly lower volume.

But she was wearing her black dress. He was a guy, after all—maybe he wouldn't notice it was the same dress. He'd just be mesmerized by her skin.

At the mere thought of his skin, her own skin seemed to buzz with yearning.

And then the door of the Misty Cat opened again.

The entire world went soft focus and slo-mo.

For this time it was him.

And all at once her heart was pounding bruisingly hard (surely not even Jude could editorialize about that). It saw what she wanted.

It was a funny paradox that a suit could make someone look so sexy that you immediately wanted to strip them of it.

He found her pretty quickly. Though he had an advantage in height, too, so locating a dumbstruck redhead, glowingly pale in a black dress, wasn't too much of a challenge.

It took him about three seconds to get to where she was standing, and still it wasn't quite fast enough.

He arrived, and she wanted to tip face forward into his chest and maybe inhale deeply to get a hit of the smell of him.

She tipped her face up instead.

His lips were *right* there.

He used them to speak.

"Have I ever fallen in . . . ?" he prompted. Sounding just a little tense.

". . . love," she completed.

When she could get a word out.

He cupped his hand to his ear and said, "Sorry?"

"LOVE," she all but bellowed.

Causing heads to swivel.

"Ah," he said. "That's what I thought. Oh yeah, a thousand times."

Suddenly, like a cane at a gong show, an arm was looped through his and he was dragged backward by Meredith Blevins.

"Gabe Caldera, these two fellas want to be involved in next year's fund-raiser. Come on over and real quick meet Darius and Ray of Canyon Collectibles."

He flashed a mischievous look over his shoulder as he went.

She stood and unabashedly watched him, on fire with curiosity over how he was going to explain that "a thousand times." She had to hand it to him. He was the least boring principal of a school possibly ever.

She remained tucked next to the snack table, semi-camouflaged in her black dress, because she didn't want to talk to anyone else, the way she didn't want to hear, say, death metal on the heels of "Nights in White Satin." Not yet.

When Gabe returned approximately two minutes later, he said, conversationally, "Okay, the first time I fell in love with you was when you stopped to watch a squirrel and a blue jay fight over a french fry. And again when you told me about how your heart broke over and over again for Annelise. And how it had broken for me and my fiancée. And when you told me why you had only one cat. And when you told Jan that some people think that a man's heart is just as important as his penis. And again when I kissed you for the first time. And again when you whispered my name against my hand because you couldn't scream, the first time we made love. And when you asked me why I was being a dick. And when a baseball in a pink box was delivered to me this morning. A thousand little earthquakes, all reshaping my heart over and over. How can this be happening? I asked myself. But I fall in love with you over and over, a little deeper, a little harder, every single time."

His voice had gotten a little quieter, a little hoarser, and his voice, which had begun with bravado, was now tender, uncertain.

Holy—!

Talk about weaponizing strengths!

Who on earth could withstand that kind of cut-to-the-chaseness without dissolving completely. She *never* cried in front of anybody if she could possibly help it, and now all her fellow Hellcat Canyon merchants were impressionistic smears.

He used his fingertips to collect them from her lashes.

"I'm sorry I hurt you. I was scared to death of losing you, and I didn't want to admit it to myself or to you."

"I figured that out. And I know I wasn't entirely fair to you, either. I'm sorry, too." She sniffled.

A few of the people in the room were copping on to the fact that something momentous was happening between the principal and the florist. Either that, or he was helping her reinstall a contact lens.

"How about you? Ever been in love?"

"Only once. With you." Short words were the only ones she could handle at the moment.

"Keeping it brief, Ms. Harwood?"

"Force of habit."

"We could make forever our new habit."

"Damn. You don't mess around, do you, Your Excellency?"

"Nope. Scared yet?"

"Nope. Never with you."

"Huh. I am, a little," he confessed.

"Don't worry, Gabe. I'll be brave for you."

They didn't know it, but with every word their bodies were moving closer, and closer, and then her arms, magically, looped around his neck, and his arms wrapped around her waist, and just the way, say, even a sudden little fire started in a crowded room would inevitably command your attention, pretty soon they were surrounded by wide eyes and dropped-open mouths and motionless people.

The only person who wasn't surprised was Greta. She just smiled knowingly and used that distraction to help herself to the last Rice Krispies treat.

The music played on but conversation stopped.

"Best sex you ever had?" he murmured into her ear.

"Just you wait."

He kissed her, right there in the middle of the Chamber of Commerce mixer, a fog-up-the-windows kind of kiss, and a romance didn't really get much more official than that in Hellcat Canyon.

EPILOGUE

Six months later, eight something (but who cares about the time?) on a Sunday morning . . .

Eden was still sleeping, her eyelashes shivering against her cheeks, her mouth parted and smushed against her pillow, her hair swirled every which way above her head, as if some guy with a camera shouting "Now sexy! Now pouty!" and an actual wind machine had styled her. One creamy shoulder and just a crescent moon of pink nipple peeked saucily from the sheet.

She was a side sleeper.

So was he.

It made spooning so much easier.

Not that it would have been a chore.

Still.

They were both still conscious of the preciousness of the milliseconds of time they saved getting into snuggle position, which would add up to minutes or even hours over the years, or so they decided, during one meandering, urgency-free conversation, of which they in fact had several over the past few months. Meandering with Eden was as fun as cutting to the chase with her.

For a second, he wallowed in the still-novel luxury of admiring her flushed and only a little drooling pink and white loveliness, striped in shadow and light from the slightly parted blinds.

What a shame it would be to wake her up.

Gabe leaned over and licked her nipple.

And very quickly lay flat again and closed his eyes.

There was a rustle from the next pillow over.

He cracked an eye.

She opened one eye, and then the other.

She smiled sleepily and stretched her arms up over her head like a wanton, letting the sheet slip down.

His head went light. Boy, that view *never* got old. "Just how I like my women. Sunny side up."

She rolled over and pressed all that warm nude lusciousness up against him. "Mmm. That's funny. I like my men over easy."

"Oh, what a pity. I'm afraid the only thing on the menu this morning is over hard," he said with great, solicitous regret.

They were shamelessly dorky.

Her hand slipped down under the sheets to investigate the veracity of this.

He sucked in a breath as her hand languidly stroked.

"I might be open to substitutions," she decided musingly as he stirred, and swelled, beneath her clever fingers that now knew him so well and yet found ways to surprise him.

She burrowed her face in his throat. "You *smell* better than toast."

"Yes, but how do I *taste*?" he said gravely.

She kissed him. Slow, slow. The sheer decadence of being leisurely was still erotic as hell. And she kept up the handiwork under the covers so that mad hunger took over both of them, and it was an effort to pace themselves.

Annelise had spent the night at Caitlynn Pennington's house, and they were picking her up at ten.

They could do this for the next two hours.

So that's exactly what they did.

A t about nine forty-five they were just about to head to the door to pick up Annelise at Caitlynn Pennington's when Eden laughed and touched his arm. "Gabe, look . . ."

She pointed to the whiteboard.

Which was crowded with even more doodles and abbreviations than before. Funny thing, though: somehow life itself seemed infinitely roomier. Love somehow expanded the depth and breadth of every day.

But in a square three weeks from the square representing today, heretofore occupied only by a little drawing of a wedding bell, were pink words in Annelise's handwriting.

Mr. Caldera is my dad!!!!

With an arrow stretching on into infinity, through all the squares.

He'd be Mr. Caldera at school. Right now, he was "Gabe" at home.

He'd be "Dad" forever after that.

This they'd all decided, after a confab, and because Annelise had a sense of ceremony, his new title would go into effect right after they both said "I do" and not sooner.

After which the whole Harwood household, whiteboard, Peace and Love and the Barbies and Annelise's guitar, everything, would move into Gabe's big yellow house with the tire swing and room for a horse.

One square per week on the whiteboard featured a sketch that was basically a little circle with a smile and a snarl of hair on top.

That was their symbol for Jasper.

Annelise Skyped with him once a week since he'd left, for a half hour or an hour or so, whatever the two of them could spare, and Jasper had been surprisingly diligent about it. Eden always hovered nearby. Or Gabe. Their relationship had settled into a sort of goofy rhythm. Jasper was a lot like a big kid, and he liked to show her stuff on the guitar, and the songs she wrote seemed to just slay him. He genuinely got a kick out of Annelise, naturally, because Annelise was awesome.

Word that Jasper Townes had a daughter still hadn't reached any gossip sites.

And it was fine. Good, even. Eden genuinely hoped they grew to love each other in the safety of a quiet relationship. More love in the world was better than less.

"I think my dad Jasper is going to be kind of like Snuffleupagus," Annelise had told Eden thoughtfully.

"From *Sesame Street*? That big furry elephant-type beast?"

"Yeah. Only Big Bird can see him. And he's kind of funny looking, and hairy, but he's nice, you don't see him very often, but when you do it's fun. And then he's gone again."

Sesame Street was indeed educational programming.

She was pretty sure Jasper's role in their lives would get a little more complicated than that as Annelise got older.

For now, it suited all of them. And Jasper was clearly pretty wary of getting on the wrong side of Gabe, so there was that.

So for the past several months, happiness wasn't an emotional state so much as it was the weather they moved through every day of their lives.

An hour or so later the three of them were heading up to Firelight Falls for that long delayed, longed-for picnic, a backpack loaded with a picnic lunch.

Annelise was taking the opportunity to pretend to be a horse. She galloped ahead of them, tossing her head and whinnying, pausing to pretend to eat a thistle.

"Baby, you might want to pace yourself. It's about a forty-five minute hike."

Little did Annelise know, but Gabe and Eden had already looked into getting a horse for her eleventh birthday. A patient one, with a few years on it.

"Hey, Leesy, you know how you can get the best view of the canyon from here?" Gabe asked.

"Stand on your toes?" Leesy asked.

"Guess again."

"Go up to the tippy top of Whiplash Peak?"

"Nope. Liiiiiiike . . . *this*."

Annelise gave a happy little shriek when he swooped down, scooped her up, and planted her atop his shoulders.

"Don't kick or grab my ears and we'll be good."

Eden laughed at them. If she were to make a totem pole of the loves of her life, it would look a lot like that one.

"Hey, I'm taller than you now, Mom," Annelise called down.

"Well, that was bound to happen sooner or later."

"HIYA, Thunder! Giddyup!" Leesy commanded.

"I am *so* calling you Thunder from now on," Eden told Gabe.

He shot her a quick smoldery glance that told her he was actually kind of looking forward to the circumstances under which that might occur.

"Pretend I'm more like a plow horse, Leesy," Gabe said. "The sturdy kind. Maybe a little hard of hearing. I'm gonna plod. Don't kick. We'll get there."

She settled in happily.

And as they made their way up the trail to the falls, Gabe steadied Annelise with one hand and reached for Eden's hand with the other.

And for a few moments all was just sun, and trees, and rightness, and Annelise pivoting her head to and fro, gulping in the view, awestruck. "Wow, Mom, I can totally see forever!"

Eden and Gabe exchanged a glance that was pure contentment, happily possessive, all passion and promise.

"Me, too, baby," she said.

Don't miss any of Julie Anne Long's
acclaimed Hellcat Canyon romances!

HOT IN HELLCAT CANYON

A broken truck, a broken career, and a breakup
heard around the world land superstar John Ten-
nessee McCord in Hellcat Canyon. Legend has it
that hearts come in two colors there: gold or black.
And that you can find whatever you're looking
for, whether it's love . . . or trouble. J. T. may have
found both in waitress Britt Langley.

His looks might cause whiplash and weak knees,
but Britt sees past J. T.'s rough edge and sexy drawl
to a person a lot like her: in need of the kind of
comfort best given hot and quick, with clothes off
and the lights out.

Her wit is sharp but her eyes and heart—not to
mention the rest of her—are soft, and J. T. is falling
hard. But Britt has a secret as dark as the hills, and
J. T.'s past is poised to invade their present. It's up
to the people of Hellcat Canyon to help make sure
their future includes a happily ever after.

WILD AT WHISKEY CREEK

Everyone knows the Greenleaf family puts the "Hell" in Hellcat Canyon—legend has it the only way they ever leave is in a cop car or a casket. But Glory Greenleaf has a different getaway vehicle in mind: her guitar. She has a Texas-sized talent and the ambition (and attitude) to match, but only two people have ever believed in her: her brother, who's in jail, and his best friend . . . who put him there.

Sheriff Eli Barlow has secretly been in love with Glory since he was twelve years old. Which is how he knows her head is as hard as her heart is soft—and why she can't forgive him for fracturing her family . . . or forget that night they surrendered to an explosive, long-simmering passion. But when a betrayal threatens Glory's big break, Eli will risk everything to make it right . . . because the best way to love the girl from Whiskey Creek might mean setting her free forever.

DIRTY DANCING AT DEVIL'S LEAP

As Avalon Harwood's fortunes soared, Maximilian "Mac" Coltrane's plummeted, and he had to fight his way back to where they both began: Hellcat Canyon. Now Mac and Avalon will play dirty—in more ways than one—to get what they each want: the glorious old abandoned Coltrane mansion. But when Avalon snaps the house up at auction, she discovers there's something awfully familiar about the extremely hot caretaker . . .

Mac might have a heart of stone, and the abs to match, but Avalon—the dazzling girl whose heart was always too big and too reckless for her own good—was always his Kryptonite. And just like that, the stakes change: suddenly they're fighting not just for a house, but for a magic they tasted only once before and never since—long ago, with each other, at Devil's Leap.

JRY1 0618

At Avon Books, we know your passion for romance—once you finish one of our novels, you find yourself wanting more.

May we tempt you with . . .

- **Excerpts** from our upcoming releases.

- Entertaining **extras**, including authors' personal photo albums and book lists.

- Behind-the-scenes **scoop** on your favorite characters and series.

- **Sweepstakes** for the chance to win free books, romantic getaways, and other fun prizes.

- Writing **tips** from our authors and editors.

- **Blog** with our authors and find out why they love to write romance.

- **Exclusive content** that's not contained within the pages of our novels.

Join us at
www.avonbooks.com

AVON

An Imprint of HarperCollins*Publishers*
www.avonromance.com

Available wherever books are sold or please call 1-800-331-3761 to order.

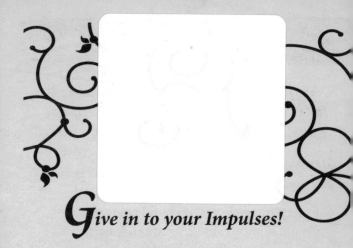

*G*ive in to your Impulses!

These unforgettable stories only take a second to buy and give you hours of reading pleasure!

Go to *www.AvonImpulse.com* and see what we have to offer.

Available wherever e-books are sold.

AVONIMPULSE

IMP 0811